THE SECRET SEVEN
ADVENTURE COLLECTION

THE SECRET SEVEN
ADVENTURE COLLECTION

ENID BLYTON

Hodder
Children's
Books

a division of Hodder Headline Limited

CONTENTS

GO AHEAD, SECRET SEVEN

CONTENTS

CHAPTER ONE

Susie is most annoying

PETER WAS going home from school one afternoon, swinging his satchel, when someone came running behind him and bumped into him.

He dropped his bag and almost fell over. He looked round crossly, expecting it to be George or Colin. But it wasn't. It was Susie with her cheeky face, standing by the kerb grinning at him.

'Sorry!' she said. 'You were in my way. How's the Secret Seven Society going?'

'You just look where you're going, Susie,' said Peter, picking up his bag. 'As for the Secret Seven, it's no business of *yours*. You're always trying to interfere!'

'Jack says there haven't been any Secret Seven meetings for ages,' said Susie, walking beside Peter, much to his annoyance. Susie was the most aggravating girl he knew.

Jack was Susie's brother, and a member of the Secret Seven. Peter was quite sure he hadn't said anything about the meetings. But Susie was right. They hadn't had any meetings for a long time. The Easter term had been rather exciting so far, and Peter hadn't thought a great deal about his secret society.

'Well, we're having a Secret Seven meeting very soon,' he said to Susie, making up his mind suddenly that they would. 'But you're not coming! And if you try any silly snooping, you'll be sorry. You don't belong to our Society, and you never will.'

'I know your last password,' said Susie, skipping over the cracks in the paving-stones. 'Aha!'

'You don't,' said Peter, racking his brains to remember what it was. Goodness – it wouldn't do for *him* to forget it!

'I do. It's Jack Sprat!' said Susie, and Peter scowled at her. She was right. Jack Sprat was the last password they had chosen – a secret password – and here was Susie shouting it out in the road. She saw his angry face and laughed.

'I'm right, aren't I? Yours is a silly society. I know your password, and so do all the girls in my class. I told them. So the next time you have a meeting we'll all be along, shout out the password, and you'll have to let us in.'

'Who told you the password?' demanded Peter. 'I know Jack wouldn't.'

'Oh no. Jack's a most annoying brother. He never tells me anything,' said Susie. 'But when I went to borrow a hanky from his drawer, I found a piece of paper there, hidden under a pile of hankies. And on it was scribbled: "Remember the password – Jack Sprat".'

'You're always snooping about, Susie!' said Peter, angrily. 'I never knew such a girl. Why can't you leave

6

us alone, and not keep trying to find out our passwords and what we're doing?'

'Well, why don't you let me belong?' demanded Susie. 'You let Janet belong, and Pam and Barbara.'

'Don't be silly. It's the Secret *Seven*. We can't have any more members, or we'd be eight,' said Peter. 'Anyway, we don't want you, Susie.'

'You're mean,' said Susie. 'Well, I'll tell Jack you're having another meeting soon. When shall I say it is?'

'Don't you go telling Jack anything!' said Peter, really exasperated with this annoying sister of Jack's. '*I* send out notices of meetings, not you. And you needn't bother to remember the password. I shall choose another one immediately, and let the members know.'

'Oh, well, Jack is sure to write it down to remember it again,' said Susie, skipping off. 'And I shall be sure to find it. Goodbye, and give my love to Jack Sprat.'

Peter glared at Susie's back. What an awful girl! He was glad that his own sister, Janet, wasn't like Susie. He walked home with a solemn face.

Certainly a meeting must be called soon. There hadn't been one for ages. It would never do to let the Secret Seven come to an end just because there weren't any meetings, or anything special happening.

But you can't solve mysteries and things unless there are some to solve, thought Peter. We'll have to think up something else to do, till one comes along. Sometimes it seems as if nothing happens for ages and ages. I'll have to change the password, too. Fancy Jack being such an idiot as to write down the password in case he forgot it. He might have known that Susie would find it.

He went home, thinking hard. Janet, his sister, was already there, and Scamper, the golden spaniel, came rushing out to greet him, barking with joy.

'Hallo, Scamper! Been a good dog today?' said Peter, fondling the long, silky ears. 'Eaten all your dinner? Been sniffing for rabbits? Barked at the dustman? You have? Ah, you're a *very* good dog, then!'

'Woof!' said Scamper, and raced round the room like a mad dog.

Janet laughed. 'He knew you were coming long before you came in at the door,' she said. 'He sat with his head on one side, listening for about three minutes before you came in. He must have known when you turned the corner up the lane.'

'Janet,' said Peter, putting down his satchel of books. 'We've got to call a Secret Seven meeting as soon as possible.'

'Oh, good! But why? Has anything happened?' said Janet, thrilled. She was disappointed when Peter shook his head.

'No – except that I met that awful sister of Jack's – Susie. And she's found out the password, and she was jeering at us because we haven't had a meeting for ages. So we simply must have one, and we must choose a new password, too! Get out your notepaper, and we'll arrange a meeting as soon as we can.'

CHAPTER TWO

Secret Seven meeting

THE SECRET Seven meeting was called for the very next day, immediately after school. Peter's mother was told, and she suggested that all the members should come to tea first, and have the meeting afterwards.

'I'll wash up every single thing after the meeting,' said Janet. 'Hurrah! Another Secret Seven meeting. How pleased everyone will be!'

The notes were sent out, and the Secret Seven were thrilled. Jack went scrabbling in his drawer to find the bit of paper on which he had written the password. He found it, but he was *most* surprised when he read it. This is what he read:

'Remember the password – Jack Sprat. No, Jack Horner. No, Jack the Giant-Killer. No – it's Jack and Jill!'

Jack stared at the bit of scribbled paper, frowning. Whatever had made him write all that? He must have been mad. And which was the password? He was sure it was Jack Sprat.

He looked closely at the paper. 'Bother Susie! She's written half of it! She's been snooping in my drawer and found the paper, and read the password! Just wait till I see her!'

But fortunately for Susie she was out to tea. Jack hunted for his badge, and at last found it. He had been afraid that Susie might have discovered that too. Really, she was the most annoying sister in the world!

The tea-party was fixed for half-past four, after school. Janet and Peter had carried everything down, and the shed looked very warm and cosy. They had a small oil stove in one corner for warmth, six candles stuck here and there, and a box for a table. Janet had put a cloth on it.

Two enormous jugs of hot cocoa stood there, with seven mugs round it. Ranged on a shelf behind were seven plates of food.

'Honey sandwiches, sardine sandwiches – and I hope you won't go for those too much, Peter, you're a pig over sardines,' said Janet. 'Buns buttered and jammed, all in halves. New doughnuts. A chocolate cake baked today. A smashing jam-sponge sandwich, already cut into seven by Mummy. Doesn't it look lovely? Oh – and a plate of mixed biscuits.'

'Woof!' said Scamper at once, and his tail thumped hard on the ground.

'*Your* dish of goodies is on the floor, but you're not to begin your tea till we do,' said Janet. Scamper looked at his own plate and sniffed longingly.

He saw two sardine sandwiches, made of the tails and little bones; one bun cut in half, with just a scraping of butter, but no jam, because Scamper liked his without; and a very large dog-biscuit smeared with potted meat. What a tea for a hungry dog!

'Here they come,' said Janet, as they heard footsteps coming down the path to the shed. She peered out of the window. 'It's Pam and Barbara.'

Rap-rap!

'Password!' called out Peter.

'Jack Sprat,' came the answer, and Peter opened the

door at once. No sooner was it shut than more footsteps were heard, and another knock.

'Password?'

'Er – I'm most awfully sorry, Peter, but it's such ages since we had a meeting that I've forgotten it,' said a voice, sounding rather upset. Janet glanced at Peter. Was he going to be cross, and perhaps refuse to let in poor Colin?

No. Peter didn't look at all cross. He opened the door, and Colin came in, looking most relieved.

'Hello!' he said, staring in delight at the tea. 'I'm sorry about the password, but, honestly, it's ages since we used it.'

'It's all right,' said Peter. 'It was my fault for not calling a meeting before. Anyway, that awful sister of Jack's knows it, so we've got to choose a new one.'

Rap-rap-rap-RAP!

'Password!' called Peter.

'Jack Sprat!' said two voices, and in came George and Jack, complete with Secret Seven badges. The door shut.

14

The candles gave a wavering light in the rather dark shed, and everything looked cosy, and rather mysterious. Just the kind of thing the Secret Seven liked!

'What's the meeting about?' said Jack, sitting on an upturned flower-pot. 'Anything special?'

'No,' said Peter. 'Nothing's turned up, worse luck – but we can't let our Society fizzle out because we wait and wait for something to happen. We'll talk about that later. Pour out the cocoa, Janet, and remember that we all like heaps of sugar.'

'Woof! woof!' said Scamper, approvingly, and got a lump of sugar from Janet at once. She poured out the cocoa, and Peter handed round the sandwiches. Soon everyone was tucking in, and Scamper gulped down his sandwiches and his bun in no time, and then settled down happily to crunch his potted-meat biscuit.

In ten minutes' time every plate was empty. Not even a biscuit was left. Jack sat back with a sigh. 'That was a scrumptious tea,' he said. 'Any more cocoa left?'

'Half a mug each,' said Janet. 'Pass yours up.'

'While we're having our last drink, we'll begin the meeting,' said Peter. 'It's not a very *important* meeting, but we've got quite a bit to discuss and to plan. If this Secret Seven hasn't any particular job to work on, it's got to find other things to do. Do you agree, members?'

'We do,' said everyone, pleased.

'Right,' said Peter. 'Well, I'll begin. Stop thumping your tail on the floor, Scamper, and you listen too!'

CHAPTER THREE

A new password – and a few ideas

EVERYONE SAT quiet. Scamper stopped his tail-thumping and sat still too, his head on one side. He was very, very proud to be at all the meetings, even though he wasn't a proper member.

'First of all,' said Peter, 'we must choose a new password, partly because Susie knows it!'

Jack was startled. How did Peter know that Susie knew it? 'Yes, she does know it,' he said, and fished the piece of paper out of his pocket, on which he had written the old password, and on which Susie had scribbled her nonsense.

'Look there, she found this bit of paper, with our password on it. I wrote it down so that I wouldn't forget it, and I hid it, and she found it and scribbled on it! But how did you *know* she knew it, Peter?'

'She told me,' said Peter. 'She seemed to think our Society was about to come to an end, or something, and she was so annoying that it made me decide to call a meeting at once. Jack, for goodness' sake don't leave our passwords about again!'

'All right. I won't,' said Jack, looking rather red in the face. 'But you don't know what it is to have a sister like Susie. I wouldn't be surprised if she isn't trying to peep in at the window this very minute.'

Everyone at once looked up at the little window, Scamper too. Peter shook his head.

'No, nobody's about. Scamper would bark if he heard the slightest sound. Well, what about a new password? Anyone got a good idea?'

'Snooper!' said Colin, thinking of Susie. 'That would be a good one.'

'Yes, we'd all remember that because of Susie,' said Janet.

'We'll have to remember the password is *Snooper*, not *Susie*,' said Pam, with a giggle. 'I'm sure I shall say "Susie" if anyone asks me the password next week!'

Jack often felt cross with his sister, but he didn't very much like the idea of the password being chosen because of Susie's snoopy behaviour. After all, she *was* his sister, and although she was very annoying at times, he was fond of her. He shook his head.

'No. I don't want that password, if you don't mind. I've got a better one. One that nobody would ever think of. What about "Beware!"? It sounds sort of *suitable* for us.'

'Yes, it does,' agreed Peter, and the others nodded their heads. They began to say the password to one another, in hollow, mysterious voices, and Scamper looked rather startled.

18

'Beware!' Janet said to Barbara, solemnly.

'Be-warrrrrrre!' hissed Colin to Jack.

'BEWARE!' said Peter to Scamper, who got up at once and sniffed in every corner of the shed, as if he had to discover what it was that everyone was warning him about. Beware! Well, he would beware all right, but what of?

'Look at Scamper. He's puzzled to bits,' said Pam, with a laugh. 'It's all right, Scamper. It's just our new password. Well, I don't think *any* of us will forget it. It's a very good one. Beware! It makes me feel quite creepy.'

'The next thing to discuss is what the Secret Seven are to do,' said Peter. 'I suppose nobody has heard of anything peculiar or mysterious or extraordinary that we could look into?'

Nobody said a word. They just looked at one another hopefully, and then shook their heads.

'Well, as there's nothing peculiar to make plans about, we'll have to decide something to *do*,' said Peter. 'I mean, it's been such a long time since we held a meeting, and societies just fizzle out if they're not kept going somehow. We must *do* something to keep up our interest or when something *does* come along, we'll miss it.'

'Yes, but what do you mean, *do* something?' asked Colin. 'We can't *make* things happen.'

'No. I know that,' said Peter. 'But we can put in a bit of practice. We can set ourselves one or two things to do.'

'What, for instance?' said George.

'Well, we could practise shadowing people,' said Peter. 'And we might perhaps have a shot at disguising ourselves, just to see if we could get away with it.'

'Disguising ourselves? But how could we?' said Pam. 'We're only children. We can't wear false beards, or ragged clothes, or pretend to walk with limps or anything. We'd be spotted at once.'

'Well, perhaps that's not such a good idea,' admitted Peter. 'We'll leave that for the minute. But we could practise spotting somebody, and then writing down a very clear description of him, so as to get practice at that kind of thing. It's always useful to be able to describe a thief in great detail, for instance.'

'But how do we know who's a thief?' said Jack.

'We don't,' said Peter, beginning to be impatient. 'We just go, say, to the railway station, and sit down on a seat. We watch the people standing there waiting for a train. We pick on somebody, it doesn't matter who. We look at them carefully, and memorise everything about them. Then, when they've gone, we write down what we've remembered. It would be very, very good practice for observing people.'

'It sounds rather dull to me,' said George. 'I'd much sooner do some shadowing or something. Anyway, I'm not much good at describing anything. I'm always bottom in composition at school. I just can't think of a thing to say.'

'All right, you can do the shadowing,' said Peter. 'Perhaps the girls would be better at spotting people and describing them.'

'Woof!' said Scamper, suddenly. 'WOOF!'

'Somebody's about,' said Peter. 'Quick, open the door and let Scamper out. If it's Susie we'll give her the fright of her life!'

CHAPTER FOUR

What fun to belong to a Secret Society!

IT WASN'T Susie. It was Peter's mother coming to say that
it was getting late, and did they know what the time was?
She was very surprised to meet Scamper flying out of the
door in the greatest excitement, barking for all he was
worth. He was quite disappointed that it was only Peter's
mother!

'Oh, Mother, it *can't* be half-past six yet,' groaned Peter.
'We haven't nearly finished the meeting. Yes, I know we
haven't done our homework, but we haven't much tonight. Can't we have another ten minutes?'

'Yes. Ten minutes, then,' said his mother, and went
away. The door was shut again, and the Secret Seven
began to talk hurriedly.

'George, you can do a spot of shadowing, and so can
Colin,' said Peter. 'You girls can do the observation idea,

go to the station or the bus-stop, or anywhere. Jack, you and I will do a bit of spying. We'll find a good spying-place, sit there, and watch what goes on without being seen. It will be good practice for when we *really* have to do it!'

'How do we do the shadowing?' asked George. 'We'd be seen following anybody in broad daylight.'

'Well, do it when it's dark, then,' said Peter. 'But don't go shadowing anyone together, you and Colin, or you'll be spotted at once. That would be silly. Go separately, choose someone you see, and follow them to their home without being seen. If you can do that, you'll be very smart!'

'I'd rather tackle a *real* mystery or problem than mess about practising,' said George, in a grumbling voice.

'I'm the head of this society, and you have to obey orders,' said Peter in rather a haughty voice. 'I've got to keep the Secret Seven going, haven't I? Well, I'm doing my best.'

'Anyway, you never know when we *might* come across something when we're putting in a bit of practice in these things,' said Jack, cheerfully. 'Things pop up most un-expectedly.'

'We'll practise our observation stunt on Saturday morning,' said Janet. 'I'll go to the railway station. I always like that, it's nice and busy and noisy.'

'I'll go to the bus-stop,' said Pam. 'You come with me, Barbara.'

'Right,' said Peter, pleased. 'Now we've all got secret jobs to do, and they'll keep us going till something turns up. Jack, I'll let you know when I've thought of a good place for us to hide and keep a watch on any goings-on nearby.'

Everyone got up, sorry that the meeting had come to an end. Pam and Barbara offered to help Janet wash up, and all the boys carried in the dirty plates and mugs for the girls.

'Now for homework,' said Peter, with a groan. 'I wish I'd listened better in class this morning. I haven't the faintest idea how to do those sums we've been set.'

Pam, Jack and George said good night, and thanked Peter's mother for the 'delicious' tea. The others washed up together, chattering at the tops of their voices. They didn't say a word of what had happened at the meeting, of course. Nobody was ever supposed to tell anything that had passed at one of the Secret Seven gatherings.

But all the members thought about it a lot. It was fun to belong to a secret society. It was something you could hug to yourself and think about before you went to sleep at

night. Janet looked at her Secret Seven badge that evening when she took it off her dress.

'S.S.,' she said. 'It should really be *five* Ss. S.S.S.S.S. For Super, Smashing, Secret, Seven, Society! I must remember to tell Peter that. I'll go to the station on Saturday morning, and watch for someone to describe perfectly. I won't miss a thing, not even the colour of his tie! I'll show the others how good I am at noticing every single thing about somebody I see just for a minute.'

Peter was thinking about what he and Jack could do, too, as he lay in bed that night. A spyhole? Now, where would an *interesting* one be? In the middle of the bush beside the main road? Yes, that would be a good place. They could take note-books and note down the cars that went by. They could put down anything they thought was interesting or suspicious. It would be fun!

Each member was planning carefully what he or she was to do. George was perhaps making the most careful plans of all. He was to go and shadow somebody. Well, he would do it really properly! He would first of all hide somewhere, and watch for somebody to come by. Then he would slip out and follow them, oh, so carefully and quietly! He would put on his rubber shoes.

'And I'll creep behind in the shadows, just like a policeman following a thief or a spy!' he thought. 'I'll be like a shadow myself. Nobody will know I'm there. I'll choose a man with a bag, to make it more real. I'll pretend he's got stolen maps in it, or jewels or something. Gosh, I'm going to enjoy this!'

All the Seven fell asleep at last. What fun it was to belong to a secret society!

CHAPTER FIVE

A little shadowing

'PETER, WHEN is the next meeting, do you suppose?' asked Janet, on Saturday morning. 'I'm going to the station now, to do my practice for the Secret Seven, you know, watching somebody and describing them, and I'd like to know when I can give my work in to the Society. I'm going to do it really well.'

'Well, I'll call the meeting for one evening next week,' said Peter. 'That will be time enough. I'm going off now to find a good spyhole with Jack. Have I got my notebook and pencil? Yes, I have. Well, good luck at the station, Janet, and don't choose just one person. That would be too easy. Choose three at least.'

'I thought I'd choose somebody we all know, too, if I can,' said Janet. 'Then you'll see if you can recognise them when I read out my notes.'

'Good idea,' said Peter. 'Well, I'm off to call for Jack.'

He set off, and Janet went in the opposite direction, to the station. She passed Barbara and Pam on the way. They were sitting on the bus-stop seat, looking rather giggly, with note-books in their hands.

'Have you begun yet?' asked Janet, in a low voice.

'No. No bus has stopped here yet,' said Pam. 'We're each going to choose one passenger getting out, and wait till the bus has gone off again. Then we're going to put down exactly what we remember about the two passengers.'

29

Colin and George were not thinking about their Secret Seven jobs just then. Both had decided to do them at night. Shadowing would be so much easier then. They were not going together, of course. Peter had forbidden that.

But when the evening came, only George set out. Colin had sneezed three times, and his mother had heard him. As she knew he caught colds very easily, she wouldn't let him go out after tea!

'But, Mother, I *must*,' said Colin, desperately. 'It's Secret Seven work. I've *got* to do it.'

'Can't it be done another night?' said his mother. 'Surely it isn't absolutely necessary to do it tonight.'

Colin hesitated. 'Well, yes, I suppose it *could* be done another night,' he said truthfully. 'All right, Mother, I won't go tonight. But you *will* let me go another night, won't you?'

So only George went out shadowing that night. He had put on rubber shoes so that he made no sound when walking or running. He had put on a dark overcoat, so that he wouldn't be seen in the shadows. He had even blacked his face. He looked most peculiar!

He stared at himself in the mirror and grinned, so that his teeth suddenly showed startlingly white in his black face. 'I'd better slip out of the garden door,' he decided. 'If Mother catches sight of me she'll have a fit! I do look strange!'

He decided to take a rubber truncheon that he had had for Christmas, to make it seem more real. Now I can really pretend I'm a policeman! he thought, swinging the rubber truncheon from his wrist. It looked exactly like a real one, but was only made of thin brown rubber!

He crept downstairs and out of the garden door. His rubber shoes made no sound. He went down the path to the back gate and came out quietly into the dark street. The street lamps were lit. He would have to keep out of their radiance.

He went along cautiously, swinging the rubber truncheon. Now then, you thieves! Now then, you spies! Look out, here comes P.C. Rubber-Soles, hard on your trail!

Who was he to shadow? Nobody seemed to come along at all. Wait a minute, was this the bus coming? Yes, it was. Good! It would set some passengers down, and he could trail one of them to his home, wherever it was.

The bus stopped up the street, and George saw some black

shadows moving as people stepped down from it. Somebody was walking towards him now, having got off the bus. He would shadow him! George pressed himself back into the hedge, and waited, scarcely daring to breathe.

The man came along. He was a tall, stooping fellow, wearing a hat, and carrying a bag. Good! Suppose there were stolen jewels in that bag! George would trail him right to his home, and he would then know where this supposed robber lived!

It seemed very real somehow, not pretence. The night was dark, the man came along without guessing that a boy was pressing himself into the shadows of a bush, and George suddenly found his heart beginning to thump. The man passed.

Now to follow him without being seen. If he spotted George, then George had failed. But George was certain he could shadow the man right back to his house without once being seen.

He came out from the bush and began to follow the man, keeping well into the darkness of the trees that lined the road. Down the road to the corner. Round the corner. Be careful now, *creep* round the corner, in case the man knows he is being followed!

George crept round cautiously, his rubber truncheon in his hand, pretending to himself that there might be great danger from a fierce thief!

He heaved a sigh of relief. There was the man, halfway down the road. George trotted on after him. Look behind you, George, as well as in front. Quick, George, look behind you!

CHAPTER SIX

A shock for poor George

BUT GEORGE didn't look behind him. He only looked in front, and followed the man steadily. Once, when he stopped to tie his shoelace, George darted into a nearby gate, afraid that the man might turn and see him.

He crept out after half a minute, and saw the man walking on again, swinging his bag. After him went George, deciding to get a little nearer, so that he could see exactly where the man lived when he went into his house.

So he crept quite near, feeling very bold and successful. And then suddenly something happened.

George heard sudden footsteps behind him, and then a heavy hand fell on his shoulder and a sharp voice spoke loudly.

'And what do you think *you* are doing, creeping along

in the dark after that gentleman in front? What's this you've got on your wrist? A truncheon! Don't tell me you meant to use it, you wicked little scoundrel!'

George was so astounded that he couldn't say a word. He stared up at the man, who dragged him to a nearby lamp-post.

'What have you done to your face?' said the man.

He was a young fellow, strong and very determined-looking, and he gave George a sudden shake.

'Have you lost your tongue?' He dabbed at George's face, and whistled. 'You've blacked it. What for? Are you one of the wretched little hooligans who think they can hit innocent people, rob them and run away?' demanded the young man, and shook George roughly again.

George found his tongue. 'Let me go!' he said, indignantly. 'Of course I'm not a hooligan! I'm only shadowing somebody for, well, just for practice!'

'I don't believe a word of it,' said the man. 'I've followed you right from the bus, you little wretch! I watched you hiding here and there, creeping round the corners, following that old fellow with the bag. Come along with me. I'll take you to the police-station. You can tell your tale there!'

George was really frightened now. He tried to wriggle away, but the man held him too tightly.

'Please don't take me to the police-station,' begged George. 'My mother would be so upset. Take me home. I'll tell you my name and address, and come with you. You'll see I'm a good boy, not a hooligan. I wouldn't DREAM of following anyone to rob them.'

'All right. I'll take you to your home,' said the young man, grimly. 'And I'll have a word with your father, young man. What you want is a good talking to!'

And poor George had to trot beside him all the way home, held so tightly by his collar that he could hardly breathe.

He didn't have at all a pleasant time at home. The young man made his harmless adventure seem very, very serious. His mother was shocked. His father was angry.

'Well, I didn't mean any harm,' said poor George, rather sulky now. 'It was only the orders I had from Peter, who is the head of the Secret Seven, our society. We were just practising several things, in case some mystery or other turned up. That's all. I had to shadow someone, and I did. But there wasn't any *harm* in it!'

'I see,' said his father. 'Well, that's the end of the Secret Society for you, George. If I'm going to have you hauled home by a member of the public, accusing you of following some harmless old fellow, and carrying a truncheon,

and with your face blacked, well, all I can say is that the
Secret Society is leading you into bad ways.'

'I agree,' said his mother. 'He mustn't belong any more.'

George looked at his parents in the utmost dismay. 'But
Dad! Mother! You don't understand. I couldn't *possibly*
not belong to the Secret Seven. They wouldn't let me go. I
must belong!'

'That's enough, George,' said his father, curtly. 'You
know I won't be argued with. Go and wash that black off
your face, and tell this Secret Society of yours tomorrow
that you no longer belong. Do you hear me?'

'Yes, Dad,' said George, shocked and miserable. He
said good night in a low voice, gave the young man a
fearful scowl, and went out of the room. He debated
whether to slam the door or not, but decided not to.
His father did not look kindly on any show of temper.

Poor George! He washed his black face, undressed, and got into bed. What a dreadful thing not to belong to the Secret Seven any more! What would they do without him? They would only be Six. Would they call themselves the Secret Six? That would still be S.S.

Or, dreadful thought, would they get someone else instead of him? George felt as if he really could *not* bear that. He buried his face in his pillow and gritted his teeth. It was too bad! He had only done what Peter had told him, and he had done it very well too, and that horrid young man had thought he was up to mischief and had hauled him home.

Tomorrow he must go and tell Peter and Janet. They would have to call a meeting on Monday night and decide what to do without him. He would be there for the last time. He would never, never attend one of those exciting secret meetings after that.

'I shall howl if I go on thinking like this,' said George fiercely, and hit his pillow hard, pretending it was the young man who had caught him. 'Take that! And that!'

He felt better then, but it was a long time before he fell asleep. Poor George!

CHAPTER SEVEN

George resigns – and a new member is elected

ON MONDAY evening, immediately after school, a meeting of the Secret Seven was called. All the Seven knew why. It was about George.

George had gone to see Peter on Sunday morning, and had told him what had happened. Peter was shocked.

'We must call a meeting as soon as possible,' he said, 'to see what we can do about it. Poor George! This is awful!'

So a very solemn, serious meeting was held down in the little shed that had the S.S. sign on its door. George gave the password in rather a trembling voice as he went in, and wore his badge for the last time.

'Beware!' he said, and as he spoke the door was opened. Everyone was there, Scamper as well.

'Hello, George,' said Janet, feeling very miserable to see George's woebegone face. 'Bad luck!'

'I expect Peter's told you what happened,' said George, sitting down on a box. 'It was just, well, what Janet said just now, bad luck!'

George took off his badge and handed it to Peter, who pinned it carefully to his jersey, beside his own badge.

'I now resign from the Secret Seven,' said George, in rather a shaky voice. 'Thank you for letting me belong. I'm very, very sorry to go, but my father says I must.'

'It's horrid of him!' said Pam fiercely, very sorry for George.

But George was not going to have anything said against his father, much as he resented being forced to leave the Secret Seven.

'He's not horrid,' he said, loyally. 'It was that young man's fault. He caused all the trouble, making such a fuss about me. He *knew* I wasn't doing any harm. He's the mean, horrid one, not my father.'

'Who was he? Do you know?' asked Jack.

'No idea,' said George. 'I'd never seen him before. When Dad asked him for his address, he said that he lived at that little hotel called "Starling's". He didn't give his name.'

'I've a good mind to go and find out who he is and tell him what I think of him!' said Jack, scowling.

'Yes. That's a good idea,' said Peter. 'Colin, Jack and I will all go. It's the least we can do for old George. We'll tell that young man what we think of him!'

'He'll just haul you home too, and get *you* into trouble!' said George, feeling rather comforted by all the interest on his behalf. 'I must say I couldn't understand why he was so

interfering. Even when I told him who I was and where I lived, he was just as mean.'

'Starling's Hotel,' said Peter, and wrote it down firmly in his note-book. 'We'll go and ask for him and tell him he's done a really mean thing.'

'I'll come, too,' said Pam, bravely; but Peter said no, the three of them could manage by themselves.

'What are you going to do about the Secret Seven now?' asked George after a pause. 'I mean, you're only six, now I'm out of it. Will you be the Secret Six?'

'No,' said Peter. 'We began as the Secret Seven, and we'll have to go on as the Secret Seven. You can't

41

suddenly change a society as important as ours.'

'I see,' said George. 'Well, you'll have to get a seventh, then. I shall hate that. Who will you have? Lennie, or Richard?'

'No,' said Peter, firmly, and everyone looked at him to see who was in his mind.

'Hadn't we better all put up somebody's name, and then we'll vote?' asked Colin. 'That's if we've got to have someone else. I shan't much like anyone in George's place.'

'You will ALL like the one that I'm thinking of, I promise you,' said Peter, and his eyes twinkled at them. 'Nobody will say no, I promise you!'

'Who is it?' said poor George, wondering who this wonderful person was that everyone would welcome.

'Yes, who is it?' said Janet, puzzled.

'He's with us tonight,' said Peter. 'But he will only be a temporary member, not a member for good, just a temporary member till we get George back again. Because I'm determined to go and find that young man and make him go and ask George's parents to let him belong to the Secret Seven again. I bet he didn't know how important it is to George to belong.'

'But who's the temporary member?' said George, puzzled. He looked all round. 'There's nobody here but us.'

'It's Scamper!' said Peter, and Scamper leapt up at his name, and wagged his tail vigorously. 'Scamper, will you please be a proper member of the Secret Seven till we get George back?'

'Woof, *woof*, WOOF!' said Scamper, joyously, as if he understood completely. Everyone began to laugh, even George.

GEORGE RESIGNS

'Oh, Peter!' he said, 'Scamper's the only person I don't mind taking my place! He's always *really* belonged to the Secret Seven, hasn't he? Oh, I do hope I come back. Still, I don't feel so bad now that Scamper's the seventh member. I just felt I couldn't bear to know that Lennie or Richard belonged instead of me.'

Everybody felt more cheerful. Scamper ran round and licked all the knees and hands he could see.

'Just as if he's saying "Thank you, thank you for this great honour,"' said Jack. 'Good old Scamper! Peter, pin the badge to his collar. Scamper, please remember the password. Let me say it in your ear, BEWARE!'

The meeting broke up. George said goodbye rather solemnly. Scamper took the members proudly to the gate, and then turned back. Wait till he showed the other dogs his magnificent badge!

CHAPTER EIGHT

A few reports

ANOTHER SECRET Seven meeting was held the next night, to hear the result of the various 'observations' and 'watchings'. All the seven were there, but the seventh this time was Scamper, not George. It seemed strange without him.

It was quite a business-like meeting. Janet spoke first. She took out her notebook and read from it.

'I was at the railway station,' she said, 'and I picked out three people to observe as they passed. They came off the 10.13 train from Pilberry.'

'First, an old woman with a round face, a big nose with a wart at one side, and grey curly hair. She wore a green coat with a belt, a hat with lots of red cherries round it and . . .'

'Mrs Lawson!' yelled everyone at once, and Janet looked pleased.

'Yes,' she said. 'Quite right. I chose her just to see if I could describe her well enough for you to recognise. Here's the second person, not very exciting. A young woman in a nurse's uniform, golden hair, doll-like face, small feet and a quick walk.'

'Well, it's quite a good *short* description,' said Peter. 'I feel as if I might know her if I saw her. I think you're good at this, Janet.'

Janet went red with pleasure. She loved Peter to praise her. 'Here's my last,' she said. 'I chose him because he really was a bit peculiar. Listen.

'A very stoopy man, who walked a bit lame, had an old soft hat pulled well down over his face, a long overcoat with the shoulders very square, small feet for his size, a funny hand . . .'

'What do you mean, a funny hand?' asked Peter.

'Well, I don't quite know what was the matter with it,' said Janet. 'It looked as if two fingers were missing, and it was sort of deformed and crooked. That's all.'

'Colour of his hair, his tie or scarf, and how did he walk – quick, slow or medium?' asked Peter.

'His hat was too low, I couldn't see his hair, and he had no tie or scarf,' said Janet. 'And he limped a bit. There! Do you think you would recognise *him* if you saw him?'

'Oh yes!' said everyone. 'Well done, Janet.'

'Now you, Barbara and Pam,' said Peter. But their notes proved to be rather silly.

'They sound as if you'd had one of your stupid giggling fits,' said Peter, reprovingly. 'Don't read any more. They wouldn't be a *bit* of use if we were *really* trying to find out something. Very poor, both of you. Now you, Colin. Did you do any shadowing?'

'No,' said Colin. 'I began a cold on Saturday night, so my mother wouldn't let me. I'm doing it tonight, after this meeting. I'm sorry, but it wasn't my fault.'

'Right,' said Peter. 'Well, that only leaves me and Jack. We found a good spyhole in a thick clump of leafy twigs springing out round the trunk of a great elm-tree. They hid us beautifully. We sat there, peeping through the leaves, and at first we saw nothing.'

'Not many people walk along that road,' explained Jack. 'It's Fairmile Road, and you know how long it is. Most people take a bus. We didn't see anyone for ages.'

'In fact, we haven't much to report,' said Peter. 'The

only possible thing of interest we saw was a car that came by, and stopped just near us.'

'But why was that interesting?' asked Pam.

'Well, it *wasn't* very interesting, actually,' said Peter. 'All that happened was that a man got out with a dog, a magnificent grey poodle, fluffy in patches and bare in patches, you know how poodles look! The dog was terribly frightened, I thought. But you could see it was only car-sick and it soon recovered, and began to sniff round quite naturally.'

'It didn't like going back into the car, though,' said Jack. 'It whined like anything and pulled away from the man as hard as it could. He was pretty rough with it, I thought.'

'I suppose the poor thing knew it would be car-sick again,' said Janet. 'Do you remember our next-door neighbour's dog, Peter? Every time it went out in the car, it cried and cried because it felt so ill.'

'Well your report doesn't seem *very* interesting,' said Barbara, rather glad to repay Peter for his candid remarks about her report and Pam's. 'Did you take the car's number? I bet you didn't.'

'There wasn't much point in taking it,' said Peter. 'But as it happens, we did. Here it is – PSD 188.'

'PSD – pretty sick dog!' said Colin. 'That's easy enough to remember!'

There was a laugh, and then a pause. Peter shut his notebook.

'Well that's all,' he said. 'I don't really feel we've done very much that is useful. Janet's reports are the best. They show how good she would be if she had to describe someone seen for only half a minute. The police are always asking for descriptions of persons seen by the public, and hardly anyone ever seems to be able to remember much about any stranger they saw.'

'But Janet would be able to tell them everything,' said Pam, rather jealously.

'The only big thing that has come out of this practice idea is George having to leave the Secret Seven,' said Colin, gloomily. 'Well, is it worth while my doing my bit of shadowing tonight, Peter? I mean, we don't seem to have done anything much, and I don't want to get caught like George.'

'George should have looked behind him as well as in front,' said Peter. 'You won't make that mistake. I think you should do your bit, Colin. I've a good mind to make Pam and Barbara do their bits again too!'

But the girls looked so crossly at him that he decided to say no more!

Colin got up. 'Well, I'm going on my job,' he said. 'What are you all going to do?'

'Let's go indoors and play a game,' suggested Janet. 'There are five of us left – sorry, Scamper, six – I forgot you! We've got an hour before it's supper-time. Come along in, Pam, Barbara and Jack.'

So they all five went in, and were soon playing a peaceful game of cards. But it wasn't peaceful for long! Who was that rapping at the window?

Tap-tap-tap! Tap-tap-tap!

'Quick! Open the window. I've something to tell you all!'

CHAPTER NINE

Colin's strange tale

'OPEN THE window!' said Janet putting down her cards. 'It's Colin! What's happened?'

Peter opened the window, and Colin climbed in. He was panting. 'Thanks,' he said. 'I didn't like to come to the front door or the back, in case your mother saw me and asked me what was up. So I tapped at the window. I saw you inside, playing cards.'

'What's happened?' said Peter. 'You're dirty, and your hand's bleeding.'

'Oh, that's nothing,' said Colin. 'Listen! You know I left you to go and find somebody to shadow, don't you?'

'Yes,' said everyone.

'Well, I didn't see anyone at first,' said Colin, 'and it began to rain and I was pretty fed up. So I chose to shadow the very first person I saw.'

'Who was that?' said Jack.

'A young man with a dog,' said Colin. 'I thought he must be taking it out for an evening walk. It didn't seem to like the walk very much. It kept whining and pulling away from the man, and I thought it might smell me, following quietly along some way behind, but it didn't seem to. I couldn't see what the dog was like at first, because it's a dark evening and raining. Then, when the man and the dog walked beneath a street lamp, I saw it.'

'What was it?' asked Janet.

'It was a bull-terrier,' said Colin. 'A beauty. A real beauty. My mother's friend breeds them, so I know a good one when I see it. Well, I shadowed the man and the dog, and it was really pretty easy, because the man was so much taken up with the dog, having to drag it along, that he hadn't time to notice I was following him!'

'Go on. What happened to get you so excited?' said Peter, impatiently.

'I'm coming to that,' said Colin. 'I followed them down Hartley Street and across Plain Square, and into a little dark alley that led between some big buildings. I went down the alley cautiously, because I couldn't see my way very well, and daren't put on my torch.'

'Was the man there?' asked Jack.

'Let me tell my story in my own way,' said Colin. 'I'm just coming to the strange part. I went right down the alley, and just as I was nearly at the end, I heard the man coming back. I knew it was him because he has the same kind of quick dry cough my Grandpa has, and he was coughing as he came.'

'What did you do?' said Janet, as he stopped for breath.

'I squashed myself into a doorway,' said Colin, 'and the
man walked right by without seeing me. But he hadn't got
the dog with him. So I wondered where he had put it, and
why he had gone down there and come straight back
again. So I went to the end of the alley myself and
switched on my torch.'

'And was the dog there?' asked Pam.

'No,' said Colin. 'The alley led into a little yard,
surrounded entirely by high walls. It was a messy place,
full of rubbish. I flashed my torch all round, expecting to
see the dog somewhere, tied up, perhaps, or even in a
kennel, but there wasn't a sign of it!'

'Where was it, then?' asked Janet, after a pause.

'That's what I don't know,' said Colin. 'I looked
absolutely everywhere for that dog. I listened for him, I
called softly, but no, not a growl, not a whine, not a

movement. And when I tell you that there was no way out of that yard except by that narrow alley, you'll guess how puzzled I was. I mean, a dog can't just *disappear* can it?'

'Woof!' said Scamper, exactly as if he was saying 'No!'

'I hunted all over that horrible yard,' said Colin. 'That's why I'm so dirty. And I cut my hand on some wire. But I tell you, there was no sign of that lovely bull-terrier, and no door or gate or anything for him to get out of. Then where was he? What had that man done with him, and why? It just beats me. I just *had* to come back and tell you.'

'There's something funny about this,' said Peter. 'I vote we go to that yard tomorrow and explore it. If there is some hiding-place there for a dog, we'll find it!'

'What a pity George isn't in this too,' said Janet. 'Peter, do go to that hotel and tell that young man he's got to go and tell George's parents they're to let him join the Secret Seven again. He'll be so upset when he knows we may be mixed up in something odd again and he won't be there to share in it.'

'All right, we'll go tomorrow after school,' said Peter. 'And then we'll go and explore that yard!'

'Yes, dogs don't just disappear,' said Jack. 'I expect there's a kennel there, or something, that you didn't notice in the dark, Colin.'

'Pooh!' said Colin. 'I'll give you fifty pence out of my money-box if you find a kennel there. You just see!'

CHAPTER TEN

The young man at Starling's

So, AFTER school the next afternoon, Colin, Jack and Peter set off to go to Starling's Hotel, to see if they could find the young man who had hauled George home the other night and caused him to leave the Secret Seven.

They discussed what to say to him. 'We'll tell him the marvellous things that the Secret Seven have done,' said Peter. 'He'll soon see that a Society that can do the things we've done would only have decent boys and girls as members. I might tell him to go and ask the police about us. They would stick up for us like anything, because we've helped them so much.'

At last they came to Starling's. It was rather a poor little hotel. There was a woman in the hall, and Peter asked her politely if there was a young man staying there. If so, could they please speak to him?'

'What's his name?' asked the woman.

'We don't know,' said Peter.

'Well, what's he like?' said the woman, sounding impatient.

'We, we don't know that either,' said Peter, feeling foolish, and wishing that he had asked George for a description of the man. 'All we know is that he's young.'

'Oh well, I suppose it's Mr Taylor you want,' said the woman, ungraciously. 'He's the only young man staying here. Go into that room and I'll ask him to come and speak to you.'

They went into a tiny room and stood about awkwardly. Soon a young man came in and eyed the three boys curiously. 'What do you want?' he said.

Peter explained. 'It's about George, our friend,' he said. 'The boy you caught the other night. You thought he was up to no good, but actually he was only putting in a bit of shadowing practice. He belonged to our Secret Society, you see, and we do all kinds of things. George's parents have told him he's not to belong, so . . .'

'Well, it's nothing to do with me,' said the young man. 'I can't do anything. He shouldn't play the fool.'

'He wasn't,' said Peter, warming up. 'I tell you, we're a very well-known society here, the police know us well; we've helped them many a time.'

'What rubbish!' said the young man.

'You ring up the Inspector and ask about us, then!' said Jack, indignantly.

The young man seemed rather astonished at this. He stared at Jack as if wondering whether to find out about them from the police or not.

'Well, whether you are friends with the police or not, I'm not having any more to do with your friend George, or whatever his name is,' said the young man. 'So that's that. He's got no right to shadow people, whether in play or not. Now clear out all of you.'

Colin hadn't said a word. He had been eyeing the young man closely, and Peter wondered why. Was he trying to do as the girls had done, and 'observe' someone closely so that he could describe him later?

As they went out, gloomy and resentful, a dog barked somewhere.

Colin turned to the young man. 'Is that your dog barking?' he asked.

'What dog? No! I haven't got a dog. And it wouldn't be any good if I had,' said the young man. 'They're not allowed in this hotel.'

Colin said no more, and the three boys walked out of the little hotel. They said nothing till they were well beyond the gate.

'He's hateful!' burst out Peter. 'Horrible cold eyes and thin mouth! As soon as I saw him I knew he was the kind of person that likes to get people into trouble. We once had a horrid teacher at school who had a mouth just like that!'

'Colin, why didn't you help us?' said Jack, as they walked down the road. 'You never said a word, till you asked about the dog that barked. Did you *have* to be unfriendly like that? You might have backed us up.'

'Wait a minute, I'll soon tell you why,' said Colin, and then the others saw that he was bursting to say something. 'Let's get right out of sight and hearing of Starling's first.'

They walked on a few hundred yards, and then Colin spoke in a low voice.

'That fellow, that young man, *he was the same one I saw last night* with the dog that disappeared!'

Jack and Peter stopped in surprise. 'What! Are you sure? But you asked him if it was his dog that was barking, and he said no he hadn't a dog!' Peter blurted all this out in far too loud a voice. Colin was afraid the passers-by might hear and he nudged Peter's arm.

'Be quiet. This may be important. Don't let's give anything away.'

'It's very interesting,' said Peter. 'Let's go to that yard at

58

once and explore. We know the young man is safely at Starling's. He won't disturb us.'

'Come on, then,' said Colin. 'Oh, *bother*! Here's Susie.'

And Susie it was, coming at them like a hurricane, all out of breath. 'Peter! I've heard that George isn't in the Secret Seven any more. Please, PLEASE let me in! Jack, tell Peter to let me be in.'

'Certainly *NOT*,' said all three boys at once. 'We've got a seventh member already, thank you,' said Peter, remembering Scamper thankfully.

'Oh, bother! I did hope I'd be in time,' said Susie, and sailed off at top speed.

'What *cheek*!' said Jack. 'Honestly, she's the limit. Come on, let's go to this yard before Susie thinks of following us. Of all the *cheek*!'

The three boys set off in the direction of the yard that Colin had told them about.

'Hartley Street first,' said Colin, 'then across Plain Square. We come to the poorer parts of the town then.'

It took them a quarter of an hour to get to Plain Square, for Starling's Hotel was away at the other end of the town.

They crossed the square, and then Colin looked for the alley-way leading between high buildings.

'There seem to be two or three,' said Peter. 'Which one was it, Colin?'

Colin hesitated. 'It all looks so different in the daylight,' he said. 'I think it's that one. But I'll soon know when we get to the yard. I'll never forget that yard, rubbishy, dirty place it was!'

They chose an alley-way, and went down it. It came out into a small enclosure that had evidently been made into a playground for children. Some little girls were there, riding tricycles and pushing prams. They stared at the three boys.

'Not this one,' said Colin, and they went back down the alley. They chose the next one and went down that. 'I think this is the one,' said Colin. 'Here's the doorway I hid in to let the young man pass!'

They came to the end of the alley and Colin gave an exclamation. 'Yes! This is the yard. I recognise that pile of old boxes, and that broken-down rusty pram. This is where the man took the dog, disposed of it somewhere, and came back without it.'

The boys gazed round. High walls enclosed the little yard. A few dusty windows overlooked it, and Peter suddenly wondered if anyone would open a window and yell to them to clear out.

'Listen,' he said, in a low voice. 'We'd better be looking for our ball, or something, in case somebody gets suspicious of us and turns us away before we've discovered anything. Anyone got a ball?'

Colin had, a very small ping-pong ball, but it would do! He carefully dropped it in among some rubbish, and then the boys pretended to hunt for it. But really they were hunting for any place where a dog might have been put.

They turned that yard upside down, growing bolder as nobody disturbed them. It was a very quiet, lonely little yard, completely enclosed, with no outlet but the alley-way, and had obviously been used for a dumping place for old boxes, crates, broken crockery, sacks, sheets of cardboard and other things.

'Everything here but the dog!' said Peter at last. 'I think we've looked into every crate and box, and into every corner where a dog could be, though no dog would keep quiet if it heard us three rummaging about. There *must* be some outlet here besides that alley-way, an outlet big enough for a dog, anyway.'

They had moved every crate and box away from the walls, hoping to find some small door, but apparently the high walls contained no opening of any kind. It was a mystery!

Jack sat down on a big box in the middle of the yard to rest. Colin fell on him in one of his sudden silly fits, and began to wrestle with him, trying to get him off the box. Both boys fell over, and the box turned over too.

'Shut up,' said Peter, crossly. 'That box made quite a crash, turning over like that.'

Colin and Jack got up, brushing the dust off themselves, and grinning. Then Peter gave a cry. He clutched Jack's arm, and pointed down at his feet.'

'Look – see that? What about *that* for pushing a dog through?'

All three were now staring down at Jack's feet. He was standing on an iron lid, a perfectly round one that fitted over what must have been a coal-hole.

'It was under that box, well hidden,' said Peter, excited. 'About the only box we didn't move, I should think. But who would have thought a coal-hole was under it? We didn't really *think* of a coal-hole, anyhow! Get off it, Jack, and let's have a look at it.'

Jack stepped off the round lid, and they all knelt down to look closely at it. 'It's been moved recently,' said Peter. 'It's not as caked with dirt round the edges as it should be. I bet that bull-terrier was shoved through here, Colin; I bet he was!'

'But why push a lovely dog down through a coal-hole?' said Colin, puzzled. 'What an extraordinary thing to do! And it seems a bit odd to me to have a coal-hole in this little yard. No coal-cart can come up that alley-way.'

'But a coal-man with a sack of coal can, stupid!' said Peter. 'Can we get this lid up? I'd like to peep down, and see if there's anything to be seen!'

It was an awkward thing to get up, besides being extremely heavy. Peter got very cross with it. But at last it was lifted, and shoved to one side. Then the boys all bent over eagerly, to look down. Their heads cracked together.

'I get first look,' said Peter, firmly. 'I'm the chief.' So the others let him look first.

He sat back, disappointed. 'Well, it's as dark and black as a, well as a coal-hole!' he said. 'Can't see a single thing. Anyone got a torch?'

'I've still got mine on me,' said Colin, and got it out of his pocket. They shone it down the dark hole. But even the light of the torch showed them nothing. Certainly there was no sign of a dog!

There was no sign of coal or coke either. It looked just a dark, horrible, deep hole.

'Er – anyone like to jump down?' said Peter.

CHAPTER ELEVEN

The coal-hole

NOBODY WANTED to jump down in the least. For one thing, the hole wasn't very big – for another, the dark ground was a long way below – and for a third thing, who knew what might lie in wait for any daring boy dropping down through that hole!

'Well, I must say I think it would be rather silly to get down there, knowing as little as we do about this affair,' said Peter, at last. 'Do you suppose this is where the dog was pushed down, Colin?'

'I don't know,' said Colin, puzzled. 'The dog's not there now, anyway, dead or alive. The hole is empty. I suppose it's really an underground cellar, and may be quite big. Anyway, what's the point of pushing a lovely dog down a coal-hole? It doesn't make sense to me.'

'We'd better put the lid back and go home,' said Peter.
'It's getting dark. I'm not sure I like this nasty lonely little
yard now it's getting towards night-time!'

He took hold of the lid, but Colin stopped him. 'Wait a
minute,' he said. 'I've got an idea.'

He put his head right down into the hole. Then he
whistled. Colin had a very shrill, piercing whistle that
usually went right through people's heads making them
angry. His shrill whistle sounded now, though it could not
be very well heard up in the yard, because Colin's head
was in the hole. It could be heard down in the cellar,
though, for the piercing noise echoed round and round!

'What are you doing that for?' began Peter, angrily, but
Jack guessed, and nudged him to be quiet. Colin was now
listening, his head still down the hole. He heard something
– what was it? Yes, there it came again. Then it stopped.

He took his head out, his eyes shining. 'The dog's down
there somewhere all right,' he said. 'It heard my whistle,
and I heard it barking, far away, somewhere, goodness
knows where.'

'Gosh! Did you really?' said Peter, amazed.

'That was a really good idea of yours, Colin. Well, we
now know for certain that the dog's down there, so that
man must have pushed him into the hole. This is a mystery
all right.'

'Yes. One that has sprung up all of a sudden, as
mysteries usually do,' said Colin. 'What do we do next?
We could get down the hole if we brought a rope-ladder,
but we'll break our legs if we just try to *drop* down.'

There was a pause. The boys sat back on their bent
knees and thought hard.

'The cellar must belong to one of these buildings,' said

Jack, at last. 'But which one? It might belong to any of these around us. The coal-hole is exactly in the centre of the yard.'

'I can't see that it matters which one,' said Peter.

'Well, it might,' said Jack. 'We could find out if any firm in these buildings is interested in dogs.'

'Well, I suppose that's an idea,' said Peter, doubtfully. 'Anyway, let's put this lid back now, and place the box over it. We don't want anyone to suspect we've come across part of their secret.'

They put back the lid as quietly as they could, and dragged the box across it. Now it was as well-hidden as when they had first come into the yard.

'It's almost dark now,' said Peter. 'We'd better get back home. My mother will be wondering where I am – and oh, bother – I've not done my homework yet. It's awfully difficult to swot at French verbs when you're thinking out a mystery all the time.'

'Look!' said Jack, as they turned to leave the yard. 'Look! Only one of these buildings has a lit window. Do you suppose the coal-cellar belongs to that one? Do you think there's anyone looking after that bull-terrier? He must be scared stiff if he's all by himself.'

The boys stared up at the lit window.

'It's the building on the left,' said Peter. 'It will be just round the corner of the block. Let's go that way and see what firm uses it. It might be a help, though, of course, the lit window may have nothing whatever to do with the mystery!'

They left the yard cautiously, went down the dark alley-way, and out into the street. They walked round the block, and came to the building that they thought must have

shown the lit window. Colin switched his torch on to the dirty brass plate in the main doorway.

'Alliance of Callinated Sack Manufacturers!' he read. 'What on earth does that mean? Anyway, by the look of the building, the sack manufacturers must have gone west long ago. What a desolate, dirty place! It hasn't had a touch of paint for years!'

'It may be one of the buildings that the Council plan to pull down,' said Jack. 'I know some of them round about here are being pulled down, they're so old. Come on, let's go.'

'Look!' said Peter suddenly, and pulled the others to one side. 'The door's opening!'

Sure enough it was. The boys stood quietly in the shadows, waiting. Someone came out and shut the door softly. He went down the few steps into the street. He kept close to the wall as he walked along, a tall, stooping man.

With one accord the boys followed, their rubber shoes making no sound. They knew that a lamp-post was round the corner. Perhaps they could see this man more clearly in the lamp-light. Who was he?

'We'll shadow him!' whispered Peter. 'Come on.'

CHAPTER TWELVE

Two interesting encounters

THE MAN came into the light of the street lamp, but only
for a second. Peter tried to take in everything at one
glance. He suddenly thought that Janet would have been
very good at that!

The man went past the lamp, and into the darkness
again.

Couldn't see very much, really, thought Peter. He had
his hat pulled so well down over his face. He seems to limp
a bit. Bother, I'd never recognise him again!

The man got along pretty quickly. He was making for
the bus-stop. It was easy for the boys to shadow him,
because now other people were walking in the street too.

'He's making for the bus-stop,' said Colin.

'We'll see which bus he catches. Shall we get on it, and
look at him more carefully?'

'Yes,' said Peter, forgetting the lateness of the evening, forgetting his homework, in fact forgetting everything except for the excitement of the moment. They were on the track of a new mystery. How could anyone stop in the middle of it and go home!

The man made for the second of the two buses that were standing at the stop.

'It's the bus for Pilberry,' said Peter. 'Come on, we'll get on too.'

The man put out his hand to the bus-rail and swung himself up. Other people followed. The boys began to get on too, but the conductor put out his arm.

'Sorry,' he said. 'Full up!'

He rang the bell, and the bus rumbled off.

'Bother!' said Peter, disappointed. 'We might have been able to shadow him all the way home.'

'Well, I don't expect he's anything to do with the dog affair, really,' said Colin. 'We might have gone on a real wild-goose chase, and found he was just a harmless old businessman, catching a bus home.'

'Peter! Colin! Did you notice his hand?' said Jack, in a voice suddenly bubbling with excitement. 'When he put it out to take hold of the bus-rail?'

'No. Why?' said both boys at once.

'Well, he had two fingers missing, and the hand was crooked,' said Jack. 'Don't you remember Janet's report, don't you re –?'

'Gosh, yes!' said Peter. 'That man she described getting off the train from Pilberry, at the station on Saturday morning! Hat well pulled down over his eyes, he walked a bit lame, a funny hand . . .'

'And very square shoulders,' said Colin. 'It all fits. He's the same man. But wait a bit, there's nothing extraordinary about us seeing the same man as Janet saw, is there? I mean, it's only just chance, and doesn't *mean* anything.'

'No, you're right. It doesn't really mean anything,' said Jack, his excitement fading. 'It just seemed strange that's all. Perhaps we're making a mountain out of a mole-hill – he's just an ordinary person going home.'

They turned to walk across the square again, and passed the little alley-way that led to the yard. Someone came out of it briskly, and almost bumped into them.

It was too dark to see what the man was like, but he

soon passed under a lamp-post, and something swinging
from his hand caught Jack's eye.

'Look, a dog-lead,' he said, in a low voice. 'But no dog!
It's the same man who lives at Starling's Hotel.'

'The one I saw with the dog yesterday!' said Colin,
excited. 'What's he doing here again? Has he taken another dog into that yard and pushed it down the coal-hole?
Gosh! This is all very peculiar, isn't it? What *is* going on?'

They went on, keeping well behind the young man.
He went round a corner, and vanished from sight. The
boys went round the corner too, and then got a sudden
shock.

The young man came out from a doorway as they
passed and caught hold of Colin and Peter by the
shoulder. He flashed a torch in their faces.

'Ha – it's you three, is it?' he said. 'Members of the
famous Secret Shadowing Gang, or whatever you call
yourselves! I *thought* you were following me! Look here, I
took that fourth boy, what's his name, George, to his
parents, and got him punished for this idiotic following of
people at night. And I've a good mind to take you to the

police, the three of you, and hand you over for making yourselves a nuisance by doing the same thing!'

'All right,' said Peter, at once. 'Take us to the police. We don't mind. Go on, take us!'

The young man hesitated. He evidently hadn't thought that Peter would challenge him like that. The boys stood there, scowling. Colin suddenly asked a question.

'Where's your dog?'

'What do you mean? I haven't a dog!' said the young man, angrily. 'You seem to have got dogs on your mind. You asked me that when you came to see me this afternoon.'

'Well, why the dog lead, if you haven't a dog?' said Colin, pointing to it.

'Look here, who do you think you are, asking foolish questions, interfering, following people? And what's all this about dogs? What's on your mind?'

The boys didn't answer that question. 'Are you going to take us to the police or not?' said Jack. 'We're ready, if you are. You can tell them anything you like. But we might tell them a few things too.'

'Pah!' said the young man, looking as if he would like to lash out with the dog-lead at the boys. 'I've had enough of you. Clear off home, and don't let me see you again!'

Off he went with angry steps. 'Well!' said Peter, staring after him. 'He certainly didn't dare to take us to the police – but why? What a very puzzling peculiar young man!'

All these exciting happenings made it necessary to call another Secret Seven meeting as soon as possible. The members simply *must* talk over everything, and try to sort things out. So, before afternoon school on Thursday, Peter called a half-hour meeting.

'What a pity George is out of it!' said Janet. 'He would so love to hear all that's happening.'

'I don't see why we can't tell him,' said Jack. 'He can't come to the meeting, of course, but I can't for the life of me see why we shouldn't tell him all that happens. After all, it was *his* first shadowing that began all this!'

'Well, he isn't a member,' said Peter, who liked the rules to be kept. 'We ought not to let anyone but the seven members know what we're doing. Otherwise we're not a Secret Society.'

'Woof,' said Scamper, thumping his tail on the floor of the shed. He seemed to think that he had to make some remark about everything, now that he was a proper member.

'Let's put it to the vote,' said Janet. 'I like rules being kept too, but it isn't George's fault he's out of this. I feel as if he really does still belong to us.'

So they put it to the vote, and fortunately everyone was of the same mind. George should certainly be told everything that happened. It would make up to him a little for being out of the Society. Scamper said 'Woof' so loudly when he was asked that everyone took it for 'Yes'. So it was solemnly recorded that the whole of the Secret Seven thought it right and proper to keep George up to date in the doings of the Society.

A very exciting discussion was held. Everyone wanted to talk at once, so Peter became very strict and insisted that only one person should speak at a time.

It was decided that the old man, who came out of the lighted-window building and got on the bus, was the same one that Janet had seen at the station.

'He probably lives at Pilberry,' said Janet. 'I saw him

getting off the train from Pilberry, and you saw him getting on the bus for Pilberry. Though I can't see that it's at all important to know where he lives. He may not have anything to do with this affair at all.'

'That's what we said,' said Jack. 'But we feel he *might* have something to do with it, so we'll keep our eyes open for him and his doings. Your description was so good, Janet, that we all recognised him for the man you saw!'

Janet was pleased, Pam and Barbara wished heartily that they had not had giggling fits at the bus-stop, but had noticed people as carefully as Janet had. Well, they would do better the next time!

The coal-hole was well and truly discussed.

'It's pretty certain that for some reason that young man takes dogs there secretly at night, and puts them through the hole,' said Colin. 'Then he leaves them. Do you suppose somebody is down there, waiting to receive them? I mean, somebody *must* look after them, surely?'

'Yes. But WHY are they taken there and hidden?' said Jack. 'That's what *I* want to know. I feel sorry for the dogs. We ought to get the RSPCA after them. It's cruel to push dogs through coal-holes and leave them there in the darkness. For all we know they have no food or drink.'

'There wouldn't be any sense in starving them,' said Peter. 'The dogs must be stolen ones. That's quite clear. We've seen one of them. You, Colin, said it was a fine bull-terrier, so it was probably a very valuable dog, and would fetch a good deal of money.'

'Yes, and the one that man must have taken last night, when we bumped into him, would have been some other kind of valuable dog, too,' said Jack. 'Gosh! Do you suppose that cellar is full of pure-bred dogs, all stolen? We'll have to do something about this!'

'Poor dogs!' said Pam. 'What happens to them down in the cellar? I do, do hope there's somebody there to see to them.'

There was a silence. Everyone was thinking the same thing. Something had got to be done about those dogs! Somehow that cellar had to be explored.

Colin, Pam and Jack began to talk loudly at the same time, and Peter rapped on the box in front of him.

'Silence! I've said you've got to talk one at a time. Has anyone any suggestions? Pam, what have you got to say?'

'Well, I've got rather a good idea,' said Pam. 'Can't we

look up the Lost and Found advertisements in the news-
papers, and see if many dogs are advertised as lost or
stolen?'

'Yes. *Very* good idea,' said Peter, and Pam felt pleased.
'We'll do that.'

'And couldn't we go to the police station and look at the
notices outside too?' asked Jack. 'They often have posters
giving particulars of lost animals.'

'Excellent,' said Peter. 'Any more ideas?'

'We *must* explore that cellar,' said Colin. 'I did wonder
if we should try to get into that building with the lighted
window and see if its cellar led to that coal-hole – but we
might get into awful trouble if we got in there. Isn't it
called "Breaking in" or something?'

'Yes. We can't do that,' said Peter, firmly. 'We can't
possibly do wrong things in order to put something right.
We'll have to explore the coal-hole, but I can't see that it
matters doing that. Now, we'd better make plans.'

'Everybody's got to do something!' said Jack. 'Give us
our jobs, Peter, and we'll do them. Hurrah – the Secret
Seven is going full speed again!'

CHAPTER THIRTEEN

Jobs for everyone

PETER GAVE each one of them a job to do. 'Pam and Barbara, hunt through every paper you can get hold of and find out if there are many valuable dogs advertised as lost or stolen,' he said.

'Yes, Peter,' said the two girls.

'And mind you do your job properly this time,' said Peter, sternly. 'Janet, you can go and look outside the police-station and see if there are any notices there, and, as it's fairly near George's house, you can go and tell him all the latest news. He didn't come to school today, because he has a cough, so he'll be glad to see you.'

'Yes, Peter,' said Janet, pleased.

'And you, Colin, and you, Jack, will come with me and Scamper to the coal-hole tonight,' said Peter, dropping his voice, and sounding suddenly serious and determined. 'Colin, bring that ropeladder you've got. It will be just right for dropping down into the hole, it's not too long. Bring torches both of you, and wear rubber shoes.'

'Yes, Peter,' said the boys, looking and feeling very thrilled indeed. What an adventure!

'Woof-woof-woof,' said Scamper.

'He said "Yes, Peter," too!' said Janet. 'You understand every word we're saying, don't you, Scamper, darling?'

'Today's Thursday,' said Pam. 'Have you forgotten that you three boys are going to Ronnie's party, all of you? You can't do anything much today.'

'Bother! I'd forgotten that!' said Peter. 'We'll have to explore the coal-hole on Friday, then. But you girls can get on with your jobs all right. Now I think that's about all, so we'll go. We'll just be in good time for school.'

They all went out of the shed, Scamper too, wagging his tail importantly. Pam and Barbara decided to go after school to the public library, where there were many papers they could read for Lost and Found advertisements. So, much to the librarian's astonishment, they seated themselves there, with copies of the daily papers and of the local papers too, around them.

They made some interesting discoveries. 'Look, Pam,' said Barbara, pointing with her finger to two advertisements. '"Lost or stolen, pedigree greyhound." "Lost or stolen, pure-bred bull-terrier." Why, that might be the very one Colin saw! It gives names and addresses here, both in our county.'

'I've found an interesting advertisement too,' said Pam. 'See – "Lost on Monday, 16th, a beautiful pedigree Saluki. Answers to name of Sally." That's in our county too. It looks as if somebody is at work, stealing pedigree dogs!'

'Here's another,' said Barbara. '"Believed stolen, pure-bred Alsatian, well-trained, answers to name of Kip." Goodness! Suppose the boys find them all down that coal-hole!'

'What do you suppose the thief does with them?' said Pam.

'Sells them again, of course. They would be worth a lot of money,' said Barbara. 'Or they might claim the reward offered. See, there's a reward of one hundred pounds for anyone finding the Alsatian!'

'I wonder how Janet will get on, looking at the police

notices!' said Pam. 'Anyway, we've done well this time. Peter can't tick us off again!'

Janet couldn't go to the police-station till the following day. She gobbled down her midday dinner and raced off. She meant to look at the police notices, and then go and see George and tell him all the latest news.

There was only one notice about dogs, and that was to say that dogs found worrying sheep would be shot. Janet hoped with all her heart that Scamper would never do such a silly thing. She didn't think he would, because her father owned a lot of sheep, and Scamper was used to them. It would be so dreadful if he was shot.

She glanced at the next notice. It described a man that the police wanted to find. Janet read it with interest.

'John Wilfrid Pace, aged 71. Small and bent. Bald, with shaggy eyebrows and beard. Very hoarse voice. Shuffles badly when walking. Scar across the right cheek.'

'I should know *him* all right if I saw him!' said Janet to herself, picturing a bent little man, bald and bearded, scarred on the face. 'Now I really must go and see George, or I'll be late for school.'

George was delighted to see Janet. He was perfectly all right except for a cough, but his mother was not going to let him go back to school until Monday.

'I've come to tell you all the latest news of the Secret Seven,' said Janet. 'Can anyone overhear us? We know you're not a member now, but we all voted that you should know what's going on. And there's plenty to tell you, George. It's all very, very exciting!'

So it was, and Janet told everything very well indeed. When she left George, he felt rather down in the dumps. All this going on and I'm not in it! he thought.

Then an idea came into his head. 'Well – why *shouldn't* I be in it? Why shouldn't I go to that coal-hole, and watch the others going down? They needn't even know I'm there! I can find it all right. Yes, I'll go. Look out, Secret Seven, I'm coming too, though you won't see me! Hurrah!'

CHAPTER FOURTEEN

Down the coal-hole!

RONNIE'S PARTY was a good one, and the three boys and Janet enjoyed themselves thoroughly. They quite forgot the exciting affair they were mixed up in, as they played all kinds of games.

But one game reminded them of the Secret Seven doings! Ronnie's mother suddenly came in with a tray of all kinds of things. 'Now look well, everybody!' she said. 'There are twenty things here. I am going to find out which of you has the best powers of observation! Look well for one minute, and then I shall take the tray away, and you must each write down what you saw on the tray, as many as you can!'

You can guess who won that competition, Janet! She remembered all twenty, and Peter was very proud of her.

'I believe you belong to a secret society, Janet,' said Ronnie's mother, giving her a box of chocolates as a prize. 'You must be one of its best members!'

That reminded the three boys of the exciting thing they were to do the next night. Down the coal-hole they would go, and what would they find there?

There was no time for a proper meeting before Friday night, so Janet, Pam, and Barbara hurriedly told Peter what they had found out about lost or stolen dogs. Peter was very interested indeed, especially when he heard that most of them were from their own county.

'That rather looks as if the thieves have their quarters in the county too,' he said. 'And if so, it may be down that coal-hole! I'd like to pay back that nasty young man for getting George into trouble. I'm sure he's mixed up in this!'

It was dark about seven o'clock. The three boys and Scamper met at the end of Peter's road, and set off together. Colin had his rope-ladder, and they all had their torches. They felt very excited.

It was a dark night, and a slight drizzle was falling. The boys turned up their coat collars. They went cautiously, in case that young man should turn up again out of some corner. They didn't like him. In fact each boy was secretly afraid of him. There was something horrid about his cold eyes and thin, cruel mouth that not one of them liked.

They went down Hartley Street and across Plain Square. A bus rumbled by and a few cars.

They came near to the alley-way. 'Do you suppose that man's coming with another dog tonight?' whispered Jack. 'We'd better keep a sharp look-out in case he does. It wouldn't do for him to find us getting down the coal-hole!'

'Well, you had better keep watch while we two get down,' said Peter. 'Then as soon as we're down you can make a run for the hole and get down yourself. I only hope that man *doesn't* come – we'd be nicely trapped if he did. He's only got to pop on the lid and we're prisoners. We couldn't possibly lift up that heavy lid from inside.'

This was not at all a nice thought. They went along even more cautiously, keeping a look-out for the young man. But there was no one to be seen near the alley-way. The boys went quietly down it and came into the yard. It was pitch-dark there.

They stood and listened for a while, with Scamper silent beside them. If the man was there they might hear a slight movement, or even breathing. But they heard nothing at all. It seemed quite safe to switch on torches and go across to the coal-hole.

Peter flashed his torch round quickly. The yard was deserted, dirty as ever, and very quiet. There was not even the lighted window to see.

They moved the box that hid the coal-hole and heaved off the heavy lid, and then Peter flashed his torch down. Nothing there but blackness and dirt. Colin undid the little rope-ladder he carried and let it drop slowly down into the hole, rung by rung. Scamper watched it going down with much interest.

They peered down. Yes, it reached the bottom nicely. Colin fastened the top end carefully to a nearby stone post.

'Now, Jack, you go to the entrance of the alley and keep guard till we're down,' whispered Peter. 'Come as soon as you hear a low whistle.'

Jack sped off obediently. Colin said he would go down first. So down he climbed, rung by rung, till he came to the bottom. He flashed his torch round. He was in a big coal-

cellar. His feet crunched a little as he stepped here and there, and he guessed that there was still coke or coal dust on the floor.

'I'm coming now,' whispered Peter. 'Look out, I'm bringing Scamper too!' Down he came, and soon stood beside Colin. He remembered Jack, and sent a low whistle to tell him he could come.

Soon they heard Jack's feet above, and then he came down too, grinning in delight. They were all very excited, Peter flashed his torch all round.

'Now, there must be a way out of this cellar. Look, is that a door over there?'

'Yes,' said Jack. 'That probably leads into the other cellars or basements. We'd better go cautiously – and listen hard as we go.'

'Nobody saw us go down, that's one good thing!' said Peter, thankfully.

But he was wrong. Somebody did see them go down. It is true that he could hardly make them out in the darkness, but he heard their low voices and knew what was happening! Who was it? George, of course!

George had done what he had made up his mind to do! He had found the yard with the coal-hole, and he was hiding to watch what happened. Somehow or other, Secret Seven member or not, George was going to be in on this!

CHAPTER FIFTEEN

Underground happenings

THE THREE boys down in the coal-hole were now carefully opening the door they had seen. Scamper was at Peter's heels, as excited as they were. Peter wished he didn't pant quite so loudly, but Scamper couldn't help that!

The door creaked as it was opened. There was no light beyond. Peter cautiously flashed his torch on and off. A passage lay before him, leading to a few steps. A closed door was at the top of the steps.

The boys went along the passage and up the few steps and then turned the handle of the door. Would it be locked? No, it wasn't. It opened towards them, and Peter peered round the crack. Still there was darkness in front of them. He flashed his torch round.

Now they were in the main cellars that lay under the big building. They stretched here and there, low-roofed, with

brick pillars standing up from floor to roof at intervals.

A noise came to Scamper's ears, and he listened, head on one side. Peter saw him listening, and listened too. But he could hear nothing. Scamper's ears were sharper than his.

They moved forward very cautiously, stopping every now and again to listen. It was very weird to be so far under a building, in the pitch darkness and loneliness of these vast cellars. They smelt strange too – musty and old and damp.

They came to another door – a wooden one – and now Scamper began to get very excited. Peter had difficulty in preventing him from barking. And then, as they opened the stout wooden door, they heard what Scamper heard!

It was the noise of whining dogs! Scamper whined too when he heard, and wanted to dash through the door. Then came a barking and a yapping. Then more whining.

'There *are* dogs shut up here,' whispered Peter. 'We were right. Go carefully now, for goodness' sake.'

They came to a long, narrow cellar, where a faint light glowed from a glass bulb. On one side was a wooden bench, on which cages were set. In them were five or six dogs, their eyes gleaming red in the faint light.

Nobody was there with the dogs. They gazed warily and snarled as the three boys came quietly near, but when Scamper gave an excited, friendly whine, they whined too, pawing at their cages in excitement.

'They've got water and food,' whispered Peter. 'Oh, look, there's the lovely car-sick poodle we saw in that car, Jack, do you remember? We saw it when we were doing a bit of practice, hiding by the road in a spyhole, watching people go by. I'm sure it's the same poodle.'

'Yes. It is,' said Jack. 'Colin, there's a bull-terrier, see? He's the same one you saw with that young man, I suppose?'

Colin nodded. He was very fond of dogs, and he was already making friends with these, allowing them to lick his hand through the wires of the cages.

'There's a greyhound, and a magnificent Alsatian!' said Peter. 'I bet those are the ones the girls read about in the papers as lost or stolen. And here's a Dalmatian – hello, Spots! You're a beauty, aren't you?'

The dogs were now all very friendly to the boys, partly because they had a dog with them who was friendly too. Peter stood and looked at the dogs, wondering what to do next.

'Should we set them free from their cages, tie them together with rope and see if we can get them out of the coal-hole?' he said.

'Don't be silly!' said Colin. 'They'd never go up the rope-ladder – and I bet they'd begin to fight if we set them free.'

'Listen, somebody's coming!' said Jack, suddenly, and Scamper gave a warning growl. The boys went into the shadows and waited.

They saw an old bent man shuffling along, carrying a lantern. His head shone in the faint radiance of the electric light above, for he was quite bald. He had a small dog with him, a mongrel of some kind, and he talked to it as he came in a curious, hoarse voice like a creaking gate!

'Come on, Tinks. We'll see if all the lords and ladies are all right. They don't think nothing of the likes of you and me, but we don't care, do we?'

The little dog trotted beside him, and they came to the

93

cages. The old man went on talking in his creaking voice, staring at the caged dogs.

'Well, my high-and-mighty ones, my lords and ladies, you're worse off than little Tinks here. You've lost your own masters, but he's got his. You may be worth your weight in gold, for all I know, but you'd give all you've got for a nice long walk, wouldn't you? Well, Tinks goes for two each day. Tell 'em, Tinks, tell 'em.'

But Tinks was not listening. He had smelt strange smells, the smells of the three boys and the golden spaniel, Scamper! In a trice he was over beside them, barking madly.

The old man held up his lantern and peered at them. 'What, more visitors?' he creaked. 'Come to see the lords and ladies, have you? Wait now, you're only lads!'

Peter came out from the shadows with Jack and Colin. He didn't feel at all afraid of this strange old man.

'Where did these dogs come from?' he said. 'Who brought them here? Who do they belong to? What are you doing with them?'

The old man gave him a helpless look.

'Them dogs, why, they comes and they goes,' he said. 'They comes and they goes. They comes in at that hole and – '

But whatever he said next was quite drowned by a sudden yelping and barking by the dogs. They had heard somebody else coming. Who was it this time?

''Ere comes the Guvnor,' said the old man, and chuckled drily. 'Now you'll be in trouble. Likely he'll lock you up in them cages!'

CHAPTER SIXTEEN

Unpleasant surprises

SOMEBODY CAME up out of the shadows very suddenly and quietly. The boys swung round at his voice.

'And what are *you* doing here?'

It was the tall, stooping man they had seen coming out of the building and getting on the bus! Yes, hat well pulled down, squared shoulders, odd hand! They couldn't see his face even now, under the shade of his black hat.

The boys, taken by surprise, didn't know what to say. The man suddenly opened a nearby cage, and spoke loudly.

'Guard them, Kip.'

The enormous Alsatian leapt out, went to the boys and glared at them, snarling and showing his teeth. Scamper shrank back, afraid. The boys didn't like it at all, either. They didn't dare to move a step.

The man laughed. 'That's right. Keep still. See my hand with two fingers off? Well, that's what an Alsatian did to me when I moved while he was guarding me!'

The boys said nothing. Peter felt wild with himself. They had thought themselves so clever, getting down to explore these cellars and see what they could find, and now they were trapped, and guarded by the fiercest Alsatian he had ever seen. He hoped and hoped that Scamper would not do anything silly. Kip would gobble him up in a mouthful.

The man fired questions at them. 'How did you come here? What for? Does anyone know you are here? Do you know the kind of things that happen to boys who poke their noses into things that are no concern of theirs? You don't? Then you soon will!'

He gave a sudden sharp order to the bald old man, who was muttering to himself in his creaking voice. 'Got your keys? Then lock these boys up in the cages. Kip, bring them here.'

Kip rounded up the boys as if they had been sheep, and hustled them in front of the man. Then one by one the Alsatian propelled each of them into a cage, snarling if they resisted. The old bald man locked them in, chortling to himself. Colin saw there was a scar across his face as the man looked up at him. There was no doubt about it, he was the old man that Janet had read about in the police notice! But not one of them could tell the police that the fellow was here, because they were all well and truly locked up.

The dogs were roaming about, growling and uneasy. The stooping man had them under control, though, and one sharp word from him was obeyed at once by any dog. He stood in front of the cages mockingly. Scamper was not in a cage, but crouched outside Peter's frightened and puzzled.

'I'm going now,' said the tall man to the little bald fellow. 'I'm taking the dogs in the car. You won't see me again. It's too dangerous here now. You don't need to know anything if anyone comes asking questions. Just play the idiot – that should be easy for you!'

'I'm afraid of the police,' creaked the old man.

'Well, hide away in the cellars,' said the other. 'It's a warren of a place. No one will ever find you. Let these kids out in twenty-four hours' time. I'll be well away by then, so it doesn't matter what kind of tale they tell! They don't know anything, anyway.'

'We do!' said Peter, boldly. 'We know that all these dogs are stolen. We know that this bald man is wanted by the police. We know the young man who brings the dogs here for you! We know you use the building above this cellar for your headquarters. We know – '

The tall man limped over to Peter's cage. For one moment the boy saw his furious, gleaming eyes and was afraid. Scamper thought he was about to harm Peter, and he flew at him and bit him hard on the ankle!

The man gave an exclamation and kicked out at Scamper. He caught him in the mouth, and the dog fled away yelping, and was lost in the shadows.

Then the man was gone, and with him went the dogs, cowed and obedient. He obviously had some extraordinary control over them – perhaps he had been a dog trainer, Peter thought. The old bald man laughed hoarsely at the frightened faces of the three boys in the cages, and his little mongrel dog sat down beside him with his mouth open as if he was laughing too.

'Boys! I don't like boys! Nasty tormenting creatures. I always said they ought to be shut up in cages!' He gave a creaking laugh. 'And now here you are, locked in my cages, and nobody knows where you are. Shall I tell you something, young sirs? If the police come after me and take me, I'll not tell them about you. I'll say to myself, "What, you'll take poor old John Pace and shut him up? Aha! Then I won't tell you about those boys!"'

He went off into a cackle of laughter, and then set off with his little mongrel at his heels. The boys were silent for a moment and then Peter spoke.

'We're properly caught. Goodness knows how long we'll be in this dark, horrible, smelly place. I wonder where Scamper's gone. He can't get up that rope-ladder by himself, or he'd go home and get help. I hope he's not hurt.'

'Sh! Listen! There's somebody else coming!' said Colin. 'I heard something, I'm sure. Gosh! I hope it's not that horrible young man. It would be just our luck if he came along with another dog for the other man!'

There was a pattering noise as well as cautious foot-steps. Was it that young man and a dog? The three boys held their breath as the footsteps came nearer and nearer. Then a torch suddenly flashed out on the cages!

CHAPTER SEVENTEEN

Good old George!

A FAMILIAR voice came to the three boys' ears. 'Peter! Colin! Jack! Whatever are you doing in those cages?'

'Why, it's George! George, is it really you?' cried Peter, joyfully. 'And Scamper! Is Scamper hurt?'

'No. But what on earth has happened?' said George, in the greatest amazement, as he gazed at the boys in the cages.

'How did *you* get in here?' demanded Jack. 'I was never so surprised in all my life as when I heard your voice.'

'I knew you were coming here tonight, because Janet told me,' explained George. 'And I thought I'd come too, even though I didn't belong to the Secret Seven any more. I thought I'd just watch. I saw you go down, and gosh! I did want to join you. I was hiding in that yard.'

'Well, I never!' said Peter. 'What made you come down into the cellars, then?'

'I waited ages for you to come back, and you didn't,' said George. 'And then I suddenly heard old Scamper whining like anything down in the hole. So I hopped out of my hiding-place and went down the ladder to him. That's all. But WHY are you in those cages? Can't you get out?'

'No,' groaned Peter. 'It's too long a story to tell you, George. You must go and get the police. Wait, though, look round first and see if that old man has hung the cage keys anywhere!'

George flashed his torch here and there, and gave a sudden exclamation.

'Yes, here are some keys, on this nail. I'll try them in the padlocks.'

He tried first one and then another in the padlock on Peter's cage door, and there was a sudden click!

'Oh good!' said Peter, as the lock opened. He pushed open the cage door. Soon the others were out too. They were most relieved.

'Now quick, we'll get the police,' said Peter. 'Come on, Scamper, old thing. Fancy you going and whining to George like that! I suppose you knew he was hiding in that yard, though *we* didn't!'

They hurried through the cellars, and came to the coal-hole. Up the rope-ladder they went. They pulled up the ladder and then picked their way through the yard, their hearts beating quickly. Scamper was very pleased with himself indeed. He felt that he had been a first-class member of the Secret Seven!

The four boys and the dog caused quite a sensation at the police-station, arriving dirty and full of excitement. The police sergeant was there. He knew them, and was far

more willing to listen to their extraordinary story than the
old policemen would have been.

They poured it out, and the sergeant called a most
interested policeman to take down notes.

The story went on and on, taken up first by one boy,
then another. 'Stolen dogs – the coal-hole – the young man
and the dog that vanished – the cellars below – the strange
bald caretaker who looked after the dogs – yes, he's the
man you've got a notice about outside the police station.
The tall, stooping man – yes, he's got away. He's taken the
dogs – in a car, he said.'

'I bet he's taken them in that car we saw the sick poodle
in the other day!' said Peter, suddenly. 'I bet he has. Wait –
I've got the number here. If you could find that car, sir
you'd probably find all the dogs *and* that man too! Gosh! I
can't find the bit of paper I wrote down the number on.'

105

He fumbled anxiously in all his pockets but the paper was not there.

'Think of the number. Try hard!' urged the sergeant. 'This is important. If we get that number, we can send out details, and the car will be stopped in a few minutes, no matter where it is. Think.'

'I know the *number*,' groaned Peter. 'It was 188. But what were the letters?'

'I know! Pretty Sick Dog!' cried Jack, suddenly remembering.

The sergeant looked astonished. 'Pretty Sick Dog?' he said. 'I don't follow.'

'PSD,' grinned Jack. 'The dog was sick, so we said the car letters must stand for Pretty Sick Dog – see? That's it – PSD 188.'

'Telephone that number to the patrol cars,' said the

sergeant to the policeman. 'Quick now! We'll get him yet. My word, we've been after these dog stealers for months. That fellow's a wonder at getting any dog to come to him, then he pops it into his car and away it goes. He hands it to somebody else, who passes it on again – '

'Yes, they go to the young man who lives at Starling's Hotel!' said Peter. 'We know he put a dog down the coal-hole to the old caretaker with the bald head and scar. You could get that young man too, Sergeant. He doesn't know about the happenings tonight! And you can get the care-taker as well. You've only to send men down the coal-hole into the cellar and up into the building above.'

The sergeant stared at Peter in awe. 'I haven't time to ask you how you know all these remarkable things,' he said. 'Car numbers – young men at Starling's – stolen dogs and their hiding place – wanted men – I just haven't time. I can't understand it.'

'Oh, well, we belong to the best Secret Society in the world, you know,' said Peter, unable to help boasting. 'We are always on the lookout for things to happen. Actually, we weren't *really* on the lookout this time. We rather *made* them happen, I think.'

The sergeant laughed. 'Well, make a few more happen. Now you'd better get home. It's late. I'll come and see you tomorrow. So long, and many, many thanks!'

CHAPTER EIGHTEEN

The jigsaw is finished

EIGHT WORRIED and amazed fathers and mothers heard the strange story of the stolen dogs when the four boys at last got home, very late, and full of excitement. Janet heard Peter come in, and flew downstairs from her bed, anxious to hear everything.

'What! You found the dogs in cages! And oh, how extraordinary that the man I read about on that police notice was there! Oh, goodness, were you really locked up in the dog-cages? And did Scamper, dear, darling, brave old Scamper, go and fetch George to your rescue? Scamper, you are one of the very, very best Secret Seven members!'

'Woof!' said Scamper, proudly, and sat up very straight.

Janet laughed at the Pretty Sick Dog business. So did everybody. It struck them as very funny. The whole

adventure seemed rather extraordinary now it was over. It was a curious mystery, a strange little adventure, that had really grown out of the 'job' and 'practices' that Peter had set all the members to do.

'In fact, we each had one bit of a jig-saw puzzle, and when we found they fitted together, we saw what the picture was!' said Peter. 'We each did our bit, even old George.'

Next morning there was a Secret Seven meeting, of course, and will you believe it, George was there too, beaming all over his face.

'I say, can I come in?' he said, when he arrived, and banged on the door. 'Oh, the password, it's still "Beware," isn't it? It was a very good one for this adventure, wasn't it? We all had to "Beware" like anything. I guessed you'd have a Secret Seven meeting this morning, so I've come too. My father says I can be a member again if you'll have me!'

'Oh, George!' cried everyone in delight, and Peter dragged him in at once. 'Did he really? Why? Because we've done such a good job again, and you helped?'

'Yes. You see, the Inspector and the sergeant both came to ask me a few questions, and they told Dad and Mother that all the Secret Seven were quite remarkable people, and Dad never said a word about having had me turned out! And after the policeman had gone, Dad said "All right, George. I give in. You can belong again. You can go and tell the Secret Seven to make you a member again." So here I am.'

'We solemnly make you a member, George,' said Janet in delight. 'Scamper, we told you you were only temporary, didn't we? So you won't mind George taking your place. But you were very, very good as a member, Scamper. Wasn't he, everybody?'

They all agreed heartily, and Scamper looked pleased and surprised to have so many pats and kind words. He gave a little whine as if to say 'Well, what about a biscuit too?'

And Janet, always ready to understand his smallest whine, at once produced a big biscuit from a tin! 'You deserve it,' she said. 'If you hadn't gone to fetch George to the rescue last night, Peter and Colin and Jack would still be locked up in the dog-cages!'

'Gosh! So we would,' said Peter. 'Hello, who's this coming?'

The big kindly face of the Inspector looked through the little window, with the sergeant alongside.

'We don't know the password,' said the Inspector, sorrowfully. 'Or we'd say it and come in.'

'It's "Beware"!' said Peter, grinning and flung open the door. 'We'll soon have to choose a new one, so it doesn't matter telling you.'

'Have you got any news?' asked Colin eagerly.

'Oh yes, that's why we came to find you,' said the Inspector. 'We thought you ought to know the results of the good work done by the remarkable Society you belong to!'

'Oh good – tell us!' said Janet.

'Well, we got the PSD 188 car,' said the Inspector. 'Got it at Pilberry.'

'Oh yes, why didn't we think of that?' said Peter. 'We *thought* that fellow lived at Pilberry!'

'Bless us, did you now?' said the Inspector. 'I'm beginning to wonder if there's anything you *don't* know! Well,

we got the car, and the dogs. The man has got a shop there, with two or three garages. He'd put the dogs into one of the garages. Goodness knows how many dogs he's stolen and sold. Ah, well PSD stood for Pretty Sick Driver by the time we'd told him all we knew about him!'

'And we also got the old caretaker fellow,' said the sergeant. 'He's a poor old stick, though, a bit feeble-minded, but clever enough to help a dog-stealer, it seems! We wondered where he had gone to earth, and there he was, in this town, under our very noses!'

'We got the young man, too, at Starling's,' said the Inspector. 'He's a bad lot. He and the other man ran this dog-stealing business between them, quite cleverly too. Covered their tracks well all the time, and bamboozled us nicely.'

'But they couldn't bamboozle the Secret Seven, could

they!' added the Inspector, getting up. 'Well, we must be off. Thanks, all of you. I wish there were more children like you, you're a grand lot to have in our town!'

The two big policemen went out, and the children shut the door and grinned happily at one another.

'Bamboozle,' said Colin, slowly. 'Bamboozle, that would be a fine word for our next password. What about it? Bamboozle, nobody would ever guess that, so long as Jack doesn't write it down for Susie to see!'

'Don't tease him,' said Janet. 'I do feel so happy, what with George back again, and all! What about a round of ice-creams? I've got my Saturday money today. I'll treat you all. Yes, and you too, Scamper darling! If anyone has earned an ice-cream, *you* have!'

'WOOF!' said Scamper, thoroughly agreeing, thumping his tail so hard on the floor that it raised quite a dust. 'WOOF!'

So there go the Secret Seven out into the sunshine, Scamper too. I do really think they're a fine Secret Society, don't you? And I can't help wondering whatever they will be up to next!

GOOD WORK, SECRET SEVEN

CONTENTS

It is illegal for fireworks to be sold to children. We recommend that fireworks should always be stored and handled by adults.

Always follow the Firework Safety Code:

1. Keep fireworks in a closed box. Take them out one at a time and put the lid back at once.
2. Follow the instructions on each firework carefully. Read them by torchlight – never a naked flame.
3. Keep pets indoors.
4. Light fireworks at arm's length – preferably with a safety firework lighter or fuse wick.
5. Stand well back.
6. Never go back to a firework once lit – it may go off in your face.
7. Never throw fireworks.
8. Never put fireworks in pockets.
9. Never fool with fireworks.
10. Site the bonfire away from the house, garage or shed.
11. Light the bonfire with firelighters – not paraffin or petrol.
12. Keep a bucket or two of water handy just in case.
13. Pour water on bonfire embers before going indoors.

CHAPTER ONE

Secret Seven meeting

'WHEN ARE the Secret Seven going to have their next meeting?' said Susie to her brother Jack.

'That's nothing to do with *you*!' said Jack. 'You don't belong to it, and what's more, you never will!'

'Goodness! *I* don't want to belong to it!' said Susie, putting on a very surprised voice. 'If I want to belong to a

secret society I can always get one of my own. I did once
before, and it was a better one than yours.'

'Don't be silly,' said Jack. 'Our Secret Seven is the best
in the world. Why, just think of the things we've done and
the adventures we've had! I bet we'll have another one
soon.'

'I bet you won't,' said Susie, annoyingly. 'You've been
meeting in that shed at the bottom of Peter and Janet's
garden for weeks now, and there isn't even the *smell* of a
mystery!'

'Well, mysteries don't grow on trees, nor do adventures,' said Jack. 'They just happen all in a minute. Anyway, I'm not going to talk about the Secret Seven any
more, and you needn't think you'll get anything out of me,
because you won't, Susie. And please go out of my room
and let me get on with this book.'

'I know your latest password,' said Susie, halfway
through the door.

'You do *not!*' said Jack, quite fiercely. 'I haven't mentioned it, and I haven't even written it down so that I
won't forget it. You're a story-teller, Susie.'

'I'm not! I'm just telling you so as to warn you to choose
a *new* password!' said Susie, and slid out of the door.

Jack stared after her. What an *annoying* sister she was!
Did she know the password? No, she *couldn't* know it,
possibly!

It was true what Susie had said. The Secret Seven had
been meeting for weeks, and absolutely nothing had
turned up. Certainly the seven had plenty of fun together,
but after having so many exciting adventures it was a bit
dull just to go on playing games and talking.

Jack looked in his notebook. When was the next meeting? Tomorrow night, in Peter's shed. Well, that would be quite exciting, because all the members had been told to bring any old clothes they could find. They were going to make the Guy for their bonfire at the next meeting. It would be fun seeing what everyone had brought.

Bonfire night was next week. Jack got up and rummaged in one of his drawers. Ah, there was his money which he kept in an old tin. Jack counted it carefully. There was just enough to buy a firework called a Humdinger. Jack was sure none of the other members of the Secret Seven would have one of those.

'Fizzzzz – whoooosh – '

'Jack! What in the world are you doing? Are you ill?' called an anxious voice, and his mother's head came round the door.

'No, Mother, I'm all right,' said Jack. 'I was thinking of a Humdinger on Bonfire Night and the noise it will make.'

'Humdinger? Whatever's that?' asked his mother.

'It's a big firework that makes lots of bangs and whooshes. I've saved up enough money to get one. Please will you ask Daddy to buy me one when he goes to do the shopping for Bonfire Night?'

'Give your father the money and he'll get you one,' said his mother. 'Oh, Jack, how untidy your bedroom is. Do tidy it up!'

'I was *just* tidying it, Mother,' said Jack. 'Hey, could you let me have some of those chocolate biscuits out of the tin, Mother? We're having a Secret Seven meeting tomorrow night.'

'Very well. Take seven,' said his mother.

'Eight, you mean,' called Jack, as she went out of the room. '*Mother*! Eight, I want. You've forgotten Scamper.'

121

'Goodness! Well, if you *must* waste good chocolate biscuits on a dog, take eight,' called his mother.

Good, thought Jack. We've all got to take something nice to eat tomorrow night, for the meeting. Choc biscuits will be fine! Now, what was the password? Guy Fawkes, wasn't it? Or was that last time's? No, that's the one. Guy Fawkes – and a jolly good password, seeing that Bonfire Night is soon coming! Why does Susie say she knows it? She doesn't!

The meeting was for half-past five, in Peter's shed, and all the Secret Seven meant to be there. Just before the half-hour five children began to file in at Peter's gate and make their way down the garden to the shed where the meetings were held.

The shed door was shut, but a light shone from inside. On the door were the letters S.S., put there by Peter. It was dark, and one by one torches shone on the door as the members arrived.

Rat-tat!

'Password, please!' That was Peter's voice inside.

'Guy Fawkes!' answered the members one by one.

Pamela was first. Then came Jack, hurrying in case he was late. Then George, carrying a bag of rosy apples as his

share of the food. Then Barbara, wondering if the password was Guy Fawkes or Bonfire Night. Oh dear!

Rat-tat! She knocked at the door.

'Password!'

'Er – Bonfire Night,' said Barbara.

The door remained shut, and there was a dead silence
inside. Barbara gave a little giggle.

'All right. I know it! Guy Fawkes!'

The door opened and she went in. Everyone was there
except Colin.

'He's late,' said Peter. 'Bother him! Look, what a spread
we've got tonight!'

The shed was warm and cosy inside. It was lit by two
candles, and there was a small oil-stove at the back. On a
table made of a box was spread the food the members had
brought.

'Apples. Ginger buns. Doughnuts. Peppermint rock, and what's in this bag? Oh yes, hazelnuts from your garden, Pam. *And* you've remembered to bring nutcrackers too. Good. And I've brought orangeade. What a feast!' said Peter.

'I wish Colin would hurry up,' said Janet. 'Oh, here he is!'

There was the sound of running feet and somebody banged at the door. Rat-tat!

'Password!' yelled everyone.

'Guy Fawkes!' answered a voice, and Peter opened the door.

Well, would you believe it! It was *Susie* outside, grinning all over her cheeky face. *Susie!*

CHAPTER TWO

That awful Susie!

'SUSIE!' CRIED Jack, springing up in a rage. 'How dare you! You – you – you . . .'

He caught hold of his sister and held her tight. She laughed at him.

'It's all right; I just wanted to give your high-and-mighty members a shock. Aha! I know your password, see?'

'How did you know it?' demanded Peter. 'Let her go, Jack. We'll turn her out in a minute. How did you know the password, Susie?'

'I got it from Jack, of course,' said Susie, most surprisingly.

Everyone stared at poor Jack, who went as red as a beetroot. He glared at Susie.

'You're a wicked story-teller! I never told you the password and I didn't even write it down, in case you found it. How *did* you know it? Were you listening in the bushes round the shed? Did you hear us say the password as we came in?'

'No. If I had, Scamper would have barked,' said Susie, which was quite true. 'I tell you, Jack, I heard you say it yourself. You were talking in your sleep last night and you kept yelling out "Guy Fawkes! Let me in! Guy Fawkes!" So I guessed you were trying to get into the meeting in your sleep and were yelling out the password.'

Jack groaned. 'I do talk in my sleep, but who would

have thought I'd yell out the password? I'll keep my bedroom door shut in future. I'm sorry, Peter. What are we going to do with Susie? She ought to be punished for bursting in on our secret meeting like this!'

'Well, we've nothing important to discuss, so we'll make Susie sit in that corner over there, and we'll have our feast, and not offer her a single thing,' said Peter, firmly. 'I'm tired of Susie, always trying to upset our Society. Pam and Barbara, sit her down over there.'

Everyone was so very cross with Susie that she began to feel upset. 'It was only a joke,' she said. 'Anyway, your meetings are silly. You go on and on having them and nothing happens at all. Let me go.'

'Well, promise on your honour you'll never try to trick us again or upset our meetings?' said Peter, sternly.

'No. I won't promise,' said Susie. 'And I shan't sit still in this corner, and I shan't keep quiet. You're to let me go.'

'Certainly not,' began Peter. 'You forced yourself in, and you can jolly well stop and see us eating all . . .'

He stopped very suddenly as he heard the sound of panting breath, and running feet coming down the garden path.

'It's Colin!' said Janet.

There was a loud rat-tat at the door, and the password. 'Guy Fawkes! Quick, open the door.'

The door was opened and Colin came in, blinking at the sudden light, after the darkness outside.

'Hey, I've had an adventure! It might be something for the Secret Seven. Listen!'

'Wait! Turn Susie out first!' said Peter.

Colin stared in surprise at seeing Susie there. She gave a sudden giggle, and Jack scowled at her.

'What's she doing here, anyway?' asked Colin, most astonished, as he watched Susie being hustled out of the shed.

The door was slammed and locked. Scamper, the golden spaniel who belonged to Peter and Janet, barked loudly. He hadn't at all approved of Susie being in his shed. He knew she wasn't a member!

'Tell you about Susie later,' said Peter. 'Now, Colin, what's all this about? Why are you late, and what's happened? And for goodness' sake, let's all talk quietly, because Susie is sure to be listening at the door!'

'I'll jolly well see that she isn't,' said Jack, getting up, but Peter pulled him back.

'Sit down! Don't you know it's just what Susie would like, to be chased all over the garden in the dark, spoiling our feast and our meeting and everything! Let her listen at the door if she wants to. She won't hear a word if we whisper. Be quiet, Scamper! I can't hear myself speak with you barking at the top of your voice. Can't *you* whisper too?'

Scamper couldn't. He stopped barking and lay down with his back to Peter, looking rather hurt. But he soon turned himself round again when Colin began his tale.

'I was coming along to the meeting, shining my torch as

I came, and when I got to the corner of Beeches Lane, I heard somebody in the clump of bushes there. You know there's quite a little thicket at that corner. There was a lot of whispering going on, and then suddenly I heard a yell and a groan . . .'

'Gosh!' said Janet, startled.

'And somebody fell heavily. I shone my torch at the bushes, but someone knocked it out of my hand,' went on Colin. 'Then I heard the sound of running feet. I went to pick up my torch, which was still shining brightly on the ground, but by the time I shone it into the bushes again, nobody was there!'

'You were really brave to pick it up and look into the bushes,' said Peter. 'What was going on, do you think?'

'I can't imagine, except that there was a quarrel of some sort,' said Colin. 'That isn't all, though. Look what I found in the bushes.'

The Secret Seven were now so excited that they had quite forgotten about whispering. They had raised their voices, and not one of them remembered that Susie might be outside. Scamper gave a little warning growl, but nobody paid any attention.

Colin was holding out a worn and battered notebook, with an elastic band round it. 'I've had a quick look inside,' he said, 'and it might be important. A lot of it is in code, I can't read it, and there's a lot of nonsense too. At least it sounds like nonsense, but I expect it's part of a code. Look!'

They all looked. Everyone began to feel excited. Peter turned the pages and came to a list written down one page. 'Look!' he said. 'Here's a list that might be a record of stolen goods. Listen . . . silver candlesticks, three-

branches, cigarette box with initials A.G.B., four silver cups, engraved . . .'

Jack sprang up. 'I know what all that is! My father read the list out at breakfast this morning. It was in the paper. It's a list of the things stolen from the famous cricketer, Bedwall, last night. Whew! Do you suppose we're on to something, Peter?'

CHAPTER THREE

Exciting plans

THE SECRET Seven were so thrilled that their excitement made Scamper begin to bark again. He just couldn't help it when he heard them all talking at once. He waved his plumy tail and pawed at Peter, who took no notice at all.

'It must be a notebook kept by one of the thieves, a list of things he stole!'

'What else does it say? I wish we could understand all this stuff in secret code. Wait, look, here's a note scribbled right across this page! See what it says?'

'"Gang meet in old workmen's shed, back of Lane's garage,"' read Peter. '"5 p.m. Wednesday." Whew! That's tomorrow. Gosh, we *are* on to something.'

Everyone began to talk excitedly again, and Scamper thought it was a very good time to sample a chocolate biscuit and perhaps a ginger bun. Before he did so he ran to the door and sniffed.

Yes. Susie was outside. Scamper could smell her. He growled a little, but as no one took any notice, and he was afraid to bark again, he went back to the good things on the little box-table.

'What are we going to do about this? Tell the police?' asked Colin, who felt most important at bringing all this exciting news to the Seven.

'No. I'll tell you what we'll do,' said Peter. 'We'll creep round to that old shed tomorrow night ourselves, and as soon as we see the gang is safely there, one of us can rush

131

round to the police-station, while the rest keep guard on the shed.'

It was decided that that would be a good, sensible and exciting thing to do. Pam gave a huge sigh.

'Excitement makes me feel so hungry. Can't we start on the buns and things? Oh, Scamper, you've been helping yourself! Thief-dog!'

'Scamper! Have you really been taking things?' said Peter, shocked. 'Go into the corner.'

'He's only taken a choc biscuit and a ginger bun,' said Jack, counting everything quickly. 'There should be eight of each thing, but there are only seven of the biscuits and the buns. So really he's only eaten what we brought for *him*, the eighth person.'

'Well, he shouldn't begin before we do,' said Peter. 'He ought to know his manners. Corner, Scamper!'

Poor Scamper retired to the corner, licking his lips for stray chocolate crumbs. He looked so woe-begone that everyone felt extremely sorry for him.

The clothes brought by the Secret Seven for the Guy were quite forgotten. The evening's events were much too exciting even to think about the Guy. The Seven made their plans as they ate.

'Gosh, we forgot all about Susie!' said Peter, suddenly. 'We've been yelling out our plans at the tops of our voices. Bother! Scamper, see if Susie is at the door!'

Scamper obediently ran to the door and sniffed. No, Susie was no longer there. He came back and sat down by Peter, putting his lovely golden head on the boy's knee, hoping for a forgiving pat.

'Oh, so she's not there. You'd have growled if she had been, wouldn't you, Scamper?' said Peter, stroking the

dog's silky head and fondling his long ears. 'Well, Susie will be most astonished to hear about our adventure when it's over – serve her right for laughing at us and trying to spoil our meeting!'

It was arranged that all the Seven should go quietly to Lane's garage the next night, after tea. Colin knew Larry, a boy who helped at the garage, and it would be quite easy for the Seven to talk to him and admire the cars until it was time to look about for the workmen's shed behind the garage. Then what would happen? A little thrill of excitement ran all the way up Peter's back when he thought of it.

The Secret Seven are on the move again! he thought.

What a good thing, after all these dull weeks when nothing happened!

It seemed a long time till the next afternoon. Everyone at the schools the Secret Seven went to was sure that something was up. The Seven wore their badges, and a lot of whispering went on. All the members looked important and serious.

Susie was very annoying. She kept looking at Pam, Janet and Barbara, who were in her class, and giggling. Whenever she passed them she whispered in their ear:

'Guy Fawkes! Guy Fawkes!'

This was very annoying because it was still the password of the Secret Seven! They had completely forgotten to change it the night before, in the excitement of making plans. Now Susie still knew it. They must change it as quickly as they could.

At four o'clock all the Secret Seven rushed home early to tea, so that they could be off again immediately to the garage. They were to meet Colin there at a quarter to five.

All their mothers were astonished to see how quickly the children gobbled their teas that afternoon, but luckily nobody was made to stop at home afterwards. One by one they made their way to the garage. Scamper was left behind, in case he barked at an awkward moment.

Everyone was at the garage at a quarter to five. Only fifteen minutes more! Now, where was Larry? They must talk to him for a little while, and then creep round to the shed at the back. How exciting!

CHAPTER FOUR

A dreadful shock

COLIN WAS already looking for Larry, the boy he knew who helped at the garage. Ah, there he was, washing a car over in the corner. Colin went over to him, and the other six followed.

'Good evening,' said Larry, grinning at the Seven. He had a shock of fair hair and a very dirty face and twinkling eyes. 'Come to help me?'

'I wish we were allowed to,' said Colin. 'I'd love to mess about with cars. Larry, can we have a look at the ones you've got in the garage now?'

'Yes, so long as you don't open the doors,' said the lad, splashing the water very near Colin's feet.

The Seven divided up and went to look at the cars near the doorway and wide windows, so that they could keep an eye on anyone passing. They might see the 'gang', whoever they were.

'Look! Doesn't *he* look as if he might be one of the gang?' whispered Barbara, nudging Jack as a man went by.

Jack glanced at him.

'Idiot!' he said. 'That's my headmaster. Good thing he didn't hear you! Still, he does look a bit grim!'

'It's five to five,' said George in a low voice. 'I think we'd better go round to the shed soon, Peter.'

'Not yet,' said Peter. 'We don't want to be there when the men arrive. Seen anyone likely to belong to the gang?'

'Not really,' said George. 'Everybody looks rather

135

ordinary. But then, the gang might look ordinary too. Gosh, I *am* beginning to feel excited!'

A little later, when the garage clock said a minute past five, Peter gave the signal to move. They all said goodbye to Larry, who playfully splashed hose-water round their ankles as they ran out.

'Bother him, my socks are soaked,' said Jack. 'Do we go down this alley-way, Peter?'

'Yes. I'll go first, and if all's clear I'll give a low whistle,' said Peter.

He went down the alley in the darkness, holding his torch, but not putting it on. He came to the yard behind the garage, where the workmen's shed was.

He stopped in delight. There was a light in it! The gang *were* in there, then! My word, if only they could catch the whole lot at once.

A DREADFUL SHOCK

Peter gave a low whistle, and the others trooped down the alley to him. They all wore rubber-soled shoes, and made no noise at all. Their hearts beat fast and Barbara felt out of breath, hers thumped so hard. They all stared at the little shed, with the dim light shining from its one small window.

'They must be there,' whispered Jack. 'Let's creep up and see if we can peep in at the window.'

They crept noiselessly up to the shed. The window was high up and Peter had to put a few bricks on top of one another to stand on, so that he could reach the window.

He stepped down and whispered to the others: 'They're there. I can't see them, but I can hear them. Shall we get the police straight away, do you think?'

'Well, I'd like to be sure it isn't just *workmen* inside,' said Jack. 'They might be having their tea there or something, you know. Workmen do have a lot of meals, and that shed's pretty cosy, I should think.'

'What are we to do, then? We can't knock on the door and say, "Are you workmen or do you belong to the gang?"' said Peter.

A loud bang came suddenly from the shed and made everyone jump. Barbara clutched at George and made him jump again.

'Was that a gun?' she said. 'They're not shooting, are they?'

'*Don't* grab me like that!' said George, in a fierce whisper. 'You nearly made me yell out. How do I know if it's shooting?'

Another loud bang came, and the Seven once more jumped violently, Peter was puzzled. What was happening in that shed? He suddenly saw that there was a keyhole.

137

Perhaps if he bent down and looked through that he would be able to see what was happening inside.

So he bent down and squinted through the keyhole, and sure enough, he got quite a view, though a narrow one, of the inside of the candle-lit shed.

What he saw filled him with such astonishment that he let out a loud exclamation. He couldn't believe his eyes. He simply couldn't!

'What is it, what is it?' cried Pam, quite forgetting to speak in a whisper. 'Are they shooting? Let *me* look!'

She dragged Peter away and put her eye to the keyhole, and she, too, gave a squeal. Then, to the amazement of all the others but Peter, she began to kick and bang at the locked door! She shouted loudly:

'It's *Susie* in there, Susie and some others! I can see her grinning like anything, and they've got big paper bags to pop. That's what made the bangs. It's Susie; it's all a trick; it's SUSIE!'

So it was. Susie, with Jim and Doris and Ronnie, and now they were rolling over the floor, squealing with laughter. Oh, what a *wonderful* trick they had played on the Secret Seven!

CHAPTER FIVE

A victory for Susie

THE SECRET Seven were so angry that they hardly knew what to do. So it was Susie and her friends who had planned all this! While Susie had been boldly giving the password and forcing her way into their meeting the night before, her friends were pretending to scuffle in the bushes to stop Colin and make him think something really serious was going on!

'They took me in properly,' groaned Colin. 'I really thought it was men scuffling there, and I was so pleased to find that notebook when they had run off! It was too dark to spot that they weren't men, of course.'

'No wonder Susie giggled all the time she was in our shed, and laughed when Colin rushed in to tell us of his adventure!' said Janet. 'Horrid, tiresome girl!'

'She's the worst sister possible,' said Jack, gloomily. 'Fancy putting that list of stolen things in the notebook, of course, *she* had heard my father read them out at break-fast-time too. Bother Susie!'

George kicked at the shed door. From the inside came the sound of shrieks of delighted laughter, and some enormous guffaws from Jim, who, like Doris, was rolling about from side to side, holding his aching sides. Oh, what a joke! Oh, to think they had brought the stuck-up Secret Seven all the way to this shed, just to see *them*!

'You just wait till you unlock the door and come out!' called Jack. 'You just wait! I'll pull your hair till you squeal, Susie. I'm ashamed of you!'

More squeals of laughter, and a loud, 'Ho, ho, ho,' from Jim again. It really was maddening.

'There's seven of us, and only four of you,' cried Colin, warningly. 'And we'll wait here till you come out, see? You hadn't thought of that, had you?'

'Oh yes, we had,' called Susie. 'But you'll let us go free – you see if you don't.'

'We shan't!' said Jack, furiously. 'Unlock the door.'

'Listen, Jack,' said Susie. 'This is going to be a LOVELY tale to tell all the others at school. Won't the Secret Seven be laughed at? Silly old Secret Seven, tricked by a stupid note-book. They think themselves so grand and so clever, but they're sure that four children in a shed are a gang of robbers shooting at one another! And we only had paper bags to pop!'

The four inside popped paper bags again and roared with laughter. The Secret Seven felt gloomier and gloomier.

'You know, Susie will make everyone roar with laughter

about this,' said Colin. 'We shan't be able to hold our heads up for ages. Susie's right. We'll have to let them go free, and not set on them when they come out.'

'No!' said Peter and Jack.

'*Yes*,' said Colin. 'We'll *have* to make a bargain with them, and Susie jolly well knows it. We'll have to let them go free in return for their keeping silent about this. It's no good, we've got to. *I* don't want all the silly kids in the first form roaring with laughter and popping paper bags at me whenever I go by. And they will. I know them!'

There was a silence. It dawned on everyone that Colin was right. Susie had got the best of them. They *couldn't* allow anyone to make a laughing-stock of their Secret Seven Society. They were so proud of it; it was the best Secret Society in the world.

Peter sighed. Susie *was* a pest. Somehow they must pay her back for this tiresome, aggravating trick. But for the moment she had won.

'Susie! You win, for the present!' said Peter. 'You can go free, and we won't even pull your hair, if you promise solemnly not to say a single word about this to anyone at school.'

'All right,' called Susie, triumphantly. 'I knew you'd have to make that bargain. What a swizz for you! Silly old Secret Seven! Meeting solemnly week after week with never a thing to do! Well, we're coming out, so mind you keep your word.'

The door was unlocked from inside and the four came out, laughing and grinning. They stalked through the Secret Seven, noses in the air, enjoying their triumph. Jack's fingers itched to grab at Susie's hair, but he kept them in his pockets.

'Goodbye. Thanks for a marvellous show,' said the irritating Susie. 'Let us know when you want another adventure, and we'll provide one for you. See you later, Jack!'

They went off down the alley-way, still laughing. It was a gloomy few minutes for the Seven, as they stood in the dark yard, hearing the footsteps going down the alley.

'We MUST find something really exciting ourselves now, as soon as possible,' said Colin. 'That will stop Susie and the others jeering at us.'

'If only we could!' said Peter. 'But the more you look for an adventure the farther away it seems. Bother Susie! What a horrible evening we've had!'

But it wasn't quite the end of it. A lamp suddenly shone out nearby and a voice said:

'Now then! What are you doing here? Clear off, you kids, or I'll report you to your parents!'

It was the policeman! Well! To think they had been turned off by the police as if *they* were a gang of robbers, and they had had such high hopes of fetching this very policeman to capture a gang in that shed! It was all very, very sad.

A VICTORY FOR SUSIE

In deep silence the Seven left the yard and went gloomily up the alley-way. They could hardly say goodnight to one another. Oh, for a real adventure, one that would make them important again, and fill their days with breathless excitement!

Be patient, Secret Seven. One may be just round the corner. You just never know!

CHAPTER SIX

A sudden adventure

NEXT DAY Peter and Janet talked and talked about Susie's clever trick. Why, oh why, had they allowed themselves to be so easily taken in? Scamper listened sympathetically to their gloomy voices, and went first to one, then to the other, wagging his tail.

'He's trying to tell us he's sorry about it!' said Janet, with a little laugh. 'Oh, Scamper, if only we'd taken you with us, you'd have known Susie was in that shed with her silly friends, and somehow you'd have found a way of telling us.'

Scamper gave a little whine, and then lay on his back, his legs working hard, as if he were pedalling a bicycle upside down. He always did this when he wanted to make the two children laugh.

They laughed now, and patted him. Good old Scamper!

Their mother popped her head in at the door. 'Don't forget you're to go to tea with old Mrs Penton this afternoon.'

'My bike's got a puncture, Mummy,' said Janet. 'It's *such* a long way to walk. Need I go?'

'Well, Daddy is going out in the car this afternoon. He can take you there, and fetch you back afterwards,' said Mummy. 'He'll call for you about six o'clock, so mind you don't keep him waiting.'

The car was waiting outside Janet's school for her that afternoon, with Daddy at the wheel. They picked Peter up

at his school gates, and Daddy drove them to
Mrs Penton's. She had been their mother's old nanny,
and she was very fond of them.

They forgot all about their annoyance with Susie when
they saw the magnificent tea that Mrs Penton had got
ready.

'Goodness – cream buns! How delicious!' said Janet.
'And chocolate éclairs. Did Mummy like them when you
were her nanny?'

'Oh yes, she ate far too many once, and I was up all
night with her,' said Mrs Penton. 'Very naughty she was,
that day, just wouldn't do what she was told, and finished
up by over-eating. Dear, dear, what a night I had with
her!'

It seemed impossible that their mother could ever have
been naughty or have eaten too many cream buns and
éclairs. Still, it would be a very easy thing to eat at least a

dozen of them, Janet thought, looking at the lovely puffy cream oozing out of the big buns, and those éclairs! She felt very kindly towards the little girl who was now grown-up, and her own mother!

They played the big musical box after tea, and looked at Mrs Penton's funny old picture-books. Then the clock suddenly struck six.

'Gosh, Daddy said we were to be ready at six!' said Peter, jumping up. 'Hurry up, Janet. Thank you very much, Mrs Penton, for such a smashing tea.'

Hoot – hoo – ! That was Daddy already outside waiting for them. Mrs Penton kissed them both.

'Thank you very, very much,' said Janet. 'I *have* enjoyed myself!'

They ran down the path and climbed into the car at the back. It was quite dark, and Daddy's headlights shed broad beams over the road.

'Good children,' he said. 'I only had to wait half a minute.' He put in the clutch and pressed down the accelerator; the car slid off down the road.

'I've just got to call at the station for some parcels,' said Daddy. 'I'll leave the car in the yard with you in it. I shan't be a minute.'

They came to the station, and Daddy backed the car out of the way at one end of the station yard. He jumped out and disappeared into the lit entrance of the station.

Peter and Janet lay back on the seat, beginning to feel that they *might* have over-eaten! Janet felt sleepy and shut her eyes. Peter began to think about the evening before, and Susie's clever trick.

He suddenly heard hurried footsteps, and thought it must be his father back again. The door was quickly opened and a man got in. Then the opposite door was opened and another man sat down in the seat beside the driver's.

Peter thought his father had brought a friend with him to give him a lift, and he wondered who it was. It was dark in the station yard, and he couldn't see the other man's face at all. Then the headlights went on, and the car moved quickly out of the yard.

Peter got a really terrible shock as soon as the car passed a lamppost. The man driving the car wasn't his father! It was somebody he didn't know at all, a man with a low-brimmed hat, and rather long hair down to his collar. Peter's father never had long hair. Whoever was this driving the car?

The boy sat quite still. He looked at the other man when they went by a lamppost again. No, that wasn't his father either! It was a man he had never seen before. His head

was bare and the hair was very short, quite different from his companion's.

A little cold feeling crept round Peter's heart. Who were these men? Were they stealing his father's car? What was he to do?

Janet stirred a little. Peter leaned over to her and put his lips right to her ear.

'Janet!' he whispered. 'Are you awake? Listen to me. I think Daddy's car is being stolen by two men, and they don't know we're at the back. Slip quietly down to the floor, so that if they happen to turn round they won't see us. Quick now, for goodness' sake!'

CHAPTER SEVEN

Something to work on

JANET WAS awake now, very much awake! She took one scared look at the heads of the two men in front, suddenly outlined by a street lamp, and slid quickly down to the floor. She began to tremble.

Peter slipped down beside her. 'Don't be frightened. I'll look after you. So long as the men don't know we're here, we're all right.'

'But where are they taking us?' whispered Janet, glad that the rattling of the car drowned her voice.

'I've no idea. They've gone down the main street, and now they're in a part of the town I don't know,' whispered Peter. 'Hallo, they're stopping. Keep down, Janet, and don't make a sound!'

The driver stopped the car and peered out of the open window. 'You're all right here,' he said to his companion. 'No one's about. Get in touch with Q8061 at once. Tell him Sid's place, five o'clock any evening. I'll be there.'

'Right,' said the other man and opened his door cautiously. Then he shut it again, and ducked his head down.

'What's up? Someone coming?' said the driver.

'No. I think I've dropped something,' said the other man, in a muffled voice. He appeared to be groping over the floor. 'I'm sure I heard something drop.'

'For goodness' sake! Clear out now while the going's good!' said the driver impatiently. 'The police will be on the look-out for this car in a few minutes. I'm going to

151

Sid's, and I don't know anything at all about you, see? Not a thing!'

The other man muttered something and opened his door again. He slid out into the dark road. The driver got out on his side; both doors were left open, as the men did not want to make the slightest noise that might call attention to them.

Peter sat up cautiously. He could not see or hear anything of the two men. The darkness had swallowed them completely. In this road the lampposts were few and far between, and the driver had been careful to stop in the darkest spot he could find. He had switched headlights and sidelights off as soon as he had stopped.

Peter reached over to the front of the car and switched them on. He didn't want anything to run into his father's car and smash it. He wished he could drive, but he couldn't, and anyway, he was much too young to have a licence. What should he do now?

Janet sat up, too, still trembling. 'Where are we?' she said. 'Have those men gone?'

'Yes. It's all right, Janet; I don't think they're coming

back,' said Peter. 'Well, I wonder who they were and why they wanted to come here in the car? Talk about an adventure! We were moaning last night because there wasn't even the smell of one, and now here's one, right out of the blue!'

'Well, I don't much like an adventure in the dark,' said Janet. 'What are we going to do?'

'We must get in touch with Daddy,' said Peter. 'He must still be waiting at the station, unless he's gone home! But we haven't been more than a few minutes. I think I'll try to find a telephone box and telephone the station to see if Daddy is still there.'

'I'm not going to wait in the car by myself,' said Janet, at once. 'Oh dear, I wish we had Scamper with us. I should feel much better then.'

'The men wouldn't have taken the car if Scamper had been with us,' said Peter, getting out. 'He would have barked, and they would have run off to someone else's car. Come on, Janet, get out. I'll lock the doors in case there is anyone else who might take a fancy to Daddy's car!'

He locked all the doors, Janet holding his torch for him so that he could see what he was doing. Then they went down the street to see if they could find a telephone box anywhere.

They were lucky. One was at the corner of the very road where they were! Peter slipped inside and dialled the railway station.

'Station here,' said a voice at the other end.

'This is Peter, of Old Mill House,' said Peter. 'Is my father at the station still, by any chance?'

'Yes, he is,' said the voice. 'He's just collecting some

parcels. Do you want to speak to him? Right, I'll ask him to come to the phone.'

Half a minute later Peter heard his father's voice. 'Yes? Who is it? *You*, Peter! But – but aren't you still in the car, in the station yard? Where are you?'

Peter explained everything as clearly as he could, and his father listened to his tale in amazement. 'Well! Two car thieves going off with my car and not guessing you and Janet were in it. Where are you?'

'Janet's just asked somebody,' said Peter. 'We're in Jackson Street, not far from the Broadway. Can you get here, Dad, and fetch the car? We'll wait.'

154

'Yes. I'll get a taxi here in the yard,' said his father. 'Well, of all the things to happen!'

Janet and Peter went back to the car. Now that they knew their father would be along in a few minutes they no longer felt scared. Instead they began to feel rather pleased and important.

'We'll have to call a Secret Seven meeting about this *at once*,' said Peter. 'The police will be on to it, I expect, and *we'll* work on it too. What will Susie do *now*? Who cares about her silly tricks? Nobody at all!'

CHAPTER EIGHT

Another meeting

IN A short time a taxi drew up beside the car and the children's father jumped out.

'Here we are!' called Janet, as her father paid the taxi-man.

He ran over, and got into the driver's seat. 'Well! Little did I think my car had been driven away while I was in the station,' he said. 'Are you sure you're all right?'

'Oh yes,' said Peter. 'We were half asleep at the back; the men didn't even spot us. They got in and drove straight to this place, then got out. They hardly said a word to one another.'

'Oh. Well, I suppose they weren't really car thieves,' said his father. 'Just a couple of young idiots who wanted to drive somewhere instead of walk. I shan't bother to inform the police. We'd never catch the fellows, and it would be a waste of everyone's time. I've got the car back; that's all that matters.'

The two children felt a little flat to have their extraordinary adventure disposed of in this way.

'But aren't you *really* going to tell the police?' asked Peter, quite disappointed. 'The men may be real crooks.'

'They probably are. But I'm not going to waste *my* time on them,' said his father. 'They'll be caught for something sooner or later! It's a good thing you had the sense to keep quiet in the back of the car!'

Their mother was a good deal more interested in the affair than Daddy, yet even she thought it was just a silly

157

prank on the part of two young men. But it was different when Peter telephoned Jack and told him what happened. Jack was absolutely thrilled.

'Gosh! Really! I wish I'd been with you!' he shouted in excitement, clutching the telephone hard. 'Let's have a meeting about it. Tomorrow afternoon at three o'clock? We've all got a half-term holiday tomorrow, haven't we? We'll tell the others at school there's a meeting on. I'll . . . Sh. Sh!'

'What are you shushing about?' asked Peter. 'Oh, is that awful Susie about? All right, not a word more. See you tomorrow.'

Next afternoon, at three o'clock, all the Secret Seven were down in the shed, Scamper with them too, running from one to another excitedly. He could feel that something important was afoot!

The oil-stove was already lit and the shed was nice and warm. Curtains were drawn across the windows in case anyone should peer in. Nobody had had time to bring things to eat, but fortunately George had had a present of a large bag of humbugs from his grandmother. He handed them round.

'I say, how super,' said Jack. 'Your granny does buy such ENORMOUS humbugs. They last for ages. Now we shall all be comfortable for the rest of the afternoon, with one of these in our cheeks.'

They sat round on boxes or on old rugs, each with their cheeks bulging with a peppermint humbug. Scamper didn't like them, which was lucky. The children made him sit by the door and listen in case anyone came prying, that awful Susie, for instance, or one of her silly friends!

Peter related the whole event, and everyone listened, thrilled.

'And do you mean to say your father isn't going to the police?' said Colin. 'Well, that leaves the field free for us. Come along, Secret Seven, here's something right up our street!'

'It's very exciting,' said Pam. 'But what exactly are we going to work on? I mean, what is there to find out? I wouldn't even know where to *begin*!'

'Well, I'll tell you what *I* think,' said Peter, carefully moving his humbug to the other cheek. 'I think those men are up to something. I don't know what, but I think we ought to find out something about them.'

'But how can we?' asked Pam. 'I don't like the sound of them, anyway.'

'Well, if you don't want to be in on this, there's nothing to stop you from walking out,' said Peter, getting cross with Pam. 'The door's over there.'

Pam changed her mind in a hurry. 'Oh no, I *want* to be in on this; of course I do. You tell us what to do, Peter.'

'Well we don't *know* very much,' said Peter. 'Excuse me, all of you, but I'm going to take my humbug out for a minute or two, while I talk. There, that's better. No, Scamper, don't sniff at it; you don't *like* humbugs!'

With his sweet safely on a clean piece of paper beside him, Peter addressed the meeting.

'We haven't really much to go on, as I said,' he began. 'But we have a *few* clues. One is "Sid's Place". We ought to try and find where that is and watch it, to see if either of the men go there. Then we could shadow them. We'd have to watch it at five o'clock each day.'

'Go on,' said George.

'Then there's Q8061,' said Peter. 'That might be a telephone number. We could find out about that.'

159

'That's silly!' said Pam. 'It doesn't look a bit like a telephone number!'

Peter took no notice of Pam. 'One man had a low-brimmed hat and long hair down to his collar,' he said. 'And I *think* there was something wrong with one hand – it looked as if the tip of the middle finger was missing. I only *just* caught sight of it in the light of a lamppost, but I'm fairly sure.'

'And the other man had very short hair,' said Janet, suddenly. 'I did notice that. Oh, and Peter, do you remember that he said he thought he'd dropped something? Do you think he had? We never looked to see! He didn't find whatever it was.'

'Gosh, yes. I forgot all about that,' said Peter. 'That's most important. We'll all go and look in the car at once. Bring your torches, please, Secret Seven!'

CHAPTER NINE

The Seven get going

SCAMPER DARTED out into the garden with the Seven. Jack looked about to see if Susie or any of her friends were in hiding, but as Scamper didn't run barking at any bush, he felt sure that Susie must be somewhere else!

They all went to the garage. Peter hoped that the car would be there. It was! The children opened the doors and looked inside.

'It's no good us looking in the back,' said Peter. 'The men were in front.'

He felt about everywhere, and shone his torch into every corner of the front of the car. The garage was rather dark, although it was only half-past three in the afternoon.

'Nothing!' he said disappointed.

'Let *me* see,' said Janet. 'I once dropped a pencil and couldn't find it, and it was down between the two front seats!'

She slid her fingers in between the two seats and felt about. She gave a cry and pulled something out. It was a spectacle case. She held it up in triumph.

'Look! That's it. He dropped his spectacle case!'

'But he didn't wear glasses,' said Peter.

'He could have reading glasses, couldn't he?' said Janet. 'Like Granny?'

She opened the case. It was empty. She gave another little squeal.

'Look, it's got his name inside! What do you think of

that? And his telephone number! *Now* we're on to something!'

The Secret Seven crossed round to look. Janet pointed to a little label inside. On it neatly written was a name and number. 'Briggs. Renning 2150.'

'Renning – that's not far away!' said Peter. 'We can look up the name in the telephone directory and see his address. Gosh, what a find!'

Everyone was thrilled. Jack was just about to shut the door of the car when he suddenly remembered that no one had looked *under* the left-hand front seat, where the man who had dropped something had sat. He took a little stick from a bundle of garden bamboos standing in a nearby corner and poked under the seat with it, and out rolled a button!

'Look!' said Jack, holding it up.

Peter gave it a glance.

'Oh that's off my father's mac,' he said. 'It must have been there for ages.'

He put it into his pocket, and they all went back to the shed, feeling very excited.

'Well, first we find out Mr Briggs' address. Then we all ride over to see him,' said Peter. 'We'll make him admit he dropped it in the car, and then I'll pounce like anything and say, "And what were you doing in my father's car?" I'm sure the police would be interested if we could actually tell them the name and address of the man who went off in Dad's car like that, and probably they would make him give the name of the other man too!'

This long speech made Peter quite out of breath. The others gazed at him in admiration. It all sounded very bold.

'All right. What about now, this very minute, if we can find his address in Renning?' said Jack. 'Nothing like striking while the iron's hot. We could have tea in that little tea-shop in Renning. They have wonderful macaroons. I ate five last time I was there.'

'Then somebody else must have paid the bill,' said Colin. 'Yes, do let's go now. It *would* be fun, but you can do the talking, Peter!'

'Have you all got your bikes?' said Peter. 'Good. Let's just go in and take a look at the telephone directory, and get the address. Mr Briggs, we're coming after you!'

The telephone directory was very helpful. Mr H. E. J. Briggs lived at Little Hill, Raynes Road, Renning. Telephone number 2150. Peter copied it down carefully.

'Got enough money for tea, everyone?' he asked.

Colin had only a penny or two, so Peter offered to lend him some. Now they were all ready to set off.

Peter told his mother they were going out to tea, and away they went, riding carefully in single line down the main road, as they had been taught to do.

Renning was about three miles away, and it didn't really take them long to get there.

'Shall we have tea first?' asked George, looking longingly at the tea-shop they were passing.

'No. Work first, pleasure afterwards,' said Peter, who was always very strict about things like that. They cycled on to Raynes Road.

It was only a little lane, set with pretty little cottages. Little Hill was at one end, a nice little place with a colourful garden.

'Well it doesn't *look* like the home of a crook,' said Jack. 'But you never know. See, there's someone in the garden,

163

Peter. Come on, do your job. Let's see how you handle things of this sort. Make him admit he dropped that spectacle case in your father's car!'

'Right!' said Peter, and went in boldly at the garden gate. 'Er – good afternoon. Are you Mr Briggs?'

CHAPTER TEN

Peter feels hot all over

AS SOON as Peter saw the man closely, he knew at once
that he wasn't either of the men in the car. For one thing,
this man had a big round head, and a face to match, and
both the other men had had rather narrow heads, as far as
he had been able to see.

The man looked a little surprised. 'No,' he said. 'I'm not
Mr Briggs. I'm just a friend staying with him. Do you
want him? I'll call him?'

Peter began to feel a little uncomfortable. Somehow this
pretty garden and trim little cottage didn't seem the kind
of place those men would live in!

'Henry! Henry, there's someone asking for you!' called
the man.

Peter saw that the other Secret Seven members were
watching eagerly. Would 'Henry' prove to be one of the
men they were hunting for?

A man came strolling out, someone with trim, short hair
and a narrow head. Yes, he *might* be the man who had sat
in the left-hand seat of the car, except that he didn't in the
least look as if he could possibly take someone else's car!

Still you never know! thought Peter.

The man looked inquiringly at him. 'What do you
want?' he said.

'Er – is your name Mr H. E. J. Briggs, sir?' asked Peter,
politely.

'It is,' said the man looking amused. 'Why?'

'Er – well, have you by any chance lost a spectacle case?' asked Peter.

All the rest of the Seven outside the garden held their breath. What would he say?

'Yes. I *have* lost one,' said the man surprised. 'Have you found it? Where was it?'

'It was in the front of a car,' answered Peter, watching him closely.

Now if the man was one of the car-thieves, he would surely look embarrassed, or deny it. He would know that it was the case he had dropped the night before and would be afraid of saying 'Yes, I dropped it there.'

'What an extraordinary thing!' said the man. 'Whose car? You sound rather *mysterious*. Losing a spectacle case is quite an ordinary thing to do, you know!'

'It was dropped in my father's car last night,' said Peter, still watching the man.

'Oh no, it wasn't,' said Mr Briggs at once. 'I've lost this case for about a week. It can't be mine. I wasn't in anyone's car last night.'

'It *is* the man we want, I bet it is!' said Pam in a low voice to Janet. 'He's telling fibs!'

'The case has your name in it,' said Peter, 'so we know it's yours. And it *was* in my father's car last night.'

'Who *is* your father?' said the man, sounding puzzled. 'I can't quite follow what you're getting at. And where's the case?'

'My father lives at Old Mill House,' began Peter, 'and he's . . .'

'Good gracious! He's not Jack, my farmer friend, surely?' said Mr Briggs. 'That explains everything! He very kindly gave me a lift one day last week, and I must

166

have dropped my spectacle case in his car then. I hunted
for it everywhere when I got back home. Never thought of
the car, of course! Well, well, so you've brought it back?'

'Oh, are you the man my father speaks of as Harry?'
said Peter, taken aback. 'Gosh! Well I suppose you *did*
drop your case, then, and not last night, as I thought. Here
it is. It's got your name and telephone number in it. That's
how we knew it was yours.'

He held it out, and the man took it, smiling. 'Thanks,'
he said, 'and now perhaps you'll tell me what all the
mystery was about, and why you insisted I had dropped
it last night, and why you looked at me as if I were
somebody Very Suspicious Indeed.'

Peter heard the others giggling, and he went red. He
really didn't know *what* to say!

'Well,' he said, 'you see, two men took my father's car last night, and when we looked in it today we found this case, and we thought perhaps it belonged to one of the men.'

Mr Briggs laughed. 'I see, doing a little detective work. Well, it's very disappointing for you, but I don't happen to be a car-thief. Look, here's fifty pence for bringing back my case. Buy some chocolate and share it with those interested friends of yours watching over the hedge.'

'Oh no, thank you,' said Peter, backing away. 'I don't want anything. I'm only too glad to bring your case back. Goodbye!'

He went quickly out of the garden, most relieved to get away from the amused eyes of Mr Briggs. Goodness, what a mistake! He got on his bicycle and rode swiftly away, the other six following.

They all stopped outside the tea-shop.

'Whew!' said Peter, wiping his forehead. 'I DID feel awful when I found out he was a friend of my father's! Dad is always talking about a man called Harry, but I didn't know his surname before.'

'We thought we were so clever, but we weren't this time,' said Colin. 'Bother! The spectacle case was nothing to do with those two men in the car, but perhaps the button is?'

'Perhaps,' said Peter. 'But I'm not tackling anyone wearing macs with buttons that match the one we found, unless I'm jolly certain he's one of those men! I feel hot all over when I think of Mr Briggs. Suppose he goes and tells my father all about this?'

'Never mind,' said Jack, grinning. 'It was great fun watching you. Let's have tea. Look, they've got macaroons today.'

In they went and had a wonderful tea. And now, what next? Think hard, Secret Seven, and make some exciting plans!

CHAPTER ELEVEN

Jobs for every member

THE NEXT day another Secret Seven meeting was held, but this time it was at Colin's, in his little summer-house. It wasn't such a good place as Peter's shed, because it had an open doorway with no door, and they were not allowed to have an oilstove in it.

However, Colin's mother had asked all the Secret Seven to tea, so it was clear they would have to have their next meeting at his house, and the little summer-house was the only place where they could talk in secret.

'We'll bring our old clothes for the Guy and decide what he should wear,' said Peter. 'We haven't even thought about him in the last two meetings and it's Bonfire Night in a few days. We'll need paper and straw for stuffing him too.'

So all the Secret Seven went to Colin's house that evening. They had a fine tea, the kind they all enjoyed most.

'Sardine sandwiches, honey sandwiches, a smashing cherry cake with cherries inside *and* on top, and an iced sponge cake. I say, Colin, your mother's a wonder,' said Peter, approvingly. 'Isn't she going to have it with us? I'd like to thank her.'

'No, she's had to go out to a committee meeting or something,' said Colin. 'All she said was that we've to behave ourselves, and if we go down to the summer-house this cold dark evening, we've GOT to put on our coats.'

'Right,' said Peter. 'Coats it will be. Mothers are always very keen on coats, aren't they? Personally, I think it's quite hot today.'

They finished up absolutely everything on the tea-table. There wasn't even a piece of the big cherry cake left! Scamper, who had also been asked to tea, had his own dish of dog-biscuits with shrimp paste on each. He was simply delighted, and crunched them up nonstop.

'Now we'll go to the summer-house. We'd better take a candle it's so dark already,' said Colin. 'And don't forget your coats everyone.'

'And the things for the Guy,' said Peter.

So down they all went to the little wooden summer-house, carrying paper, straw, string and safety pins as well as an odd assortment of old clothes. The house had a wooden bench running all round it and felt a bit cold. Nobody minded that. It was such a nice secret place to talk in, down at the bottom of the dark garden.

The candle was stuck in a bottle and lit. There was no shelf to put it on, so Colin stood it in the middle of the floor.

'Have to be careful of Scamper knocking it over!' said Peter. 'Where is he?'

'He's gone into the kitchen to see Daddy,' said Colin. 'He's cooking a stew or something, and Scamper smelt it. He'll be along soon. Now stack your things under the wooden bench for the time being. That's right. We'll look at the clothes when we've finished the meeting.'

'We'll begin it now,' said Peter. 'Owing to our silly mistake about the spectacles case, we're not as far on with this adventure as we ought to be. We must do a little more work on it. First, has anyone any idea where "Sid's place" is?'

There was a silence.

'Never heard of it,' said Jack.

'Well, it must be some place that is used by men like those two in my father's car,' said Peter.

'Perhaps Larry at the garage would know?' said Colin, who had great faith in Larry. 'He knows a lot of lorry-drivers, and they're the kind who might go to some place called "Sid's" or "Jim's" or "Nick's".'

'Yes. That's a good idea,' said Peter. 'Colin, you and George go and find out from Larry tomorrow. Now, what else can we do? What about the number that one of the men had to get in touch with – what was it now?'

'Q8061,' said Pam, promptly. 'I think of it as the *letter* Q, but it might be spelt K-E-W, you know.'

'Yes, you're right. It might,' said Peter. 'That's really quite an idea, Pam. It might be a number at Kew tele-phone exchange, Kew 8061. You and Barbara can make it your job to find out.'

'How do we set about it?' said Barbara.

'I really can't explain such easy things to you,' said Peter, impatiently. 'You and Pam can quite well work out what to do yourselves. Now is there anything else we can work on?'

'Only the button we found in the car,' said Jack.

'I told you, it's sure to belong to my father's mac,' said Peter. 'It's just like the buttons on it.'

'But we ought to make *sure*,' argued Jack. 'You know you always say we never ought to leave anything to chance, Peter. There are hundreds of different coat but-tons.'

'Well, perhaps you're right,' said Peter. 'Yes, I think you are. Janet, will you see to that point, please, and look at Dad's mac. I know he's got a button missing, so I expect it belongs to his mac, but we *will* make sure.'

'You haven't given *me* anything to do,' said Jack.

'Well, if the button doesn't match the ones on Dad's mac, you can take charge of *that* point,' said Peter, with a sudden giggle, 'and you can march about looking for people wearing a mac with a missing button.'

'Don't be an idiot,' said Jack. 'Still, if it *isn't* your father's button, it *will* be one dropped by one of those men, and one of us ought to take charge of it. So I will, if it's necessary.'

'Right,' said Peter. 'Well, that's the end of the meeting. Now let's think about the Guy.'

CHAPTER TWELVE

Oh, what a pity!

COLIN AND Jack took the bundles of clothes for the Guy out from under the wooden bench of the summer-house. The Seven knelt down on the floor to sort everything out. What a lovely job!

'I wish we had a better light than just this flickering candle on the floor,' said Pam. 'It's difficult to see what colour the clothes are.'

Colin pulled out a fearsome-looking mask from the pile of old things. 'Who brought this? It looks like the villain in that play we saw on TV last night. He put on the mask and hissed menacingly, "Your money or your life."'

'You look worse than that villain, Colin,' said Janet. 'I got the mask at a party ages ago and I put it away for Guy Fawkes. I almost forgot where I had put it.'

'It will make a really frightening Guy. I can just imagine him leering down at us from the top of the bonfire,' said Barbara.

'We'd better start making the Guy,' said Peter. 'This is a good big pair of trousers. If we stuff straw and screwed up paper down the legs we can safety pin those old slippers on the bottoms to look like feet.'

'And here's your father's old green jacket, George. We can do the same to the arms and pin my old gloves on for hands,' said Barbara, 'though his hands will look a bit smaller than the rest of him!'

'Look what I've brought,' said Pam. 'I thought it would

173

be much easier to have an old cushion for a body instead of straw and paper. Mother said I could take this old blue one that has been leaking stuffing.'

The Secret Seven began to roll up paper and stuff straw into the trousers and jacket. It was difficult to see what they were doing with only the light of the candle. As they worked, they heard the sound of a bark, and then scampering feet. Scamper had been let out of the kitchen door and was coming to find his friends. Where were they? Wuff! Wuff!

'Scamper!' called Janet from the summer-house. 'We're here!'

Scamper tore down the garden path, barking madly. Anyone would think he had been away from the seven children for a whole month, not just half an hour!

He rushed straight into the little summer-house and over went the bottle with the lit candle in its neck! Crash!

'You idiot, Scamper,' said Peter and reached to set the bottle upright again. The candle was still alight.

But before he could take hold of it, the flame of the candle had licked against a bundle of straw. It was alight!

174

OH, WHAT A PITY!

'Fire!' yelled Peter. 'Look out, Pam! Look out, Barbara!'

The straw flared up and the loose paper on the floor began to burn too. The children tried to stamp out the flames but the fire spread faster than they could stamp.

Flames licked at the wooden bench. The old clothes were smouldering, sending out black smoke that made the children cough and splutter.

The seven children hurried out of the little summer-house clutching each other. Scamper, really terrified, had completely disappeared.

They all turned to look back. Fire glowed through the doorway and windows. They could hear a crackling as their things burned.

'We'd better get some water,' said Colin, suddenly. 'The summer-house will catch fire and burn down. Quick!'

They left the fire and ran to get buckets. There was a little pond nearby, and they filled the buckets from it. Splash! Splash! Splash! The water was thrown all over the summer-house, and there was a tremendous sizzling noise. Black smoke poured out of the little house and almost choked the Seven.

'Pooh!' said Jack, and coughed. 'What a horrible smell!'

'It's a good thing your father didn't see this,' panted Peter to Colin, coming up with another pail of water. 'He would be furious about this. There, I think we've about got the fire down now. Pooooon! That smoke!'

It was a very, very sad ending to the tea and meeting at Colin's. Barbara was in tears. There was nothing left of the Guy but smoke and smell and a nasty-looking black mess.

'It's bad luck,' said Peter, feeling as if he wouldn't mind howling himself. 'Bother Scamper! It's all his fault. Where is he?'

'Gone home at sixty miles an hour, I should think,' said Janet. 'It's a pity he hasn't got a post-office savings book

like we have. I'd make him take some money out and buy another mask for us.'

'We'll have to see if we can collect some more clothes. But I don't suppose people will want to give us any more after this,' said George.

'I hope your parents won't be too cross about the summer-house,' said Jack gloomily. 'At least it didn't burn down, but everything is very black and wet. The wooden bench is a bit charred too. I'll come along tomorrow, when it's dried up a bit, and help you to clear it up.'

They were just about to go off to the front gate when Janet stopped them. 'We meant to choose a new password today,' she said. 'You know that Susie knows our last one, "Guy Fawkes", and we really *must* have a secret one. Susie has told everyone in our class.'

'Yes. I forgot about that,' said Peter. 'Well, I vote we have "Bonfire". It really does seem a very good password for tonight!'

'All right – Bonfire,' said Colin. 'I'm sorry it's been such a disappointing evening. This is definitely *not* the kind of adventure I like! Goodbye, all of you. See you tomorrow!'

It was a gloomy company of children that made their way home. Bother Scamper, *why* did he have to do a silly thing like that?

CHAPTER THIRTEEN

Sid's Place

ALL THE Secret Seven felt exceedingly gloomy next day, which was Sunday. They met at Sunday School, but none of them had much to say. They were all very subdued. Colin's parents had been very cross about the damaged summer-house and had forbidden him ever to use candles there again.

'Scamper *did* race home last night,' said Janet to the girls. 'He was behind the couch, trembling from head to foot. He is awfully frightened of fire you know.'

'Poor Scamper!' said Pam. 'Did you forgive him?'

'We simply had to,' said Janet. 'Anyway, he didn't mean to upset the candle, poor Scamper. We stroked him and patted him and loved him, and when he saw we weren't going to scold him, he crept out and sat as close to our legs as he could, and put his head on my knee.'

'He's so sweet,' said Barbara. 'But all the same it's *dreadful* to have lost our Guy.'

'It's quite put our adventure out of my mind,' said Pam. 'But I suppose we'd better think about it again tomorrow, Barbara. We've got to find out about that telephone number, Kew 8061. Though how we shall do it, I don't know.'

'Leave it till tomorrow,' said Barbara. 'I can't think of anything but our poor Guy today.'

The next day was Monday, and the Seven were back at school. George and Colin went to call at the garage after morning school, to try and find out something about

179

'Sid's Place' from Larry. He was sitting in a corner with a newspaper, munching his lunch.

'Hallo, Larry,' said Colin. 'I wonder if you can help us. Do you know anywhere called "Sid's Place"?'

'No, I don't,' said Larry. 'Sounds like an eating-house or something. There's a lorry-driver coming in soon. If you like to wait, I'll ask him.'

The lorry drove in after three or four minutes, and the man got down, a big heavy fellow who called out cheerfully to Larry. 'Just off to get a bite of dinner. Be back in half an hour for my lorry.'

'Hey, Charlie, do you eat at "Sid's Place"?' called Larry. 'Do you know it?'

'"Sid's Place"? No, I eat at my sister's when I come through here,' said Charlie. 'Wait a minute now. "Sid's" you said. Yes I remember seeing a little café called "Sid's Café". Would that be the place you're meaning?'

'Could be,' said Larry, looking questioningly at Colin.

Colin nodded. 'Probably the one,' he said, feeling suddenly excited. 'Where is it?'

'You know Old Street? Well, it's at the corner of Old Street and James Street, not a first-class place, and not the sort you boys want to go to. So long, Larry. See you in half an hour!'

'Thanks, Larry,' said Colin. 'Come on, George, let's go and have a look at this place. We've just about got time.'

They went to Old Street and walked down to James Street at the end. On the corner, sharing a bit of each street, was a rather dirty-looking eating-house. 'Sid's Café' was painted over the top of the very messy window.

The boys looked inside. Men were sitting at a long counter, eating sandwiches and drinking coffee or tea. There were one or two tables in the shop, too, at which slightly better-dressed men were having a hot meal served to them by a fat and cheerful girl.

'Oh so that's "Sid's Place",' said Colin, staring in. 'I wonder which is Sid?'

'Perhaps Sid is somewhere in the back quarters,' said George. 'There are only girls serving here. Well we know that one of those men comes here every day about five o'clock. One of us must watch, and we'll be bound to see the man.'

'It'll have to be Peter,' said Colin. 'We wouldn't know the man. He would probably recognise him at once.'

'Yes. It's going to be very difficult for him to hang about here, watching everyone,' said George. 'People will wonder what he's up to. Two of us would seem even *more* suspicious.'

'Well that's up to Peter!' said Colin. 'We've done *our* job

181

and found Sid's place. Come on, we'll be awfully late for lunch.'

Peter was very pleased with Colin and George when he heard their news. 'Good work!' he said. 'I'll get along there at five o'clock this afternoon. How have Pam and Barbara got on?'

Janet told him while they had a quick tea together after afternoon school. 'They just couldn't think *how* to do anything about KEW 8061,' said Janet. 'They simply couldn't.'

'Couple of idiots!' said Peter, munching a bun quickly. 'Hurry up, I must go.'

'Well, Pam asked her mother how to find out if there *was* such a number, because she and Barbara really didn't feel they could wade all through the telephone directories,' said Janet. 'And her mother said, "Well, just ring up and see if there's an answer!"'

'Easy,' said Peter. 'Simple!'

'Yes – well, they rang up the number, feeling very excited, because they thought they could ask whoever answered what his name and address were, but there was no reply,' said Janet. 'And the operator said it was because there was no telephone with that number at present! So Q8061 is *not* a telephone number, Peter. It must be something else!'

'Bother!' said Peter, getting up. 'It would have been marvellous if KEW 8061 *had* answered. We'd have been able to get the name and address and everything. That clue isn't much good, I'm afraid. I must be off, Janet. Wouldn't it be wonderful if I spotted one of the men going into Sid's place?'

'It *would*,' said Janet. 'Oh, I DO hope you do, Peter!'

CHAPTER FOURTEEN

A wonderful idea

PETER WENT as quickly as he could to the corner of Old
Street and James Street. Yes – there was Sid's Café, just as
Colin had said. What was the time?

He glanced at his watch – six minutes to five. Well, if the
man came at five o'clock, he ought just to catch him. Of
course, he might come any time after that. That would be
a nuisance, because then Peter would have to wait about a
long time.

Peter lolled against the corner, watching everyone who
came by, especially, of course, the men who went in and
out of 'Sid's Café'. They were mostly men with barrows of

fruit that they left outside, or drivers of vans, or shifty-looking men, unshaved and dirty.

He got a shock when someone came out of the café and spoke roughly to him.

'Now then, what are you doing here, lolling about? Don't you dare take fruit off my barrow! I've caught you boys doing it before, and I'll call the police if you do. Clear off!'

'I wouldn't *dream* of taking your fruit!' said Peter, indignantly, looking at the pile of cheap fruit on the nearby barrow.

'Ho, you wouldn't, would you? Well, then, what are you standing here for, looking about? Boys don't stand at corners for nothing! We've been watching you from inside the shop, me and my mates, and we know you're after something!'

Peter was shocked. How dare this man say things like that to him! Still, perhaps some boys did steal from barrows or from fruit-stalls outside shops.

'Go on, you tell me what you're standing about here for,' said the man again, putting his face close to Peter's.

As the boy couldn't tell him the reason why he was standing at that corner, he said nothing, but turned and went off, his face burning red. Horrible man! he thought. And I haven't seen anyone yet in the least like that man who went off in our car. Of course, all I've got to go on really is his hat and long hair, and possibly maimed finger on his right hand.

He ran back home, thinking hard. After all, that man might go to Sid's place each night and I'd *never* know him if he had a cap instead of a hat, and had cut his hair shorter. And most of these men slouch along with their hands in their pockets, so I wouldn't see his hand either. It's hopeless.

Peter went round to see Colin about it. Jack and George were there, doing their homework together.

'Hallo!' they said, in surprise. 'Aren't you watching at Sid's place?'

Peter told them what had happened. 'I don't see how I can go and watch there any more,' he said, rather gloomily. 'That man who spoke to me was really nasty. And how can I watch without being seen?'

'Can't be done,' said Colin. 'Give it up! This is something we just can't do. Come on out to the summer-house and see what I've made! We cleared away the mess from the fire, and I've got something else there now!'

They all went out to the summer-house, with their torches. Colin shone his on to something there, and Peter jumped in astonishment, not at first realising what it was.

'Gosh! It's a Guy!' he said, in admiration. 'What a beauty!'

The Guy certainly was very fine. He was stuffed with straw, and wore some of Colin's very old clothes. He had a mask, of course, and grinned happily at the three boys. He had a wig made of black strands of wool and an old hat on top. Colin had sat him in a garden barrow, and he really looked marvellous.

'He's not man-sized because I only had my very old and small suit, but he's the best I could do,' said Colin. 'I bought another mask with my pocket money. Dad said we can have a bonfire at the bottom of the garden as long as he is there. You can all come and help build it tomorrow.'

The Guy seemed to watch them as they talked, grinning away merrily.

'It's a pity *he* can't watch outside Sid's place!' said Jack. 'Nobody would suspect him or bother about *him*. He could watch for that fellow all evening!'

They all laughed. Then Peter stopped suddenly and gazed hard at the Guy. An idea had come to him, a really WONDERFUL idea!

'Hey!' he said, clutching at Colin and making him jump. 'You've given me an idea! What about ME dressing up as a Guy, and wearing a mask with eye-holes – and one of you taking me somewhere near Sid's Café? There are heaps of these Guys about now, and nobody would think our Guy was *real*. I would watch for ages and nobody would guess.'

'Whew!' said the other three together, and stared at Peter in admiration.

Colin thumped him on the back. 'That's a brilliant idea!' he said. 'Super! Smashing! When shall we do it?'

'Tomorrow,' said Peter. 'I can rush here and dress up

186

easily enough, and one of you can wheel me off in the barrow – all of you, if you like! What a game!'

'But my mother doesn't like the idea of children taking Guys and begging for money,' said Colin, remembering. 'She says that begging is wrong.'

'So it is,' said Peter. 'My mother says that too, but if we *did* get any money we could give it to a charity.'

'Oh well, that's all right, then!' said Colin. 'Gosh, this is grand! Mind you don't leap up out of the barrow if you see that fellow going into Sid's place, Peter!'

'I'll keep as still as a real Guy!' said Peter, grinning. 'Well, so long. See you at school tomorrow.'

CHAPTER FIFTEEN

The peculiar Guy

PETER RACED home to tell Janet of the new idea. She was so thrilled that she couldn't say a word. What an idea! How super! She stared in admiration at her brother. He was truly a fine leader for the Secret Seven!

Scamper wuffed loudly, exactly as if he were saying, 'Great, Peter, splendid idea!'

'*I've* got something to tell you, too,' said Janet, suddenly remembering. 'I looked on Daddy's mac and he *has* got a button missing; but it's a small one on his sleeve, not a large one like we found. And also it's not quite the same colour, Peter.'

'Ah, good! That means it probably *was* a button that dropped from that man's mac!' said Peter, pleased. 'Jack will have to take the button, Janet, and work on that clue, if he can! So give it to me, and I'll hand it to him tomorrow.'

'I wish we could find out about Q8061,' said Janet. 'I'm pretty sure it must be someone's telephone number, but it's very difficult to find out.'

'There's Mother calling,' said Peter. 'I bet it's to tell me to do my homework!'

It was of course, and poor Peter found it very difficult indeed to work out arithmetic problems when his head was full of dressing up as a Guy!

All the Secret Seven were thrilled to hear of Peter's new plan, and next evening they were round at Colin's to see him dress up. He really did look remarkably good!

He wore an old pair of patched trousers, and a ragged jacket. He wore a pair of great big boots thrown out by Colin's father. He had a scarf round his neck, and a big old hat over a wig made of black wool.

'You look quite *dreadful*!' said Janet, with a giggle. 'Put the mask on now.'

Peter put it on, and immediately became a grinning Guy, like all the other Guys that were appearing here and there in the streets of the town. Scamper took one look at Peter's suddenly changed face, and backed away, growling.

'It's all right, Scamper,' said Peter, laughing. 'It's me! Don't be afraid.'

'You look horrible,' said Pam. 'I really feel scared when I look at you, though I know you're really Peter. Nobody, *nobody* could possibly guess you were alive!'

190

Peter got into the barrow. 'Gosh, it's very hard and uncomfortable,' he said. 'Got any old cushions, Colin?'

Colin produced an old rug and three rather dirty garden cushions. These made the barrow much more comfortable. Peter got in and lolled on the cushions in the limp, floppy way of all Guys. He really looked extremely Guy-like!

The others shrieked with laughter to see him.

'Come on,' said Colin at last. 'We really must go, or we shan't be there till long past five.'

The three boys set off, taking turns at wheeling Peter in the barrow. He kept making horrible groans and moans, and Jack laughed so much that he had to sit down on a bus-stop seat and hold his aching sides.

An old lady there peered at the Guy. 'What a good one!' she said, and fumbled in her purse. 'I'll give you some money for fireworks.'

'Oh, any money we get is going to charity,' explained George quickly.

She gave him fifty pence, and then, as the bus came up, waved to them and got on.

'How nice of her!' said George. 'Fifty whole pence.'

They went on down the street, with Peter thoroughly enjoying himself! He lolled about, watching everything through the eye-slits of his mask, and made silly remarks in a hollow Guy-like voice that made the others laugh helplessly.

At last they came to Sid's Café. The barrow was neatly wedged into a little alcove near the door, from which Peter could see everyone who went in or out.

The boys stood nearby, waiting to see if Peter recognised anyone. If he did, he was to give a sign, and two of the Seven would shadow the man to see where he went, if he happened to come *out* of the café. If he went inside it they were to wait till he came out.

The men going in and out of the eating-house were amused with the Guy. One prodded him hard with his stick, and gave Peter a terrible shock. 'Good Guy you've got there!' said the man and threw five pence on to Peter's tummy.

'Colin! Jack! You're NOT to let people prod me like that,' said Peter, in a fierce whisper. 'It really hurt.'

'Well, how are we to stop them?' said Colin, also in a whisper.

All went well till two young men came by and saw the Guy sitting there. 'Hallo! He's a good Guy!' said one. 'Nice pair of boots he's got. I've a good mind to take them off him!'

And to Peter's horror, he felt the boots on his feet being tugged hard. He gave a yell, and the young men looked extremely startled. They disappeared quickly.

'CAN'T you look after me better?' said Peter to the others. 'Heave me up a bit on the cushions. Those men pulled me off.'

Colin and George heaved him into a more comfortable position.

'Anyway, you've made quite a bit of money,' said George, in Peter's ear. 'People think you're jolly good, we've got quite a few pounds.'

Peter grunted. He was cross with the others. Why didn't they guard him from pokes and prods and pullings? Then, quite suddenly, he caught sight of somebody, and stiffened all over.

Surely, SURELY, that was one of the men who had taken his father's car? Peter stared and stared. Was it? Oh, why didn't he stand a bit nearer so that he could see?

CHAPTER SIXTEEN

The two men

THE MAN was standing by the window of the café, as if he were waiting for someone. He had on a hat and his hair was rather long. Peter looked as closely at him as he could.

The man who drove the car had a low-brimmed hat, he thought and long hair. This man somehow *looks* like that man we saw in the car.

The man moved a little nearer, and coughed impatiently. He took a handkerchief from his pocket and blew his nose. The top of one middle finger was missing. Peter knew for *certain* that it was the man he was looking for! It *must* be the man! Perhaps he's waiting for the other man.

Almost before he had finished thinking this, the second man came up! There was no mistaking that cap and the short, cropped hair, grown a little longer now. The cap was pulled down over his face exactly as it had been when he was in the car. He wore an old mac, and Peter tried to see if it had a button missing.

The two men said a word of greeting and then went into the café. They went right through the room to a door at the back, opened it, and disappeared.

'Colin! George! Jack! Those were the two men,' called Peter in a low voice full of excitement. 'One of them had half a finger missing. I saw it.'

'And the other had a button off his mac!' said Jack. 'I noticed that, though I didn't know he was one of the men we're after! But seeing that I'm in charge of the button

193

now, I'm making a point of looking carefully at every mac I see! I believe our button matches his exactly.'

'Good work!' said Peter. 'Now listen. The next move is very, very important. Two of you must shadow these men. If they separate, you must separate too, and each go after one of them. Colin, you must wheel me home.'

'Right,' said the three, always willing to obey Peter's

leadership. He really was very good at this kind of thing.

'Get as close to those men as you can and see if you can hear anything useful,' said Peter. 'And track them right to their homes if you can. Report to me at the Secret Seven shed as soon as you can.'

'Right,' said George and Jack, feeling as if they were first-class plain-clothes policemen!

The two men were not long in Sid's. They came out after about ten minutes, looking angry. They stood in the doorway, taking no notice of the Guy and the boys.

'Sid's let us down,' said the man with the missing finger. 'He said he'd give us two hundred and now he's knocked it down to fifty. Better go back to Q's and tell him. He'll be wild.'

The boys listened intently, pretending to fiddle about with the Guy.

'I'm not arguing with Sid again,' said the other man. 'I reckon I'm an idiot to come out of hiding, yet, till my hair's grown. Come on, let's go.'

They went off down the street, and George and Jack immediately set off behind them, leaving Colin with Peter.

'Did you hear that?' said Peter, in great excitement, forgetting he was a Guy. 'They've stolen something and want to sell it to Sid, and he won't give them what he promised. So they're going back to Q, whoever he is, probably the chief, to report it. Well we know that Q is a man, now!'

'And did you hear what the other man said about his hair growing?' said Colin, bending over Peter. 'I bet he's just come out of prison, it's so short. They always shave it there, don't they? Or perhaps he's an *escaped* prisoner, in hiding. Gosh, Peter, this is super!'

'Wheel me to our shed,' commanded Peter, wishing he could get out and walk. 'Hurry up. The girls will be there already, and George and Jack will join us as soon as they can. Do hurry up! . . . I'm going to get out and walk,' announced Peter. 'It's a nice dark road we're in. Stop a minute, Colin, and I'll get out.'

Colin stopped, and Peter climbed out of the barrow. Colin shone his torch to help him, and an old man with a dog saw the Guy stepping out of the barrow. He stared as if he couldn't believe his eyes, and then hurried off at top speed. Good gracious! A Guy coming alive. No, surely his eyes must have deceived him!

It wasn't long before Colin and Peter were whispering the password outside the shed at the bottom of Peter's garden. The barrow was shoved into some bushes, and Peter had taken off his mask.

'Bonfire!' said the boys, and the door opened at once. Pam gave a little scream as Peter came in, still looking very peculiar with a black wool wig, an old hat, and very ragged clothes.

'We've got news!' said Peter. 'Great news. Just listen, all of you!'

CHAPTER SEVENTEEN

Good work!

PETER QUICKLY told the girls all that had happened, and they listened in silence, feeling very thrilled. Now they were really finding out something, even that button had helped!

'I think the short-haired man has either just come out of prison or escaped from it,' said Peter. 'He may have committed a robbery before he went in, and have hidden what he stole, and it's these goods he and the other man are trying to sell to Sid.'

'Well, who's Q, then?' asked Janet. 'Where does *he* come in?'

'He's probably holding the stolen goods,' said Peter, working everything out in his mind. 'And I expect he's sheltering the thief, too. If only we could find out who Q is and where he lives. He's the missing link.'

The five of them talked and talked, and Scamper listened and joined in with a few wuffs now and again, thumping his tail on the ground when the chatter got very loud.

'When will George and Jack be back?' asked Pam. 'I ought not to be too late home, and it's a quarter past six now!'

'Here they are!' said Colin, hearing voices outside. A knock came at the door.

'Password!' shouted everyone.

'Bonfire!' said two voices, and in went George and Jack,

beaming all over their faces, glad to be out of the cold,
dark November night.

'What happened? Did you shadow them?' demanded
Peter, as they sat down on boxes.

'Yes,' said George. 'We followed them all the way down
the street, and away by the canal and up by Cole Square.
We only once got near enough to hear them say anything.'

'What was that?' asked Peter.

'One of them said "Is that a policeman lying in wait for
us over there? Come on, run for it!"' said George. 'And
just as a bobby came out of the shadows they ran round
the corner, and the policeman never even noticed them!

We shot after them, just in time to see them trying the handles of some cars parked there.'

'Then they slid quickly into one and drove off,' finished Jack. 'That was the end of our shadowing.'

'So they stole *another* car!' said Colin.

'You didn't take the number by any chance, did you?' asked Peter.

'Of course!' said Jack, and took out his notebook. 'Here it is, PLK 100. We didn't go back and tell the policeman. We thought we'd race back here and let you decide what we ought to do next.'

'Good work,' said Peter, pleased. 'If only we knew where Q lived, we'd know where the men were, and could tell the police to go and grab them there. They'd get the stolen goods too. I bet they're being held by our mysterious Q!'

'I know! I know!' suddenly yelled Pam, making everyone jump. 'Why can't we look up all the names beginning with Q in our local telephone directory? If Q lives somewhere here, his name would be there, and his number.'

'Yes but there might be a lot of Qs, and we wouldn't know which was the right one,' objected Janet. 'Why, we ourselves know a Mrs Queen, a Mr Quigley and a Miss Quorn.'

'But don't you see what I *mean*!' said Pam, impatiently. 'We'll go down all the list of Qs, and the one with the telephone number of 8061 will be *our* Q! Don't you *see*?'

Everyone saw what she meant at once.

Peter looked at Pam admiringly. 'That's a very good idea, Pam,' he said. 'I've sometimes thought that you're not as good a Secret Seven member as the others are, but now I know you are. That's a Very Good Idea. Why didn't we think of it before instead of messing about with K.E.W.?'

'I'll get our telephone directory with all the numbers in,' said Janet and raced off.

She soon came back, gave the password and joined the others. She opened the book at the Qs, and everyone craned to look at them.

There were not very many. 'Quant,' read Pam, 'telephone number 6015. Queen, 6453, Quelling, 4322, Quentin, 8061 . . .! That's it. Look, here it is, Quentin, 8061, Barr's Warehouse East End. Why, that's only about two miles away, right at the other end of the town.'

'Gosh!' said Peter, delighted. 'That's given us JUST the information we wanted. A warehouse, too. A fine place for hiding stolen goods! My goodness, we've done some excellent work. Pam, you deserve a pat on the back!'

She got plenty of pats, and sat back, beaming. 'What do we do now?' she said.

Before anyone could answer, there came the sound of footsteps down the path, and Peter's mother's voice called loudly: 'Peter! Janet! Are Colin and George there, and Pam? Their mothers have just telephoned to say they really must come home at once, it's getting late!'

'Right, Mummy!' called Peter. 'Wait for us. We've got a wonderful tale to tell you! Do wait!'

But his mother had gone scurrying back to the house, not liking the cold, damp evening. The seven children tore after her, with Scamper barking his head off.

Just as they went in at the back of the house, there came a knock at the front door.

'See who that is, Peter!' called his mother. 'I've got a cake in the oven I must look at.'

Peter went to the door, with the others close behind

202

him. A big policeman stood there. He smiled at the surprised children.

'I've just been to Jack's house,' he said, 'and Susie told me he might be here. I saw you tonight in Cole Square – you and this other boy here. Well, not long after that somebody reported to me that their car had been stolen near where you were, and I wondered if either of you had noticed anything suspicious going on.'

'Oh, come in, come in!' cried Peter, joyfully. 'We can tell you a whole lot about the thieves, and we can even tell you where you'll probably find the car. Come in, do!'

CHAPTER EIGHTEEN

Don't worry, Secret Seven!

THE POLICEMAN went into the hall, looking extremely surprised. Peter's mother came from the kitchen and Peter's father looked out of his study.

'What's all this?' he said. 'Nobody has got into trouble, surely?'

'No,' said Peter. 'Oh, Daddy, you must just listen to our tale. It's really super!'

They all went into the study, the policeman looking more and more puzzled.

'I *think* you'll find that stolen car outside Barr's Warehouse, at the East End of the town,' said Peter. 'And in the warehouse you'll probably find a Mr Quentin, and quite a lot of stolen goods on the premises.'

'And you'll find a man with half a finger missing, and another whose hair is so short that he looks like an escaped prisoner,' put in Colin.

'Wait! Wait a minute! What's this about a man with a missing half-finger?' said the policeman, urgently. 'We're looking for him – Fingers, he's called, and he's a friend of a thief who's just been in prison. He escaped last week, and we thought he might go to Fingers for help, so we've been keeping an eye open for him too.'

'They met at Sid's Café,' said Peter, enjoying everyone's astonishment.

'WHAT?' said his father. 'Sid's Café? That horrible place! Don't dare to tell me you boys have been in there.'

'Not inside, only outside,' said Peter. 'It's all right, Daddy. We *really* haven't done anything wrong. It all began with that night when you left Janet and me in your car in the station yard, and two men got in and drove it away.'

'And we wanted you to go to the police, but you didn't think you'd bother,' said Janet. 'So we've been trying to trace the two men ourselves, and we have!'

Then the whole of the story came out how they found Sid's Café, how Peter dressed up as a Guy to watch for the men, how they saw Fingers with his missing half-finger, and how George and Jack followed them and saw them steal the car near Cole Square.

'And we know where they've gone, because they have a friend called Q, a Mr Quentin,' said Peter. 'They mentioned his telephone number, it was 8061, and we looked

up the number and found the address. We only did that a
little while ago, actually. The address is Barr's Warehouse,
as we said.'

'Amazing!' said the policeman, scribbling fast in his
notebook. 'Incredible! Do these kids do this kind of thing
often?'

'Well, you're a fairly new man here,' said Peter's father,
'or you'd know how they keep poking their noses into all
sorts of things. I don't know that I really approve of it, but
they certainly have done some good work.'

'We're the Secret Seven Society, you see,' explained
Janet. 'And we really do like some kind of adventurous
job to do.'

'Well, thanks very much,' said the policeman, getting
up. 'I'll get a few men and ask the Sergeant to come along
with us and see what we can find in Barr's Warehouse.

You'll deserve a jolly good Bonfire Night tomorrow! I hope you've got a wonderful collection of fireworks, you deserve the best!'

'Our families are joining together for a big bonfire party. We all saved up for the fireworks and Colin's father is keeping them for us – though I expect all our fathers will take turns letting them off!'

'Well, have a good evening then – and mind you all take care not to get too close!' said the policeman, going to the door. 'I'm much obliged to you all. Good night!'

'What a tale!' said Peter's mother. 'I never heard of such goings-on! Whatever will you Seven do next? To think of you dressing up as a Guy, Peter, and watching outside Sid's Café! No wonder you look so DREADFUL! Take that black wig off, do!'

'Mummy, *can't* the others stay and have a bit of supper?' begged Peter. 'We've got such a lot to talk about. Do let them. Sandwiches will do. We'll all help to make them.'

'Very well,' said his mother, laughing at all the excited faces. 'Janet, go and telephone everybody's mothers and tell them where they are!'

The Seven were very pleased. In fifteen minutes' time they were all sitting down to potted meat sandwiches, oatmeal biscuits, apples and hot cocoa, talking nineteen to the dozen, with a very excited Scamper tearing round their legs under the table. What an unexpected party! thought Scamper, delighted, and what a wonderful selection of titbits!

The telephone suddenly rang, and Peter went to answer it. It proved to be a very exciting call indeed! He came racing back to the others.

208

'That was that policeman! He thought we'd like to know what happened.'

'What? Tell us!' cried everyone.

'Well, the police went to Barr's Warehouse and the first thing they saw in the yard was the stolen car!' said Peter. 'Then they forced their way in at the back door, and found Mr Quentin, scared stiff, in his office. When they told him they knew that Fingers and the escaped prisoner were somewhere in the warehouse, he just crumpled up!'

'Have they got the others?' asked Colin.

'Oh yes. Quentin showed the police where they were hiding,' said Peter. 'Down in a cellar, and the stolen goods were there too. It was a wonderful raid! By the way, the police want to know if we can identify the second man, the close-cropped man, and I said yes, if he was wearing a mac with a missing button, because we've got the button!'

'Goody, goody!' said Barbara. 'So we have. We forgot to tell the policeman about that! Where *is* the button?'

'Here,' said Jack, and spun it on the table. 'Good old button, you did your bit too! Gosh, this is one of the most exciting jobs the Secret Seven have ever done. I'm jolly sorry it's ended.'

So was everyone. They didn't want that exciting evening to come to a finish, but they had to say goodbye at last.

'Tomorrow is Bonfire Night,' said Peter to Janet as they shut the front door on the others. 'We'll all have a wonderful party and Colin's Guy will look down on us all from the top of the bonfire.'

'Shall we put you there instead, Peter? You'd look even better!' said Janet, smiling.

'I'd much rather watch the Guy than be him tomorrow night,' said Peter, 'though it was exciting being a Guy just for one night! Come on, Janet, let's go up to bed and dream about all those super fireworks – '

They both ran upstairs shouting at the tops of their voices, 'Bang! Whoosh! Bang-Bang-Bang!'

SECRET SEVEN WIN THROUGH

CONTENTS

CHAPTER ONE

The holidays begin

'EASTER HOLIDAYS at last!' said Peter. 'I thought they were never coming. Didn't you, Janet?'

'Yes. It was a dreadfully long term,' said Janet. 'We've broken up now though, thank goodness. Don't you love the first day of the hols, Peter?'

'You bet! I get a lovely *free* sort of feeling,' said Peter, 'and the hols seem to stretch out in front of me for ages and ages. Let's have some fun, Janet!'

'Yes, let's! April's a lovely month – it's warm, and sunny too, and Mummy will let us off on picnics any day we like,' said Janet. 'Scamper, do you hear that? Picnics, I said – and that means rabbit-hunting for you, and long, long walks.'

'Woof!' said Scamper at once, his tail thumping on the floor, and his eyes bright.

'You're the best and finest golden spaniel in the whole world!' said Janet, stroking his silky head. 'And I do so love your long, droopy ears, Scamper. You like it when we have holidays, don't you?'

'Woof!' said Scamper again, and thump-thump-thump went his tail.

'I vote we have a meeting of the Secret Seven as soon as we can,' said Peter. 'Tomorrow, if possible. Picnics and things are much more fun if we all go together.'

'Yes. Let's have a meeting,' said Janet. 'What with exams and one thing and another all the Secret Seven have forgotten about the Society. I haven't thought a word about it for at least three weeks. Gosh – what's the password?'

'Oh, Janet – you haven't forgotten that *surely*?' said Peter.

'You tell me,' said Janet, but Peter wouldn't. 'You don't know it yourself!' said Janet. 'I bet you don't!'

'Don't be silly,' said Peter. 'You'll have to remember it by tomorrow, if we have a meeting! Where's your badge? I expect you've lost that.'

'I have *not*,' said Janet. 'But I bet some of the others will have lost theirs. Somebody always does when we don't have a meeting for awhile.'

'Better write out short notes to the other five,' said Peter. 'And tell them to come along tomorrow. Got some note-paper, Janet?'

'Yes, I have. But I don't feel a bit like sitting down and writing the first day of the hols,' said Janet. 'You can jolly well help to write them.'

'No. I'll bike round to all the others and deliver the notes for you,' said Peter.

'Now it's *you* who are silly,' said Janet. 'If you're going to everyone's house, why not *tell* them about the meeting. All this note-writing! You just *tell* them.'

'All right. It just seems more *official* if we send out notes for a meeting, that's all,' said Peter. 'What time shall we have it?'

'Oh, half-past ten, I should think,' said Janet. 'And just warn Jack that he's not to let his horrid sister Susie know, or she'll come banging at the door, shouting out some silly password at the top of her voice.'

'Yes. I'll tell him,' said Peter. 'The worst of it is, Susie is

so jolly sharp. She always seems to smell out anything to do with the Secret Seven.'

'She would be a better person to have *in* a club than out of it,' said Janet. 'But we'll never, never let her into ours.'

'Never,' said Peter. 'Anyway, we can't be more than seven, or we wouldn't be the Secret Seven.'

'Woof!' said Scamper.

'He says he belongs, even if we're seven and he makes the eighth!' said Janet. 'You're just a hanger-on, Scamper, but we simply couldn't do without you.'

'Well, I'm going to get my bike,' said Peter, getting up. 'I'll go round and tell all the others. See you later, Janet. Coming, Scamper?'

Off he went, and was soon cycling to one house after another. He went to Colin first, who was delighted to hear the news.

'Good!' he said. 'Half-past ten? Right, I'll be there. I say – whatever's the password, Peter?'

'You've got all day to think of it!' said Peter, with a grin, and rode off to Jack's. Jack was in the garden, mending a puncture in the back wheel of his bicycle. He was very pleased to see Peter.

'Meeting of the Secret Seven tomorrow morning in the shed at the bottom of our garden,' said Peter. 'I hope you've got your badge, and that your awful sister Susie hasn't found it and taken it.'

'I've got it on,' said Jack, with a grin. 'And I wear it on my pyjamas at night, so it's always safe. I say, Peter – what's the password?'

'I *can* tell you!' said a voice from up a near-by tree. The boys looked up to see Susie's laughing face looking down at them.

'You don't know it!' said Jack fiercely.

'I do, I do!' said the annoying Susie. 'But I shan't tell you, and you won't be allowed in at the meeting. What a joke!'

Peter rode off to the rest of the Seven. That Susie! She really was the most AGGRAVATING girl in the whole world!

CHAPTER TWO

A dreadful blow

NEXT MORNING Peter and Janet began preparing for the meeting. Meetings weren't proper meetings, somehow, unless there was plenty to eat and drink while they talked. Their mother was always generous in giving cakes or biscuits and lemonade, and the two children went to find her.

'Hello,' she said, looking up from chopping parsley on a board. 'What are you two after now?'

'We're going to have a Secret Seven meeting,' explained Peter, 'and we wanted something to eat and drink.'

'Well now, let me see – you can have that tin of ginger biscuits – they've gone soft,' said Mummy smiling. 'And you can make yourself some real lemonade – there are plenty of lemons and sugar in the larder.'

'Ooh, good!' said Janet. 'I'll do that. I'll make it with hot water, and let it go cool. Anything else we can have?'

'Jam-tarts,' said Mummy, chopping away hard at the parsley. 'Only four though, I'm afraid. That's all that were left from supper last night.'

'Four – well, we'll halve them,' said Peter. 'There'll be one half over, so . . .'

'Woof! woof!' said Scamper, at once. The children laughed.

'All right, you shall have the half left over,' said Peter. 'You never miss a word of what we say, do you, Scamper?'

Janet made the lemonade, and Peter got the tin of

biscuits and found the tarts. He cut them carefully into exact halves and put them on a plate.

'Come on, Janet,' he said. 'It's nearly half-past ten.'

'Peter, please do tell me the password!' said Janet. 'I'm very, very sorry I've forgotten it.'

'No. I shan't tell you,' said Peter. 'You'll have to be in the shed, anyhow, and you can jolly well listen to the others coming along and saying the password, and feel ashamed of yourself!'

'You're mean!' said Janet. 'Isn't he mean, Scamper?'

Scamper didn't answer. 'There,' said Peter, 'he won't say I'm mean. He never will. Do come on, Janet. I'm not going to wait a minute longer.'

Janet was ready. She put the jug of lemonade and seven unbreakable mugs on an old tray and followed Peter out of the kitchen. 'Thanks, Mummy!' she said, as she went carefully down the steps outside the kitchen door.

Peter was ahead of her. He went along the path that wound between the bushes right down to the bottom of the garden, where the old shed stood that they used for their meetings. On the door was always pinned the sign 'SS'. How many, many times the Secret Seven had met there and made exciting plans!

Janet followed a little way behind, carrying her tray carefully. She suddenly heard Peter give a startled shout, and almost dropped the tray she held.

'What's the matter?' she called and tried to hurry. She came in sight of the shed – and stared in horror.

The door was wide open, and so were the windows. Everything had been turned out of the shed! There were boxes and cushions and sacks, all strewn on the ground in untidy heaps! Whatever had happened?

Janet put her tray down, afraid that she might drop it in her dismay. She looked at Peter in despair.

'Who's done this? Just as we were going to have a meeting too! It's too bad.'

Peter looked into the shed. It was quite empty, except for the shelves round the sides. He was puzzled.

'Janet – it couldn't be Susie, could it?' he said. 'I mean, this is an awful thing to do, throw everything out of our shed. I don't think even Susie would do that.'

'She might,' said Janet, almost in tears. 'Oh, our lovely meeting-place!'

'Here come the others,' said Peter, as Pamela and Barbara appeared down the path together. They stared in amazement at the untidy mess on the ground.

'What's happened?' said Barbara. 'Are we too early?'

'No. We've only *just* seen all this ourselves,' said Peter. 'Hello – here's Jack. Jack, look here.'

'Gosh!' said Jack. 'Who's done this? It can't be Susie. She's been with me all morning till I left just now.'

Colin and George came up just then, and the seven looked ruefully at the boxes and cushions thrown out so untidily. 'We'd better put them back,' said Janet. 'And we'll find out who's done all this to our secret meeting-place.'

They began to put everything back, and then they heard footsteps coming along down the path. Who was it? Peter looked to see.

It was the gardener, carrying a strong broom over his shoulder, a pail of water in his hand, and some cloths hanging on the side of the pail. He stared at the seven in annoyance.

'Hey, you! What are you doing? I've only just thrown all that rubbish out!'

'But why?' demanded Peter, indignantly. 'This shed is our meeting-place, and this isn't rubbish. We use it.'

'Oh, well, I don't know anything about that,' said the gardener. 'All I know is that your father told me to clear out this place, burn all the rubbish, and do a spot of painting. He said it was going to rack and ruin, and he wanted it cleaned up.'

'I see,' said Peter, his heart sinking. If his father had planned this, there was nothing to be done. He turned to the others. 'Come on, let's find somewhere to talk,' he said. 'We can't meet in our shed for a while, that's certain. How annoying!'

'Never mind! We'll think of somewhere just as good,' said Colin. But nobody agreed with him. They thought the shed was the finest place in the world for Secret Seven meetings!

The Seven, followed by Scamper with his tail well down, went slowly up the garden path. Somehow it seemed dreadful not to have their usual meeting-place.

'We'll go to the summer-house,' said Peter. 'Oh, look, there's Mummy, Janet. We'll ask her about the shed.'

'Mummy!' called Janet. 'Why didn't you tell us the shed was going to be cleaned and painted – our own shed, I mean, where we meet? I do think *somebody* might have told us.'

'Oh dear, I quite forgot to tell you that Daddy wanted it cleaned and mended,' said Mummy. 'It was almost falling to bits here and there, you know. But you can have it for a meeting-place again when it's finished. It will look nice and bright and clean then.'

'But we like it old and dark and untidy,' said Peter mournfully. 'And I do think it's a pity to have it done in the holidays, Mummy, just when we want to use it.'

'Yes, I agree that that's a pity,' said Mummy, looking very sorry. 'I would have stopped it if I'd known that it was to be done just now. Well – you'll have to find another meeting-place. What about the attic?'

'Oh no,' said Janet. 'It's no fun meeting in a *house*, Mummy, with other people in near-by rooms. We want a secret, lonely place, we do really.'

'Yes . . . I suppose you do,' said Mummy. 'Well, I can't suggest one, I'm afraid. Go to the summer-house just for now.'

'We were going to,' said Peter, still very doleful. Soon they were all squashed into the little old summer-house. They didn't much like it, because it was rather earwiggy.

They began to eat the ginger biscuits. 'Rather soft, I'm afraid,' said Janet.

'Oh, I like them soft and squidgy,' said Pam. 'I hate them when you have to bite so hard they splinter in your mouth. Hey, this is good lemonade! Did your mother make it, Janet?'

'No. I made it myself,' said Janet proudly. 'Peter, hadn't we better talk about where to have a new meeting-place?'

'Yes,' said Peter. 'And I vote that we all of us have a good hunt round to find somewhere, some absolutely secret place that even Jack's sister Susie won't find. It mustn't be too far away. I'll give you today to find one. Meet here this evening, in this summer-house again, at six o'clock.'

'Right,' said Colin. 'I think I know of one already.'

'Well, don't tell us now,' said Peter. 'We'll each give in

our ideas this evening and put it to the vote to see which is the best. We must do these things properly.'

'Yes,' said everyone, and took a drink of Janet's lemonade.

'What about the password?' said Jack. 'We were all so upset about the shed that we never even gave the password.'

'We've all got our badges on,' said Pamela. 'I had an awful hunt for mine. I put it in such a safe place that it was almost too safe for me to find!'

'Where was it?' asked George.

'I buried it in the pot of maidenhair fern my mother has in the drawing-room,' said Pam, with a giggle. 'And then forgot about it. It took me ages to remember it.'

'I thought it looked a bit grubby,' said Peter. 'I think that's a silly place.'

'Oh, I wrapped it in paper,' said Pam. 'But I forgot that Mummy watered it twice a week – so, of course, the paper soaked off and made my badge messy.'

'It's a good thing it didn't put out roots and grow!' said Peter. Everyone laughed.

'Peter, could we have a new password?' said Jack. 'Susie knows our last one. I'm most dreadfully sorry, and I don't know how she knew it, unless she hung round our last meeting and heard it.'

'All right. We'll choose a new one,' said Peter. 'It's time we did, anyway. I must say that your sister Susie is getting worse and worse, Jack. I hope she's nowhere about just now.'

Jack got up and went out of the summer-house. 'Nobody's anywhere near,' he said. 'Quick – what's the new password?'

'Easter-egg,' said Peter. 'That's easy to remember, because it's the Easter holidays.'

'Easter-egg,' repeated everyone, in low voices. Pam took out a notebook and began to write it down.

'Don't *you* write it down, Jack!' said Janet, 'or Susie will find it. I wonder how she knew our last password?'

'Well, she called out, "Your password is Sugar-mouse" just as I was leaving,' said Jack. 'And I don't mind owning up now that I was really glad to hear it, because I'd forgotten it completely.'

'Sugar-mouse!' said Peter, in astonishment. 'It was nothing of the sort. Susie just made that up because she knew you'd forgotten it. She hoped you would rap on the door of the shed and yell out "Sugar-mouse" and make a fool of yourself.'

Jack went red. 'What was the password then?' he said. 'Janet, you tell me. Peter won't.'

Janet went red too. '*I've* forgotten it as well,' she said.

Pam blushed as red as Janet, so Peter knew she had forgotten too! He rapped on the summer-house table.

'The last password was a very simple one,' he said. 'It was "Thursday". Just that, "Thursday".'

'Gosh, so it was,' said Barbara. 'I just couldn't remember if it was "Thursday" or "Friday".'

'*I* thought it was Sunday,' said Colin, with a laugh. 'It was a silly password to choose, Peter, too easy to muddle up with the other days of the week. "Easter-egg" is much better.'

'Well, let's hope that Barbara and Colin don't mix it up with "Christmas present" or "Birthday gift"!' said Peter. 'Now – we've eaten everything, and Scamper's had his half-tart, and we've drunk all the lemonade – what about separating and hunting for a new meeting-place?'

'Right,' said everyone and got up. They all went off up the path to the front gate, and most of them were murmuring two words to themselves as they went.

'Easter-egg! Easter-egg! I must remember Easter-egg!'

CHAPTER THREE

Plenty of ideas

AT SIX o'clock that evening there was a continual noise of footsteps up the path to the little summer-house. Janet, Peter, and Scamper were inside, waiting.

'Easter-egg,' said Jack, walking inside. There was no door, for the summer-house was three-sided, with its fourth side open to the garden.

'Easter-egg,' said Barbara, walking in, too.

'Where's your badge?' asked Peter sharply.

'Oh – I've got it, it's all right,' said Barbara, feeling in her pocket. 'I don't know why I forgot to pin it on.' She pinned it on carefully and sat down.

The other three came along, each solemnly giving the password.

'For once nobody *yelled* it out,' said Peter. He took a notebook out of his pocket, and licked his pencil. 'Now then. I want your reports on any likely places to meet secretly. Colin, you begin.'

'Well, there's a fine big tree at the bottom of our garden,' began Colin hopefully. 'It's a great chestnut, and . . .'

'No good, I'm afraid,' said Peter, 'but I'll put it down. It would hardly be a secret meeting-place! Everyone would see us going down the garden to it, and people passing the wall nearby would hear us up there. Barbara, what's *your* idea?'

'Oh, it's a silly one,' said Barbara. 'There's an old hut in a field nearby our house, and . . .'

229

'I know it,' said Peter, scribbling in his notebook. 'Not a bad idea, Barbara. You, Pam?'

'I simply haven't any idea at all,' said Pam. 'I've thought and thought, but it's no use.'

'*Not* very helpful,' said Peter, putting a cross against Pam's name in his notebook. 'You, George?'

'Well, there's an empty caravan in a field not far from here,' said George. 'I know who owns it – it's a friend of my father's. I think I could get permission for us to use it.'

This sounded exciting. Everyone looked admiringly at George, who seemed quite pleased with himself.

'You, Jack?' said Peter. 'And please don't suggest any-where near *your* house, because of Susie.'

'I'm not going to,' said Jack. 'I'm not quite so silly as that. I've chosen somewhere a long way away, down by the river. It's an old boathouse that nobody ever uses.'

This sounded exciting too. Peter wrote it down so-lemnly. 'Now we've heard everyone's idea except mine and Janet's. We went out hunting together, and Scamper came too – and we've all got the same idea.'

'What?' asked everyone.

'Well, it's a cave in the quarry near the field where we

grow potatoes,' said Peter. 'So it's on my father's farm, and not very far. It's absolutely lonely and secret, and goes back into the hill behind the quarry. Scamper found it, actually.'

'That sounds good – a secret cave,' said Pam.

'Well, we'll now put all our ideas to the vote,' said Peter,

and handed round slips of paper. 'Please write down on these papers what ideas you like best – but nobody must vote for their own idea, of course. I'll just go shortly over them again: 'Colin suggests a tree, but it's not a very *secret* place. Barbara suggested that old hut in the field near her house – but the roof's almost off and the rain would come in. Pam has no ideas. George suggests the caravan owned by his father's friend, a very good idea, but I don't honestly think we'd be allowed to use it because it's still furnished. I'd be afraid of breaking something.'

Peter paused for breath. 'Jack suggested the old boathouse by the river. Fine – but isn't it rather far away for a meeting-place? It's at least a mile away. And you know what Janet and I suggest – the cave. But that isn't a really comfortable place. There you are – please vote on your papers, fold them in half, and give them to me.'

Everyone solemnly wrote something on their papers, then handed them to Peter. He opened them and read them. When he looked up, his eyes were shining with pleasure.

'Er – well – it's very funny, but everyone except me and Janet have voted for the cave. We couldn't vote for our own idea, of course. So it's five votes for the cave – and the cave it will be. I'm glad – it's a great place really!'

'Is it? Let's go and see it straight away!' said Jack. 'It's not very far.'

'All right, come on then,' said Peter. 'We'll have a quick look, and then plan what to bring to it tomorrow. We'll settle into it at once.'

This was exciting. They all got up and went out into the bright sunshine. It was almost half-past six, and as warm as could be.

'This way,' said Peter, and led the way down his garden and through a gate into a field. His father owned the farmland at the back of the house, and it stretched away over the hills, the fields green with growing corn and rootcrops.

Peter took them down a grassy path, past a pond with ducks on it, and then turned to the right towards the old quarry. Sand had been dug from it years ago, and it had then been abandoned. They all filed into the quarry and looked round.

Scamper ran in front. 'He'll show you,' said Peter. 'Just as he showed me and Janet this morning!' Scamper ran up to what looked like a rabbit path, over a little sandy hill, then down into a hollow behind. The others followed. Scamper stood waiting for them, his tail waving to and fro.

He ran through a gap in some thick bushes and disappeared. The others went through the gap too and looked for Scamper. He had gone!

'He's gone into the cave,' said Peter, grinning. 'You can see the entrance just there. It's all hung over with some plant that has sent long, trailing stems down, and has almost hidden the entrance to the cave. Come on – it's really quite exciting!'

CHAPTER FOUR

In the cave

THE SECRET Seven crowded together to see the cave. There was no proper path to it, and they had to squeeze through close-growing bushes of bright yellow broom to get to it. The bushes grew almost up to the cave entrance.

'No wonder Janet and I never spotted this cave before,' said Peter. 'We've been in this old sand quarry heaps of times, but never found the cave. It was only because old Scamper disappeared and we went to look for him that we found it. We were standing here, calling him, when he suddenly appeared under the trailing leaves that hide the cave! Didn't you, Scamper?'

'Woof!' said Scamper, and ran into the cave and back, as if to say, 'Do come on, it's a fine place!'

The trailing stems that hung down over the entrance certainly hid it very well. Peter pulled the greenery aside. 'It's like a curtain,' he said. 'Look – now you can see into the cave properly.'

Everyone bent their heads and looked in. It certainly was a fine cave!

'Nice and big, and with a lovely sandy floor!' said Jack. 'I don't see why you said it's not comfortable, Peter. Sand is lovely to sit on.'

'Oh well, I had to say *something* against it, as it was Janet's suggestion and mine,' said Peter.

By now they were all in the cave. Pam flung herself down on the sand. It was very soft indeed.

235

'Lovely!' she said. 'I'd like to sleep here in this sand. I could burrow my body down into it and make a lovely bed. It's a *wonderful* meeting-place, I think.'

'Nobody would EVER find it!' said George, looking round. 'It's a bit dark, that's the only thing. It's that green curtain over the entrance that makes it so dark.'

Janet obligingly held the curtain back, and the sun streamed into the cave.

'Fine!' said Colin. 'We can have the curtain back when we're just playing about, and draw it when we're having a secret meeting. Couldn't be better. A cave with a ready-made curtain!'

'And look, the cave has a rock roof, all uneven, high here and low there,' said Barbara. 'And there are rocky shelves round the walls; we can use those to put our things on. We'll bring all kinds of things here! I expect we'll have to use this cave all the Easter hols, so we'll make it a kind of home as well as a meeting-place. Shall we?'

Everyone thought this was a very good idea. 'We'll bring the shed cushions here,' said Janet. 'And a box for a table.'

'And keep food here, and lemonade or orangeade,' said Jack. 'Won't it be fun?'

'Yes, and you'll have to be careful not to let Susie follow you here,' said Peter warningly. 'She'd just love to come here and mess things about, bring her silly, giggling friends with her too, I expect, and have a picnic or something in the middle of the cave.'

'I'll be very careful,' promised Jack. 'Well, I must say this is a brilliant place for the Secret Seven. Not too far away, perfectly secret, quite lonely, and our very own. Can any of us come here when we like, Peter? When there's not a meeting or anything planned? I'd love to come and read here by myself.'

'Yes. I don't see why this shouldn't be a kind of head-quarters as well as a meeting-place,' said Peter. 'Anyone can come whenever they like, but please leave it tidy, and don't go and eat all the food we leave here!'

'Of course not,' said everyone at once.

'If we come alone and want something to eat we'll bring it ourselves,' said Colin, and everyone agreed.

'Now, let's see. We'll come tomorrow at half-past ten,' began Peter, but Jack interrupted before he could say any more.

'Oh, earlier than that, Peter! It's going to be fun; I'd like to come earlier. Can't we make it half-past nine?'

'No, because Janet and I have jobs to do for our father and mother,' said Peter. 'We'll say ten, if you like. We can get our jobs done by then, I expect.'

'I've got jobs to do as well,' said Pam. 'I always help Mother with the housework in the hols. So does Barbara.'

'Well, say ten,' repeated Peter. 'And bring what you can to make the cave comfortable and homely. Bring books if you like – the cave's quite dry – and games.'

Everyone was sorry to leave the exciting cave. It really was a nice one, spacious, though the roof was not very high, and it was only in places that the Seven could stand upright – clean, with its floor of soft sand – and reaching back into a very nice, mysterious darkness, quite out of reach of the sunshine.

Peter held back the curtain of greenery till everyone had gone out. Then he let it drop into place and arranged it so that hardly a bit of the entrance showed. Nobody at all would ever guess there was a big cave behind it, going right into the hill beyond!

Scamper came out last of all, his tail wagging madly. He liked the cave. It was exciting. There was no smell of rabbits in it, which was disappointing, but it was good fun to pretend there was, and to scrabble hard at the sand with his front paws, and send it showering into the air!

The Seven all walked back to the gate at the bottom of Peter's garden, and then up the garden to the front gate.

They said goodbye, and went off to their different homes, thinking exciting thoughts.

Susie met Jack as he came in, and looked at his sandy shoes.

'Where have you been?' she demanded. 'I've been looking for you everywhere. Where did you get that sand on your shoes?'

'Ask no questions, and I'll tell you no lies,' said Jack, pushing by her.

'You've been with the Secret Seven, I know you have,' said Susie, and she laughed. 'What's the password? Is it still Sugar-mouse? Ha, ha – I tricked you nicely over that, didn't I?'

CHAPTER FIVE

Settling in

NEXT DAY Peter and Janet felt very excited. They went down the garden to collect the old cushions they had in the shed. The gardener had put them into another shed, together with the boxes, sacks, and other things.

He was very busy repairing the old shed. The two children peeped inside. It would certainly be nice and clean when it was all finished.

'I'd rather have the cave for the holidays though,' said Peter, and Janet nodded.

They were very laden indeed as they made their way down to the quarry. Scamper carried a bone in his mouth. He knew quite well they were going to the cave, and he wanted to take something too!

Peter and Janet were there before the others. They drew aside the curtain of greenery and went in. The curtain fell behind them.

'Don't draw it back yet, till the others come,' said Peter. 'They'll have to give the password outside the curtain before we pull it back. Otherwise we'd never know who was coming in! But the password will tell us it's the Secret Seven.'

Janet set down the cushions. Peter put down the box he had brought. It was heavy, because he had filled it with all kinds of things. He began to unpack.

'Hand me the things,' said Janet. 'I'll arrange them nicely on these rocky shelves. There's no hole we can use

241

for a cupboard, but that won't matter. Gosh, isn't this going to be fun?'

Peter looked at his watch. 'It's almost ten,' he said. 'You go on arranging things, and I'll wait just at the entrance, behind the curtain, and ask for the passwords. The sand outside is so soft that we shan't hear anyone coming. I must watch for them.'

Almost immediately there came a soft shuffle outside. 'Password,' said Peter, in a low voice.

'Easter-egg!' said Colin's voice. Peter pulled aside the curtain of greenery, and Colin came staggering in, carrying a big cardboard box. He collapsed on the soft, sandy floor.

'Gosh! I never knew books were so heavy! I've brought my whole set of "Famous Five" books to put on the shelves for anyone to borrow, and they've nearly dragged my arms out!'

'Oh, fine, there's one I want to read again,' said Peter, pleased. 'Find a nice even shelf of rock somewhere along the wall there, Colin, and put the books up neatly.'

A small cough came from outside the cave. Someone was waiting to be allowed in. 'Password!' said Peter, at once.

'Easter-egg!' said two voices together, and Peter lifted the green curtain. In came Pam and Barbara carrying parcels.

'Janet will see to those,' said Peter, taking up his post by the curtain again. Soon he heard the soft sound of feet coming quietly over the sand outside, and heard, too, the noise of people squeezing through the thick bushes of yellow broom.

'Password!' he said, and two voices answered together. 'Easter-egg!'

'Not so loud, idiots!' said Peter, and pulled aside the green curtain, grinning widely at Jack and George. He peered cautiously behind them.

'It's all right. I slipped off while Susie was at the bottom of our garden,' said Jack, staggering in. 'I've brought two bottles of juice and two bottles of water. Mother said I could, as her share towards the Secret Seven goings-on!'

'Goodo!' said Peter, pleased. He drew back the curtain and tied it with a bit of string, so that the sunshine flooded into the cave. He looked all round outside to make sure that no one was about.

'I think we're absolutely safe and secret here,' he said. 'This quarry has been deserted for years, and I don't expect that anyone remembers there was ever a cave here.'

'Scamper would bark if anyone wandered near,' said Janet. 'Then we could quickly pull the curtain over the entrance and lie as quiet as anything!'

'Yes. Scamper would certainly warn us,' said Peter. 'Now, how are you all getting on?'

The cave was beginning to look quite cosy and furnished. The box-table was in the middle. Cushions were here and there on the sandy floor, ready for anyone to sit on. Arranged on the uneven ledges of the rocky wall were Colin's books and some of Jack's. Plastic cups had been neatly put in a row by Janet, and on a wider ledge she had put Jack's bottles.

A tin stood in one corner. It had in it some of the food that the Seven had brought, and on another ledge stood a tin of boiled sweets, a packet of oatmeal biscuits, and two bars of chocolate brought by Pam. A small jar of potted crab paste stood next to a jar of home-made strawberry jam.

'It all looks very good,' said Peter approvingly. 'Very good indeed.'

'Yes. We've found places for everything,' said Janet, pleased. 'That corner over there belongs to Scamper, by the way, that's where he's buried the big bone he brought with him. Please don't disturb it, anyone. You can stop sitting on it, Scamper. I've told everyone it's your own special corner.'

Scamper still sat there, however. To him a bone was a very precious possession indeed, and he had to make *quite* sure that everyone understood it was *his* bone.

'I'm hungry after all this,' announced Jack, 'I vote we choose something to eat. We've got very well-filled cupboards!'

'I'll have a ginger bun,' said Colin. 'My mother made them yesterday. They're lovely. Let's begin with those.'

So there they sat, all the Secret Seven, happily munching ginger buns. The sun streamed in at the cave entrance, for the green curtain was still pulled back. What a lovely meeting-place – the best they had ever had!

CHAPTER SIX

Jack is very puzzled

THE CAVE was a great success. On rainy days it was a wonderful place to lie in and read, or play games. Each of the seven burrowed into the sand and made his or her own bed or hole. Each had a cushion for their head. The shelves were always kept stacked with papers and magazines, and with food and drink.

'We couldn't have found a better place,' said Colin. 'Jack, does Susie ever bother about where you disappear to for hours on end?'

'Goodness, yes,' said Jack. 'She keeps on and on about it. She knows our old shed is no longer a meeting-place, because she went to have a look at it. I have to be awfully careful not to let her follow me when I come here. Yesterday I turned round and there she was, keeping to the bushes beside the road, hoping I wouldn't see her.'

'What did you do?' asked Pam.

'I turned a corner and went off to the sweet shop instead of coming here,' said Jack. 'I do hope she won't find our cave.'

'Let's go into the quarry and play hide-and-seek,' said Janet, getting up. 'The sun's out again, and I'm longing to stretch my legs.'

So off they all went. Jack was chosen to shut his eyes and count a hundred before he began looking. The cave was to be Home.

Jack stood by a tree at the other side of the quarry,

counting nice and slowly. When he had counted a hundred, he looked round. Could he see anyone behind a bush, or lying in the lush grass nearby?

No – not one of the others was to be seen. He moved cautiously round his tree, keeping his eyes open for a sudden movement somewhere.

He glanced towards the cave, which he could just see between a gap in the broom bushes that hid it so well. Then he stared. Someone was slipping into the cave! Who was it? He just couldn't see.

That's not fair, thought Jack. They haven't given me a chance to find them. Well, I'll soon find out which of the seven it is, and tell them what I think of them!

He saw a patch of blue nearby and recognised Pam's dress behind a bush. He rushed at her, but she escaped and ran squealing to the cave.

Then he found Barbara, Janet, and Scamper together, crouching behind a great hummock of sand. He ran to catch them and fell headlong over a tuft of grass. They rushed away, the girls squealing and Scamper barking.

He nearly caught Colin behind a tree, but Colin was too quick for him. Let's see – that only leaves one more, said Jack to himself. The first one I saw going into the cave – then the three girls – then Colin – myself – and so there's just one more. It's Peter or George.

He hunted here and there, and then suddenly fell over two giggling boys. It was Peter and George, half-buried in the soft sand. Jack grabbed at Peter and caught him, but George escaped to the cave.

'I'm caught all right!' said Peter, grinning. 'I'll be "He" next. Let's call out to everyone in the cave.'

'Wait a minute,' said Jack, looking puzzled. 'There's something I don't understand. Let's go up to the cave.'

Peter went with him to the cave, where the other five were waiting.

'What don't you understand?' asked Peter.

'Well, listen – first I saw someone slipping into the cave immediately after I'd finished counting,' said Jack, 'which wasn't really fair. Then I found Pam, then Janet and Barbara, then Colin, then you and George, Peter.'

'Well – what's puzzling you?' asked Peter.

'Just this – that makes *eight* of us, not counting Scamper,' said Jack. 'And what I want to know is, who was the eighth?'

They all counted. Yes, Jack was right. That made eight, not seven. Everyone said at once that they hadn't slipped into the cave before Jack discovered them.

'Well, who was that first person then, if it wasn't any of us?' said Jack, really puzzled. 'I tell you I saw somebody go into the cave before I discovered *any* of you. Who was it?'

Everyone began to look round uneasily. Peter pulled the green curtain back as far as he could, and the sunshine filled the cave, except for the dark places at the back.

'There's nobody here,' said Pam. 'Oh, Jack, do you suppose it could have been Susie?'

'I don't know. I only just saw *somebody*, but I haven't

any idea who it was,' said Jack. 'And look here, surely that somebody must still be in here! I found Pam almost immediately, and she rushed off to the cave. You didn't see anyone here, did you, Pam?'

'Of course not,' said Pam. 'If I'd seen Susie I would have been furious with her!'

Peter took down a torch from the shelf of rock nearby and switched it on. He flashed it towards the dark corners at the end of the cave. 'Come forth!' he said, in a hollow voice. 'Come forth, O wicked intruder!'

But nobody came. The far corners of the cave, now lit brilliantly by the torch, were quite empty.

'It's odd,' said Jack, frowning. 'Very odd. Give me the torch, Peter. I'll go and see if there's any corner or hole at the end of the cave that we haven't noticed.'

'Well, there isn't,' said Peter, giving him the torch. 'Janet and I had a good look when we first found the cave!'

All the same, Jack went to the far end and had a very good look round, flashing the torch everywhere. There seemed to be nowhere that anyone could hide.

He came back, still looking puzzled. 'Cheer up,' said Peter. 'You must have imagined someone, Jack. Anyway, *would* anyone come to that cave while we were all of us here, in plain view?'

'But that's just what we were not,' said Jack. 'We were playing hide-and-seek, and there wasn't a sound, and all of us, except me, were well hidden. Anybody coming here just then would not have heard or seen anything of us. They would have thought the place deserted.'

'Yes. I see what you mean,' said Peter. 'All the same, there's nobody here. So cheer up, Jack, and let's go on with the game. My turn to find you all. Go and hide!'

CHAPTER SEVEN

A real mystery

NOBODY SAID any more about Jack's idea that someone had slipped into the cave. Jack began to think he really must have imagined it. Perhaps it was a shadow from a cloud or something? They all played the game of hide-and-seek again and again, and nobody saw mysterious people slipping into the cave any more!

'It's time to tidy up and go home,' said Peter, at last. 'What a mess we seem to make when we've been in the cave for even a short time!'

The girls shook up the cushions, and the boys gathered up the rubbish and put it into a bag to take home. Then Janet put the rest of the food back on the shelves, and tidied up Colin's set of 'Five' books.

'There!' she said. 'Everything tidy! If our mothers came and looked in they would be most astonished.'

They all laughed. They went out of the cave, and Peter pulled the green curtain carefully across. Then off they went home.

'Same time tomorrow!' called Peter, when they all said goodbye to him and Janet and Scamper at his front gate.

'No! You've forgotten – we're all going to bike over to Penton and see the circus come through,' said Colin. 'We're meeting at eleven at my house.'

'Oh, yes, how could I forget!' said Peter. 'We'll go to the cave after dinner tomorrow afternoon.'

Next day they had a good morning, watching the long

251

circus procession passing through the little town of Penton. Then they biked back for their dinners, and, at various times, set off to the cave.

Pam and Barbara arrived first, Pam, very pleased because her granny had given her a tin of peppermints for the Secret Seven to enjoy.

'I'll put them beside the other tins,' she said. 'Hello – look, Barbara, there's a tin on the floor of the cave. Who do you suppose knocked that down? We're the first here today!'

'Perhaps it overbalanced,' said Barbara.

'And gosh, look – we left a whole bar of chocolate, a very big one, just *here*,' said Pam. 'I put it there myself. That's gone!'

'It's probably somewhere else,' said Barbara. Then she herself noticed something. 'Gosh, look – three of our cushions are missing! Has somebody been here?'

'It's Susie,' said Pam frowning. 'That's who it is. She didn't come with us to Penton today, so she must have come here instead! She has followed Jack sometime or other, and found out our meeting-place. Bother Susie!'

'Here are the others,' said Barbara. 'Let's tell them.'

They heard the password being murmured outside the cave. 'Easter-egg' – then the curtain was pushed aside and in came Colin and George.

'Susie's been here!' said Pam angrily. 'Look, there are cushions missing, and our big bar of chocolate is gone, and a tin was on the ground.'

'And look, those currant buns we were saving for today are nearly all gone!' said Barbara, opening a tin. 'Would you believe it!'

Soon Peter, Janet, and Jack arrived and were also told the news. 'But it needn't have been Susie,' said Peter, trying to be fair, though he felt perfectly certain it was. 'It could quite well have been a tramp.'

'He'd have taken lots more things,' said Pam. 'And what would he want with *cushions*! We might meet him down a lane carrying them, and we'd know he was the thief at once. No tramp would be as silly as that.'

'That's true,' said Peter. 'Well, Jack, you'll have to find out if it's Susie.'

'All right,' said Jack, looking troubled. 'I'll go now. But somehow I don't think it *is* Susie, you know. I can't help remembering that person, whoever it was, that I saw slipping into the cave yesterday.'

Jack went off to find Susie. The others each took a peppermint from the tin that Pam offered them, and settled down to read. Colin finished his book and went to get another. He gave an exclamation.

'One of my "Famous Five" books has gone! Has any-one borrowed it? It's *Five go down to the sea*.'

Nobody had. 'I know it's not Jack,' said Colin. 'He's

just finished reading it. Well, if that's Susie again I'll have something to say to her!'

Jack came back in about an hour. 'Easter-egg' he said, outside the cave, and Peter called him in.

'Well,' he said, throwing himself down on the sandy floor. 'I've had an awful time. Susie says she's never been *near* our new meeting-place, she says she doesn't even know where it is! She flew into such a temper when I accused her of coming and taking things, that Mother heard her, and came to see what was the matter.'

'Oh, bother!' said Peter. 'You might have kept your mother out of this. What happened next?'

'Mother made me tell where our meeting-place is,' said poor Jack, looking really miserable. 'I couldn't help it, Peter, really I couldn't. She *made* me.'

There was silence. Everyone knew that it was wrong, and also quite impossible, to refuse to tell mothers anything they wanted to know. But to give away their wonderful new meeting-place! How truly shocking.

'Was Susie there when you told?' asked Peter.

'Yes,' said Jack. 'She was, and she said she was jolly well coming to find the cave and make a real mess of it! I don't think she did come here this morning. She was with Jeff all the time in the garden. Mother said so.'

'Well then, who did?' said Peter, puzzled. 'It's a strange thief who comes and takes three *cushions*!'

There was a silence. Pam glanced round the cave fearfully. Who was it who came here? Jack had seen someone yesterday, and now the someone had come again today. WHO was it?

'Now that Susie knows about our cave, I think that someone must be here on guard whenever we're not here,' said Peter. 'I mean – we can't let Susie come and mess everything up. I can quite see that if it wasn't her who came and took the things this morning, she must be really furious with us for thinking it was.'

'I wouldn't be surprised if she brought Jeff with her and turned the whole place upside down now,' said Jack gloomily. 'You don't know Susie like I do.'

'Well, let's make things jolly unpleasant for them if they do come,' said George. 'Let's balance a jug of water on that ledge over the green curtain. As soon as the curtain is moved, the jug will overbalance and pour water all over them.'

Pam giggled. 'Yes. Let's do that!'

'And let's do what my cousin once did to someone he didn't like,' said Colin. 'He got a reel of cotton and wound it all over and across the entrance to our summer-house – and he dipped it in honey first! Then when this awful boy walked into the summer-house, he walked right through the sticky threads and thought that an enormous spider's web had caught him!'

'How horrible!' said Pam, shuddering. 'To have sticky thread all over you like that!'

'Susie would hate it,' said Barbara. 'She loathes getting caught in spider thread. But who's got cotton or honey? Nobody here!'

'I can run indoors and get a reel of silk from my work-box,' said Janet, 'and there's some honey in a jar in our kitchen, I know. But aren't we being rather horrid to Susie?'

'No, Susie will only get caught in our tricks if she finds the cave and comes to turn it upside down,' said Pam. 'It will be her own fault if she gets caught. Nobody else's.'

'It's no good being soft-hearted with Susie,' said Jack gloomily. 'Actually, sometimes I think she's cleverer than any of us!'

Janet ran off to get the honey and the reel of silk. Barbara complained because her cushion was gone and she now had nothing to rest her head on.

'I suppose whoever took our cushions did it for some kind of silly joke,' she said. 'And probably threw them into the bushes somewhere.'

'I'll go and look,' said Colin, and got up. But the cushions were nowhere to be seen, and he soon came back. Janet came with him, having got the reel and the honey.

'We'll get the tricks ready when we go home to tea,' said Peter. 'I'll slip up after tea to make sure that no one's been into the cave, and I'll come last thing at night too.'

Just before they left they arranged the booby-traps. Janet ran the grey silk thread through the sticky honey, and the boys wound it back and forth across the entrance to the cave, twisting it round the plants that lined the edges of the cave entrance from top to bottom.

'There!' said Peter, at last. 'No one can get in without getting covered with thin, sticky threads! And what a shock they'll get too, when they draw back the curtain and get swamped with water from that jug! I've balanced it very carefully, so that at the slightest pulling back of the green curtain the water will pour out!'

Everyone giggled and wished they could be there to see the booby-traps catch any intruder. 'I hope Jeff comes with Susie, I can't bear him,' said Jack. 'And shan't I laugh if Susie comes back sticky and wet! Come on, let's go.'

After tea Peter went up to the cave to examine the booby-traps. They were still there! The jug of water, half-hidden by leaves, was still in place, and he could see the grey, sticky threads gleaming behind the green curtain.

'Susie and Jeff haven't been yet,' he told Janet, when he got back. 'I'll slip up again just before it gets dark and have another look.'

So up he went once more to the cave, but again the booby-traps were still there, untouched. Susie won't come now, he thought. I'll be up here before nine o'clock tomorrow morning and watch out for her in case she comes then.

CHAPTER EIGHT

Scamper is a help

JACK CAME to see Peter just before nine the next day. 'I
came to tell you that Susie's not been near the cave,' he
told Peter. 'I kept an eye on her all yesterday evening and
this morning. She's gone off to her music lesson now, so
we're safe till twelve o'clock anyhow.'

'Right,' said Peter. 'Well, help me with the few jobs I
have to do, and then we'll go up with Janet and Scamper.
We'll try to get there just before the others come.'

So at five to ten, Peter, Janet, Scamper, and Jack made
their way to the quarry and then up to the cave.

They looked up to where the jug was so carefully balanced on a ledge, and grinned.

'I'll get it,' said Jack, and climbed up to remove it.

'We'll have to break these threads ourselves,' said Janet. 'What a waste of booby-traps, wasn't it? Ooh, be careful, you'll get honey all over you!'

They broke the threads as carefully as possible, so as not to get themselves sticky, and went into the cave. And then they stood there in astonishment, gazing round as if they could not believe their eyes!

The tins were all opened – and emptied! Some were flung on the floor. Two more of the cushions had gone. A bottle of orangeade had disappeared, and so had a bottle of water. The tin of peppermints had completely vanished, and also some more books. A torch that Colin had left on a shelf had gone too.

'But – but – how could anyone get *in*?' stammered Peter, utterly astonished. 'Our booby-traps were still there – those threads were quite unbroken. NOBODY could have come in, and yet look at this. I don't like it. There's something very strange going on in this cave – and I just don't – like – it!'

The three children felt scared. It was quite clear that *no one* had gone into the cave, because the sticky silk threads would certainly have been broken. But how could their belongings have been taken, and their tins emptied, if no one had been in the cave?

'You know,' said Jack, looking all round him fearfully, 'you know, Peter, I was quite certain I saw somebody slipping into the cave that time we played hide-and-seek. You kept saying I must have imagined it, but I didn't.'

'Well, certainly *somebody's* about, somebody who likes

eating and drinking,' said Peter. 'And if he didn't get into our cave from the *outside*, he must know a way in from the *inside*!'

'But that's silly too,' said Janet. 'We know there's no way into the cave from the inside. We've had a jolly good look.'

'Scamper seems very interested in the cave this morning,' said Jack. 'Look at him sniffing and nosing round.'

Scamper certainly was interested. He ran here and there excitedly, giving little barks and whimpers, as if to say, 'I could tell you such a lot if only I could speak!'

He ran over to the place where he had buried his bone, dug it up, and carefully took it to another corner and buried it there. Peter laughed.

'He's afraid our visitor might find his bone – see how deep he's burying it this time! Hey, Scamper, you're sending sand all over us!'

Janet looked round at the untidy cave with its empty tins and scattered books. Tears came into her eyes. 'I made it all so nice,' she said. 'And we had such a lot of good food here. WHO is this horrible visitor who comes when we're not here and steals like this? Where does he come from? How does he get here if he doesn't come in at the entrance?'

'Let's look all round the cave again, very, very carefully

to see if there's another entrance somewhere,' said Jack. 'There might be a small hole that someone could wriggle through, covered with sand.'

They looked thoroughly, Scamper sniffing too. But no, no matter how Scamper sniffed all round and about, or how the children dug here and there to find a hole under the rocky walls, nothing was found that would help to solve the mystery.

'And a very strange mystery it is too,' said Peter. 'I said I didn't like it, and I don't. I vote we clear up this cave and find another meeting-place. It's going to be no fun if we keep having our things stolen and messed about by some unknown visitor.'

'Yes. *I* don't feel as if I want to be here any more either,' said Janet. 'It's a shame. It's such a good place. Well, the others will be along soon, so let's just clear up a bit, and we'll tell them when they come.'

It wasn't long before the others came, all four of them, chattering and laughing as they walked through the old quarry.

As soon as they arrived at the cave, Peter told them what had happened. They stared at his grave face and listened in astonishment to what he told them.

'It's very odd,' said George. 'I don't understand it. Taking food – and cushions – and books! It sounds like someone hiding somewhere and needing food, and something soft to lie on.'

'If one or two of us hid here in the cave tonight, we might see whoever it is that comes,' said Colin.

There was a silence. Nobody liked the idea at all. This mysterious visitor didn't sound a very nice person to lie in wait for.

'Well,' said Peter at last, 'I'm no coward, but considering that there really isn't any place in this cave that we could hide in without being seen almost at once, I don't see much point in your suggestion, Colin. I mean the intruder, whoever he is, would probably see *us* before we spotted him. Anyway, I don't like the sound of him.'

'Nor do I,' said Jack. 'I vote we clear out of here and have another meeting-place. What's the sense of bringing stuff here and having it taken as soon as our back's turned?'

They began to clear up the cave. It was really very sad.

Scamper watched them in surprise. Why were they looking so miserable? Why were they packing up everything? Well, he'd certainly better get his bone then! He couldn't leave that behind if everyone was leaving the cave!

He ran over to the corner where he had buried it. His sharp nose sniffed something else not far off on a low ledge of rock. Did it belong to the children? It didn't really smell like any of them. Scamper could always tell what shoe or glove belonged to any of the Seven just by sniffing it!

Scamper sniffed at this thing on the ledge, and then picked it up in his mouth. Perhaps it did belong to one of the children after all. He ran with it to Peter and dropped it at his feet with a little bark.

'Hello, Scamper, what is it?' said Peter. He bent down and picked up a small, dirty notebook with a frayed elastic band round it. 'Anyone own this?' he asked, holding it up.

Nobody did. Jack came up, excited.

'Peter! It might have been dropped by our strange visitor! Look inside!'

Peter slipped off the elastic band and opened the little notebook. His eyes suddenly shone. 'Yes!' he said, in a low voice. 'It *does* belong to our visitor – and here's his name – look. Wow, this *is* a find! He dropped it when he came raiding our cave last night!'

They all crowded round him in excitement. Peter's finger pointed to a name scribbled at the front of the notebook.

'Albert Tanner,' he said. 'He must be our mysterious visitor. Albert Tanner! Who can he be? Well, we'll find out *somehow*!'

CHAPTER NINE

An exciting plan

'LET'S CLEAR out of here quickly,' said Colin, in a low voice, looking nervously all round the cave. 'If Albert Tanner, whoever he is, is anywhere near, as he does seem to be, we don't want him to know we've found his notebook. We're all ready to go. Let's scoot off quickly, and examine the notebook in secret.'

'Good idea,' said Peter. 'Ready everyone? Come on then! Scamper, to heel!'

They left the cave and went out into the bright sunshine, each carrying a load. The tins, alas, were now empty, and very light to carry. Half Colin's *Famous Five* books were gone, so he hadn't a great load, either. Most of the magazines had disappeared too. Evidently their mysterious visitor was quite a reader!

They went through the quarry and into Peter's garden. 'We'll go to the summer-house, I think,' said Peter. 'It's not very comfortable, but at least we can talk in secret there.'

Soon they were all sitting on the little bench that ran round the old summer-house, with Scamper panting on the floor in a patch of warm sunshine.

Peter took the worn notebook out of his pocket and opened it. The others crowded as near as possible to see what was in it. Peter turned over the pages.

'Albert Tanner has written his name in the front as you know,' he said. 'Which was kind of him, I must say – we at

265

least know the *name* of our visitor now! There doesn't seem much else in the book, actually. Just a few notes of money and various dates, and a few words scribbled here and there. Let's see – yes – "potatoes, turnips, tomatoes, flour", just a shopping list, I suppose.'

He turned over a page or two. 'Another shopping list, and some figures jotted down. It doesn't seem as if this notebook is going to be of any use at all!'

Jack took it from him and looked through it too. At the back was a folded-in piece of leather to hold paper money. Peter hadn't noticed it. Jack slipped his fingers in to see if anything could be there.

Yes, a slip of paper, small and torn, with something scribbled on it in a different handwriting from Albert Tanner's.

'Look here!' said Jack. 'This was in the back of the notebook. See what it says? It's a note to Albert Tanner.'

'What does it say?' asked Janet, excited. 'Anything of use to us?'

'It's just scribble,' said Jack, screwing up his eyes. 'It says, "Daren't write it. Jim knows the place. He'll tell you. Meet him on post office seat 8.30 p.m., 15th. Ted."'

'The 15th! That's today,' said Peter. 'Read it again, it's evidently an important message, but how mysterious! What's this "place" Jim is going to tell Albert? My word, if only we could know it! We could go to the "place" Jim says and have a good snoop round.'

A little feeling of excitement began to stir in everyone. Colin caught hold of Peter's sleeve.

'I'll go to the post office seat tonight and sit there. Perhaps I shall see this "Jim" and hear what he says to Albert. I shall *see* Albert too!'

There was a silence, and the excitement suddenly grew stronger. 'A few of us should go,' said Peter. 'Not just you.'

'You can't,' said Janet. 'You're going to see "*Westward Ho!*" at the cinema. Mother's taking us both. And George is coming too, don't you remember?'

'Bother!' said Peter. 'Well, we can't get out of that without giving the whole thing away. Colin, you and Jack must go. And for goodness' sake listen hard and hear what's being said!'

'Right,' said Colin, thrilled. 'Can you come, Jack?'

'Oh yes!' said Jack. 'And what about us shadowing Albert and Jim, Peter? One of us could follow Albert, and the other one could follow Jim. It might be useful to know where Jim lives, and I must say I'd like to follow Albert if he goes back to the cave!'

'A jolly good idea,' said Peter. 'I only wish I could come too. But it's no good. I begged and begged to go to "*Westward Ho!*" and I can't get out of it now.'

They pored over the little note again, written in a bad handwriting, hurried and careless. Peter read it out aloud once more.

'Daren't write it. Jim knows the place. He'll tell you. Meet him on post office seat 8.30 p.m., 15th. Ted.'

'Would there be something hidden in this "place" that is in the note, do you think?' said Janet.

'Yes. Probably,' said Peter, thinking hard. 'And if it's hidden, it's valuable. And if it's valuable it may be stolen goods.'

'Yes. Goods stolen by Ted, whoever he is, and hidden away!' said Colin. 'Or stolen by Ted *and* Albert – and Ted hid them – then got caught, perhaps, and went to prison. And now he wants Albert to find them.'

Everyone laughed. 'You've made quite a story of it!' said Jack. 'I don't expect it's anything like that really. All the same, as soon as we know the place we'll certainly go there – if only we can get there before Albert does!'

'Yes, that's not going to be so easy!' said Peter. 'Maybe Albert will go there at once.'

'I hope he does!' said Colin. 'We'll be shadowing him, and he'll lead us right to this mysterious "place", wherever it is!'

'I wish I was going to be with you tonight,' said Peter longingly. 'It's an adventure, you know, and they don't come very often. I WISH I was going to share it!'

CHAPTER TEN

What happened at half-past eight

COLIN MET Jack that evening at eight o'clock outside the post office. It was dark, and there was no moon. They spoke together in low voices as they went over to the wooden seat nearby.

'What shall our plans be?' said Colin. 'The seat is just by that big chestnut tree. Shall we hide behind the tree, or get under the seat, or what?'

'We mustn't both of us be in the same place,' said Jack. 'Otherwise if the men see us and send us off, we'll neither of us hear a word. I vote one of us gets *behind* the tree, and the other *up* the tree!'

'That's a very good idea,' said Colin. 'You'd better climb up the tree. I've got a stiff knee, and it's bandaged. I fell down our cellar steps today, and Mother made a tremendous fuss, and I was afraid she'd make me rest in bed or something! I nearly had a fit, thinking I might not be able to come this evening!'

'All right. I'll climb the tree,' said Jack. 'But I'd better do it now, before anyone comes. There's nobody about at all. I'll stand on the back of the seat, and you can give me a leg-up to that big branch that overhangs the seat.'

It wasn't long before Jack was perched in the thick branches of the chestnut tree. Colin went behind the tree and leaned against the trunk, waiting. The church clock chimed a quarter past eight. Colin's heart began to beat faster – this *was* fun!

Ten minutes went by, and then someone came up. No, two people, arm-in-arm. Colin stiffened and held his breath. The two people passed talking together. Then someone else walked by smartly with a dog.

And then somebody came slouching along in rubber-soled shoes, a shadowy someone who kept out of the light of the street-lamps. He sat down on the seat, and Colin almost stopped breathing!

Jack peered down cautiously from the tree, but it was so dark that he could make out very little except that the man was wearing a cap.

Another shadowy figure appeared from across the road, walking silently. It joined the man on the seat. The two men sat a little apart, saying nothing, and the listening boys held their breath again.

After a few minutes of silence, the first man spoke. 'You're Albert. That's right, isn't it?'

But, before Albert could even nod his head, something happened that made the two men almost jump out of their skins.

Colin sneezed! He always had a very loud sneeze indeed, but this one was tremendous! He didn't even know it was coming, and it gave him almost as much of a shock as it gave the two men!

'A . . . WHOOOOOSH – ooo!'

In a trice Albert had whipped behind the tree and got hold of the startled Colin. He held him in a grip of iron. 'What are you doing here? Hiding behind this tree?'

He shook poor Colin until the boy felt as if his head would fly off. The other man came round the tree too.

'It's only a kid,' he said. 'Let him go. We don't want any noise here.'

Colin got a blow on the head and went staggering away, almost falling. Albert ran at him again, and the boy fled for his life, terrified. Jack, up in the tree, felt very scared too. Should he go to Colin's rescue? No, by the time he'd got down the tree it would be too late. Ah, Colin had run away, so he was all right. Jack clung to the branch, trembling a little.

The men stood under the tree together. 'Better clear off,' said the first man, in a low voice to Albert.

'You've got something to tell me,' said Albert.

'Yes. The scarecrow!' said his companion, lowering his voice. 'That's where it is. Look by the scarecrow.'

'Thanks,' said Albert, and slouched off silently, and was soon lost in the shadows. Jack wished Colin could have shadowed him. *He* certainly couldn't shadow Albert, because it would take him a minute or two to get cautiously down the tree. Perhaps he could follow the first man, though.

By the time Jack was safely down the tree both men had completely disappeared. Jack made off as quickly as he could, feeling decidedly scared. Was Colin all right? He'd better go to his house and see if he could find out, without letting anyone else know why he had come!

When he arrived at Colin's house he saw a light in Colin's bedroom window. Good! He threw up a pebble and hit the window-pane first time. The window was opened cautiously, and Colin's head came out.

'Colin! It's me, Jack! Are you all right?' called Jack, in a low voice.

'Yes. Quite. That man gave me a jolly good box on the ear, but I got home all right, and no one saw me coming in. What about you? Did you hear anything?'

'Yes, but nothing *really* helpful,' said Jack. 'What a terrific sneeze that was of yours, Colin!'

'Yes, my goodness. I thought I . . .' began Colin, and

then drew his head in quickly. Jack heard him speaking to someone in his bedroom, and ran out of the gate as quickly as he could.

The *scarecrow*! he thought. What does that mean? *I* don't know! Perhaps Peter will. Gosh, I can hardly wait until tomorrow morning to tell him!

CHAPTER ELEVEN

Off they go again!

THE MEETING in the summer-house the next morning was quite exciting. Peter and Janet and Scamper waited impatiently for Jack and Colin to come. Pam and Barbara came together as usual, then came George, and last of all Colin and Jack.

'Sorry we're a bit late,' said Jack. 'I went to call for Colin. His leg's still stiff so he couldn't walk very fast, though you ran fast enough last night didn't you, Colin?'

Colin grinned. He had a bruise on the left cheekbone near his ear, where he had been struck the night before. He felt rather proud of it.

'We've got some news,' said Jack, feeling extremely important as he looked round at the expectant faces of the others.

'Well, hurry up and tell us then,' said Peter impatiently. 'Did those two men meet? What did you hear?'

'Tell it all from the beginning,' begged Janet. 'I like to know every single thing so that I can see it in my mind's eye.'

'All right,' said Jack. 'Well, Colin and I met by the post office at eight o'clock, and the men came at half-past. Colin hid behind a tree, and I climbed up into it.'

'Well done,' said Peter approvingly.

'Just as the men were beginning to talk Colin did the most TERRIFIC sneeze you ever heard,' said Jack. 'Honestly, I nearly fell out of the tree!'

275

'Gosh!' said Janet. 'Whatever happened then?'

'The men ran round the tree and found poor old Colin, and that bruise on his cheek is where he got hit,' said Jack. Everyone gazed in awe at Colin's bruise, and he felt very proud indeed.

'He had to run for his life, and there was I, stuck up the tree,' went on Jack, enjoying himself immensely. 'I can tell you, it was quite an adventure! Well, then the men spoke in low voices again, but I managed to hear the important thing.'

'What was it?' demanded Peter. 'You're so long-winded. Get to the point.'

'The first man – he must have been the Jim mentioned in the letter – he said "*The scarecrow!*"' said Jack, lowering his voice just as the men had done. '"The scarecrow! That's where it is!" he said. "The scarecrow!" Then the two men went off, and I hadn't time to shadow them because I was up the tree.'

'You did very well,' said Peter. 'Extremely well! It was a pity about Colin's sneeze. Still, you heard the main thing, Jack – and that was the word "scarecrow".'

'What does it mean, though?' asked Jack. 'Do *you* know? Does it mean a *real* scarecrow?'

'No. There's a tiny inn called "The Scarecrow" up on the common,' said Peter. 'I've often passed it when I've been in the car with my father. We'll go up there and snoop round. I bet that's where something is hidden, loot from some robbery, probably.'

'Oh, yes, *I* remember seeing that inn too, and thinking what an odd name it had,' said Janet. 'Peter, let's go *now*! Before Albert gets away with anything!'

'Yes. We'd certainly better go now, this very minute!'

said Peter. 'We may find Albert there, digging away in some corner of the garden. It would be very interesting to see what he digs up!'

Everyone felt the delicious surge of excitement that always came over them when adventure was in the air. 'Get your bikes,' ordered Peter. 'Colin, is your knee too stiff to bike, do you think?'

'I can pedal all right with one leg,' said Colin, who wasn't going to be left out of this morning's excitement for anything. 'Come on, let's get our bikes, those of you who didn't come on them.'

'Meet at the crossroads by the old barn,' said Peter. 'Wait for each other. Then we'll all set off together. We're really on to something now!'

George was the only one who had come on a bike. The others set off to get theirs. Peter and Janet fetched their two from the shed, and set off with George to the crossroads, Scamper running excitedly behind them. He knew when adventure was about, he always knew!

Soon everyone was at the cross-roads, even Colin, who could only pedal with one leg. Jack came last, looking hot and cross.

'What's up?' asked Janet, seeing how upset he looked. 'Did you get into trouble at home about anything?'

'No. It's Susie,' said Jack, with a groan. 'She says that she and Jeff went up to our cave this morning, you know I had to tell Mother about it in front of Susie, and when she saw we'd gone, she and Jeff decided to have it for their meeting-place! Isn't that maddening?'

'Well, let them if they want to!' said Peter. 'Much good may it do them! Albert will probably visit them as he did us and take their things! Serve them right!'

'I wonder how Albert gets into the cave if he doesn't use our entrance!' said Janet. 'We know he used it once, because Jack saw him that time, when we were playing hide-and-seek. But he didn't use it when he robbed us of all those things. Those silk threads at the entrance weren't broken, you remember!'

'I imagine that our dear friend Albert may be some-where at the inn called "*The Scarecrow*"!' said Peter. 'He probably won't be using the cave much more if he finds what he's looking for!'

'Look, there it is – "*The Scarecrow*"!' said Pam, riding ahead. 'What a funny old inn, hundreds of years old, I should think. Come on, everybody – isn't this EXCITING!'

CHAPTER TWELVE

The Scarecrow Inn

THE SECRET Seven came near to the old inn. It was certainly a strange place, almost tumble-down. Outside a sign swung in the wind, creaking dismally. On it was painted a scarecrow in a field, and printed on it in big letters was the name.

'The Scarecrow,' said Peter, leaping off his bicycle. 'Here we are. Look out for Albert, everyone!'

They leaned their bicycles against a hedge and walked over to the inn. No one was about. The whole place looked completely deserted.

'But there must be somebody about!' said Colin. 'Look, there are a few hens pecking around.'

They went right up to the old inn. 'It seems to be shut,' said Peter, puzzled. 'Yes, look, there are bars across the windows and across the front door too, wooden bars, nailed on.'

'It must be closed down,' said Jack. 'Let's go round to the back. We can ask for a drink of water, or how to get to Penton, or something like that.'

So they all went round to the back door of the inn. A woman was in a little yard there, hanging out some washing, an old, grey-haired woman with a very disagreeable face.

'Er, could we have a drink of water, please?' asked Peter, in his politest voice.

'There's the well. Help yourself,' said the woman.

'Thank you. Is the inn closed now?' asked Peter.

'Yes. Been closed for months,' said the old woman, pegging up a sheet. 'I just caretake, and it's a lonely job up here on the common. You're the first people I've spoken to for about six weeks, except for the milkman and the grocer's boy.'

'Oh, then you don't know anyone called Albert, I suppose?' asked Peter, as innocently as he could.

'Now, don't you be cheeky,' said the woman angrily. 'Who told you my old man was called Albert? You call him Mr Larkworthy, and mind your manners. See, there he is. I'll send him after you if you're cheeky!'

The Secret Seven saw an old bent man coming out of the inn with a stick in his hand, on which he leaned heavily. Goodness, they hadn't meant to be cheeky! How could they have guessed that the old woman's husband was called Albert?

'We didn't mean your husband,' said Peter hurriedly. 'We really didn't. We're just looking for someone called Albert that we thought we might see here this morning.'

'Well, I won't have any cheek from children,' said the old woman. 'You clear off, now, before I tell my husband to chase you.'

The Seven went away slowly, taking a good look at the little place as they went. They walked to their bicycles by the hedge.

'What do you think, Peter,' asked Jack. 'Do you suppose Albert came here at all?'

'No,' said Peter. 'We're on the wrong track. I think that cross old woman was speaking the truth. She probably hasn't seen anyone here for weeks! Gosh, I did feel awful when she said her husband's name was Albert! No wonder she thought we were cheeky!'

'I had a good look at that little garden,' said George. 'And it's quite plain that nobody has been digging in it to get anything buried there. Nothing but enormous weeds.'

'Yes. I had a look too,' said Peter. 'No, we're on the wrong track, as I said. The thing is, what do we do next? If only we knew where Albert was at this moment, it would be a great help!'

'It might not be,' said Jack, with a grin. 'He might be scaring Jeff and Susie in our cave!'

'I hope he is,' said Peter grimly. 'Just like those two to try to annoy us!'

'What are we going to do now?' asked Janet. 'Peter, do you suppose it's a *real* scarecrow we have to look for?'

Peter considered. 'Yes, it might be. I was so sure that the old inn was the place meant, that I didn't really think about proper scarecrows. But we can't go chasing over the countryside looking for all the scarecrows in the fields!'

'Yes, we can,' said Colin. 'Quite easily. All we've got to do is to separate, and bike all over the place, and whenever we see a scarecrow, get off and see if anyone has been disturbing the ground by it. I *bet* whatever is hidden is well dug-in beside a scarecrow.'

'Yes. It would be such a good place if the thief wanted to get the loot again,' said Peter. 'I mean, if stolen goods were hidden in a field in the ordinary way, they couldn't be marked in case anyone wondered what the mark was for. A stick or a post or something would call attention to the place and make the farmer examine it. But a scarecrow is a *natural* mark and anything hidden beneath it wouldn't be found until the field was reaped!'

'Yes. And the thief meant to get it before that, as we know!' said George. 'Well, shall we go scarecrow-hunting?'

281

'Yes,' said Peter, getting on his bicycle. 'But look out for farmers. They mightn't be too pleased to see us walking all over their fields to get to a scarecrow!'

They all rode off together, Peter calling out orders as they went.

'You take the west road, Colin and Jack. You the east, Pam and Barbara. You take the north, George, and Janet and I will turn at the crossroads and take the south. We shall cover most of the countryside then. Meet at half-past two this afternoon in the summer-house.'

Off they all went. 'Scarecrow-hunting!' said Jack to Colin. 'What a game! I do wonder how many scarecrows we shall find!'

The Seven had a strange time, hunting for scarecrows! Pam and Barbara found a most fearsome one in the middle of a field, his coat flapping like mad in the wind.

They went to examine him, but as the soil was quite hard all round him they knew that nothing had been hidden and dug up beside *him*! So off they went to find another.

Colin and Jack found two. One was in an allotment, and although they were sure that it couldn't be the one they were looking for, they went up to him all the same, and examined the ground nearby.

A man came into the allotment with a spade over his shoulder. When he saw the two boys there he shouted at them angrily:

'You clear off, you two! These allotments are private. Are you the kids who've been taking broccoli from here?'

'No!' shouted the two boys. 'We were just having a look at the old scarecrow.'

'I'll scarecrow you if you come here again!' yelled the man, and Colin and Jack fled for their bicycles. The next scarecrow they found was in a field of young wheat, and no sooner had they walked over the field to the scarecrow than a farmer appeared with a dog. The boys just had time to make sure that the earth round the scarecrow was undisturbed before the dog flew at them.

'Ha! He'll bite you next time!' called the farmer, as the boys leapt on their bicycles.

'I don't think I like this scarecrow-hunting much,' said Colin, whose stiff leg was hurting him. 'That's twice we've had to run, and I just can't bend my knee properly.'

George, cycling quickly up and down country roads, thought he spied a scarecrow at the end of a field. He jumped off his bicycle and squeezed through the hedge – only to face a surprised and angry farm-labourer, hoeing vigorously.

'Oh – sorry – I thought you were a scare-crow,' said George very foolishly, backing away through the hedge. The farm-labourer, angry at being called a scarecrow, flung a clod of earth at George. It shattered into bits all over him. George spat some out of his mouth.

'Phoo! That was a good shot on his part!' said George, riding away. 'I don't know that I like this scarecrow business much!'

Peter and Janet had examined four scarecrows, for their particular roads ran between big farms, and great fields lay on either side. One scarecrow had thrilled Janet because a thrush had built a nest in the dented crown of the old scarecrow's hat. Peter could hardly get her away from it!

The other three they had found were not interesting, and quite plainly no one had been into the field to disturb the earth near any of the scarecrows.

Peter felt disheartened as he rode home beside Janet. 'All those scarecrows and not one of them any good to us,' he complained. 'I only hope the others have found the right one.'

They got home just in time for their dinner. Their mother looked in horror at their shoes, which were covered in mud from the soil in two very wet fields they had walked over.

'Where *have* you been?' she said. 'And what in the world

were you doing to get your shoes so filthy? Take them off at once, and leave them outside.'

'We went to look at scarecrows, Mummy,' said Janet, 'and we found one with a thrush's nest in his hat! That's how we got our shoes so dirty. But we'll clean them ourselves.'

'You should go and see the scarecrow old James has put up in the oat-field,' said her father, who was already at the table. 'He tells me it's got a robin's nest in each pocket!'

'But how did he know?' said Janet in astonishment. 'He's almost blind, poor old man – he can't even see the clouds now, to tell him the weather.'

'Well, he's not too blind to see that somebody had been walking over his precious oat-field,' said her father. 'He followed the footsteps, and they led him right to the scarecrow – and that's how he found the two robins' nest in the pockets!'

Peter pricked up his ears at once. 'Somebody walking over our oat-field to the scarecrow?' he said. 'Who, Dad – and why?'

'Goodness knows,' said his father. 'There are plenty of foolish townspeople who think they can walk all over growing fields! It was one of them, I expect.'

But Peter felt sure it was Albert! He looked at his mother. He really must go and see! 'Er – please could I just go quickly and look at those robins' nests?' he said desperately.

His mother looked at him in amazement. 'What – *now*? Just as dinner's ready? Don't be silly, dear. The nests won't fly away – they'll be there after dinner!'

Peter looked at Janet, who had read his thoughts. 'WHY didn't we think of our own scarecrow!' she blurted out. 'We see it from our bedroom windows each day. We—'

Peter gave her a sharp kick under the table, and she stopped at once. Goodness, she had nearly given the game away!

'Why all this sudden interest in scarecrows?' inquired her mother. 'I hope it soon wears off. I can't allow you to get your shoes like that again.'

Peter and Janet longed for dinner to be over. As soon as they were allowed to go, they shot out into the garden, and slipped on their dirty shoes.

'It was *our* scarecrow we should have looked at!' said Peter. 'I could kick myself! Come on – let's go now and examine the soil round it. We'll take a fork, in case we may find something, though I'm afraid that Albert has got there first. Hurry up!'

CHAPTER THIRTEEN

Everything seems dull now

PETER AND Janet ran down the garden and out of the gate at the bottom. Round the potato-field and over a stile they went, and there was the oat-field, its green rows as bright as emerald!

In the middle of it stood the scarecrow put up by old James. He was a fine one, and wore one of James's old hats, cocked over on one side. He wore a ragged red jersey and an old tweed coat with sagging pockets. A robin flew out of one of them as the children went near.

The scarecrow's ragged trousers flapped in the wind against his two wooden legs. His head was a turnip in

287

which old James had scraped eyes and mouth. He seemed to be grinning at them as they came up, and the wind shook him and made him jig to and fro.

But Peter and Janet didn't look at the scarecrow, or even at the robin's nests in the sagging pockets. They looked at the ground around his wooden legs.

And Peter gave a deep groan that really might have come from the old scarecrow! 'We *are* too late, Janet. Look, someone's been here. There are footprints all around and about, not only old James's hobnailed ones, but somebody with rubber-soled shoes – Albert's!'

'Yes,' said Janet, her eyes on the ground. 'And the soil has been well dug up. Something was hidden here, beside the old scarecrow. Oh, Peter, WHY didn't we look here first?'

'It wouldn't have been any good,' said Peter gloomily. 'I expect Albert came last night. He wouldn't come digging here in the daytime. He knew which scarecrow was meant, of course. We didn't! And all the time it was our own scarecrow!'

'Just dig round a bit and see if there's anything left,' said Janet.

'There won't be,' said Peter dolefully. 'I expect whatever it was was in a bag, a strong bag too, to resist the damp.' He dug about with his fork, but brought up nothing except a surprised worm. '*Bother!*' he said. 'I was so excited about this scarecrow business. Now we're too late, Albert has got the stuff, whatever it was, and will be off and away.'

'Yes, I suppose he will,' said Janet dismally. 'I wouldn't be surprised if he knew that it was hidden in this district and that was why he came and hid in our cave, so as to be on the spot to speak to that other man, what was his name? Jim? And to get the stuff easily.'

'I think you're absolutely right, Janet,' said Peter. 'And if you are, the stolen stuff, or whatever it was, must have *come* from this district too. I wonder if there have been any robberies lately.'

They had a look at the two cosy robins' nests, both of which had tiny feathered nestlings inside, and then walked back home. It was about half-past two, and the other members of the Secret Seven were waiting in the summer-house.

They were very downcast at Peter's news. 'Well, we were none of us successful in our scarecrow-hunt this morning,' said Jack, 'and no wonder, if the loot had been buried by *your* scarecrow, Peter. What back luck! If only we'd been able to dig by your scarecrow last night, perhaps we'd have got the hidden goods before Albert.'

'What shall we do now?' asked Pam. 'Everything seems dull suddenly, now that we've not got our cave any more, and the adventure has faded away.'

'I'm going up to the cave,' said Jack, standing up. 'I think I left my torch there, high up on a ledge. I hope Albert hasn't taken it! It's rather a nice one, and I'd like to get it if it's still there.'

'Right, we'll all come, just for the walk,' said Peter. 'We could take spades and dig in the old quarry, the sand is moist in parts, and you can model quite well with it. Let's do that.'

So they took four spades from the shed and three trowels, and off they went to the quarry. Jack went up to the cave and then stopped short in surprise.

Someone was there! He could hear excited voices. Then

he frowned. He knew *one* voice – it was Susie's! Bother her, now she would mess about round them, and make silly remarks. Who was with her? It sounded like Jeff. What cheek to come to the cave! Just like Susie!

He went into the cave, still frowning. Susie and Jeff were right at the back, scrabbling about. Whatever were they doing?

'Susie!' he called sharply. 'What are you doing here?'

Susie turned round and then came quickly over to her brother. 'Jack! I *am* glad you've come. Something peculiar has happened!'

'What?' asked Jack impatiently. 'I think it's pretty peculiar that you and Jeff should come to *our* cave, even though we've left it.'

'Don't be cross, Jack. I really am glad you've come,' said Susie. 'Listen. Jeff and I came here, and we thought it was a lovely place. We made deep holes for ourselves. Mine's over there, look, and Jeff's is opposite, by the rocky wall. We thought perhaps you others might be coming, so we practically *covered* ourselves with sand, just left our noses out to breathe, and we waited for you so that we could give loud yells and leap out at you when you came in thinking nobody was here – '

Jack gave a snort. 'Is that all you've got to tell me? *Not very interesting.*'

'Oh, *do* listen, Jack,' said Susie. 'Well, we lay like mice, only our noses out, waiting for you to come in at the front entrance there, and then somebody came out from the *back* of the cave, and trod heavily on poor Jeff and went out of the entrance!'

'And yet we *know* the cave was empty when we came in,' said Jeff. 'We looked to make sure. But there's nowhere for anyone to hide or to come from, so who was this person, and how did he get here?'

Jack was now listening intently. This was news! He turned to the entrance of the cave and yelled loudly: 'PETER! JANET! EVERYBODY! COME HERE QUICKLY! QUICKLY, I SAY!

291

CHAPTER FOURTEEN

What an excitement!

PETER, JANET, and all the others threw down their spades and trowels and raced to the cave at top speed. 'What is it?' cried Peter.

Then he saw Susie and Jeff and stopped. 'Clear out,' he cried. 'This is our cave, not yours.'

'Wait, Peter,' said Jack. 'Susie's just told me something strange.' He told the others what Susie had said, how she and Jeff had buried themselves all but their noses in the empty cave, and then someone had come from the back and walked out!

'So there *is* some way into this cave from the back,' he said. 'I know we've looked and looked, but there *must* be! Susie, did you hear anything at all before this man walked out of the cave?'

'Yes,' said Susie. 'I heard a kind of thud – so did Jeff.'

'As if someone had leapt down to the sandy floor,' said Jeff. 'Like this!' He jumped into the air and came down, making a soft thud.

'Then the way in from the back must be from some-where up near the roof,' said Peter. 'Anyone got a torch?'

'Here's mine,' said Jack. 'I found it on the ledge where I'd left it.'

Peter took it. 'Come on,' he said. 'We're jolly well going to solve this mystery. Wait though – Colin, keep guard at the front of the cave, in case that man comes back. Take a good look at him if he does.'

'Right,' said Colin, and limped to the front of the cave, though he would dearly have liked to be with the others.

There was quite a crowd at the back of the cave. Peter shone his torch on to the roof there. It was fairly high. He saw a rocky ledge jutting out and thought he would climb up to it. 'Give me a hand,' he said to Jack. 'Hold the torch for a minute, Janet.'

He was soon up on the ledge, and then shone the torch on to the roof again. He gave a sudden exclamation.

'What is it?' shouted everyone, almost dancing with excitement.

'There's a round hole here. You can't see it from where you are,' said Peter. 'And there's a rope-end hanging down. I can just reach it.'

The others craned their necks to see what Peter saw, but they couldn't. The hole was hidden by a jutting-out piece of rock, and it was only because Peter was high up on the ledge that he could see it at all. He shone his torch on the thick rope-end. It was well within his reach from the ledge on which he stood.

He stuffed the torch into his pocket. 'I can get hold of the rope,' he called down, 'and I think I can pull myself up by it. I'll try anyway.'

He caught the rope in both hands, and then by means of treading on first one narrow ledge of rock and then another, he managed to get right into the hole. He let go of the ledges with his feet and swung on the rope with his hands. He climbed up it as he did at gym, and came to a broad ledge, where he rested for a moment or two.

Then he stood on the ledge, putting his head up through the hole that still went upwards, and found that he was

294

looking out of the hole into another cave above! He shone his torch around.

He gave a yell to the others down below, but to them his voice sounded curiously muffled and hollow. They were quite startled to hear it.

'Hey! There's another cave here, a much smaller one! And some of our food's here, and all our cushions, and books and magazines! And there's a bag too, a small mail-bag that looks full of something!'

'What? What do you say?' yelled the others, almost overcome with excitement at all this shouting, and not being able to make out a word.

'PETER! What have you found?' cried Janet.

Peter came down from the rope, found the ledge he needed to climb down from, and leapt to the ground. He pushed the others away as they crowded round him, and went to get some air at the front of the cave.

'Tell us! What did you find?' said Jack. 'We heard you yelling.'

'There's a cave up there with all our things in it. That man Albert used the cushions to lie on, because the floor is of hard rock, not soft sand,' said Peter. '*And* there's a bag, a mail-bag, I think. Probably full of registered envelopes! Goodness knows how long it was buried beneath our scarecrow.'

'Well, that's a find!' said Janet, her eyes shining. 'Now we know how our mysterious visitor got into the cave without passing through the front entrance, when he wanted to steal our things. How thrilled he must have been to find food and cushions and books!'

'Now listen,' said Peter. 'He may come back at any minute, he won't dare to come into the cave while people are there. I'm going to tell Dad, and he'll phone the police. You stay here, all of you, till I come back, then Albert won't be able to remove the stolen mailbag! I'll leave Scamper with you too.'

'Right,' said Jack, taking charge. 'We'll make a good bit of noise too, shall we, to scare him off if he comes! Well done finding that cave above, Peter. You *are* clever!'

'Well, *I* really put you on to it,' said Susie. 'Gosh, I was glad to see you, Jack.'

'You were wrong to come to our cave, but for once in a way you were right to tell me what you'd seen,' said Jack sternly. 'Now, if you want to stay with us, behave yourself, Susie. Do you hear?'

'Yes, teacher,' said Susie demurely. 'I'll be a good, good girl. I'll—'

'Be quiet,' said Jack, 'or out you both go, you and Jeff!'

Susie looked at Jack's face and was suddenly quiet. They all were for a minute or two, thinking over the startling happenings of the last few minutes. Then they remembered that Peter wanted them to make a noise, so that Albert would not come to the cave to try to get that mailbag! They began to talk and laugh.

Peter ran at top speed to find his father. 'Dad!' he called, seeing him by the barn. 'Hey, DAD! Quick, I want you!'

CHAPTER FIFTEEN

A wonderful finish!

PETER'S FATHER could not make head or tail of the boy's breathless story at first. But at last he made out enough to call his wife.

'Will you telephone to the police and tell them to come at once, and go to the cave in the quarry?' he called. 'I'm off there with Peter. Tell you what's up when I get back!'

He went off with the excited Peter. Soon they were at the cave, where the others, talking loudly, were waiting anxiously. The green curtain was tied back now, and Peter's father gazed into the cave.

'I'd forgotten this old cave,' he said. 'I used to love it when I was a boy. Do you really mean to say there's a cave *above* it, Peter? I never knew that, and yet I played here heaps of times.'

'So did we,' said Janet. 'Come and see where the hole is that leads into the cave above, Daddy.'

'We had this cave for our Secret Seven meetings,' explained Peter, 'and we *couldn't* make out who took our things, or why. We didn't guess someone was in hiding in a cave above us! There's a mail-bag up there, Dad. Do you think the man stole it?'

'Probably. You'd better shin up and get it when the police come,' said Peter's father. 'I wonder how long it's been hidden there? Quite a long time, maybe.'

'No, only since last night,' said Peter. 'It was buried beside that scarecrow in the oat-field, Dad!'

299

'So *that's* why you were so interested in scarecrows all of a sudden,' said his father. 'I wonder if your mother has telephoned the police yet. Run back and see if they're coming, Peter.'

Peter set off through the quarry with Scamper at his heels, but halfway through Scamper left him and ran behind a hummock, barking madly. Peter followed him. He saw a curious mound in the sand, which, as Scamper leapt on it, put out hands and feet – and head!

'Call him off!' said a voice. 'Call him off!'

'Who are you?' demanded Peter, catching Scamper by the collar. 'Hey, *I* know who you are, you're Albert, aren't you? Waiting till we're all gone so that you can fetch that stolen mail-bag and empty it! You meant to leave the bag up in that cave, stuff your pockets with the contents, and slip away free! You'll—'

'Now, now,' said a deep voice, 'what's all this, and who is this fellow lying in the sand? Ah, surely it's Albert Tanner! We've been looking for you, Albert, ever since that last mail robbery.'

It was the big Inspector of Police! Behind him was a

stolid village constable, looking as if this kind of thing was very ordinary indeed.

The Inspector turned to Peter and beamed at him. 'Hello, Peter! I knew as soon as your mother phoned that you were caught up into one of your adventures. Is Albert here anything to do with it?'

'Yes,' said Peter. 'Look, my father's over there, by the cave. He's waiting for you.'

'Bring Albert along,' said the Inspector to his policeman, and Albert was duly brought along to the cave. As soon as Peter's father saw him, he gave an exclamation.

'Why! It's Albert Tanner! I thought I told you never to show your face in this district again, Albert!'

'You know him, sir, do you?' said the Inspector, getting out a big note-book.

'I should think I do!' said Peter's father. 'He was brought up here on this land, in a cottage not far off, and worked for me for a few years. But he was so dishonest I had to dismiss him.'

'That's how he knew this cave then!' said Peter. '*And* the one above. He must have explored like we did.'

Albert didn't say a word. He stood there, sullen and angry. The Inspector threw a glance at him. Then he turned to Peter's father.

'This man and another did a mail-bag robbery,' he said. 'The other man hid the bag somewhere, meaning to get it when the commotion about it died down. He worked on this farm once too, sir – his name's Ted Yorks.'

'Ted Yorks! Yes, he was here for years,' said Peter's father. 'He was a bad lot too, but a fine hedger and ditcher, which is why I kept him so long.'

'Well, as I said, these two planned this robbery,' said the

Inspector, 'and the mail-bag was hidden, ready to be found and the contents shared between the two of them in due course. But Ted got caught and put into prison, where he is still.'

'But he managed to get a note out of prison to Albert, to tell him how to find out where he had hidden the bag!' cried Peter. 'I see it all now! Albert came to this cave to hide till he heard from Ted, because he knew the police here were still looking for him, and he didn't dare to show his face – '

'And when he got Ted's note, he went to meet that man Jim, the one on the seat by the post-office, and learnt that he had to look by the scarecrow!' said Jack. 'I heard Jim say "The Scarecrow. That's where it is." And of course, Albert knew it was *our* scarecrow!'

'These kids know all about you, you see, Albert,' said the Inspector, looking at the surly man. 'Where did you put that mail-bag after you'd dug it up, Albert?'

'I'm not saying anything,' said Albert, 'except that I don't know anything about any mail-bag, and it's no use asking me.'

'I'll get the mail-bag, shall I?' said Peter, much to the Inspector's surprise. He looked at Peter, quite astounded.

'The mail-bag? Don't tell me you know where *that* is?' he said. 'Right, get it.'

So off went Peter to the back of the cave, shinned up the wall, caught hold of the rope, and disappeared. Then a voice came down the hole.

'Stand by, everyone! Mail-bag on the way!' There was a

heavy thud on the soft sand, and there was the mail-bag! Its fall had broken it open, and registered envelopes and packets came tumbling out.

'Whew!' said the Inspector, amazed. 'This is magic! Hey, Peter, any more mail-bags to come?'

Peter came down the hole, laughing. 'No. That's the only one. Is it the stolen one?'

'Yes,' said the Inspector. 'Well, I'm afraid Albert won't be able to steal any more mail-bags for a long, long time. Take him away, Constable!'

Albert was marched away, still sullen and silent. 'Come in and have a word with my wife, Inspector,' said Peter's father. 'She must be longing to know what all this excitement's about. Peter, here's some money. Take all the Secret Seven out and give them a thumping good tea, ice-creams and all. You've done well, my boy!'

He went off with the Inspector, who waved a cheery hand to them. Peter turned to the others, beaming. He waved the money at them.

'Look at that! We'll have a feast. Come on!'

Susie and Jeff went out of the cave with the others. Jack gave his sister a little push.

'You're not coming with *us*, Susie. We're the Secret Seven, and you don't belong. You go home.'

'Oh,' said Janet, seeing Susie's downcast face, 'couldn't she come just for once? I mean, she did tell you about Albert coming out of the back of the cave when she and Jeff were there, Jack, and it was because of that that we managed to find the other cave at last. *Couldn't* she come?'

'No. We're the Secret Seven,' said Jack, 'and Susie would only laugh and sneer at us all the time, like she always does. And Jeff too. No.'

'I won't! I think you're wonderful!' said Susie. 'Let me come. Just this once, Jack. I DO want to hear all about this exciting adventure.'

'You can come, Susie,' said Peter, taking command. '*And* Jeff too. Just this once. It's a story worth telling, I promise you. It will take us at least four ice-creams each before the tale is told. It's a jolly good adventure, you'll have to admit that, Susie!'

It was, and Susie's going to say so, too, when she's heard it. Good old Secret Seven – they always get there in the end, don't they?

THREE CHEERS, SECRET SEVEN

CONTENTS

CHAPTER ONE

No meeting after all!

'I DON'T see much sense in calling a Secret Seven meeting,' said Janet to Peter. 'There's really nothing to discuss – no adventure or mystery anywhere – and I did want to finish reading my book.'

'We haven't had a meeting for three weeks,' said Peter. 'And if you've got something better to do than to belong to the Secret Seven and attend the meetings, well, do it! We can easily get somebody instead of you.'

'Peter! Don't be so cross!' said Janet, quite horrified at the thought of not being a Secret Seven member. 'Of *course* I want to belong. But it's only *really* exciting when something is happening. Or if we've got plenty to eat and drink.'

'Well, if the others bring what they promised we should have quite a nice feast,' said Peter. 'Do help me to tidy the shed ready for the others, Janet – you just sit there and do nothing!'

The two of them and Scamper were down at the meeting-shed getting ready for the other five. On the door were the big letters, SS, and Scamper, the golden spaniel, sat outside as if guarding the shed. It was quite an ordinary shed in the usual way, but it seemed very important to Scamper when the Secret Seven held a meeting there.

'Here comes someone,' said Peter, as Scamper gave a small bark of welcome.

'Rat-tat!' There came a sharp knock on the closed door of the shed.

311

'Password!' called Peter. 'And don't yell it, please!'

'Lollipops!' said a voice, with a little giggle at the end.

'That's Pam,' said Janet. 'Come in, friend!'

Pam came in, carrying a small bag. 'Hallo!' she said. 'Am I the first? I've brought some biscuits – but there aren't many, I'm afraid.'

'Wuff-wuff!' said Scamper, from outside, and more footsteps could be heard.

'Lollipops!' said a low voice. And then another voice said, 'Peppermints!' and laughed.

Peter went to the door at once. George and Colin were there. 'Come in, George,' said Peter. 'Stay out, Colin; you didn't know the password.'

'Oh, come on! That was only a joke!' said Colin, hastily. 'Honestly it was, Lollipops is such a silly password – I just improved on it by saying "peppermints". Ask George if I didn't *really* know the password. I told him it coming along. Didn't I, George?'

'Yes – he does know the password really, Peter,' said George. 'Let him in.'

'Well, I will *this* time,' said Peter. 'Hallo, here comes Barbara – and Jack. But who's that waiting about over there?'

'It's *Susie*!' said Janet. 'That horrid sister of Jack's. I bet she'll try to come to the meeting.'

'Password, Barbara,' said Peter. Barbara and Jack both remembered it and went into the shed. Peter watched Susie for a few moments, but she didn't come any nearer, so he went in and shut the door of the shed. He left Scamper on guard outside.

'On guard!' he said, and Scamper sat down and waited, knowing perfectly well that he must bark if anyone came near. He watched Susie intently. If she dared to come one step nearer he would bark in his very fiercest voice!

Peter turned on Jack as soon as the shed-door closed. 'Whatever do you want to bring that awful sister of yours here for?' he demanded. 'You know how often she's upset our meetings, and got to know our passwords!'

'Well, she's promised not to come *near* our shed,' said Jack. 'And though I agree she's an awful nuisance, she does keep her word, you know. She won't disturb us, really she won't.'

'But why did you want to bring her at *all*?' said Peter. 'I don't trust her one bit. I bet she wants to play some silly trick on us.'

'She doesn't. But I'll tell you why I *had* to bring her,' said Jack. 'An American cousin of ours has sent her an aeroplane, and she can't fly it by herself. I'm longing to have a go at it. So we're going to fly it after the meeting somewhere. We've left it under your hedge till the meeting is over.'

'An aeroplane? What sort?' said George, eagerly.

'A *fantastic* one,' said Jack. 'As big as this!' and he held his arms out wide. 'And it's got some kind of clockwork to wind up the elastic bands that help it to fly. I tell you, it's super!'

'Fancy sending an aeroplane to *Susie!*' said Peter, amazed. 'Why didn't your cousin send it to you, Jack?'

'Well, we were each asked what we wanted,' said Jack. 'I chose a cowboy outfit – it's fine – and Susie chose an aeroplane. Just like Susie to choose something *I* want when it comes. It's miles nicer than my cowboy-suit.'

'Would Susie let us come and see you fly it?' asked George.

Jack looked doubtful. 'I don't know. She's always rather cross about the Secret Seven, you know, because we keep her out of it.'

'I tell you what!' said Peter, quite changing his mind about Susie, now that she owned such a wonderful aeroplane. 'Let's *not* make this a Secret Seven meeting. Let's take our food into the garden somewhere, and tell

Susie she can join us – if she'll let us help with the aeroplane.'

'Right,' said Jack. 'I'll ask her,' and out he went to speak to Susie.

He came back at once. 'Yes! She says she'll join our feast, and we'll go and fly the plane afterwards,' he said, putting his head in at the shed. 'Come on, bring out the food!'

So out they all went, and Susie joined them, grinning all over her freckled face.

'Hallo!' she said cheekily. 'We're not the Secret Seven this morning – we're the Exciting Eight!'

CHAPTER TWO

The beautiful aeroplane

PETER DIDN'T like Susie's remark that they were not the
Secret Seven at the moment, but the Exciting Eight.
However, it wouldn't do to make her cross by snapping
at her just when they all wanted a favour from her.

'Where's this super plane?' he asked.

'Where's this super food?' said Susie at once. 'We'll
have that first before we fly the plane.'

'All right, all right. We meant to, anyhow,' said Peter.
'Where shall we have it? Over there under that tree?'

'No. I tell you what we'll do,' said Jack. 'Susie and I

were going to fly the plane in the big field behind our house, so what about taking the food there and sitting on the grass? It's a nice field.'

'Yes. Good idea,' said Peter, and the others agreed. 'Come on, Scamper, walkie-walk!'

'Wuff!' said Scamper, pleased, and acted like his name, scampering off at top speed to the front gate. He stopped and gazed suspiciously at something hidden under the hedge, and then barked again.

'It's all right, Scamper, it's only my aeroplane,' said Susie, proudly. The Seven stopped to admire it. It stood there under the hedge, the biggest toy aeroplane they had ever seen, gleaming silver-bright in the sun.

All the children thought the same thing. Fancy that beautiful plane belonging to *Susie*. What a dreadful waste! But none of them said that, knowing perfectly well that if they did, the annoying Susie would pick up the plane and march off with it all by herself.

'Well, what do you think of it?' asked Susie. 'Better than a silly cowboy-suit, isn't it?'

Jack went red and glared at his sister. 'If I'd known that *this* was the kind of aeroplane our American cousin was going to send . . .' he began, angrily, but Peter stopped him.

'Don't go up in smoke, Jack,' he said, anxious to keep the peace. 'I bet your suit is super. But gosh, WHAT an aeroplane! It's even got retractable landing wheels, look!'

'Yes,' said Susie, proudly. 'In the leaflet about the plane, it says that the wheels go up into the body as soon as the plane starts flying, and are put out again automatically when it lands. I bet no one in the whole country has a model aeroplane that does that.'

The Secret Seven felt sure she was right. Susie picked up the beautiful plane and went out of the front gate.

'*I'll* carry it for you,' said Peter. 'I'm sure it's too heavy for you!'

Susie laughed in her usual annoying way. 'What you *really* mean is that you're longing to carry it yourself so that everyone we meet will think it's *yours* and envy you!' she said. 'Ha, you're going red! *I* know you boys. But the plane is *mine* and *I'm* doing the carrying, thank you.'

Nobody said any more. What a pity Jack had such a clever sister. You could never get the better of Susie! She always had a smart answer ready. The little procession set out down the road, Susie first with the plane, then the others straggling behind and Scamper last of all, sniffing into all the corners as usual.

They came to Jack's house, went in at the side gate, and down to the bottom of the garden at the back. There they had to climb over a fence to get into the vast field that lay beyond.

'Food first,' said Susie, when they were all over, and Scamper had been lifted safely down to the ground.

'What food have *you* brought?' said Pam, who was beginning to feel annoyed with Susie.

'None. *I've* brought the aeroplane,' said Susie. 'I hope *you* haven't brought the miserable biscuits you bring to school to eat at break!'

'Shut up, Susie,' said Jack, uncomfortably. 'We've got a jolly good feast. You can have a very fair share, and remember that it doesn't cost you anything to be polite.'

319

The feast was certainly quite good. There were the biscuits, of course, some rock buns, pieces of gingerbread, an enormous bar of nut chocolate, jam-tarts, two bottles of lemonade, and a bag of toffees.

'Give Scamper a toffee,' said George. 'That will keep him quiet for ages.'

But Scamper wanted a bit of everything, and got it too. He had only to lie down by any of the Seven and look at them beseechingly out of his great brown eyes to get anything he wanted! Even Susie gave him a titbit and patted him.

'Now we'll fly the plane,' she said, when every crumb had been finished, and every drop of lemonade had been drunk. At once everyone stood up, excited. Jack took up the leaflet about the plane and studied it, while the other three boys tried to look over his shoulder.

'It seems easy enough,' said Jack.

'All I want is for you to show me what to do the *first* time and I'll know forever afterwards,' said Susie. 'Now, what happens?'

'Well, you turn this, that's to make sure the wheels go back as soon as the plane is in the air,' said Jack. 'And you

press this, look, Susie. And you wind up the key here –
that's the mechanism that winds the elastic bands up
tightly so that they give the plane the energy to fly,
and . . .'

'I don't want all those explanations,' said Susie, impatiently. 'I just want to know how to *fly* the plane.'

Jack said no more, but pressed this and that, and wound
the little key till it would wind no more. Then he held the
beautiful plane high above his head and pressed a little
button at the back.

'Fly!' he shouted, and threw the plane forward. It rose
high into the air at once, with a loud, humming noise. It
circled round beautifully while the children watched it in
delight. Then it rose high into the air and flew off across
the field to the other side, for all the world like a real
plane.

'It will turn and circle back to us,' said Jack. 'That's what the booklet said.'

But it didn't! It kept straight on, flew over a high wall at the other side of the field, and disappeared completely!

'Oh no!' said Jack, horrified, 'It hasn't come back. *Now* what are we to do?'

CHAPTER THREE

Where is the aeroplane?

'IT'S GONE!' said Susie, looking quite heart-broken. 'My beautiful aeroplane! Oh, I wouldn't have let you fly it, Jack, if I'd thought you'd lose it on its very first flight. It will be smashed to pieces!'

'*I* didn't know it would do that!' said Jack. 'Whoever saw a model plane fly like that before? I never guessed it would be able to fly right across this big field. Oh, Susie, I'm awfully sorry, really I am.'

'Who lives in that place?' asked Peter, looking towards the high wall. 'Is there a house there?'

'Yes. It's called Bartlett Lodge, and it's a very big house,' said Jack. 'It's been shut up for ages, because the owners left to go abroad.'

'Oh, well, we could easily go and get the plane then,' said George. 'No one will shout at us or chase us if we look for it.'

'There's a gardener there,' said Jack, doubtfully. 'He's not very nice. When Susie and I lost our ball over there he wouldn't even let us climb over the wall to get it, though *he* couldn't find it. So we lost it.'

'*I'm* not going over,' said Barbara. 'I'd be scared. I don't like cross gardeners.'

'No one has to go if they don't want to,' said Peter firmly. 'Perhaps only four of us should go anyway. Eight is too many to make a quick getaway if necessary. We'll climb up to the top of the wall and see if the gardener's there. If he is,

323

we'll be awfully polite, and apologetic, and ask if he's seen our plane. If he's *not* there, we'll go over and hunt.'

'Hadn't you better ask permission before you do that?' said Janet.

'Who from?' said Jack. 'There's nobody in the house to ask. Come on – we'll see what we can do.'

All the eight, and Scamper too, went across the field to the high wall. 'How are you going to climb that?' said Barbara. 'It's terribly high.'

'We'll shove each other up,' said Jack. 'I'll go first and have a look from the top of the wall to see if the gardener is anywhere about.'

George and Peter pushed him up, and at last he was on the top of the wall. He looked down into the overgrown shrubbery on the other side. Through a gap he could spy an unmown lawn, but there was no gardener to be seen. He put his hands to his mouth and shouted.

'Hey! Anybody there?' He listened, but there was no answer. Jack called again. 'Can I come over the wall and look for our aeroplane, please?'

Then a voice suddenly shouted back.

'Who's that? Where are you?'

'Here, on the top of the wall!' yelled Jack. He turned and looked down at the others. 'I can see the man. He's coming. Perhaps he's got the plane.'

A man came quickly through the gap in the trees. He was thick-set, and broad-shouldered, and had a ruddy, surly face, with screwed-up eyes. In his hand was a spade.

'Now then, what are you doing on that wall?' he said, threateningly. 'You get off. This here is private property and well you know it! Do you know what I do to children who come in here? I chase them with a spade!'

'We don't want to come in,' said Jack, rather alarmed.
'We just wanted to know if you've seen our aeroplane. It
flew right over the . . .'

'No. I've not seen *any* aeroplane, or *any* ball, or *any*
kite, and what's more if I find one it can stay here,' said the
surly man. 'You've got a big enough field back there to
play in without throwing things over here. If I find a plane
I shall put it on my bonfire.'

'Oh, *no!*' said Jack, in horror. 'It's a very valuable plane,
a real beauty. Oh please, *do* let me come down and look
for it, it belongs to my sister, and I . . .'

'If it belonged to the Queen of England I'd not let you
come in here,' said the man. 'Understand? I've got my
orders, see? I'm in charge of this place while it's empty,

and I'm not having any boys coming in here to steal the fruit, or . . .'

'I'm not a thief!' said Jack, indignantly. 'I just wanted our plane. I'll tell my father, and *he'll* come and get it for me.'

'*That* he won't,' said the surly gardener. 'Now you clear off that wall this minute, or I'll tip you off!' He held up his spade as if he meant what he said. Jack didn't want to be shovelled off like a sack of potatoes, and leapt down very hastily into the field.

'What a beast!' said Peter, to poor Jack, as the boy sprawled heavily on the grass, for it was a high jump down from the wall.

'YOU SEND BACK MY AEROPLANE!' suddenly shouted Susie, stamping her foot on the grass, tears in her eyes at the thought of losing the aeroplane on its very first flight. But there was no answer at all from over the wall.

'Oh, Susie, I'm so sorry,' said Jack, getting up. 'Listen, I'll go and get the plane for you, really I will, as soon as that horrible man has gone off for his dinner. I expect he goes at about twelve o'clock.'

WHERE IS THE AEROPLANE?

Everyone crowded round Susie, feeling really upset about the lovely plane. 'Didn't you even *see* it anywhere?' asked Susie, in a fierce voice, turning to Jack. He shook his head dolefully.

'Listen,' said Peter, taking command again. 'Two of us will go and watch at the front gates of that house, and then, as soon as we see that horrible gardener going off for his midday dinner, we'll know it's safe to slip over the wall and hunt for the plane. We won't go in at the front gates in case anyone sees us and tells the gardener.'

'Good idea,' said Jack, cheering up. 'You and I will go, Peter. What's the time? Gosh, it's almost twelve now! Come on, let's sprint down that little lane to the road that the house faces on. Hurry up!'

Jack and Peter set off down a narrow little lane that led from the field to the road on which the big house faced. They turned to the left in the road and came to the big gate that led into the drive of Bartlett Lodge. There was a second gate farther on that also led into the drive.

'You watch that gate, I'll watch this one,' said Peter. 'But hide behind a tree or something. You don't want that gardener to see you. He's already seen you up on the wall, and he may recognise you and chase you.'

'Don't worry, I won't let him spot me, and if he does, I bet I can run faster than he does!' said Jack, and set off towards the second gate.

There was a workmen's shed a little farther down the road, and he decided to hide behind that. So he posted himself there. Peter went across the road and hid behind a bush that most conveniently grew there. Now, would that tiresome man soon come out?

They had waited about ten minutes when they saw

327

someone coming out of the gate nearest Peter. Jack
signalled to Peter, and he nodded back. It was the gardener, no doubt about that. Jack recognised the burly figure
at once, and drew back behind the shed.

The man set off down the road and turned the corner.
Jack whistled to Peter, and the two ran to the little lane
together, to go and tell the others that the gardener had
gone.

They were in the field, playing with a ball, waiting
impatiently for the boys to come back. Susie was still
upset about her plane, and had been making quite a lot of
rude remarks about the Secret Seven. They were getting
rather tired of her!

'Here are the boys!' said Janet, as they appeared in the
field. 'Any news, Peter?'

'Yes. That man's gone to his dinner, as we hoped,' said Peter. 'Now we can try and get Susie's plane. We'll go over the wall as before.'

'I'm coming too,' said Susie, unexpectedly.

'You are *not*,' said Jack at once.

'Well, it's my plane, isn't it?' said the irritating Susie. 'I've got every right to go and look for it. I'm coming too.'

'YOU ARE NOT!' said Peter, in the voice that all the rest of the Secret Seven knew well, and didn't dream of disobeying. But Susie wasn't going to take orders from Peter.

'I shall do as I like,' she said, defiantly. 'I shall climb the wall too.'

'Well, I don't know how,' said Peter, 'because I shall certainly forbid anyone to give you a shove up.'

He and Jack were quickly hoisted up to the top of the wall by George and Colin. Susie stood by, looking sulky. She turned to the two boys near her. 'Now give *me* a shove,' she said.

'Nothing doing,' said Colin, cheerfully. 'Peter's our chief, as you jolly well know, and he's given his orders. Don't be an idiot, Susie.'

'I'll climb up by myself then,' said Susie, and she very nearly did, using every little hole and crevice for her feet and fingers! The others watched her angrily – but to their delight she could not reach the top, and fell down when she was half-way up.

'Have you hurt yourself?' asked Janet, anxiously. But Susie refused to cry or to say she was hurt. She made a rude face at Janet and stood up, brushing her skirt with her hand. She walked a little way away from the others, and leaned against the wall, whistling as if she didn't care tuppence for any of the Secret Seven.

The boys had now disappeared from the top of the wall. There was a most convenient tree that leaned towards the wall just there, and one by one the boys gave the little leap towards it that enabled them to catch hold of a branch and then swing themselves neatly to the ground.

They stood there, all looking cautiously towards the house, through the gap in the shrubbery. No one was to be seen, of course, and as the house was not overlooked by any other, they felt that they could go safely forward and hunt for Susie's aeroplane.

'I hope it's not smashed to bits,' said Jack to Peter, as they made their way through the trees and bushes towards the great untidy lawn. 'If it is I'll never hear the last of it from Susie. She never forgets a thing like that!'

They began to hunt for the aeroplane. First they searched the beds round the lawn, but no plane was there, only masses of weeds that made the boys wonder what the gardener did for his wages! They hunted in the bushes, they looked up into the trees, wondering if the plane had caught in some high branch.

'This is maddening!' said Jack, at last. 'Not a *sign* of the plane! Do you suppose that gardener found it and hid it away?'

'I shouldn't be surprised!' said Peter. 'He's surly enough for anything!'

They were now fairly near the great house. It looked very forbidding, for all the curtains were drawn straight across the windows. And then Peter suddenly saw the aeroplane.

It had landed neatly on a little balcony on the second floor of the house, and there it was, balanced on the broad stone ledge.

'Look, there it is!' said Peter, pointing. 'And if we climb this tree that goes right up to the balcony we can easily get it. It's not smashed. It looks perfectly all right!'

'You go up, and I'll keep watch down here,' said Jack. 'I don't know why, but I suddenly feel nervous. I hope that gardener hasn't come back!'

CHAPTER FOUR

Something rather strange

PETER BEGAN to climb the tree. It was quite easy and safe. Jack stood at the bottom, watching him, looking all round now and again in case that bad-tempered gardener came back!

It didn't take Peter long to get up as far as the second-floor balcony. He climbed over it, and examined the aeroplane. Was it broken in any way?

Most miraculously it seemed to be perfectly all right, nothing bent or broken at all. It had, in fact, made a perfect landing in a very difficult place! Peter called down to Jack.

'Hey! The plane's not damaged at all. Isn't that a bit of luck? I'm wondering what is the best way to get it down. I can't very well climb down the tree with it because I need both my hands.'

'Got a piece of string?' called back Jack. 'If you have, you could tie one end to the tail of the plane, and let it down carefully to me.'

'Oh, yes, of course! Good idea!' said Peter. He always carried string about with him, of course, as did all the Secret Seven; you never knew when it might come in useful in any sudden adventure, and, in the opinion of the Secret Seven, adventures were nearly always sudden!

Peter took the string out of his pocket and undid it. Yes, it would just about reach down to Jack. He began to tie one end to the tail of the plane, marvelling at the beautiful workmanship in it as he did so. No wonder Susie was proud of such a model. But oh, what a *waste* for it to belong to her!

He carefully let the plane down to Jack, who stood with his hands outstretched, waiting to receive it, most thankful that it wasn't damaged. Now perhaps Susie would hold her tongue!

'I've got it! Thanks awfully, Peter!' he called up. 'Come on down, and we'll take it back to Susie.'

Peter glanced round the balcony to make sure that he was leaving nothing behind. The curtains of the balcony room were drawn across, just as they were in all the rooms of the house – but they did not quite meet in the middle. And then just as Peter was turning away to climb over to the tree, something caught his eye. Something red and glowing, shining between the cracks of the curtains just where they did not meet.

He stopped, astonished. Why, that looked like a light, or a fire burning in the balcony room! But it couldn't be – the house was shut up and empty!

Gosh, I hope a fire hasn't started up somehow, thought Peter, alarmed. I'd better peep through the window and see. Perhaps I can open the balcony window.

He went to the window and peered through the crack of the curtains. Yes, he was right, there *was* a fire glowing in the room! But wait a minute – it was a gas-fire, surely?

He pressed his face against the glass of the window, and, when his eyes became used to the dimness of the curtained room, he could see quite clearly that a gas-fire was burning brightly in the fireplace. What a very extraordinary thing!

He tried the window to see if he could open it, but it was fastened inside. Gosh, had the people left that fire on when they went away? What a terrible waste of gas! It certainly ought to be turned off.

He was just peering to see what else he could spy between the curtain when he heard Jack's voice.

'Peter! What on earth are you doing? Do come down!'

'I'm just . . .' began Peter, when Jack called again, suddenly sounding scared.

'Peter! I can hear someone whistling. I think it's that gardener coming back. HURRY UP!'

Peter had a shock. Gosh, it would never do to get caught by that awful man! He shot over the balcony at once, and was climbing down the tree before Jack could call again!

'Come on,' said Jack, urgently. 'Whatever made you so long? I'm sure it's that gardener about somewhere!'

But there was no sign of the man, much to Peter's relief. It must have been someone else whistling. He and Jack tore down the garden to the bottom, and stopped to get their breath in the shrubbery by the wall.

'Listen, Jack,' panted Peter. 'I saw something rather odd in that balcony room. I think we'll call a meeting about it. So can you make Susie go off with her plane, and then we'll be able to plan a meeting this afternoon?'

'Oooh, what did you see? What's up?' said Jack, at once.

'No time to talk about it now,' said Peter, looking at his watch. 'Anyway, I'd rather tell it to everybody at a meeting. Come on, let's shin up this tree and get over the wall. I'll hold the plane and hand it to you when you're at the top.'

He called over the wall. 'Hey, are you there, Colin and George?'

'Yes! Have you found the plane?' called the two boys on the other side.

'Yes. We're coming over. Stand by to help,' said Peter.

He waited till Jack had climbed the tree and was sitting on the wall, and then handed him the precious plane, which Jack then handed down carefully to Colin. There was the sound of delighted voices at once!

Then up went Peter and was soon on the wall grinning

down at the others. He saw Susie proudly holding her plane again, smiling all over her face.

'Better take it home straightaway, Susie,' said Jack, remembering that he had to get rid of his sister somehow.

'I'm jolly well *going* to,' said Susie. 'I'm not letting the Secret Seven fly it again!' And off she went, head in air!

'Listen, Secret Seven,' said Peter, urgently. 'Meet this afternoon at half-past two. I've got something to tell you all. Not a word to Susie, though!'

'Right!' said everyone, excited, and Scamper barked too. Ah, was something going to happen at last?

CHAPTER FIVE

A proper meeting

THE SECRET Seven met very punctually indeed that afternoon, for they were all very anxious to know why Peter had called such a sudden meeting. Jack arrived first, ten minutes early and quite out of breath.

'Lollipops!' he panted, and was let into the shed at once. 'I've given Susie the slip – I *hope*!' he said. 'She wanted me to go fishing in the ponds with her this afternoon, and I had an awful bother trying to put her off. I think she half suspects there's another meeting on. I ran like a hare as soon as I could give her the slip!'

'Bother Susie!' said Peter. 'We'll put old Scamper on guard again outside the door. And, by the way, Jack, there's no food for the meeting to have this afternoon, because we ate it all this morning, and my mother won't let me have another lot.'

'Same here,' said Jack. 'Listen, here are the others. Goodness, aren't we nice and early! It's only twenty-five past two.'

'Wuff-wuff!' said Scamper, as the usual knock came at the door of the shed, and the password was muttered by the other four members.

'Pass, friends!' called Peter, and in they all came, with Scamper at their heels. He always knew when the whole seven were there!

'Sorry, Scamper, old thing, but I want you to keep guard outside,' said Peter, and gave him a gentle push.

'Bark if Susie so much as puts her nose in at the front gate!'

Scamper put his tail down mournfully, and went to sit outside. He sensed that there was excitement about and he wanted to share it. Still Peter was the chief, and Scamper, like the others, obeyed him at once.

They were soon all sitting round on boxes and flower-pots, their eyes fixed expectantly on Peter.

'What's this sudden meeting for?' asked Colin. 'Is something up?'

'I don't know. But I thought I'd tell you and we'd discuss it,' said Peter. 'There may be absolutely nothing in it – but if there is, it's only fair that you should all share. Listen!'

They listened eagerly while Peter told them what he had seen when he had climbed up to the balcony to get Susie's aeroplane.

'As soon as we saw the plane sitting so nicely on the balcony, I shinned up a tree to get it,' said Peter. 'And when I was there I noticed that there was a red glow shining in the balcony room. There was a crack in the curtains, you see, that's how I spotted the glow.'

'But what *was* the glow? Could you see?' asked Janet, eagerly.

'Yes. It came from a gas-fire, a *lighted* gas-fire!' said Peter. 'Now, what do you make of that?'

'Somebody left it on when the house was closed, and the people went abroad,' said Barbara, promptly. 'Easy!'

'Yes. That's what *I* thought at first,' said Peter. 'But now I'm not so sure. I have a sort of feeling that I was just about to notice something else odd when Jack suddenly called me, and I was scared the gardener would come back, so I rushed away to climb down the tree.'

There was a short silence. 'But what do you mean, you were *about* to notice something,' said Colin. 'What sort of something?'

'I don't know. I've been thinking and thinking, but it's like something in a dream. You nearly remember it and it slips away,' said poor Peter, frowning hard and trying to remember what it was that had so nearly attracted his attention. 'I *think* it was something on a table.'

'A cloth,' said Barbara, not very brightly.

'Four legs,' said Pam, with a giggle.

'Don't be silly,' said Peter, impatiently. 'It was something *unusual*, I'm sure.'

'Well, what are we going to do about this gas-fire?' said George. 'It ought to be turned off, that's certain. It's a frightful waste of gas, and there might be a danger of fire from it.'

'That's what *I* think,' said Peter. 'But how do we get it turned off?'

'Tell the gardener!' said Jack, promptly. 'Or whoever's got the keys. I suppose, Peter, there can't be anyone in the house, can there? I mean, it *is* all locked up, isn't it?'

'Yes, as far as I know,' said Peter. 'All the curtains to the windows were drawn, anyhow, and that usually means a house is locked up. I wonder who the owners are?'

'Somebody called Hall,' said Jack. 'I heard my mother say so.'

'Would your mother know who had the keys?' asked Peter. 'I mean, sometimes people give the keys to neighbours, don't they? Or to estate agents?'

'She *might* know,' said Jack. 'I'll ask her. Suppose she says the estate agents have them, we could go and tell *them* about the gas-fire then. And if it's neighbours, perhaps my mother could telephone to them and get them to go in and turn off the fire.'

'And if we *can't* find out who has the keys, we'll have to tell that old gardener,' said Janet. 'For all we know, *he* has the keys himself! Perhaps he pops into the house and lights a gas-fire to warm his toes by when he's cold!'

'Fool!' said Peter. 'Look out, that's Scamper barking. Someone's coming!'

There was a knock on the door. 'If that's you, Susie, I'll pull your hair till you yell!' shouted Jack, fiercely.

But it wasn't Susie. It was Peter's mother. 'I don't know your password!' she called, 'but I've come to say that if you'd like to ask the Secret Seven to tea, Peter, they can all stay!'

'Mother! Come in! You don't need a password if you bring news like that!' said Peter, joyfully, and flung the door wide open. 'The meeting's over. Report any news from your mother tomorrow, Jack.'

CHAPTER SIX

A good half-hour's work

NEXT MORNING the Secret Seven met again, very promptly. The password was muttered five times to Peter and Janet in the shed, and five times Scamper barked a welcome.

'Well,' said Peter, when the door was shut and they were all sitting in a circle in the dark little shed. 'Any news to report, Jack?'

'Not much,' said Jack. 'I asked my mother about Bartlett Lodge, and she said the owners have gone abroad for a year, and they left the keys at their bank. Mother said no one is allowed to go into the house except by permission of the bank.'

'Really?' said Peter. 'Not to clean or anything?'

'I asked her that,' said Jack. 'And she said no, not even to clean. She said that Alice, a woman who comes to do some cleaning each week, went in and cleaned it thoroughly, top to bottom, before it was locked up.'

'Ah, then what about asking Alice if she left the fire on!' said Peter, at once. 'Couldn't you ask her that, Jack? Could you talk about the house and then sort of lead round to gas-fires and electric lights and so on?'

'Well, I don't mind trying,' said Jack. 'But wait a bit, no, I can't. She's broken her arm and isn't coming for a bit.'

'Bother,' said Peter. 'Now how can we get round *that*?'

Everyone thought hard. 'Why can't you go and ask her how she is, and take her some sweets or something?' said

Janet at last. 'When our old nanny is ill we always pop round with a little present.'

'All right,' said Jack, feeling that he was being asked to do rather a lot. 'Anyway, why don't you all come with me? It would be easier then. She's seen most of you.'

'Perhaps on the whole it might make things easier if we *did* all go,' said Peter, considering. 'We could tell her about the aeroplane going into the garden. That would introduce the subject, so to speak. But we wouldn't say anything about climbing up to the balcony, of course.'

'Gosh no!' said Jack, horrified. 'She might tell my mother, and I'm sure I'd get into a row if she thought we'd gone there and climbed up like that!'

'Well, what about going straightaway?' said Peter, who liked doing things at once. 'Anyone got any money to buy sweets or something? We could buy her peppermints.'

'Oh, yes, Alice likes peppermints,' said Jack. 'That's a good idea. Come on – let's go. It's a lovely sunny afternoon, and I've had enough of this shed.'

So they all went out to buy the peppermints and were given quite a lot for fifty pence. Off they went to the little cottage down Green Lane where Alice lived. She was very pleased indeed to see them.

'Well, there now! It's a treat to see your smiling faces!' she said. 'And you're just in time to have one of my bits of gingerbread. As sticky as can be, it is, and I know Jack likes *that*!'

The children felt that Alice was giving them as much a treat as they hoped to give her with the peppermints! She was, however, so delighted with their unexpected gift that they couldn't help feeling pleased.

'And what have you been doing, you and Susie, since I broke my arm?' she said to Jack. 'Into mischief again,

I'll be bound! And have you worn your cowboy-suit yet?'

This was a wonderful opening for what they wanted to say. Jack plunged in at once. 'Oh yes, and we've flown that lovely aeroplane that Susie got. And will you believe it, it flew right over the wall into Bartlett Lodge!'

'Did it, now? That's the house belonging to the Halls,' said Alice, offering the tin of gingerbread round generously. 'I cleaned it down from top to bottom after they went. My, that was a job!'

'Did you have to draw all the curtains?' asked Peter. 'We noticed they were drawn.'

'Yes, I drew them all,' said Alice. 'The house looked so dark and dreary then that I was glad to lock it up and leave it behind me!'

'I suppose you had to turn off the electricity and water and gas?' said Janet, feeling rather clever.

'Oh, yes, I turned everything off,' said Alice. 'So if any of you are thinking of moving in there, you'll have to get me to come and turn things on again for you!'

Everyone laughed heartily at this little joke, and Peter

looked triumphantly at Jack as he, too, laughed. So the gas *had* been turned off, had it? Then how did that gas-fire come to be burning there, up in the balcony room? Well, they had learnt quite a bit from Alice!

'Isn't there *anyone* there?' asked Jack.

'Nobody at all. It's all locked up now. I tell you, I locked every window and door myself,' said Alice. 'The only person who goes there is old Georgie Grim, the gardener, and a good name he's got too! Grim by name and grim by nature. But he's honest, I'll say that for him. Have another piece of gingerbread, Jack?'

'No thanks,' said Jack. 'We must be getting off. I hope your arm will soon be all right, Alice. Goodbye – see you soon again, I hope!'

And with that the Secret Seven marched off, feeling that they had done quite a good half-hour's work! And now, WHAT ABOUT THAT GAS-FIRE?

CHAPTER SEVEN

An unlucky encounter

'LET'S GO into this field and talk,' said Peter, as soon as they left Alice's house. 'We've learnt quite a few things from her. It was a good idea to go and see her. She's awfully nice, isn't she, Jack?'

'Yes. I told you she was,' said Jack. 'But look – if she locked and . . .'

'Wait till we're in the field,' said Peter. 'We don't want *anyone* to overhear this. At the moment it's our own little mystery, and we'll keep it to ourselves.'

So nobody said a word till they were all sitting down in the field. Then Peter began the talk.

'It's quite clear that *Alice* didn't leave the fire on,' he said. 'And if she did as she said, and turned off water, gas, and electricity when she left, then SOMEONE has turned on at least the *gas* since she locked up the house.'

'That's right,' said George. 'But who? And what for? Surely nobody is living in the house, unknown to anyone?'

'You'd have thought old Georgie Grim would have spotted any stranger about,' said Colin, thoughtfully. 'Alice said he was honest, didn't she? Well, if he'd noticed anyone lurking about, he'd surely have reported it?'

'I think he's horrid,' said Pam. 'I bet he wouldn't bother about reporting anything!'

'Don't be silly, Pam,' said Peter. 'Just because *we* think he's horrid, because he wouldn't let us get Susie's plane, isn't any reason to think he's dishonest.'

There was a silence. Nobody could think what should be done next.

'Do you think we should tell Mother?' said Janet at last, turning to Peter. Peter hesitated.

'I don't think she'd believe I really *did* see that gas-fire burning,' he said. 'It sounds rather unbelievable after all that Alice told us.'

'Well, we can easily prove it's true,' said Jack. 'Easily! Let's wait till that gardener goes home for the night and slip over the wall and up that tree again. We can easily peep through the curtains.'

'Yes! And if the fire *is* burning there, though we know from Alice that the gas is turned off, *then* we'll tell your mother, Peter,' said George. Everyone nodded gravely.

'Yes. It's about the only thing to do,' said Peter. 'All right. Jack and I will scout round there this evening after Georgie Grim has gone home. Jack, I'll be round at your house about half-past six. It'll still be light, and we can shin up that tree in a second.'

'Who's going to boost us up the high wall?' said Jack. 'We can't climb it without help.'

Peter considered. 'Have you a light ladder you could lug out of your shed?' he asked. 'We could easily take it into the field – it's only just behind your house! And we could go up the ladder and clamber on the wall one after the other.'

'Right,' said Jack. 'I only hope Susie isn't about. If she sees me dragging a ladder out of the shed she'll stick to me like a leech to see where I'm going with it!'

'Bother Susie!' said Peter, feeling very glad that Janet was not like the tiresome Susie. 'Well, I'll see you about half-past six, Jack. We'll have a meeting tomorrow morning at ten-thirty, down in the shed.'

'Make it eleven,' said Colin. 'I've got to go to the dentist.'

'Right. Eleven o'clock,' said Peter. 'And tonight Jack and I will have a look at the Mysterious Gas-Fire. I bet it will be burning away merrily!'

They all went home to their dinners, feeling pleasantly excited. Jack went to his garden shed to see if there was a ladder there. Yes. There was the old one that his father used when he pruned some of the taller fruit trees.

'Hallo! What are you doing in here?' said Susie's voice, just behind him. He jumped, and Susie laughed.

'Oho! You've gone quite red! What are you up to?' said Susie, annoyingly. 'Are you doing some job for that silly Secret Seven club of yours? Do you want a ladder by any chance?'

Susie was altogether too good at guessing! Jack picked up a little fork and a basket and marched out. He would do some weeding and show Susie she was wrong about the ladder! She followed with great interest, calling out as she went.

'Oh, what a good little boy! He's going to do some weeding! And he doesn't know the difference between seedlings and weedlings!'

'Will you be quiet, Susie,' roared Jack, really exasperated, and pulled up a wallflower quite by mistake.

'That's a wallflower,' said Susie at once. 'Oooh, you *will* get into trouble if you're going to pull up all the wallflowers.'

And then Jack lost his temper and pulled up two more hefty wallflower plants and shook the earth from their roots all over his aggravating sister. Susie fled, howling in dismay.

At half-past six Peter came round to the garden door at Jack's home. He saw Jack waiting for him behind some bushes. He put his finger to his mouth to warn Peter to be quiet.

'Susie's about,' he whispered, and led the way to the shed on tiptoe. He opened the door and there, sitting half-way up the ladder he so badly wanted, was Susie, pretending to read a book, grinning all over her face!

'Hullo! You don't want the ladder, do you?' she said. 'I'll get down if you do.'

Jack glared at her, and then the two boys walked out and banged the door hard. 'Now we can't even have the ladder!' said Jack, fiercely. 'I'm so sorry, Peter.'

'Don't worry,' said Peter, cheerfully. 'We'll simply not go over the wall, that's all. We'll go in at one of the front gates. It can't be helped. Come on, and do cheer up, Jack. This may be rather exciting!'

The two boys made their way out of Jack's garden and walked across the field till they came to the little lane that led to the front of Bartlett Lodge. Now they were in the road into which the drive-gates opened. They looked cautiously up and down the road.

'Not a soul in sight,' said Jack. 'I think if we walked smartly up to the first drive-gate and darted inside we'd be safe from anyone's view. Come on. If anyone appears in the road we'll simply walk past the gates, and then come back again when the coast is clear.'

They walked quickly up to the first drive-gate. Nobody appeared at all, so they darted in quickly and hid in some bushes to make sure that no one had seen them. Nobody shouted at them, so they felt sure they were safe. Keeping carefully to the bushes, they made their way round the side of the big, silent house.

'It's a gloomy place, isn't it?' said Jack, in a low voice. 'The curtains are still drawn across every window. Now, look out! We've got to sprint across this yard, so be quick.'

They sprinted across the little yard, and ran straight into two big men! One was Georgie Grim, and the other was a big, well-dressed man, wearing a suit, and carrying a slimly rolled umbrella. They both gaped at the two surprised boys.

'Here you! What are you doing here?' said the gardener at once, and pounced on Jack before he could get away. He gripped Jack's arm so hard that the boy cried out.

'Ha! You're the boy who said his aeroplane had flown into the garden, aren't you?' said Grim, and shook Jack as if he was a rat. 'Yes, you sat up on that wall and cheeked me! Now what are you doing here? If you . . .'

'Let me go!' cried Jack. 'You're hurting me.'

Grim shook him again. 'Yes, and I mean to! Was it you who came into this garden and walked over the bed at the bottom of that old tree? Was it you who climbed up the tree to the balcony? Oh, I saw the footmarks below, and I saw the marks where you'd climbed the tree! That I did! What were you doing up there, I'd like to know?'

'Our aeroplane landed on that balcony, that's all!' said Peter. 'We climbed the tree to get it. We couldn't help treading on the bed below, but there weren't any plants in it, only weeds!'

'Now look here, my lad,' said the other man in a pleasant, well-spoken voice, 'it's a serious thing to come trespassing into a private place, you know. And if this is the second time, as Grim here says, I'm afraid you're going to get into trouble. What are your names and addresses?'

Peter's heart sank. Gosh, now his father would hear about this and be angry, and Jack would get into trouble too.

'Honestly, sir, we weren't going to do any harm,' he said.

'Either you tell me honestly what you are doing here this evening, or I shall get Grim to go for the police – with you, boy, still in his grip,' said the stranger, sternly. 'I'm not the kind of person that lets bad boys get away with anything. If you tell me the truth, though, I may think twice about the police.'

'Well,' said Peter, desperately, 'I *will* tell you! Our aeroplane flew over the wall, and landed up there on that balcony. And Jack and I came to get it. I climbed up the tree to the balcony, and just as I was going to get down again, I had a look round at the balcony room, and I saw something odd.'

Both Grim and the stranger looked at him sharply. 'And what was the odd thing you saw?' asked the second man.

'The curtains up there don't quite meet,' said Peter.

'And when I peeped between them I saw a gas-fire burning
in the room. I really did!'

'And we came back tonight to climb up again and see if
it was still burning,' said Jack, still in Grim's steely grip.
'And if it was we were going to tell our parents, and they
would ring up the police and . . .'

Grim gave a sharp exclamation. 'What! You saw a gas-
fire burning? Impossible!' He turned to the other man.
'You're from the bank, aren't you? You've come to see if
everything is all right? Well, it *is*, and what's more all the
gas is turned off at the main, so this boy is telling lies! You
can't have a gas-fire burning without gas!'

'I tell you I DID see it,' said Peter. 'And I was jolly
astonished.'

'Well, this is a most amazing story,' said the man in the
suit. 'I'm Mr Frampton, from the bank, and I came here to

357

pay Grim his wages this evening and to see if everything was all right. You seem decent lads, not the little hooligans I thought you were at first. But really, if there's no gas it's difficult to believe your tale.'

'Have you got the keys with you?' asked Peter, eagerly. 'Couldn't you unlock the place, see if the gas really *is* turned off, and go up to that balcony room where I saw the fire? Just in case.'

'Hm, well, it seems rather a waste of time,' said Mr Frampton, putting his hands into his coat-pocket, and bringing out a Yale key labelled Bartlett Lodge No 2. 'But I think on the whole that I'd better go into this. Let that boy go, Grim. I'm inclined to believe they are not after any mischief. Now, where is the front-door key? Ah, here it is. We'll go in and see if there's any truth in this extraordinary tale!'

In a short while they were all in the big hall of Bartlett Lodge. Grim, looking as dour as his name, marched Mr Frampton to the kitchen, and showed him the gas-meter, the electricity switch, and the tap to the water main.

'Every one turned off, as you can see,' he said. Mr Frampton looked at them, and nodded.

'Right. Now let's go upstairs to this balcony room where the mysterious gas-fire is supposed to be burning. Lead the way, Grim, lead the way!'

CHAPTER EIGHT

Peter is very angry

GRIM LED the way, first up one wide flight of steps and on to a fine long corridor, and then up another flight of stairs to the second floor. The house seemed very dark because of the drawn curtains, and Mr Frampton stumbled once or twice. It smelt musty and shut up, too.

'Here's the balcony room,' said Grim, opening a door. A crack of light came in through the place where the curtains did not quite meet. Grim went across and drew them apart with a noise that made everyone jump.

Peter looked for the gas-fire. Yes, there it was, but no red light glowed from it! It stood there, unlit and cold! He

stared at it in silence, unable to believe his eyes, for he had felt certain that it would be just as red and glowing as it had been when he had peeped in from the balcony and seen it.

Mr Frampton made a clicking noise of exasperation. 'Well! You've been making up a nice little story, haven't you, my boy? This fire is certainly not alight and can't have been before either, because all the gas is turned off. You should know better than to make up tales like that. I'm ashamed of you. You seem quite a decent lad, too. Well, Grim, shall we hand them over to the police and let them tell their fairy-tale to *them*, and see what the police have to say about it?'

Grim shook his head. 'I reckon the police have enough to do these days, without having to listen to silly tales like this. The boy made the whole thing up to amuse all his friends, and then made the tale an excuse to come trespassing.'

'I did *not!*' said Peter, angrily. 'And I'd like to tell you . . .'

'That's enough!' said Mr Frampton, sharply. 'And now, just listen to me. I will NOT have you children trespassing like this, whether it's to fetch balls or aeroplanes or anything. And I'm not listening to any more excuses or tales. If Grim had wanted to hand you over to the police I would have done so with pleasure, but he's let you off, and so will I – just this once! Grim, if you have any more trouble with these boys, ring me up and I'll deal with them.'

'Right,' said Grim, sounding extremely pleased.

'But I've got something else to . . .' began Peter, desperately, but Mr Frampton snapped at him at once.

'Silence! I will not listen to another word. I thought you

were a decent lad. I'm mistaken, it seems. Get down the stairs and out of the gates before I chase you out with my umbrella.'

Peter gave Mr Frampton such a glare that Jack was quite astonished. Whatever was the matter with Peter? He had been proved wrong, so why did he go on arguing and interrupting? He took Peter's arm and pushed him to the stairway.

'Come on, idiot,' he said. 'Let's go while the going's good. You made a mistake. It's no use arguing about it!'

Looking very angry indeed, Peter went down the stairs with Jack, and out of the front door. He slammed it hard, and the noise echoed all around. It made Jack jump in fright, and he stared at Peter, really astonished.

'What *is* the matter?' he said. 'Surely you're not in a rage because you were proved wrong, Peter, old chap?'

Peter didn't answer. He took Jack's arm and led him at top speed down the drive and into the road. He didn't say a word all the way down the little lane to the field, and not until they were well out in the middle of the field did he open his mouth to the puzzled and rather scared Jack.

Then he turned and faced him. 'So *you* think I was mistaken too, do you?' he said. 'Well, I'm *not*. That fire was alight when I saw it. I don't care tuppence if the gas and the electricity and the water and everything else is turned off – *that fire was alight*. SOMEBODY had turned it on and lit it. SOMEBODY had been in that room – and done other things, besides lighting the gas, too!'

Jack stared at Peter, amazed. '*What* other things?' he said. 'And why didn't you tell Mr Frampton?'

'I *tried* to. You know I did!' cried Peter. 'And everytime I tried he snapped at me and shut me up! I shan't tell him anything! I'll solve the mystery myself!'

'Wait a minute, Peter. Tell me. What other things did the person do besides lighting the gas-fire?' asked Jack, wondering if Peter had gone slightly mad.

'Listen. Do you remember I said that I had *almost* noticed something in that room, besides the gas-fire, yesterday morning?' demanded Peter. 'And I couldn't call to mind what it was because just as I was noticing it, you shouted at me?'

'Yes. I remember,' said Jack. 'What was it, then?'

'Well, I noticed a plant in a pot,' said Peter. 'A plant my mother grows in her greenhouse, called a primula. The flowers are rather like big polyanthus. And I noticed that the plant was alive and healthy, not all dead and withered as it *should* have been, left in an empty house for weeks. Primulas need a lot of water.'

'You mean someone had been watering it?' asked Jack.

'Yes,' said Peter, beginning to calm down. 'I looked into the pot just now and the soil was wet. Someone had watered it not later than yesterday. AND I noticed something else, which *you* should have noticed too if you'd been a *good* member of the Secret Seven!'

'What?' asked Jack, surprised again.

'I noticed that the clock on the mantelpiece was going,' said Peter. 'And it's only an eight-day clock. So *someone* must have wound it up during the last week, mustn't they? And I thought the room smelt of tobacco smoke too. Oh, somebody has been living in that room, I'm pretty sure!'

'Gosh!' said Jack, astounded. 'But who, Peter? And why?'

'That's for the Secret Seven to find out,' said Peter. 'Go round to everyone and remind them that there's an important, MOST IMPORTANT meeting at eleven o'clock sharp tomorrow morning. And don't let that tiresome Susie know a *thing* about it! This is very, very secret!'

CHAPTER NINE

Peter gives his orders

AGAIN THE Secret Seven were extremely punctual, and the password, 'Lollipops', was said briskly as all the members arrived at the meeting-shed, greeted excitedly by Scamper.

'What's up, Peter?' said George, seeing Peter's rather grim expression as he sat waiting in the shed for everyone. 'You look sort of boiling up inside.'

'Well, I am,' said Peter, relaxing into a short grin, and then looking grim again. Clearly something big was happening, and the Secret Seven settled down expectantly, feeling little thrills as they looked at their chief. Whatever was he going to tell them?

Very shortly and clearly Peter told them of his and Jack's visit to Bartlett Lodge, and how they had been caught by Grim the gardener and Mr Frampton from the bank, the man who held the keys of the locked house.

Then he told them how he had persuaded Mr Frampton to go into the house and find out whether the gas really was turned off or not (and what a sigh all the members gave when he had to confess that it *was* turned off after all); and then went on to describe how they had gone up to the balcony room, and seen the fire unlit (another disappointed sigh!) and then, and then . . .

The next part was truly exciting, of course, especially when he told about the ticking clock. The members gazed at Peter in real admiration. Here was a chief indeed! Why, he had behaved like a first-class detective, and he had stood up to Grim and the man from the bank like a hero!

'You should have *seen* Peter when he came out of that house!' Jack said, when Peter had finished his tale. 'He was in such a rage that he slammed the front door till it nearly fell off its hinges! And his face was as red as fire, and . . .'

'That's enough,' said Peter, his face looking almost as red as fire once again, he was so embarrassed at Jack's praises. 'Anyone would have felt as I did. Honestly, I kept *on* trying to tell Mr Frampton about the clock, and the plant, and the smell of smoke, but he simply wouldn't listen.'

'What a stupid man!' said Barbara. 'To think he could have noticed all those things and didn't. Still, *Jack* didn't notice any of them either, did he?'

'That's enough, Barbara,' said Peter again, seeing *Jack's* face go red now! 'We've got a most peculiar mystery on our hands, and we've got to get to the bottom of it ourselves. This is something that the Secret Seven really *can* rack their brains over. Now, how can we find out who's been in the house, and if he was still there, hidden somewhere while Grim and Mr Frampton went in and out, and if Grim knows anything about it? And if anyone *is* hiding there, what's his reason?'

'We'd better try and find out if Grim really *has* got a name for honesty,' said George. 'If he has, and everyone speaks well of him, we'll know it's nothing to do with *him*.'

'Yes. That's a good point,' said Peter. 'Does anyone know somebody who has employed Grim at any time?'

'Yes. My granny did for a year,' said Pam. 'I didn't like him at all then, because he wouldn't let me pick even an unripe gooseberry when I went to tea with Granny!'

'Hm! That sounds rather honest than otherwise!' said Colin.

'Or mean!' said George. 'Hadn't Pam better go and ask her granny a few questions, Peter?'

'Yes. That's a job for you to do today, Pam,' said Peter, looking at her. 'I want a report this afternoon about that.'

'Right,' said Pam, feeling important, and writing it down in her notebook, though she knew she couldn't possibly forget.

'We really ought to find out where Grim lives and see if we can discover if he's at home each night,' said Peter. 'It might *possibly* be Grim making himself nice and comfortable at Bartlett Lodge. I mean, he might have a horrid wife who nags him, say, and he goes and sleeps in that house just to get away from her, now he's got the chance. I bet he knows how to get into the house, even though he hasn't got the keys.'

'I think that's a bit far-fetched,' objected Barbara. 'About his nagging wife, I mean.'

'We can't leave anything to chance,' said Peter, firmly. 'Nothing is too far-fetched to examine. Grim is an important person in this mystery. The more we know about him, the better.'

'All right,' said Barbara, hastily. 'But all I hope is that I don't have to go and interview a nagging wife!'

'Well, you *will*,' said Peter, to Barbara's horror. 'You and Janet can go together, once we've found out where he lives. Pam's granny will be able to tell her that, I expect.'

'Do we have to find out if Mr *Frampton* is all right?' asked Jack, beginning to feel that there was going to be a lot of snooping round in this mystery!

'Yes. I can ask my father that,' said Peter. 'I expect he'll know him, or know *of* him. But I don't somehow think Mr Frampton *really* comes into this.'

'What else do we do?' asked George.

'Well, when we've found out all we can about Grim, and have made up our minds about him, I shall probably decide to set a watch on Bartlett Lodge,' said Peter, in a most business-like tone. 'There's a good shed there, within view of the kitchen-door, which, I imagine, would be the likeliest place for any mysterious person to enter or leave the house. One or other of us must be on watch all the time. I am quite DETERMINED to track down the person who lives secretly in that balcony room.'

'It's terribly exciting,' said Pam, feeling quite breathless with all this sudden planning. 'I think you're a very good chief, Peter. I do really.'

'So do I,' said Jack, and the others agreed.

'Well, we'll soon see if I am or not,' said Peter, getting

up. 'Time will tell! Oh, by the way, there's a new password for next time, as we've had our last one for a long time.'

'What is it?' asked Jack.

'Grim!' said Peter, smiling. 'Just that. Grim! And don't you forget it, anyone!'

CHAPTER TEN

The girls do very well

PAM FELT very important as she went off to see her granny immediately after her midday dinner. She had her notebook in her blazer pocket, and a freshly sharpened pencil. I may have to write down all kinds of details for Peter, she thought. What fun it is to belong to the Secret Seven. We just NEVER know what kind of job we'll have to do next.

Her granny was in her back garden, snipping off dead daffodils. She was very pleased to see Pam.

'Why, Pamela!' she said. 'I didn't expect you this afternoon. Have you come to have tea with me, dear?'

'No, I'm afraid not, Granny,' said Pam. 'I've got orders from Peter to interview you about someone.'

'Good gracious!' said Granny, surprised. '*Interview me*? What about?'

'About a gardener you once had, called Georgie Grim,' said Pam, taking out her notebook. 'You see, Granny, the Secret Seven is on to a mystery again, and we're interested in Grim because we think he's got something to do with the mystery.'

'You and your mysteries!' said Granny, laughing. 'You really amuse me. Well, well, if it's Peter's orders, you must do as you're told. Now, what do you want to know?'

'Was Grim honest, Granny, when he was with you?' asked Pam.

'Absolutely,' said Granny, and Pam wrote that down,

371

wondering if she was spelling it right. 'Abslootly honest,' she wrote.

'Er – did he ever have to look after the house when you went away?' asked Pam.

'Yes. During the year that he worked for me, he and his wife came and lived in the house for a month, while we were away,' said Granny. 'And the wife kept the place spotlessly clean. She was a thin, pale woman, with a cough, I remember.'

'Wait a bit, you're going too quickly,' said Pam, writing down all this at top speed. 'How do you spell "spotlessly"? Oh, it's all right – I know.'

'Any more questions?' said Granny, amused. 'I feel as if you were a policeman questioning me, Pamela!'

Pam laughed. She was quite enjoying this, and couldn't help feeling that she was doing it very well. She bit the end of her pencil and wondered what to ask next.

'Er – did you miss anything from the house when you came back?' she said.

'Not a thing!' said Granny. 'And what was more, Mrs Grim had made a lot of jam for us, and bottled a great deal of fruit, and wouldn't take a penny for it, because she said she had enjoyed staying in the house so much. I must say the little woman looked a good deal better for the month she spent here. Dear me, am I going too fast for you, darling? Let *me* write it all down for you.'

'Oh, *no*,' said Pam at once. 'This is *my* job, Granny. Just say it all again slowly, and I'll soon get it down. Are there two Ts in "bottle", do you suppose?'

'There are usually,' said Granny. 'Well, well, I must say that I admire you Secret Seven. You certainly go into things thoroughly. *Do* stay to tea.'

'I wish I could, but Peter wants this information this afternoon,' said Pam. 'Well, thanks awfully, Granny. You've given me some surprising news. We all suspected Grim might be doing something he'd no right to do.'

'And what was that?' said Granny, quite overcome with curiosity.

'Oh, it's a secret,' said Pam. 'We're never supposed to talk about our mysteries while we're solving them. Goodbye, Granny, and thank you very much.'

She skipped off happily, her notebook safely in her pocket. Pam was not often entrusted with important things by Peter, and she felt rather proud of the way she had written down Granny's answers to her questions. In fact, she thought herself quite clever!

Peter and the three boys were in the shed with Scamper when Pam arrived. 'Lollipops!' she said, as she knocked at the door. There was no answer.

'Let me in!' called Pam. 'I said the password.'

'You didn't, whoever you are,' called Peter's voice.

'I'm Pam, and you *know* it's me!' said Pam indignantly. 'I've got a lot of news. Let me.'

'Password, please,' said Peter.

'But I've already s . . .' began Pam, and then she suddenly remembered the *new* password. 'Oh, sorry, Peter – Grim, Grim, GRIM!'

'Once is quite enough,' said Peter, and opened the door. 'Well, did you see your granny?'

'Yes,' said Pam, and beamed round happily. 'Here are my notes, with my questions and Granny's answers. I wrote everything down.'

Peter took the notes and read them out aloud, much to Pam's delight. He shut the little notebook and nodded at Pam.

'Very good, Pam. A very nice piece of work. Well, it seems as if Grim is honest enough, and his wife too. In fact the wife sounds really nice. It's rather surprising, really, because I couldn't help feeling that bad-tempered old Grim was the one who had broken into Bartlett Lodge somehow. Now it seems as if somebody *else* must be there, someone that Grim knows nothing about, for if he did he would certainly report it, as your granny says he's absolutely honest.'

'It's funny, isn't it?' said George. 'Well, we'll certainly have to find out who it is.'

'Yes, we must keep a watch on the kitchen-door, as I said,' decided Peter. 'Hallo, here comes Janet and Barbara. They've been to find out about Mrs Grim. I wonder if they'll remember the new password!'

A knock came at the door. 'Grim,' said Janet's voice, and then came a giggle. '*Mr Grim.*'

'And *Mrs* Grim!' said Barbara. Peter opened the door, grinning.

'Come in, idiots,' he said, 'and tell us your news!'

The two girls came in and sat down. Scamper gave them an enormous welcome.

'Hallo, Pam!' said Janet. 'What did your granny say about Grim?'

'Oh, she says he's absolutely honest,' said Pam. 'Here are my notes about it. I wrote them down.'

Janet and Barbara were impressed with the notes. 'You didn't spell the word "absolutely" the right way,' pointed out Barbara. 'Oh, Peter, *we* didn't make notes. We only just asked questions and remembered the answers.'

'That's all right,' said Peter. 'Janet, what happened? Make your report, please.'

'Well, we went down to where Grim lives,' said Janet. 'I found out from the postman; it was quite easy. Oh, Peter, it's a *dreadful* little cottage. Really dreadful.'

'Why? What's it like?' asked Peter.

'It's near the canal, and built so low that it's on a level with the water,' said Janet. 'And you know we've had a lot of rain this year, so the canal water has risen quite a bit, and it has overflowed into the little cottage garden . . .'

'And the ground floor of the cottage must be TERRIBLY damp,' said Barbara. 'And do you know, we even saw fungus growing all the way up one wall! It's really horrible.'

'It's in very bad repair too,' said Janet. 'Daddy would never let *his* cottages get like that, Peter. Our farm-men's cottages are palaces compared with Grim's. I can't think how he stands it. There's quite a big hole in the roof, where some tiles have fallen off.'

'No wonder they were so happy when they looked after my granny's house one summer,' said Pam. 'And no wonder Granny said Mrs Grim looked thin and ill. Anyone would, if they lived in that damp, smelly cottage down by the canal!'

'I wonder they don't move,' said Jack.

'Well, it's hard to get a cottage these days,' said George, 'especially at a low rent. Did you find out anything about Mrs Grim, Janet? Did you see her?'

'No, we didn't,' said Janet, 'but we talked to the woman next door. Her cottage is built much higher than the Grim's, and it's quite dry. She saw us looking round the Grim's place, and called out to know what we wanted.'

'And we just said we were looking at the quaint old cottage!' said Barbara. 'Which was perfectly true, of course. And we asked her who lived there, though *we* knew it was Grim's cottage.'

'You did well,' said Peter, approvingly. 'Go on. What did the woman tell you?'

'Well, she told us what we already knew – that Grim has a daily job, keeping that big garden going at Bartlett

376

Lodge, and that he comes home about six o'clock each night. And that his wife isn't well, so he does all the shopping in his dinner-hour, and cooks a meal at night. And she said that Mrs Grim was a nice little woman . . .'

'And she's very fond of Grim,' said Barbara, anxious not to be left out. 'Gosh! Fancy anyone being fond of surly old *Grim*.'

'Mrs Grim must be quite ill,' said Janet. 'Her neighbour says she hasn't been out to hang her washing up for a whole week. Grim even does that, too!'

'Well, *I* think he sounds rather a nice old boy, even though he's so bad-tempered with us,' said Peter, rather astonished at all this news. 'Pam's granny says he's quite *honest*, and if he does all that for his wife, he must be kind as well.'

'I expect it's living in that dreadful damp cottage that makes him surly,' said Barbara, who really had been shocked to think of anyone living in such a horrid little hole. 'Peter, you wouldn't even let one of your *pigs* live in a place like that.'

'I should think not!' said Peter. '*Our* pigs have wonder-ful sties, and they're cleaned out twice a day.'

It suddenly began to dawn on everyone that their reports had not helped the mystery in the least. In fact, what they had learnt actually wiped Grim right out of the picture, and left them with nobody to suspect at all, except perhaps Mr Frampton the man from the bank. But Peter had something to say about him.

'*He's* all right. My father's known him for years,' said Peter. 'I just mentioned casually that I'd met him, and Dad said, "Oh, Frampton, he's a fine chap, quite a friend of mine. Where did you meet him?"'

'Gosh, what did you say to *that*?' asked Jack, remembering their meeting with the man, and how nearly they had got into serious trouble. 'How did you answer?'

'Well, Scamper barked at that very moment, and I just didn't answer the question, but asked Scamper one instead!' said Peter, with a laugh. 'I said. "Who's coming, Scamper, who's coming, old boy? Let's go and see who you're barking at!" And out of the room we went.'

There was another silence. A cold, flat feeling slowly came over the Seven. Where did they go from here? Was there anything they could do to solve the mystery now, except what Peter had suggested before – watch the door of Bartlett Lodge from the little shed opposite it? But they *knew* it wasn't Grim going into the house. Would they ever see any intruder at all? They couldn't watch the doors and windows! It would have been easy enough just to watch

378

the kitchen-door when they felt sure it was Grim going in and out; but suppose the intruder, whoever he was, never came and went at all, but simply stayed hidden in the house, turning on the gas at the main whenever he wanted a little warmth, or to boil a kettle!

'Let's talk and plan,' said Peter, at last. 'Now, has anyone a good idea, a really good one?'

No one said a word at first, and then Jack spoke up. 'Well, Peter, the only thing *I* can think of is for one of us to climb that tree up to the balcony tonight, and watch for a light to come on in that room, and peep through the crack in the curtains to see who it is. That's my idea!'

CHAPTER ELEVEN

An astonishing discovery

THE REST of the Seven stared at Jack in admiration. 'Why ever didn't we think of that before?' said Peter. 'Of course whoever is hiding there would feel quite safe at night, with Grim gone home, and nobody about at all. We might see something really interesting if we watch up on the balcony!'

'Bags I go,' said George, at once.

'*Four* of us will go,' said Peter. 'One of us must be on guard at the gate to warn the others if someone comes in there. We don't want to be caught. One of us must also be at the bottom of the tree to warn the ones on the balcony if anyone comes. I think Jack and I will climb the tree and be the balcony watchers – we've been up there before.'

'Can I come too?' said Janet, longingly. 'It's beginning to sound awfully adventurous!'

'No you can't come,' said Peter, 'or there will be too many. The four of us will go together when it's really dark.'

'Let's ask if we can go to the cinema,' said Jack. 'And not stay till the end, but slip out about eight o'clock and go to Bartlett Lodge.'

'Good idea,' said Peter. 'Right, we'll all meet at the cinema. You others can come too, if you're allowed, but you'll have to sit right through the programme, if your parents will let you stay as late as that.'

'Mine won't,' said Barbara, sadly. 'At least I don't think

381

so. Oh, I shan't be able to sleep tonight for wondering what's happening to you four boys.'

A very pleasant feeling of excitement warmed the hearts of the Secret Seven for the rest of that day. Even Scamper felt it, and was most bitterly disappointed when Janet and Peter went off to the cinema without him after tea.

He sat down sadly in a corner. Now he would have a long, long wait till he could bark and jump and wag his tail again!

None of the Secret Seven paid that much attention to the picture at the cinema, and yet it was a good one, all about a wild pony, the kind they usually loved. The four fidgeted and looked at their watches, wishing the time would go quickly, so that they might leave, and go about their night adventure!

At ten to eight Peter whispered to Jack. 'We'll go! I can't sit still a moment longer! Tell the others.'

Peter led the way. It was dark outside now, and they needed their torches. It was a cloudy night and not even a star showed in the sky.

They made their way to Jack's house and slipped in at the back gate. 'Watch out for Susie!' said Jack, in a low tone. 'She's in tonight.'

But there was no sign of the aggravating Susie, much to Peter's relief. They went across the field at the back of Jack's house and down the little lane into the road beyond, where Bartlett Lodge stood.

'Now,' said Peter, halting. 'You know your orders, all of you. Colin, watch by the gate. Hoot like an owl if anyone comes in. George, you're to stand at the foot of the tree that we're going to climb to the balcony. You're to hoot too, if you see or hear anything suspicious. Jack, have you got your torch ready? We'll need it to climb the tree.'

Jack put his torch between his teeth, and so did Peter, as soon as they began to climb the tree that grew up to the second-floor balcony. This meant that they could use both their hands for climbing, and yet could see where they were going, though rather awkwardly.

Colin was at his post by the gate, hiding behind a bush. George was at the foot of the tree, listening intently for any unusual sound. He could hear Jack and Peter cautiously climbing the tree. Then he could hear the slight scrape of their rubber shoes as they climbed over the stone balcony. Now a great disappointment for Peter and Jack – no longer could they see through the crack in the curtains! Someone had pulled them carefully together, so that not the tiniest chink remained for them to peep through! The boys were bitterly disappointed!

'Look at that! We can't possibly see into the room now,' whispered Jack.

'Yes, but it shows someone has been into the room again!' said Peter. 'It may even mean that somebody is there *now*.'

They pressed their noses against the closed window, trying in vain to see inside. They saw nothing, but they suddenly heard sounds, sounds which surely came from the inside of that little room!

'Listen!' whispered Jack. 'What is it?'

'It's a radio being played very, very quietly,' said Peter. 'We can hardly hear it. I'm sure that's what it is. Would you believe it! Who in the world is in there?'

They had now switched off their torches, and were in complete darkness. They stood there, wondering what to do. How did the intruder get into the house? Mr Frampton appeared to be the only one with the keys of the house; not even Grim had one. And anyway they had proved that he was absolutely honest. Then had some outsider a key? Or did he perhaps get in through a coal-hole? Or was there an unfastened window somewhere? All these things went through the boys' minds very quickly, and then something happened that made them jump violently.

An owl's hoot sounded from the front of the house! It must be Colin giving the arranged warning. The two boys stiffened at once. And then, to their horror, another hoot came, this time so near to them that they jumped in fright again. It came from the bottom of the tree.

'Danger!' said Peter. 'Keep quite still, Jack. Something's going to happen!'

The two boys on the balcony stood absolutely still, and hardly breathed. And then they heard a sound that made them stiffen again in fright.

'Someone's climbing up the tree!' whispered Peter to Jack. 'I can hear him – and see the light of his torch!'

'What can we do?' said Jack, trembling. 'He will see us here. We can't hide anywhere on this balcony.'

'No. But we can quickly scramble up the tree a bit higher and hide in the leaves,' said Peter, pulling Jack to the tree. He could now hear the climber's heavy breathing farther down the tree. Thank goodness he was slow at climbing!

'Quiet now!' whispered Peter, as he and Jack climbed back into the tree and went upwards for about six feet. They then stayed quite still, peering through the leaves down at the balcony below.

A man was climbing up the tree to the balcony, his torch in his mouth. As he came, a warning owl-hoot sounded again from below. The man was now climbing over the little stone pillars of the balcony, and stood below the boys, taking his torch from his mouth. Jack and Peter in the tree above could see the light shining brightly.

The man went to the window and knocked. It was a special knock – three long ones, two short ones and then two long ones. Knock-knock-knock. Knock-knock. Knock-knock.

The boys held their breath and peered through the leaves cautiously. They saw the curtains drawn back from the window, and immediately a light streamed out from the room inside. Then someone unfastened the window and opened it.

As the light streamed out on to the balcony, Jack and Peter saw the man who stood there, saw him quite clearly and recognised him! They could hardly believe their eyes!

The man went swiftly through the window, shut it behind him and

drew the curtains across so that not a chink of light showed. Only when the window was shut did the two boys dare to breathe. Then Peter clutched Jack.

'Did you see who it was, Jack?'

'Yes. *Surely* it was old Grim the gardener!' said Jack, quite astounded. 'What did *you* think?'

'Yes – it *was* Grim! But who would have thought it! *Grim*! The honest Grim! No wonder he was angry when he discovered our footmarks at the bottom of this tree, and saw that *we* had climbed it too, and had used his own private way into the house!'

'But who's *in* there?' said Jack, feeling bewildered. 'It must be the someone who lit the gas-fire and wound up the clock, and watered that plant! Is it some burglar there busy packing up things for Grim to take away?'

'Goodness knows!' said Peter, as puzzled as Jack. 'I suppose it was Grim who had carefully turned off the gas

387

at the main last night when we all went in to see the house. He must have seen our footmarks under the tree by then and have been afraid we might have seen the gas-fire and tell tales about it. So he quietly turned off the gas at the main, in case anyone said they'd seen the fire, because it's plain there couldn't be a fire without gas. I was jolly puzzled about that, weren't you?' 'Very,' said Jack. 'Well, what do we do now? Better climb down, I think, because I'm sure we can't see anything more here at the moment. We'd better find Colin and George – they'll be worried about us.'

So they climbed carefully down the tree again, making no noise at all, nor daring even to switch on their torches. They felt carefully with their feet before they made a step downwards, and were soon at the bottom.

There was no sign of George. 'He may think we are the man who climbed up,' whispered Jack. 'What about saying our password, Peter? He'll know it's us, then.'

'I was just going to,' said Peter. 'Grim!' he said, in a piercing whisper. 'Grim!'

'Here I am!' said George, from a nearby bush. 'Gosh, I was glad to hear the password! I was afraid it might be that man again! Did you hear my hoot?'

'Yes. And Colin's too,' said Peter. 'Let's go and find him. This mystery has got very mysterious, all of a sudden!'

They found Colin hidden by the front gate, and gave him the password. He appeared as soon as he heard it. They all slipped out of the gate and down the road, and were soon in the little lane leading to the field behind Jack's house.

They stopped in the middle of the field, having been completely silent since leaving the front gate.

'Who was that man? Did you see?' said Colin at once.

'It was Grim!' said Peter. 'Would you believe it! Grim, the man we had ruled out completely. What *can* he be doing there?'

'Pretty mean of him to leave his sick wife all alone each night in that horrible cottage,' said Colin. 'He must have a pal in Bartlett Lodge and be planning to rob the house in peace and quiet while the owners are away. There's nothing to stop them taking things bit by bit.'

'Shall we tell the police?' asked George.

'I don't know. I rather think I'll tell my father,' said Peter. 'You see, he knows Mr Frampton, the man who has the keys of the place. We'd better leave it to them as to what to do. Gosh, who'd have thought it was Grim after all!'

'Well, I never liked him,' said Colin. 'Horrid, bad-tempered man. Come on, let's get on. I'm beginning to feel as if there may be quite a lot of Georgie Grims in this dark field, waiting to pounce on us. Hurry up!'

'We'll go to my house and tell my father straightaway,' said Peter. 'You must all come with me. There'll be a lot to tell, and you'll have to back me up. Let's go by the cinema and see if the others are out. They really ought to be in on this.'

They went down the road that led to the cinema, and saw the people streaming out – and the three girls with them! Peter ran up.

'Hey, you three! You're to come with us. Something very strange has turned up, and we're all going to my house to tell my father. *He'll* know what to do!'

CHAPTER TWELVE

Peter's father takes over

THE FOUR boys told the excited girls what had happened. When they came to the part where Jack and Peter had actually heard someone climbing up to the very balcony on which they were standing, Pam gave a loud squeal.

'Oh! I should have been scared stiff! Oh, who was it? I'm jolly glad I wasn't there!'

'It was old Georgie Grim!' said Peter. 'What do you think of *that*? And to think we'd quite decided that he was honest and kind and all the rest of it! Anyway, it's a serious matter now. That's why we're going back to tell my father.'

Peter's father and mother were most astonished to see everybody coming in together. 'Why Colin – Jack – Pam, Barbara, George – whatever are you doing back here instead of going home?' said Peter's mother.

'Mother, we've got something to tell you,' said Peter. 'Dad, you'll be surprised when you hear it! You see, the Secret Seven have . . .'

'Don't tell me you've tumbled into another adventure!' said his father. 'You haven't got yourselves into trouble, have you?'

'Oh, no,' said Peter. 'And – well, I hope you won't be cross when you hear the things we've done.'

'Begin at the beginning,' said his mother, taking down a tin of biscuits and handing them round. 'You're the chief of the Seven, aren't you, Peter? Well, you begin, then.'

391

So Peter began the strange story, right from the morning when Susie's aeroplane had flown over the wall into the garden of Bartlett Lodge, and disappeared. He told of the angry gardener, of how he and Jack had discovered the aeroplane on the balcony and climbed up to get it . . .

'And it was *then* that the mystery really began,' said Jack, interrupting. 'Wasn't it, Peter? Because when Peter peeped in between the drawn curtains of the balcony windows he saw a gas-fire merrily burning away there!'

How astonished Peter's parents were to hear the story and to listen to the way the Seven had proved Grim's honesty, and his kindness to his wife, and then, to cap everything, they heard the astonishing ending!

'There we were, up in the tree six foot above the balcony, trying to see who it was coming knocking on the window of that curtained room, and when the curtains were pulled and the light streamed out we saw who it was.'

'And who *was* it?' said Peter's father, really excited.

'It was *Grim*,' said Peter. 'Yes, it really was, Dad! Someone from inside opened the window, and he got in, and the curtains were drawn across and the window fastened!'

392

'And we thought we'd better come and tell you because you know Mr Frampton, who has the keys,' said Jack. 'We felt sure you would know the best thing to do.'

'That was sensible of you,' said Peter's father. 'Well, I'm blessed! The things you Seven get up to! And yet I can't find fault with you for anything you've done in this matter. You were very sensible and most courageous, and now, of course, we must at once go after this fellow Grim, and see what he's up to. Thanks to you, we shall catch him in his lair with his burglarious friend, whoever he is!'

'His burglarious friend!' said Pam. 'That sounds exciting. What are you going to do, please?'

'I'm going to ring up Mr Frampton, get him to come round with the keys of Bartlett Lodge, and he and I will go together to surprise Grim and his friend in their cosy lair,' said Peter's father, getting up to go to the telephone.

'Dad! Dad, can we go too?' cried Peter, afraid that at this most exciting moment he was going to be left out.

'I'll see what Mr Frampton says,' said his father, and dialled his number. The children listened to the one-sided conversation in silence, their hearts beating fast. What an adventure this had suddenly turned into! Oh, if only they were allowed to see the end of it!

Peter's father rang off and turned to the waiting children. 'Mr Frampton is extremely interested, as you can imagine. He's coming round straight away and will pick me up here in his car. He says Peter and Jack may come too, as they will be able to state again that they actually saw the gas-fire burning the day before yesterday. They'll be what we call witnesses.'

'Can't we others come?' said Janet, dolefully. 'Oh, I do want to, Dad.'

'I dare say you do,' said her father. 'But you must realise that we can't have the whole Seven of you trailing after us in what may be quite a serious matter. Mr Frampton is going to ring up the police, and ask them to stand by in case he telephones from Bartlett Lodge for help. We shall have to find out first if it really *is* a police matter – and it probably is.'

Jack and Peter felt a great big surge of excitement welling up inside them. They grinned at one another in joy. They were going to be in at the end. What would happen? What would Grim say? And who was his 'burglarious friend'?

In a few minutes there came the sound of a car hooting at the front gate. Peter, his father, and Jack hurried out, followed by the envious gazes of the others. Then Janet's mother set to work to ring up the other children's parents and tell them not to worry; the Secret Seven were at her house!

Jack and Peter got into Mr Frampton's car, and sat silently in the back. They still remembered how angry he had been with them only a short time ago! He said nothing to them, but spoke briefly to Peter's father, and then drove off to Bartlett Lodge.

Jack squeezed Peter's arm in excitement. 'We're bang in the middle of a real adventure!' he said, in a low voice. 'Whatever do you suppose is going to happen next?'

CHAPTER THIRTEEN

Inside the empty house

THE CAR drew up outside Bartlett Lodge. The house looked absolutely dark, not a light to be seen anywhere. They all got out, and Mr Frampton spoke quietly as they stood beside the car.

'I propose that I unlock the front door, and that we all go in silently,' he said. 'It is imperative that we make no noise at all, for we don't want to give any warning to those fellows inside. We will go straight up to the same room that these boys took me up to before and surprise the men there, and demand an explanation. Now, follow me.'

They followed him in at the drive-gate, and up to the front door. He cautiously slid the key in, turned it, put a second key into a lock below, and turned that also. The door opened with a small creak.

Mr Frampton walked in quietly. The others followed, and he shut the door silently. He switched on his torch and spoke in a whisper.

'The telephone is here, in that corner. You, boy – what's your name, now?'

'Peter,' said Peter.

'Well, you, Peter, will have to be the one to nip down to the phone and call the police if we have any trouble,' said Mr Frampton. 'Just say that I want someone sent along here at once. Is that clear?'

'Yes,' said Peter, and again felt the uprush of breathless excitement that all adventures bring.

'Now, quiet,' said Mr Frampton, and led the way upstairs, his torch shining steadily in front of him. The stairs were well carpeted, and their footsteps made no noise at all. The men went first, the two boys followed. Jack was so excited that he felt quite breathless.

Up the first flight of stairs, on to the wide landing, and then very, very quietly up the second flight. Again there was a landing, but not such a wide one. Mr Frampton stood quite still at the top, and then switched off his torch.

A line of light showed under one door, the door of the balcony room! From inside came a murmur of voices and then suddenly the voices became raised, and the four outside could hear shouts and threats!

What was going on in that closed room? Jack felt himself shaking at the knees. 'It's all right,' whispered Mr Frampton, feeling Jack trembling against him.

'They've got the radio on, they're listening to a play. Don't be scared!'

Jack was most relieved. Only the radio! Of course! He and Peter had heard it before, when they had stood outside on the balcony! Mr Frampton now strode forward to the closed door and turned the handle, but he turned it in vain! The door was locked on the inside!

Mr Frampton raised his hand and knocked most imperiously on the door, shouting at the same time, 'Open this door at once!'

The radio in the room was switched off suddenly and now there was nothing but silence. Mr Frampton knocked again. 'I said OPEN THIS DOOR!'

'Who's there?' said a voice from inside.

'Open the door, and you'll soon see,' roared Mr Frampton, making both boys jump violently. 'I know your voice, Grim! The game's up. Open the door, or it will be the worse for you and your friend!'

There was a silence for a few seconds, and then Grim's voice came again, sounding most upset. 'It's you Mr Frampton, isn't it? You haven't got the police with you, have you? You know I'm an honest man, you . . .'

'I've no police here at the moment,' thundered Mr Frampton, 'but I'm sending someone down to telephone them in one minute's time, if you do not open this door! As for your honesty, I fear it will be difficult for you to prove that, Grim.'

There sounded a hurried few words from inside the room, as if Grim were reassuring someone. Then he spoke again, in a most beseeching voice.

'Mr Frampton, I'll open the door and come out to you,

if you'll let me shut it after me and will not come into the room till I've spoken to you.'

'You'll open this door, and we shall come in straight-away,' said Mr Frampton, angrily. 'What nonsense is this? And I warn you, Grim, that if you let your friend get away through that window it will be the worse for you. Have done with this nonsense, man, and OPEN – THIS – DOOR!'

The door still did not open. Mr Frampton turned to Peter and spoke to him in a loud voice, so that Grim could hear it inside the room.

'Peter, go down into the hall and ring up the police as I told you. Tell them to send someone here immediately.'

'Right,' said Peter, but before he could take more than two steps there came a cry from Grim.

'No! Don't get the police! I'll open the door. Wait, wait!'

'Wait, Peter,' said Mr Frampton, in a low voice. 'I think he's come to heel.'

Nobody moved. They heard a key turning in the lock on the other side of the door, the handle turned, and the door opened. Grim stood there, his surly face lined and worried.

'Once more, I beg of you, don't come into this room,' he said, holding the door so that no one could see into the room. 'I do beg of you.'

'Stand aside, man,' said Mr Frampton, and pushed him sternly to one side. He stepped into the room, followed by Peter's father. The two boys came last, wondering whatever they were going to see.

Nobody in the least expected to see what was there! They stood silent, staring in astonishment.

CHAPTER FOURTEEN

A great surprise

THE LITTLE balcony room looked clean and cosy. The gas-fire burned steadily, and the clock on the mantelpiece ticked merrily. The table was set with a small white cloth, and on it was a loaf of bread on a wooden platter, a dish of butter, and a plate of yellow cheese.

But these were not the things that surprised the four visitors. Their eyes were fixed on one corner of the room, where there was a couch near the fire. On it lay a woman, a little old woman with white hair and white face, whose hands trembled as her scared eyes watched the four come into the room.

Mr Frampton stopped abruptly in astonishment. He, like the others, had expected to see another man, some 'burglarious friend'. But there was no one to see except the frightened old woman.

'Please,' she said, in a trembling voice. 'Please, it's all my fault. Don't be hard on Georgie.'

Mr Frampton spoke in a surprisingly kind voice. 'Now don't get upset, old lady. We've only come to see what's happening here.'

Tears suddenly rolled down the old woman's cheeks. Grim went over to her and took her hand. 'Now, now,' he said, 'don't you fret. I did it for the best.'

Then he turned to Mr Frampton. 'You see, it was like this. My wife, she's not strong, and her cough has been bad all winter. The doctor said I'd have to take her away from that cottage of ours, too damp he said it was, and he said he'd get her into a hospital . . .'

'And I wouldn't go,' said the old woman. 'I can't be separated from Georgie. I'd die, I know I would.'

'And then the canal water rose with all the rain we had, and the water came into the house,' said Grim, in a desperate voice. 'And some tiles came off and the rain came through into our bedroom. Well, what was a man to do? I couldn't find another place to go to, and here was this big house, all empty, and we only need one small room, and I was at work here . . .'

'I see,' said Mr Frampton, sitting down on a chair. 'Yes, I see. So you managed to get your wife here, into a warm, dry room, and you turned on the gas and the electric light and the water . . .'

'Yes. I got in through the coal-hole the first time, and went up into the kitchen, and unlocked the door,' said Grim. 'You had taken the key, but I knew where a spare one hung on a hook on the dresser. And I brought my old wife here one night, and a terrible walk it was for her . . .'

'And you made her comfortable here, Grim?' said

Mr Frampton. 'And did the shopping, and the washing, and hung it out behind your old cottage? Yes, I know all about that, you see! And then you climbed in each night through the balcony window.'

'Yes,' said Grim, dolefully. 'And I was in a rare temper with these boys here, when I knew they'd been up that tree outside, and on to the balcony, and what a fright I had when they told you about seeing the little gas-fire here. I tell you, I've been in a real state all the time. Yes, I know I did wrong, but what was a man to do?'

'You could have come and asked me, Grim,' said Mr Frampton.

'And you'd have said no!' cried Grim. 'Look here, and you too,' he said, turning to Peter's father. 'My old woman, she's done what she could in the house while she's been here. She's dusted every day, ill as she is, and she's watered every plant, and she's polished every bit of furniture. She was scared to death all the time, but I will say this, her cough's better.'

Peter suddenly found that there were tears in his eyes. Poor Grim! And his poor, ill old wife, in that dreadful damp cottage with a hole in the roof. After all, they had done no harm. In fact, Mrs Grim had dusted and polished and watered, and done as much as she could!

There was a little silence. Then Mr Frampton spoke in a gentle voice. 'Well, Grim, I shall have to report this to the owners, of course, but I shall point out your difficulties, and say that Mrs Grim has kept the house dusted and polished, and . . .'

'You won't get the police, will you?' pleaded the little old woman, from her couch. 'My Georgie, he's a good man, honest as the day, and kindness itself. He's got a temper that gets him into trouble now and again, but he's a good honest man, and *I* ought to know!'

'I shan't get the police,' said Mr Frampton. 'But as you know, perhaps, the owners are coming back next week. You will not be able to stay here then.'

'I'll go back to my old cottage then,' said Mrs Grim. 'My cough's better since I've been here, this warm, dry place. I'll be all right now in our cottage.'

'You won't!' said Grim, suddenly sounding desperate again. 'They'll put you somewhere away from me. They'll say you're ill, and they'll take you away!'

'Now, listen, stay here until I hear from the owners,' said Mr Frampton. 'I can see you are to be trusted. But if you're in trouble another time, ask for help from some friend, Grim. Don't do things like this.'

'I'd have done that, but I thought my wife might be taken away from me,' said Grim. 'I'm sorry for the trouble I've caused, but we've done no harm, that I can promise you.'

Peter's father stood up. 'Come along, Frampton,' he said. 'Let's leave them in peace. Grim, come along to me tomorrow and I'll see that you are supplied with milk and eggs for your wife. Good night, Mrs Grim. Cheer up. We'll see what can be done for you and Grim. Good night, Grim.'

'Good night,' said Grim, and the two men, followed by the two boys, went out of the room, leaving Grim standing at the door, worried and anxious.

'Dad!' said Peter, looking as anxious as the old gardener. 'Dad, can't we do *some*thing? I shan't be happy till we do!'

CHAPTER FIFTEEN

Three cheers for the Secret Seven!

THE NEXT morning there was another Secret Seven meeting in the old shed. One after another the knocks came, and the password.

'Grim!'

'Grim! It's me, Pam.'

'Grim! Can I come in?'

Peter opened the door five times, and Scamper barked five times too. Soon everyone was there. They all looked rather nervous, for the events of the night before had surprised and shocked them.

'To think that we hated Grim so much, and all the time

he was worried in case we found out his poor, precious secret!' said Janet.

'I *can't* bear to think of them having to go back to that awful cottage,' said Barbara. 'Old Mrs Grim will get a dreadful cough again. But they'll have to turn out of Bartlett Lodge in a few days. Oh dear, this mystery is having a rather horrid end.'

'We've GOT to do something to help them,' said Jack. He pulled a purse out of his pocket, and emptied some money on to the top of a wooden box. 'Look, I've emptied my money-box and Susie's too, and I've brought all the money along in case it will be any use.'

'*Susie's* money-box!' said Janet, amazed. 'But did she say you could?'

'Yes. I told her all about last night when I got home,' said Jack. 'After all, you know, it *was* her aeroplane that started this adventure. Wasn't it?'

'Yes,' said everyone, nodding.

'So I thought Susie ought to hear the story,' said Jack. 'And she told me to take *all* her money, too.'

'Gosh! People are most surprising!' said Barbara. 'Good old Susie!'

'Well, now,' said Peter, 'does everyone want to give money to help the Grims? And is there anything else we can do? I dare say our money would help to mend that hole in the cottage roof. We've got to do *some*thing! I shan't feel happy till we've tried to make up for spying on old Grim, and bringing his precious secret to light.'

Everyone most willingly

agreed to help. Peter felt proud of his Secret Seven. There wasn't a mean, ungenerous person among them! Jolly good!

Scamper suddenly began to bark, and a knock came at the door.

'Password!' shouted Peter.

'I don't know it,' said his father's voice.

'Oh, it's you, Dad! We'll let you in without the password!' said Peter, and opened the door. His father came in, and smiled round at everyone. He saw the money on the top of the box and raised his eyebrows.

'My word, somebody's rich!'

'Oh, that's money to help old Grim and his wife,' said Peter. 'Jack brought it, half is from Susie too. We're all going to bring some, Dad. We're so sorry for thinking those awful things about Grim, and for spying on him, when all he was doing was taking care of his wife.'

'Yes. It was a very sad story, wasn't it? said his father. 'I felt as upset as you did, Peter. I'm glad you want to help. So do I!'

'How can *you* help, Dad?' said Peter, astonished.

'I'll tell you,' said his father. 'You know that little cottage that our old cowman has just left? Well, I'm going to have it done up straightaway, and offer it to old Grim. We need a man to trim the hedges and so on, and if he likes to come to our farm here and work, he can have the cottage and live there with his wife. It's sunny and dry, and she'll be all right there.'

'Dad! Oh Dad! I do love you!' cried Janet, and almost knocked her father over with a great bear-hug. 'We couldn't *bear* to let the Grims go back to that dreadful old place of theirs. Oh, how wonderful to be a grown-up and do things like that!'

411

'And how wonderful to be young and to belong to the Secret Seven!' said her father. 'You're a set of meddling youngsters, you know, but somehow your heads and hearts are sound, and you do the right thing in the end! Well, I'm glad you found out Grim's secret. Now we can set his mind at rest, and our own too.'

'And we'll give you all our money to help to pay for putting the cowman's old cottage right,' said Jack. 'We meant to help somehow with the money, and we will!'

'Thank you,' said Peter's father. 'Give it to Peter, and he can give it to me. And let me say this, all of you. You've had many adventures before, you Secret Seven, but I don't think you'll ever have one that has such a satisfactory ending. And one more thing – I'm very, very proud of you all!'

He stood up, smiled round at everyone's pleased face, and went out. Peter looked round, his face glowing.

'Did you hear that, Secret Seven?' he said. 'Did you hear that, Scamper? Three cheers for the Secret Seven! Hip-hip-hip . . .'

'HURRAH!' shouted everyone, and Scamper barked madly. What a curious adventure it had been – and all because of Susie and her aeroplane!

SECRET SEVEN MYSTERY

CONTENTS

CHAPTER ONE

Something interesting

PETER AND Janet were having breakfast with their father and mother one lovely spring morning. Scamper, their golden spaniel, was lying as usual under the table.

'Dad,' began Peter, but his mother frowned at him.

'Your father is reading the paper,' she said. 'Don't bother him just now!'

His father put down the paper and smiled. 'Do the Secret Seven want to make themselves really useful?' he asked. 'Because I've just read something in my paper that may be right up their street!'

'Oh, Dad – what?' cried Peter, and Janet put down her egg-spoon and looked at him expectantly.

'It's about a girl who's run away from home,' said their father, looking at his paper. 'She stole some money from the desk of her teacher, but when the police went to see her aunt about it, she ran away.'

'But – what can the Secret Seven do about it?' asked Peter, surprised.

'Listen – I'll read you the piece,' said his father, and propped the paper up in front of him. 'Elizabeth Mary Wilhemina Sonning, after being accused of stealing money from the desk of her teacher, was found to be missing from her aunt's house. She took nothing with her but the clothes she was wearing, and is in school uniform and school hat. It is stated that her parents are abroad, and that she has a brother who is at present away in France.'

417

Peter's father looked up from the paper. 'Now comes the bit that might interest *you*,' he said. 'Elizabeth was seen on the evening of that day in Belling Village, and it is thought that she might be going to her grandmother, who lives not far off.'

'Belling Village! Why that's the next village to ours,' said Janet. 'Oh – you think that the Secret Seven could keep a look-out for Elizabeth, Daddy! Yes – we could! What's she like?'

'There's a photograph here,' said her father, and passed the paper across. 'Not a very good one – but in her school uniform, which is a help.'

Peter and Janet stared at the picture in the paper. They saw the photograph of a merry, laughing girl a little older than themselves, with a mass of fluffy hair round her face. They thought she looked rather nice.

Though she can't be really, if she stole money and then ran away, thought Janet. She turned to her father. 'Whereabouts in Belling Village does her granny live?'

'It doesn't say, does it?' said her father, reaching for his paper again. 'You'll have to read this evening's paper and see if there are any more details. If the child goes to her granny's she'll be found at once, of course. But if she hides somewhere around the place, you might be able to spot her.'

'Yes. We might,' said Peter. 'The Secret Seven haven't had *anything* interesting to do lately. We'll call a meeting tomorrow. Good thing it's Saturday!'

That evening, Janet sat down to write notices to each of the Secret Seven to call them to a meeting the next day. Each notice said the same things.

'Dear S.S. Member,
'A meeting will be held tomorrow morning, Saturday, at ten sharp, in the shed. Wear your badges and remember the password.'

Peter signed each one, and then he and Janet fetched their bicycles and rode off to deliver the notices, Scamper trotting beside them. They felt pleasantly excited. This new affair might not come to anything – but at least it was something to talk about and to make plans for.

'We'd better buy an evening paper on our way back and see if there's anything else in it about Elizabeth Mary Wilhemina Sonning,' said Peter.

So they stopped at the little newsagent's shop and bought one. They stood outside the shop, eagerly looking through the pages for any mention of the runaway girl. At last they found a small paragraph, headed 'MISSING GIRL'.

'Here it is,' said Peter, thrilled. 'Look, Janet, it says, "Elizabeth Sonning is still missing, and her grandmother states that she has not seen her. Anyone seeing a child whose appearance tallies with the following description is asked to get in touch with the police." Then, see, Janet, there's a good description of her. That's fine – we can read it out to the Seven tomorrow.'

419

'Good!' said Janet. 'Come on, Scamper – we'll have to bike home pretty fast, so you'll have to run at top speed!'

Scamper puffed and panted after them, his long silky ears flopping up and down as he ran. He wasn't a member of the Secret Seven, but he certainly belonged! No meeting was complete without him.

'What's the password, Peter?' asked Janet, as they put their bicycles away. 'It's ages since we had a meeting.'

'It's a jolly good thing *I* never forget it,' said Peter. 'I shan't tell it to you – but I'll give you a hint. Think of *lamb* – that ought to remind you!'

'Lamb?' said Janet, puzzled. 'Well – it reminds me of sheep, Peter – or Mary had a little lamb – or lamb chops. Which is it?'

'None of them!' said Peter, grinning. 'Have another shot, Janet – and tell me at the meeting tomorrow!'

CHAPTER TWO

Knock – Knock

'HAVE YOU remembered the password yet?' asked Peter next morning, when Janet and he were tidying their shed ready for the meeting.

'No, I haven't,' said Janet. 'And I think you might tell me, because you know jolly well I've got to come. I've been thinking of lamb – lamb – lamb for ages, but it doesn't remind me of anything except what I've already told you. Tell me the word, Peter, do!'

'No,' said Peter firmly. 'You're always forgetting. It's

time you were taught a lesson. I shan't let you into the meeting unless you remember it. Look – go and ask mummy if we can have some of those biscuits she made last week.'

'Go yourself,' said Janet, crossly.

'I'm the head of the Secret Seven,' said Peter. 'Obey orders, Janet!'

Janet went off, not feeling at all pleased. She was quite afraid that Peter *wouldn't* let her into the meeting! He was very strict about rules.

She went into the kitchen, but mummy wasn't there. Some lamb chops lay on the table, and Janet looked at them frowning. 'Lamb! Oh dear – whatever ought you to remind me of? I simply can't think! Oh – here's mummy. Mummy, *may* we have some of your ginger biscuits, please? Oh, what's that you've got? Mint – let me smell it. I love the smell. I wouldn't mind mint scent on my hanky!'

'It's for mint sauce with the chops,' said mummy. 'Now I'll just –'

'Mint sauce! Of *course*! That's the password, Mint sauce! What an idiot I am!' said Janet. Then she grew serious and looked solemnly at her mother.

'I shouldn't have said the password out loud! We're not supposed to tell a soul. Mummy, don't remember it, will you?'

'What are you gabbling about?' said her mother, and went to get her tin of ginger biscuits. 'Here you are – you can have all of these. I'm making some more for tomorrow.'

'Oh, *thank* you!' said Janet, delighted, and skipped off down the garden with the tin. As she came near the shed she shouted out to Peter.

'Mint sauce, mint sauce, mint sauce!'

'Have you gone mad?' said a cross voice, and Peter looked out of the shed, frowning. 'Shouting out the password for everyone to know! I'm glad you've remembered it at last.'

'Well, mummy came in with mint to make mint sauce. Wasn't it lucky?' said Janet. 'Oh, Scamper, you know I've got some ginger biscuits, don't you? I expect there'll be one for you. Peter it's almost ten o'clock.'

'I know,' said Peter. 'I'm just ready. Are there enough things to sit on? You'll have to sit on that big flower-pot, Janet. The gardener must have taken our seventh box.'

Scamper began to bark. 'That's someone coming already,' said Peter. 'Shut the door, Janet, please. We'll have to ask the password as usual.'

Knock – knock!

'Password!' called Peter.

'Mint sauce!' said two voices.

'Enter!' said Peter, and Janet opened the door. 'Hello, George and Colin. You're very punctual.'

Knock – knock.

'Password!' shouted Peter. A cautious voice came in through the keyhole.

'I've forgotten. But I'm Pam, so you can let me in.'

'No, we can't. You know the rule,' said Peter, sternly.

'Think of lamb chops!' called Janet, before Peter could stop her.

A giggle was heard. 'Oh, yes – of course. MINT SAUCE.'

Janet opened the door, but Peter looked quite cross. 'How dare you remind Pam like that?' he demanded.

'Well, *you* reminded me!' said Janet, indignantly. 'You said, "Think of lamb chops", didn't you?'

'There's someone else coming,' said Peter, changing the subject hurriedly.

Knock – knock! 'Mint sauce,' said two voices.

'Come in!' shouted Peter, and in came Jack and Barbara together. Scamper greeted them with pleasure, and then everyone sat down and looked expectantly at Peter.

'Anything exciting?' asked Jack, eagerly.

'Yes – quite,' answered Peter. 'But what about that awful sister of yours, Jack? Is she anywhere about? This is quite an important meeting.'

'No. She's gone shopping with my mother,' said Jack. 'She doesn't even *know* there's a meeting on. So we're quite safe. She won't come snooping round.'

'Have a ginger biscuit.' asked Janet, and the tin was handed round.

Peter cleared his throat. 'Well, now,' he began, 'it was my father who thought we should inquire into the matter

I'm going to tell you about, so you can see it's quite important. It concerns a girl who has run away from her aunt's home, after stealing some money at school. She's been seen near here, at Belling Village, where her grandmother lives – but so far hasn't been to see her granny.'

'Oh – and I suppose it's up to the Secret Seven to keep a look-out for her – and find her!' said Jack. 'We ought to be able to do *that* all right. What's she like – and what are your plans, Peter?'

'That's just what this meeting is about,' said Peter. 'Now listen!'

CHAPTER THREE

Mostly about Elizabeth

PETER EXPLAINED everything clearly.

'The girl's name is Elizabeth Mary Wilhemina Sonning,' he said. 'Her parents live abroad, and she is a weekly boarder at school and spends her week-ends with an aunt. She has a brother who is away in France. She was accused of stealing money from her teacher's desk, and when the police went to speak to her aunt about it, she ran away.'

'What was she dressed in?' asked Pam.

'School uniform,' said Peter. 'Here's her photograph in it. Ordinary navy school coat, navy felt hat with school band round it, ordinary shoes, and socks. It says here that she wore a grey skirt underneath, with a white blouse – well, really she's dressed just like Janet and Pam and Barbara when they're at school, it seems to me!'

'She might have taken some other clothes with her,' said Jack. 'Her Sunday coat or something.'

'No. Her aunt said that no other clothes were missing – only the ones she went in,' said Peter. 'You may be sure the aunt would look carefully, because it would be difficult to spot the girl if she were not in her school uniform.'

'Where's the description of what she's like?' asked Janet. 'It was in the evening paper last night, Peter.'

'Oh yes. Here it is,' said Peter, and began to read out loud. '"Elizabeth can be recognised by her mass of soft, dark, curly hair, her brown eyes, straight eyebrows, and scar down one arm. She is tall for her age, and strong. She

427

swims well and is fond of horses." Well – there you are –
do you think you'd spot her if you saw her?'

'We might,' said Colin, doubtfully. 'But lots of girls
have dark, curly hair and brown eyes. If only the girl
would wear short sleeves we might spot the scar – but
that's the one thing she will certainly hide!'

'How do we set about looking for her?' asked George. 'Do
we bike over to Belling Village and hunt all over the place?'

'That's what we've got to discuss,' said Peter. 'I don't
actually think that just biking up and down the streets is
going to be the slightest good – Elizabeth will be sure to
find a hiding-place. She won't wander about in the daytime, I imagine – she'll lie low.'

'Where?' asked Pam.

'How do *I* know?' said Peter, who thought that Pam
was sometimes very silly. 'Use your brains, Pam. Where
would *you* hide if you ran away from home?'

'In a barn,' said Pam.

'In the woods under a thick bush,' said George.

'Wuff, wuff, wuff-wuff,' said Scamper, wagging his
tail.

'What did you suggest – in a *kennel*?' said Peter. 'Thank you, Scamper – quite a good idea of yours.'

Everyone laughed, and Scamper looked pleased.

'I thought it would be sensible if we thoroughly explored Belling Village and round about,' said Peter. 'If Elizabeth has already actually been *seen* in Belling, she must be hiding *some*where near. I expect the police have already hunted pretty well everywhere, but we know better where to look than they do – because we know where *we'd* hide if we wanted to – but they wouldn't. Grown-ups seem to forget the things they did when they were young.'

'Yes, they do,' said George. 'But I *never* shall. I'm determined not to. What about the grandmother, Peter? Should one of us go to see her, do you think? She might have something helpful to say.'

'Yes, I think that's a good idea,' said Peter, considering it.

'Bags *I* don't go,' said Pam, at once. 'I wouldn't know what to say. I should just stand there and look silly.'

'Well, you'd find *that* quite easy,' said Colin, and Pam scowled at him.

'Now just you tell me what you –' she began, but Peter stopped the argument before it began.

'Shut up, you two. Jack and I will go, probably. And listen – there is another thing we might do.'

'What?' asked everyone.

'Well, this girl is fond of horses, it seems. We might go to the two or three stables we know of and see if any girl has been seen hanging around. She might even try to get a job at one.'

'That's a *good* idea,' said Janet, warmly. 'Well – there seems quite a lot we can do, Peter.'

'The next thing is to give each one of us a section of the countryside to hunt,' said Colin. 'It's no good us all going together – for one thing anyone in hiding would hear us coming and lie low. And for another thing we'd never cover all the countryside! What particular places must we search, Peter?'

'Well – you'll use your own common sense about that, of course,' said Peter. 'Anywhere that looks likely – a deserted shack – an empty caravan – a copse – anywhere in the woods where there are thick bushes – barns – sheds – even a hen-house!'

'Wuff, wuff, wuff-wuff,' put in Scamper.

'You mentioned a kennel before, Scamper, old thing,' said Peter. 'We'll leave *you* to examine those. Now, Secret Seven, there are two hours before dinner. Arrange between yourselves where you're going to search. Jack and I are going off to the grandmother's house. Everyone report back at half-past two – SHARP! Now – get going!'

CHAPTER FOUR

Jumble for Mrs Sonning

PETER AND Jack went out of the shed together. 'Do you know the address of the grandmother?' asked Jack.

'No, I don't,' said Peter. 'But I know her name is Sonning, the same as the girl's – so I vote we look it up in our telephone book.'

'Good idea,' said Jack. 'We'll get our bikes afterwards.' The two boys went down the path to the garden door, and Peter looked for the telephone book. He found it and began to hunt for the name of Sonning.

'What are you looking for, dear?' asked his mother, coming into the hall. 'Can't you find a number?'

'I was looking for the phone number of that runaway girl's grandmother,' said Peter. 'But she's not on the phone apparently.'

'But Peter, dear – you can't telephone her house and ask

her questions about her granddaughter!' said his mother, quite shocked.

'I wasn't going to, Mother,' said Peter. 'I was going to call there with Jack – but I don't know her address.'

'I know it,' said his mother, surprisingly. 'She often runs jumble sales for Belling Women's Institute, and it was only last week that she wrote and asked me for some old clothes.'

'Some jumble?' said Peter, excited. 'Oh, Mother – what a chance for us! Can't we take some over to her, and say it's from you – and maybe she'll tell us a lot about Elizabeth, her granddaughter. We're looking for her, you know, just as Daddy suggested.'

'Oh dear – you and your Secret Seven!' said his mother. 'Very well – I'll give you some jumble, and you can say I've sent it by you. But you're to be polite and kind, and if she doesn't want to say a word about Elizabeth, you are NOT to ask questions.'

'All right, Mother. We'll be quite polite, really we will,' said Peter. 'Where's the jumble?'

'In those two boxes,' said his mother. 'I dare say you can strap them on the back of your bicycles if they won't go into your baskets. The address is "Bramble Cottage, Blackberry Lane".'

The two boys hurried off jubilantly with the jumble. 'Wasn't that a bit of luck?' said Peter. 'Come on – we've got a wonderful excuse for calling on the old lady!'

They rode off with Scamper running beside them, panting. They soon came to Belling Village, and asked for Blackberry Lane.

It was a little winding lane, with fields on one side and a wood on the other. Bramble Cottage was the last house in the lane, a pretty little place with tulips and wallflowers in the garden, and creepers climbing up the whitewashed walls.

'Here it is,' said Peter, seeing the name on the gate. 'Get your jumble, Jack.'

They carried the two cardboard boxes up the path, and rang the bell beside the green front door. They heard footsteps coming, and then someone in an overall opened the door and looked inquiringly at them.

She couldn't be the grandmother, Peter was certain. She looked a good deal too young.

'We have brought some jumble for Mrs Sonning's sale,' he said. 'May we speak to her, please? I have a message from my mother.'

'Come in,' said the woman, and led the way to a small sitting-room. 'Put the boxes down there, please. You can't see Mrs Sonning – she's in bed, not very well. I'm Miss Wardle, her companion, and *I'll* tell her you brought these.'

'I suppose she's very upset about her grand-daughter,' said Peter, plunging in at once. 'My mother was sorry to hear about it too.'

'Ah, yes – the old lady is very troubled,' said Miss Wardle. 'She's so fond of Elizabeth, and is longing for the child to come to her. She doesn't believe all that nonsense about stealing money. Neither do I!'

'Do you know Elizabeth, then?' asked Peter.

'Know her! I've known her since she was so high!' said Miss Wardle. 'And a nicer, more honest, straightforward child I've never seen. A bit of a rascal at times, but none the worse for that. Poor child – I can't bear to think of her hiding away somewhere, afraid to come out.'

'Do you think she's somewhere about here?' asked Jack. 'She has been seen in the district, hasn't she?'

'Yes – and, what's more, it's my belief she's been here,

434

to this very house!' said Miss Wardle, lowering her voice. 'I haven't told Mrs Sonning about it, it would worry her. But some of my tarts went last night and a meat pie – and a tin of biscuits! And a rug off the backroom sofa!'

This was news indeed! Peter looked at Jack. Elizabeth must certainly be in the district!

'Why do you suppose she won't come to her grandmother and stay with her instead of hiding away?' asked Peter. 'People usually hide when they feel guilty. But you say you don't believe Elizabeth *is* guilty of stealing that money!'

'That's true – I don't,' said Miss Wardle. 'But the pity of it is – the money was found in her chest of drawers! So what are you to believe?'

'Who's that, Emma, who's that?' a voice suddenly called from upstairs. 'Is there any news of Elizabeth?'

'That's Mrs Sonning. You must go,' said Miss Wardle, and ran up the stairs at once.

'Come on,' said Peter to Jack. 'We've got quite a lot of information! And on Monday we'll see if there's any more! I'll find another boxful of jumble, Jack – and we'll bring it to Miss Wardle and see if she has anything more to report – maybe another rug gone, or a pie! Come on, Scamper – we've done well!'

CHAPTER FIVE

Pam and Barbara are busy

Now HOW had the others been getting on? Well, Pam and
Barbara had been having a very busy time. They had
planned to explore the woods and the fields on the east
side of Belling, while the boys and Janet explored the rest
of the countryside – or as much as they could!

'There's an old shed on that field, look,' panted Barbara, as she toiled up a hill on her bicycle. 'Let's go and see
if it looks as if someone is camping there.'

They left their bicycles by a gate and climbed into the
field. The shed was in good repair – and the door was
locked!

'Hm,' said Pam. 'Locked! I wonder why. Field sheds
aren't usually locked. How can we look inside, Barbara?'

'There's a tiny window this side,' reported Barbara. 'But
too high up to peep through. Let's look through the keyhole.'

There was nothing whatever to see through the keyhole,
for the inside of the shed was pitch dark. It would have to
be the window or nothing! Pam fetched her bicycle from
the gate and proposed to stand on the saddle while
Barbara held it steady. She was just about to stand on
the saddle when a loud shout made her lose her balance in
fright and fall off.

'Hey, you! What are you doing?'

The two girls turned round and saw a farm labourer
leading a horse towards them. Pam couldn't think of any
excuse but the truth.

'We – we were only just wondering what was in the shed,' she stammered. 'We weren't doing any harm.'

'Well, that's the shed where I lock up my tools,' said the man. 'Little nosy-parkers! Get off this land before I call the police!'

The girls left that field at top speed, Pam riding her bicycle over the bumpy clods! Gosh – what a cross person!

'We'd better be careful of the next shed we want to look into,' said Pam, as they cycled along. 'Look, there's an empty caravan – see, in that field there. That would be a good place for anyone to hide in. Now for goodness' sake let's be careful this time. I'll keep guard while you look inside. Hurry up!'

Pam stood on guard near the dirty, broken-down old caravan, which looked as if no one had lived in it for years.

Barbara went cautiously up the steps and looked inside. She beckoned to Pam in excitement.

'Pam! Someone *does* live here! There are a couple of dirty old rugs – or blankets – and a tin mug and plate – do come and look!'

Pam came up the steps too. 'Pooh!' she said, and held her nose. 'What a DREADFUL smell! Come down, Barbara. You know jolly well you'd never hide in a place like that, nor any other schoolgirl either. I think I'm going to be sick.'

'You're right, I'd rather sleep in a ditch than in there,' said Barbara. 'Don't be sick, Pam. It's not worth it. Come on, let's get on with our job. We want to have plenty to report to the others this afternoon.'

Pam decided not to be sick after all, and they rode on again, keeping a sharp eye out for any kind of hiding-place. But except for a roadman's hut, they saw nothing else that was possible to hide in. They didn't even stop at the little hut, because the roadman himself was there, sitting in it and having some kind of snack.

'What about the woods?' asked Pam, at last. 'There's Thorney-Copse Wood – and it has plenty of thick bushes in it. We might go there. We've still got an hour to look round in.'

So they went to the nearby woods, and left their bicycles beside a tree. 'Now let's be as quiet as possible,' said Pam, in a low voice. 'You go that way, and I'll go this. Whistle twice if you see anything interesting.'

She went quietly in and out of the trees, looking behind any thick bush and even under them. But there was nothing at all interesting or exciting to be seen. Pam found an empty cigarette packet, and Barbara found a dirty handkerchief with J. P. on it, but neither of them felt that they were of any value in the hunt. Now if E.M.W.S. had been marked on the handkerchief, what a thrill!

And then Pam suddenly clutched hold of Barbara, making her jump violently, and hissed in her ear. 'Quiet! Somebody's coming, and it's a girl – look!'

They crept under a thick bush at once, and made little peep-holes through the leaves. Yes, it was a schoolgirl – in navy blue coming down a path towards their bush.

'Keep still – and then we'll follow her!' whispered Pam. 'I bet that's the girl we want!'

The girl's hat was pulled well down over her eyes. She walked boldly up to the bush – and then suddenly fell into it, almost squashing Pam and Barbara. She began to roar with laughter.

'Oh, it's Susie. Jack's horrible sister Susie!' cried Barbara, indignantly. 'Get off us, Susie – you've nearly squashed us flat. What did you do that for?'

'Well, you were lying in wait to jump out at me, weren't you?' asked Susie. 'I spotted you crawling into the bush!'

'We were *not* lying in wait for you,' said Pam.

'Well,' said Susie, 'what were you doing then? Come on – you've *got* to tell me!'

CHAPTER SIX

Up at the stables

PAM AND Barbara glared at Susie. It was *just* like her to interfere. Pam rubbed her shoulder.

'You've given me a big bruise,' she said. 'And we shan't tell you a thing!'

'It's something to do with the Secret Seven, isn't it?' said Susie. 'Go on, tell me – I know it is. You've got some kind of secret on again, haven't you? Jack has gone off without saying a word to me. Tell me, and I'll help you.'

'Certainly not!' said Pam indignantly. 'We keep our secrets to ourselves!'

'Well – I'll get it out of Jack,' said the irritating Susie, and walked off, tipping her hat over her face once more. 'Good-bye – and don't lie in wait for me again!'

'Now she knows we're in the middle of another excitement,' said Barbara, brushing herself down. 'She's so sharp that I'm sure she'll find out what it is. I do hope we don't keep meeting her looking for Elizabeth too!'

'Time's getting on,' said Pam, looking at her watch. 'We'll just hunt in a few more places, and then we'll have to go home!'

They did quite a lot more hunting, and found an exciting hollow tree which, they decided, would have made a fine place for a runaway girl if she had happened to see it.

'We'll remember it for ourselves, in case we ever need a place like this,' said Barbara. 'Now let's go home. We've nothing to report – except about Susie – but at least we've done our best. I wonder how Colin got on? He was going round the farms and looking into the barns.'

'And George and Janet were going to visit the riding stables in the district,' said Pam. 'That would be quite a nice job. I love stables.'

George and Janet thought it was quite a nice job too. They had looked up the riding stables in the district, and found that there were three.

'Belling Riding Stables,' said Janet. 'And Warner's Riding Stables – and Tiptree's. We'll go to all three, shall we?'

So off they went on their bicycles, feeling, as usual, very important to be on Secret Seven work again. They came to Tiptree's Stables first. Janet knew the man who ran it, for he was a friend of her father's.

He was rubbing down a horse and smiled at Janet and

George. 'Well – come to have a look at my horses?' he
said. 'I've a foal in there, look – Silver Start, she's called,
and a bonny thing she is.'

They admired the lovely little foal. 'I do wish I worked
at a stables,' said Janet, artfully. 'Do you ever let school-
girls work here – perhaps in the school holidays,
Mr Tiptree?'

The riding master laughed. 'No! I get plenty of help
from my wife and two daughters – they're all mad about
horses. They do all the work there is to do – I don't need
anyone from outside. This is quite a family stables! Why –
did you think you'd come and help? Your father has surely
got plenty of horses for you to play about with?'

'Well, yes, he has,' said Janet, stroking the little foal. 'I
only just wondered if you ever gave jobs to girls – lots of
girls I know love horses and wish they could work in a
stables.'

'Come on, Janet,' said George, seeing that they could
get no useful information from Mr Tiptree. Obviously the
runaway girl would not be able to get a job here, even if
she wanted one.

'Thank you for showing us the foal, Mr Tiptree,' said
Janet. 'I'll tell my father about her – he'll be interested.'

They rode off again, and George looked at his list of
stables. 'We'll go to Warner's Stables next,' he said.
'That's not far from the old granny's house. It might
be a good place for Elizabeth Sonning to hide in – or get a
job at.'

'I hardly think she'd go anywhere so close, would she?'
said Janet. 'She might be recognised. It's more likely she'd
go farther off – to Belling Stables, the other side of the
village. Still – we'll go to Warner's first.'

They rode up to the
stables on the top of the
next hill. Below them were
spread fields of all kinds
and shapes looking like a
big patchwork quilt.

Warner's Stables were
quite big, and looked busy
as they came up to them.
Some horses were going
out with riders, and others
were coming in. Nobody
took much notice of the
two children.

'Let's have a snoop round,' said Janet. 'And if we see
any stable-girls, we'll have a good look at them.'

'Wouldn't Elizabeth have to wear riding things if she wanted a job at a stable?' said George. 'We know that she was wearing her school clothes when she left – she took no others.'

'Well – she might have borrowed some at the stables,' said Janet. 'Though that's rather unlikely, I think. Look – there's a stable-girl – see – cleaning out that stable.'

They stood and stared at the girl. Her back was towards them, and she was doing her job well. She turned round to fetch something, and at once they saw that it was not Elizabeth.

'Far too big!' said Janet, disappointed. 'Look – there are two stable-boys over there. Let's go and talk to them – we may learn something, you never know.'

CHAPTER SEVEN

Tom has some news

GEORGE AND Janet made their way between the horses and their riders to where the two stable-boys were. One was carrying a great load of straw on his back. The other was helping a small girl down from a pony. They took no notice of George and Janet.

'Hello, Janet!' said the small girl, and Janet turned in surprise. It was Hilda, a little girl who went to her school, and was two years below her.

'Hello, Hilda,' said Janet, feeling pleased to see her. Now she could pretend she was with her, and it wouldn't matter that she and George were not in riding clothes. Everyone would think they had come to meet Hilda.

'Thank you, Tom,' said Hilda to the boy who had helped her down. He took the pony off to a nearby stable, Hilda followed him, accompanied by Janet and George.

'I like the other boy best,' Hilda said. 'He talks to me, but this one won't. Come and see me give my pony some sugar. He's a darling.'

They walked over to the stable with her, following Tom and the pony. The other lad had gone into the same stable with his straw, and was now spreading it on the floor of a stall. He whistled as he worked, and had a merry look in his eye.

'You talk to this boy, and I'll talk to the other one,' said George, in a low voice to Janet. 'Talk to Hilda too – find out if any new girl is here helping in any way – or if she has seen any strange girl wandering about, watching, as we are doing.'

447

'Right,' said Janet, and went to Tom and Hilda.

'It must be fun working with horses,' she said to the boy, who was now fastening the pony to the wall. He nodded.

'Not bad,' he said.

'It's funny that so many more girls ride than boys,' went on Janet. 'I can't see a single boy here except you, and the other stable-boy. Are there any others?'

'No,' said the boy. 'Just us two.' He began to clean out the stall next to the little pony, turning his back on Hilda and Janet. Janet thought he was rather rude. So did Hilda.

'He's like that,' she whispered to Janet. 'The other boy, Harry, doesn't mind telling you anything. He's talking to George as if he's known him for years.'

So he was. George was getting on very well indeed!

'Do they have many stable-girls here?' George asked, when he had a good chance. The burly fellow shook his head.

'Only one – and she's over there. One came the other day to ask for a job, but Mr Warner turned her down at once. Why, she wasn't any bigger than you! And yet she said she could handle this big cob over there.'

George pricked up his ears. He wasn't interested in the cob, but he was interested in this girl who had come for a job. Could it have been Elizabeth?

'What was she like?' he asked. Harry called across to the other stable-boy.

'Hey, Tom – what was that girl like who came and asked for a job the other day?'

'Was she brown-eyed?' asked George, eagerly. 'Had she masses of dark, fluffy hair? And did you notice if she had a scar down one of her arms?'

The stable-boy swung round sharply and stared at George. 'What girl's that?' he asked. 'Is she a friend of yours?'

'No, not exactly,' said George. 'It's – er – well, it's just someone we're looking out for. Do tell me, was this girl like my description of her?'

'I didn't see her,' said Tom, much to Janet's and George's disappointment. 'I wasn't here the day she came.'

'Oh, no – that's right,' said Harry. 'Well, I know she hadn't got dark hair – she had yellow hair, and she was lively as a monkey. Very cross too, when Mr Warner turned her down. She couldn't have been your friend.'

449

'I saw a girl like the one you described when I was in Gorton the other day,' said Tom suddenly. 'Mass of fluffy brown hair, you said, didn't you – and a scar down one arm.'

'Did you? Did you *really* see her?' cried Janet, coming up, looking thrilled. Now they were really getting warm! 'How did you manage to see her scar?'

'Oh – she sat in a tea-shop, and it was hot there – so she took off her coat,' said Tom. 'I saw her scar then.'

'But hadn't she a long-sleeved school blouse on?' asked Janet, surprised.

'Maybe. But her sleeves must have been rolled up if so,' said Tom, and bent to his work again.

'Tom – this is really very important,' said George, joining in. 'Could you tell us anything she said – did she speak to you?'

'She said she was going to catch a train to London and see if she could fly to France to join a brother of hers,' said Tom, to Janet's and George's surprise and excitement. Why, the girl *must* have been Elizabeth, then. A scar on her arm – and a brother in France! There was no doubt about it!

'Tom! I want you!' called a voice, and Mr Warner looked into the stable. 'Come and show this child how to saddle her horse.'

Tom went off, and Janet and George looked at one another, delighted. 'Well – we've got something to report to the meeting this afternoon!' said Janet. 'Come on, George – we needn't stay here any longer.'

CHAPTER EIGHT

Another meeting

EVERYONE WAS early for the two-thirty meeting, and the password was muttered five times as Janet and Peter opened and shut the door of the shed. Scamper barked a welcome to everyone. Then the door was locked and the meeting began.

'I hope everyone has something to report,' said Peter. 'I'll begin with my report. Well, Jack and I went to the grandmother's house, but the old lady wasn't well, so we didn't see her. We didn't find it difficult to ask questions, and her companion was quite friendly.'

'That was a bit of luck!' said George.

'It was,' said Peter. 'We learnt quite a few things – for instance, that Elizabeth is definitely hiding somewhere in the district – not far from her granny's, I should think – because she has got into the house at night and taken pies and things, and an old rug!'

George and Janet looked astonished. 'But, Peter – ' began George and Janet together. Peter frowned. 'Please don't interrupt,' he said. 'You and Janet can have your say in a minute. Well, as I was saying – the old lady's companion, Miss Wardle – told us quite a lot about Elizabeth, and said that she was a very nice, straightforward girl.'

'She can't be!' interrupted Pam. 'You can't call a thief straightforward! She was only just *saying* that!'

'Be quiet,' said Peter, exasperated. 'The point I'm trying

451

to make is that there's no doubt that Elizabeth is hiding somewhere near her grandmother's – and getting food from there. And she'll do that at night as often as she needs food! I suggest that we go and watch one night, and see if we can catch her. Jack and I are going to take some more jumble to the grandmother's on Monday, and if Elizabeth has been getting into the house again, we could perhaps watch that night.'

'Yes. Jolly good idea!' said Pam, Barbara, and Colin. George and Janet said nothing, but looked meaningly at one another.

'Well, that's my report – mine and Jack's,' said Peter. 'What about you, Colin?'

'Nothing to report at all,' said Colin, in a rather apologetic tone. 'I examined about six sheds, all kinds of barns, and wandered over a whole caravan colony the other side of Belling Hill – but didn't find out a thing. Not a thing. I'm sorry, Peter.'

'That's all right,' said Peter. 'You and Pam, Barbara – what's your report?'

'Well, nothing much, either,' said Barbara. 'We looked in a locked shed – or tried to – and got turned off by a man with a horse. And we found a terribly smelly old caravan with a rug inside and a tin cup and plate. And we hunted all through Thorney-Copse Wood, looking into and under bushes.'

'And that awful sister of Jack's was there, too,' said Pam. 'We saw her coming along, dressed in the same uniform as we wear – navy blue coat and hat – and we thought it might be the runaway girl, so we hid in a bush – and Susie jumped right into it on purpose and fell on top of us – you should see the bruise I've got!'

452

'So *that's* why Susie was pestering the life out of me at
dinner to find out what the Secret Seven are up to!' said
Jack. 'You *are* a couple of idiots to make her think there is
something up, you two. Now I shan't have a moment's
peace. Susie is bound to find out what we're after – she's as
sharp as a needle.'

'She certainly is,' said Peter, who had a healthy respect
for Susie's sharpness. 'I wouldn't be a bit surprised if she's
not snooping outside somewhere now, listening for all
she's worth.'

'Scamper would bark,' began Janet – and just at that
very moment Scamper *did* bark as a face looked in at the
window of the shed! It was Susie, of course.

'Hello, Secret Seven,' she called. 'I *thought* you'd be
here, Jack. I know what you're all up to. I found your
newspaper cutting! Ha, ha.'

Peter looked furiously at Jack. 'Do you mean to say you
left that newspaper report about?' he said.

'That's right, tick him off!' said the annoying Susie,
pressing her face closer to the window. 'Hey, you do look a
lot of sweetie-pies sitting down there. Shall I tell you my
news of Elizabeth Mary Wilhemina Sonning?'

Jack leapt up in a fury, flung open the door, and raced out with Scamper at his heels. The others went to the door.

Susie was a fast runner. She was running out of the gate, laughing, before Jack was half-way there. He knew it was no good chasing after her. He went back to the shed, red in the face.

'Do you suppose she heard what we were all saying?' asked Jack. Peter shook his head.

'No. Scamper would have barked. Susie could only just that moment have come. I must say it's very annoying. Now Susie will be hunting too. Bother! If she finds Elizabeth before we do, I shall be jolly furious.'

'She won't,' said George, bursting to tell what he had heard from Tom the stable-boy. 'You just wait till you hear what Janet and I have to report.'

CHAPTER NINE

Reports and plans

'GIVE YOUR report, George and Janet,' said Peter. 'It sounds as if it may be an important one.'

'It is,' said Janet, proudly. 'You begin, George.'

'Well,' began George, 'Janet and I went to Tiptree Stables first, but as they don't employ anyone there except their own family, we knew Elizabeth wouldn't have got a job there. So we left at once and went on to Mr Warner's stables.'

'And we saw a stable-girl there, but she was much too big to be Elizabeth,' put in Janet.

'Then we saw two stable-boys – one a big, burly fellow called Harry, and the other smaller, called Tom. He was a bit surly, we thought, but Harry wasn't. He was nice. We asked him if any girl had been asking for a job at Mr Warner's, and one had, but she had yellow hair not brown, so we knew that was no good.'

'And when we told Harry what the girl was like that we wanted, the other boy, Tom, who was listening, suddenly said that *he* had seen a girl like the one we were describing – and she even had a scar down one arm!' cried Janet unable to resist joining in.

'What!' cried everyone, and sat up straight.

'This *is* news,' said Peter, delighted. 'Go on, George. Where had he seen Elizabeth – because it must be her if the description tallies.'

'He said he met her in a tea-shop in Gorton – that's not

455

very far from here, is it? She was having tea, I suppose. It was hot and she had her coat off – that's how he noticed the scar down one arm. She talked to him.'

'What did she say?' demanded Peter, his eyes shining.

'She told him she was going to London to see if she could get a plane to fly to France to see her brother,' said Janet. 'She did really! So it *must* have been Elizabeth, mustn't it?'

'Yes. Of course it must,' said Peter, and the others nodded their heads. A brother in France – a scar on one arm – it could *only* be Elizabeth.

'Well, now you see why Janet and I don't think that Elizabeth is hiding anywhere in the district,' said George. 'She's probably hiding somewhere in London, trying to find out about planes.'

'Well – can you answer this question then, if that's so,'

said Peter, looking suddenly puzzled. 'If Elizabeth is in London, waiting to fly to France, who is it who is taking pies and a rug from her grandmother's house at night?'

There was a deep silence. Everyone looked at Peter, even Scamper.

'I hadn't thought of that,' said Janet. 'Well, of course, George and I didn't know anything about the pies till you told us in your report, Peter. Bother! One of our reports is wrong somehow. If Elizabeth is hanging round her granny's house at night, she can't be going to fly to France!'

'She might have found that she hadn't enough money to get to London and buy a seat on a plane,' said Jack. 'She might have changed her mind and gone to Belling, after all. She might even have hoped to get money from her grandmother's house. After all, if she had stolen once, she could easily do so again.'

'That's true,' said Peter. 'Yes – I think you're right, Jack. She may have made that plan at the beginning and then found she hadn't enough money – and so she came to this district. We know she was seen somewhere about here.'

There was another silence. The Seven were trying to sort things out in their minds. 'What about that girl who came to ask Mr Warner for a job – the one Harry told you about,' said Janet to George. 'He said she had golden hair, didn't he? Well, I suppose she might have had it dyed, mightn't she – I mean, that *might* have been Elizabeth, after all. I know my auntie once had her hair dyed golden when it was brown. So Elizabeth could have done the same, couldn't she?'

Nobody knew very much about hair being dyed, and Peter made up his mind that the next thing to do was to go and interview the two stable-boys himself. They might be able to tell him something they hadn't thought of telling Janet or George.

'I shall go and see those boys,' he said. 'What are they like to look at?'

'I told you Harry was big and burly, and the other smaller,' said George. 'They've both got dark hair, rather untidy. They ought to exchange riding-breeches too – Harry's are too small for him, and Tom's are too large! Wasn't it a bit of luck Tom meeting Elizabeth at Gorton – now we know for certain she must be somewhere about, still wearing her school things.'

'Well, she's *got* to be somewhere near, or she couldn't raid her granny's house at night,' said Peter. 'Now, what do we do next? Tomorrow's Sunday, we can't do anything then. It will have to be Monday after school.'

'You and I will go to old Mrs Sonning's with some more jumble,' said Jack, 'and find out the latest news from *that* quarter.'

'And after that we'll go and see the stable-boys,' said Peter. 'The others can come too, so that it won't seem too noticeable, us asking questions. Meet here at five o'clock on Monday. Well – I *hope* we're on the trail – but it's not very easy at the moment!'

CHAPTER TEN

Miss Wardle has more news

SUNDAY PASSED rather slowly.

When Peter and Janet came back from morning church, Peter had an idea.

'Janet – George and I are going to take some more jumble to old Mrs Sonning tomorrow, you remember – to make an excuse for asking about Elizabeth again – so shall we hunt up some? What sort of things does Mother give for jumble? Old clothes mostly, I suppose.'

'Yes. But we can't give away any of our clothes without asking her,' said Janet. 'And she would want to know why we were doing it – she'd guess it was an excuse to go to old Mrs Sonning again, and she might not approve.'

'That's just what I was thinking,' said Peter. 'I know – let's turn out our cupboards and see if there's anything we can find that would do for jumble.'

They found plenty! It was astonishing what a lot of things they had which they had quite forgotten about and never used.

'Two packs of snap cards,' said Peter. 'A game of snakes and ladders – we've never even *used* it, because we always preferred our old game. And look here – a perfectly new ball! Shall we give that?'

'Well, jumble isn't really supposed to be *new* things,' said Janet. 'Let's give our old ball instead. And look, here are my old sandals I thought I'd left at the seaside! I can't get into them now – *they* can go.'

In the end they had quite a big box full of jumble and felt very pleased with themselves. They longed for Monday to come!

It came at last, and then there was morning school to get through, and afternoon school as well. They raced home to tea and were down in the shed just before five o'clock. All the Seven were there, very punctual indeed!

'Good,' said Peter, pleased. 'Well, Jack and I will bike to Bramble Cottage, and see if we can get any more news out of Miss Wardle, the companion, or Mrs Sonning, the granny. The rest of you can bike up to Warner's Stables and wait for us there. Chat to the stable-boys all you can. We'll join you later.'

They all set off, Peter with a neat box of jumble tied to the back of his bicycle. They parted at the top of Blackberry Lane, and Jack and Peter went down the winding road, while the others rode up the hill to where Warner's Stables were, right at the top.

Peter and Jack left their bicycles at the gate of Bramble Cottage and went to the front door. They knocked, hoping that Miss Wardle would come, not old Mrs Sonning. Mrs Sonning might not be so willing to talk about Elizabeth as Miss Wardle was!

Thank goodness it was Miss Wardle who opened the door again. She seemed quite pleased to see them.

'Well now – don't say you've been kind enough to bring us some *more* jumble!' she said. 'Mrs Sonning was *so* pleased with the boxes you brought on Saturday. I'll give her these – she's still in bed, dear old lady.'

'Oh, I'm sorry,' said Peter. 'Hasn't she heard any more of her granddaughter?'

'Not a word,' said Miss Wardle. 'The police say she seems to have disappeared completely – and yet she came here again last night – *and* the night before!'

This was indeed news! 'Did she?' asked Peter eagerly. 'Did you see her? Did she leave a note?'

'No. Not a note, not even a sign that she was here,' said Miss Wardle, 'except that more food was gone. How she got in beats me. Every door and window I made fast myself. She must have got a key to the side-door. That's the only one with no bolt.'

'What do the police say about that?' asked Jack.

'Nothing,' said Miss Wardle, rather indignantly. 'It's my belief they think I'm making it up, they take so little notice. Why don't they put a man to watch the house at night – they'd catch the poor child then, and what a relief it would be to the old lady to know she was safe!'

'They probably *do* put a man to watch,' said Peter, 'but I expect Elizabeth knows some way into the house that they don't. I bet she knows if there's a policeman about – and where he is and everything. *I* would! Why don't you watch, Miss Wardle?'

'What? Watch every door and window?' said the companion. 'Nobody could do that. And I'm not one to be able to keep awake all night, even if I had to.'

'Well – we'd better go,' said Peter. 'I *do* hope Elizabeth is soon found. It must be awful hiding away in some cold, lonely place all by herself, not daring to come home because she feels ashamed.'

They said good-bye and went. 'Well,' said Peter, as soon as they were out of the front gate, 'I know what *I'm* going to do tonight! I'm going to hide somewhere in the garden here! I bet I'll see Elizabeth if she comes – but I shan't tell the police. I'll try and get her to go and tell everything to her granny!'

'Good idea! I'll come too!' said Jack, thrilled. 'Let's go up to the stables now and find the others. I bet they'll want to come and watch as well!'

CHAPTER ELEVEN

Tom – and a bit of excitement

PETER AND Jack saw the others as soon as they pushed open the tall double-gate and went into the big stable-yard. They had evidently been sent to fetch hay and straw, and looked very busy indeed, carrying it over their shoulders. The two stable-boys were there as well, helping.

'Hallo, Peter – hallo, Jack!' called Janet. 'Aren't we busy? We're having a lovely time. Mr Warner said we could take the ponies down to the field later on, with Harry and Tom, the stable-boys.'

'Good. I'll come too, with Jack,' said Peter, pleased. He loved anything to do with horses, and often helped old Jock, the horseman, in his father's farm-stables. He went over to the two stable-boys. Harry grinned at him, but Tom just nodded. Peter looked at him keenly. So this was the boy who had actually seen Elizabeth!

'Hey – I hear you saw that girl, Elizabeth Sonning, at Gorton the other day,' began Peter. 'That's very interesting.

The police haven't found her yet – I should think her grandmother must be feeling ill with worry, wouldn't you?'

'What about the girl, then?' said Tom, in a gruff voice. 'I reckon she must be feeling pretty awful too.'

'Well, if she stole that money, she deserves to feel awful,' said Peter. 'The funny thing is that Miss Wardle, who is the old lady's friend, says Elizabeth is an awfully nice girl, straightforward as anything! Here – let me help you with that saddle.'

'Thanks,' said Tom. 'I feel interested in that girl – seeing her in Gorton just by chance. I reckon she's in France by now. She said she wanted to go to her brother.'

'Well, she's *not* in France,' said Peter, struggling with the heavy saddle. 'She goes each night to her granny's house and takes things. Miss Wardle told me that. She says she can't *think* how Elizabeth gets into the house – everything's locked and fastened. She thought maybe the girl might have a key to the side-door, which has no bolts.'

Jack joined in then. 'And we thought we'd go and watch the house ourselves tonight,' he said. 'We're sure *we* should see her getting in, if she comes in the dark – and we'd try and get her to go and talk to her old granny, who loves her. We hate to think of a girl camping out somewhere all alone, feeling miserable.'

'Are you really going to watch tonight?' said Tom, sounding surprised. Peter nodded. He hadn't wanted Jack to tell a Secret Seven plan to the stable-boy – that was really *silly* of him, thought Peter, and gave him a stern frown, which startled Jack very much.

'Well, if you're going to watch the house, I'd like to come too,' said Tom, most surprisingly. 'I bet *I* could see anyone creeping into a house at night. I'll come with you.'

Peter hesitated. He wanted to say that Tom could certainly *not* come! But how could he prevent him if he wanted to? It was just a nice little adventure to him, and possibly a chance to show how clever he was at spotting anyone breaking into a house!

'All right,' he said, at last. 'We shall be there at half-past ten. I'll give an owl-hoot when we arrive – and if you're there, hoot back.'

'I'll be there,' said Tom. 'And I suppose a policeman or two will, as well! Well, you stick up for me if I get seen by the police, and say I'm a friend of yours, not a burglar!'

'All right,' said Peter, wishing more than ever that Jack hadn't said so much. 'Do we take the ponies down to the fields now?'

Apparently they did, and a long trail of children riding or leading ponies went over the hill and down to the fields, bright in the evening sun.

After they had safely fastened in the tired ponies, the Seven, with Tom and Harry, walked back to the stables. Tom looked tired and spoke very little. Harry cracked jokes and slapped the other stable-boy on the back several times. Peter whispered to Tom when he had a chance.

'Don't forget the owl-hoot!' Tom nodded and turned away. The children shouted good-bye and fetched their bicycles, riding them down the hillpath.

In the distance they saw someone climbing over a stile – someone with a suitcase – someone in a navy blue coat and hat – someone who looked round and then, seeming scared, ran hurriedly down the road.

'Look!' said Colin, pointing. 'Is that Elizabeth – with a suitcase, too! Quick, let's follow!'

They rode along the path, bumping up and down as

they went, for it was very rough. They came to the stile. By it lay something white.

Janet picked it up. 'A handkerchief!' she said. 'LOOK! It's got E in the corner, embroidered in green! It *was* Elizabeth! Her hiding-place *is* somewhere near here. Quick, let's follow her.'

They lifted their bicycles over the stile into the road and looked to see if they could spy a running figure in navy blue.

'There she is – at the corner – by that old cottage!' shouted George. 'If only we can get her to be friends and come with us! Ring your bells, all of you, so that she'll hear us coming!'

CHAPTER TWELVE

How very annoying!

THE WHOLE Seven cycled as fast as they could after the disappearing figure in navy blue, ringing their bells loudly to attract her attention.

The figure reached the corner, and vanished round it. When they came to it, the girl was nowhere to be seen. The Seven dismounted from their bicycles and looked at one another.

'Wherever has she gone? She's nowhere down the road!' said Janet. 'She must have slipped into some hiding-place. But I can't see any near by.'

'Yes, look – there's that ruined old cottage,' said Colin, pointing. 'Can't you see it – among that little thicket of trees. I bet she's there!'

'We'll go and look,' said George, and, putting their bicycles beside the hedge, they squeezed through a gap and ran over to the old stone cottage. It had very little roof left, and there were only two rooms below and one above. A broken stone stairway went up in one corner to the room above.

'There's nobody here!' said Pam, surprised. 'Oh, but look – there's an old stone stairway. Perhaps she's up there!'

George ran up – and gave a shout. 'The girl isn't here – but her suitcase is! And it's got E.M.W.S. on it! It *was* Elizabeth we saw!'

Everyone tore up the stairs in a hurry. They looked at

the cheap little suitcase on the dirty floor. Yes – it certainly had E.M.W.S. printed on it in black.

'Elizabeth Mary Wilhemina Sonning,' said Barbara, touching the initials. 'But where *is* Elizabeth?' she called loudly. 'Elizabeth! Where are you?'

There was no reply. 'That's odd,' said Janet. 'There really isn't anywhere for her to hide here. Why did she throw her case up these stairs and then rush away. She might guess we'd find it. Where *is* she? ELIZABETH!'

'I'm going to open the case,' said Peter. 'I feel there's something peculiar about all this. I hope it isn't locked.'

It wasn't. It snapped open easily enough. The Seven crowded round to look inside. One small box was there, and nothing else. It was tied up with string.

'Perhaps this is the money she stole!' said Colin. 'Gosh – look! It's got "THE MONEY" printed on it in big letters. Open the box, Peter.'

Peter undid the string and opened the box. Inside was a smaller one, also tied with string. He undid that, and inside found once again another box. He looked puzzled. It seemed strange to put money inside so many boxes!

He opened the third box – and inside that was a card, laid on its face. Peter picked it up and turned it over. He stared at it as if he couldn't believe his eyes!

'What does it say? What does it say?' cried Pam, trying to see.

Peter flung it down on the floor and stamped on it, looking very angry. 'It says "*Lots and lots of love from Susie!*" OH! I'd like to slap her! Making us chase after her – leaving that silly hanky by the stile – and making us undo all those boxes!'

The Secret Seven were very, very angry, especially Jack.

'How *dare* she play a trick like that!' he said. 'Just wait till I get home. I'll have something to say to her!'

'Where's she gone?' said Barbara. 'I didn't see her after we turned the corner. She must have had her bicycle hidden somewhere here.'

'She planned it all very well,' said George. 'I must say she's jolly clever. Gosh – I really *did* think we'd got hold of Elizabeth that time!'

'Susie must have laughed like anything when she printed the initials E.M.W.S. on that cheap old suitcase,' said Jack. 'I recognise it now – it's been up in our loft for ages.'

'Well, come on – let's get home,' said Janet. 'I'm tired of talking about Susie.'

They left the little ruined cottage and rode away. Peter began to arrange the night's meeting with George, Jack, and Colin. The girls were sad that they could not come too.

'You always leave us out of these night adventures,' complained Janet. 'I do so wish we were coming. It will be so exciting to wait in that dark garden – let me see – there will be five of you counting that boy Tom – though I really do think it's a pity to have him, too.'

'There may be a policeman or two as well,' said George. 'I vote we get there before they do – or they'll get rather a shock when they hear a whole collection of people taking up their positions here and there in the garden!'

Everyone laughed. 'Don't you DARE to let anything out to Susie about tonight,' Peter warned Jack. 'We can't have her ruining everything. I do wonder how Elizabeth gets into the house. She must have an extra key.'

They arranged to meet at ten past ten at the corner and bicycle all together to Belling. 'We'll hide our bikes under the nearby hedge and get into the garden at the back,' planned Peter. 'Remember to hoot if there's any danger.'

'This is awfully exciting,' said Jack. 'I only hope Susie doesn't hear me getting up and going downstairs.'

'Jack – if you do anything silly so that Susie follows you, I'll dismiss you from the Secret Seven!' said Peter – and he REALLY meant it!

CHAPTER THIRTEEN

Waiting and watching

THAT NIGHT Peter, Jack, George and Colin slipped silently
out of their houses. Jack was very much afraid that Susie
might hear him, but when he put his ear to her door, he
could hear gentle little snores. Good – she was asleep! He
remembered Peter's threat to dismiss him from the Secret
Seven if he wasn't careful about Susie, and he felt very
glad to hear those snores!

The boys met together and then cycled quickly over to
the grandmother's house in Belling. They met nobody at
all, not even a policeman, and were very thankful. The
four of them dismounted quietly and put their bicycles
into the hedge beyond Bramble Cottage. The cottage was
in complete darkness.

'The only person to hoot is *me*,' whispered Peter. 'If we
all hoot when we hear or see something interesting or
suspicious, it would sound as if the garden was *full* of owls
– and any policeman would be most suspicious!'

'All right,' whispered back George. 'Can we choose our
own hiding-places? What about two of us going to hide in
the garden at the front of the house, and two at the back?'

'No – two at the back, one in the front – you, Colin –
and one at the side where the side-door is,' said Peter, in a
low voice. 'Don't forget that Miss Wardle said she thought
Elizabeth might have a key to that door – and there are no
bolts there on the inside!'

'Oh, yes!' said Jack. 'I'll go and hide in the hedge beside

the garden door, Peter. There isn't any door on the fourth side. We shall be watching every door there is – and every window.'

'It's very dark,' said Peter, looking up at the sky. 'There's no moon, and it's a cloudy night, so there are no stars either. We shall have to keep our ears wide open, because it may be pretty difficult to see anything.'

'Our eyes will soon get used to the darkness,' said Colin. 'Hey – listen, what's that?' He clutched at Peter and made him jump.

A slight noise came from near by, and then a shadow loomed up. A voice spoke. 'It's me – Tom. I was waiting here, and I heard you. Where are you hiding?'

They told him. 'Well, I think *I'll* climb up a tree,' said Tom, in a low voice. 'That will be a very good place to watch from – or listen from! I don't think any policemen are about. I've been here for some time.'

'Hoot if you hear anyone coming,' Peter reminded him. 'I'll hoot back. But only you or I will hoot.'

'I'll find a tree to climb,' whispered Tom. 'See – that one over there, near the wall. I shall have a good view from there – if only the clouds clear and the stars shine out!'

The four went to find their own hiding-places, feeling pleasantly excited. This *was* fun! They heard Tom climbing his tree. Then there was silence. Peter was snuggled into a bush, from where he could keep good watch.

A sudden screech made everyone jump, and their hearts beat fast. Whatever was it? Then a white shadow swept round the dark garden, and everyone heaved a sigh of relief.

'Only a barn-owl!' thought Peter. 'Gosh – it made me jump. Good thing it doesn't hoot, only screeches – or we would all of us have thought that someone was coming!'

Nothing happened for a while – then a low, quavering hoot came across the garden. 'Hoo! Hoo-hoo-hoo-hoooooooo!'

'That's Tom!' thought Peter, and he and the others in hiding stiffened, and listened hard, trying to see through the darkness.

Then someone brushed by Peter's bush and he crouched back in fright. He heard a little cough – a man's cough. It must be a policeman who had come along so quietly that no one but Tom had heard him. Peter waited a few seconds till he was sure that the man had found a hiding-place, and then he hooted too.

'Hoo! Hoo-hoo-hoo-hooooooo!'

Now everyone must guess that at least one policeman was in the garden! Peter's heart began to thump. Suddenly things seemed very strange and very exciting – all the dark shadows around, and so many people waiting! He half hoped that Elizabeth would not come to her granny's house that night. It would be so frightening for her to be surrounded suddenly by complete strangers!

Then suddenly he stared in amazement. Was that a *light* he saw in one of the upstairs rooms of the house? A light like that made by a torch? Yes – it was! He could see the beam moving here and there behind the drawn curtains!

Elizabeth must be there – she must have got in somehow, in spite of everyone watching! Or could it be Miss Wardle creeping about with a torch? No – surely she would switch on a light!

Peter gave a hoot again. 'Hoooo! Hoo-hoo-hoo-hoooooooo!' That would make certain that everyone was on guard. If Elizabeth had got in, then she would have to get out – and surely one of them would see her!

The light in the upstairs room disappeared – and reappeared again in another room. Peter thought it was the kitchen. Perhaps the hungry runaway girl was looking for food again?

How HAD she got in? But, more important still – where was she going to come out?

CHAPTER FOURTEEN

A real mystery

THE LIGHT from the torch inside the house moved here and there. Then it disappeared completely, as if it had been switched off. All the watchers listened, and strained their eyes in the darkness. Now Elizabeth would be leaving the house, and they must stop her. What door – or what window – would she creep from?

Nothing happened. No door opened. No window creaked or rattled. For ten minutes the watchers stood silent and tense. Then a man's voice called from somewhere in the garden.

'Will! Seen anyone?'

To Peter's intense surprise another man's voice answered. 'No. Not a thing. The kid must be still in the house. We'll knock up Miss Wardle and search.'

So there were *two* policemen in the garden then! How very quiet the other one had been! The boys were most surprised. *Now* what should they do? They watched the policemen switch on torches and heard them go to the front door of the house.

Peter hooted once more, and the others, realising that he wanted them, left their hiding-places and came cautiously to find him. Tom slid down the tree and joined them too.

'The policemen didn't hear or see anyone – any more than we did!' said Peter. 'We could only have seen what they saw – a light in the downstairs of the house. Tom, did *you* see anything else?'

'Not a thing,' said Tom. 'Look – I'll slip off, I think. The police don't know me, and they might wonder what I'm doing here with you. So long!'

He disappeared into the night and left the four boys together. They went near to the front door, at which the policemen had rung a minute ago, keeping in the dark shadows. The door was being opened cautiously by a very scared Miss Wardle, dressed in a long green dressing-gown, her hair in pins.

'Oh – it's you!' the boys heard her say to the police. 'Come in. I'm afraid I was asleep, although I said I'd try and keep awake tonight. Do you want me to go and see if anything is taken?'

'Well, Miss Wardle, we know that *someone* was in your house just now,' said one of the policemen. 'We saw the light of a torch in two rooms. One of us would like to come in and search, please – the other will stay out here in case the girl – if it is the girl – tries to make a run for it. We haven't seen her come out – or go in either for that matter! But we did see the light of her torch.'

'Oh, I see. Well, come in, then,' said Miss Wardle. 'But please make no noise, or you'll scare the old lady. Come into the kitchen – I can soon tell if food is gone again.'

The policeman disappeared into the cottage with Miss Wardle, leaving the other man on guard in the garden. The four boys watched from the safety of the shadows. Surely Elizabeth must be in the house? She couldn't have left by any door or window without being seen or heard! They watched lights going on in each room, as Miss Wardle and the policeman searched.

After what seemed like a very long time, they heard voices in the hall. Miss Wardle came to the door with the policeman.

'Nothing to report, Will,' said the policeman to the man left on guard. 'Nobody's in the house. Miss Wardle even went into the old lady's room to make sure the girl hadn't crept in there, feeling that she was cornered.'

'Well – nobody's come *out* of the house,' said Will, sounding surprised. 'Has anything been taken?'

'Yes – more food. Nothing else,' said the first policeman. 'Strange, isn't it? How could anyone have got in
under our very eyes and ears – taken food – and got out
again without being heard or seen going away? Well –
thanks, Miss Wardle. Sorry to have been such a nuisance
for nothing. How that girl – and it *must* be the girl – gets in
and out like this beats me. And where she's hiding beats
me too. We've combed the countryside for her! Well – her
brother's coming over to this country tomorrow – not that
he can do much, if we can't!'

The police departed. The front door shut. The light went
off in the hall, and then one appeared upstairs. Then that went
out too. Miss Wardle was presumably safely in bed again.

'What do you make of it, Peter?' whispered Jack.
'Peculiar, isn't it?'

'Yes. I can't understand it,' said Peter. 'I mean – there
were us four hiding here – and two policemen – and Tom
up the tree – and yet not one of us saw Elizabeth getting in
and out – and not one of us even *heard* her.'

'And yet she must have come here, into this garden,'
said Jack. 'She broke in somewhere – or unlocked a door –
she even put on her torch in the house to see what she
could take – and then she got out again, with us all
watching and listening – and disappeared. No – I don't
understand it either.'

'Come on – let's go home and sleep on it,' said Peter. 'I feel
quite tired now, with all the waiting and watching – and the
excitement – and now the disappointment. Poor Elizabeth –
what must she be feeling, having to scrounge food at night,
and hide away in the daytime? She must be very miserable.'

'Well – maybe her brother can help,' said Colin. 'He'll
be here tomorrow. Come on – I'm going home!'

480

CHAPTER FIFTEEN

Crosspatches

THE FOUR boys belonging to the Secret Seven, overslept the next morning. They were so tired from their long watch the night before! Janet was cross when Peter wouldn't wake, because she was longing to know what happened!

'Gosh – I'll be terribly late for school,' groaned Peter, leaping out of bed. 'You might have woken me before, Janet.'

'Well, I squeezed a sponge of cold water over you, and yelled in your ear, and pulled all the clothes off!' said Janet indignantly. 'And Scamper barked his head off. What *more* would you like me to do? And what happened last night?'

'Nothing. Absolutely nothing!' said Peter, dressing hurriedly. 'I mean, we didn't get Elizabeth – she got into the house, took what she wanted, and got out again – and disappeared. And although there were seven people altogether in the garden, watching, nobody saw her. So you see – nothing happened. ALL RIGHT, MOTHER! I'M JUST COMING.'

He tore downstairs with his mother still calling him, ate his breakfast standing up, and then cycled to school at top speed. He yelled to Janet as he left her at the corner.

'Meeting tonight at five-thirty. Tell Pam and Barbara!'

The meeting was not very thrilling. After such high hopes of something really exciting happening the night before, everyone felt flat. Pam made them all cross by saying that if *she* had hidden in the garden she would certainly have heard or seen Elizabeth creeping by.

481

'You must have fallen asleep,' she said. 'You really must. I mean – *seven* of you there! And nobody heard a thing! I bet you fell asleep.'

'Be quiet,' said Peter crossly. 'You don't know what you're talking about, Pam. Now don't start again. Be QUIET!'

'Well,' said Pam, obstinately, 'all I can say is that if Elizabeth *really* didn't get in or out, and it seems like that to me, or you'd have heard her – then she must be hiding in some secret place *inside* the house.'

'The police searched all over it,' said Peter. 'I did think of that bright idea myself – but I gave it up when the policeman hunted all through the cottage last night without finding Elizabeth. After all, it's only a small place – no cellars – no attics. We did hear *one* thing of interest, though. The brother who's in France is arriving in this

482

country today. Maybe he'll have something to say that will be of help.'

'Well – why don't you go and see him, then?' said Pam, who was in a very persistent mood that day. 'You could tell him what *you* know – about Tom the stable-boy seeing Elizabeth in Gorton, for instance.'

'H'm. That's the first sensible remark you've made, Pam,' said Peter. He turned to Jack. 'Will you come with me, Jack? I'd like to see the brother, I must say.'

'Wuff-wuff-wuff!' said Scamper, suddenly.

'*Now* what's the matter?' said Peter, whose late night had made him decidedly impatient that day. 'What's Scamper barking for? If it's Susie I'll have a few sharp words to say to her about playing that stupid trick on us with the suitcase!'

It *was* Susie. She stood grinning at the door when Peter opened it. 'Mint Sauce!' she said promptly. 'Let me in. I've some clues – great big ones. I know where Elizabeth is and what she's doing. I . . .'

'You do NOT!' yelled a furious Peter, and called for Jack. 'Jack get her out of here! Pam, Barbara, Janet – get hold of her dress and pull, too. Come on! Get going!'

And for once in a way the cheeky Susie was taken by surprise and found herself being dragged to the gate, and not very gently either!

'All right!' she yelled, kicking and hitting out as vigorously as she could. 'I shan't tell you my big clues. But you'll see I'm right! And I know your password, see! Mint sauce, Mint sauce, Mint sauce!'

She disappeared up the lane, and the Seven went back to the shed, feeling better for the excitement. 'Now we shall have to alter our password,' said Peter, in disgust. 'How

did Susie know it, Jack? Have you been saying it in your sleep, or something?'

'No,' said Jack, still angry. 'She must have hidden somewhere near the shed and heard us saying it. Bother Susie! You don't think she really *does* know something, do you?'

'How can she?' said Peter. 'And why can't you keep her in order? If Janet behaved like that I'd give her a piece of my mind.'

'You would *not*,' said Janet, indignantly. 'You just try it!'

'Gosh – we really are crosspatches today!' said Barbara, surprised. 'The boys must be tired after their late night! Well – have we any plans?'

'Only that Jack and I will go and see Elizabeth's brother, if he's arrived at the grandmother's,' said Peter, calming down. 'He'll be sure to go there, because his sister is known to be somewhere near. Come on, Jack – I'm fed up with this meeting. Let's go!'

CHAPTER SIXTEEN

Unexpected news

PETER AND Jack arrived at Bramble Cottage on their bicycles, and at once heard voices there. They put their cycles by the gate and looked over the hedge.

Three people were sitting in deck-chairs in the little garden, enjoying the warm evening sunshine. One was Miss Wardle – one was an old lady, obviously the grandmother – and one was a youth of about eighteen, looking very worried.

'He must be the brother,' said Peter. 'Good, he's arrived! Come on. We'll go up the front path, and if Miss Wardle sees us, she'll call us and we'll go over and talk.'

Miss Wardle did see them, and recognised them at once. 'Oh,' she said to the old lady beside her, 'those are the two nice boys who brought all that jumble. Come here, boys – I'm sure Mrs Sonning would like to thank you.'

Peter and Jack walked over. 'Good evening,' said Peter, politely. 'I do hope you have news of your granddaughter, Mrs Sonning.'

'No. We haven't,' said the old lady, and to Peter's alarm, a tear rolled down her cheek. 'This is my grandson, Charles, her brother. He's come over from France to see if he can help, because Elizabeth is very fond of him. If she knows he is here, she may come out of hiding.'

'We met a boy the other day who saw her in Gorton,' said Peter. 'She must have been on her way here then.'

'What!' said the boy Charles. 'Someone actually saw her in *Gorton*! But that's *not* on the way here. Who was this boy?'

'One of the stable-boys up at Warner's Stables there,' said Peter, pointing up the hill. 'He said Elizabeth told him she was going to France to see you.'

'But she didn't know where I *was* in France,' said Charles. 'I've been travelling around all the time! Even the police only got in touch with me with great difficulty! I'm certain that Elizabeth wouldn't have been mad enough to try to find me when she didn't even know what part of France I was in!'

'Well,' said Peter, 'that's what *Tom* said she told him, and he couldn't very well have made it up, because he had never met her before!'

'I'll go and see him,' said Charles, and got up – but just then the telephone bell shrilled out, the noise coming clearly into the garden.

'Answer it, Charles, there's a dear,' said old Mrs Sonning, and the boy went indoors. Peter and Jack waited patiently for him, and were immensely surprised to see him come running out again at top speed, his eyes shining and his face aglow.

'Granny! It was Elizabeth's headmistress. She . . .'

'Oh – has the child gone back to school – or gone back to her aunt?' said the old lady.

'No! But all that upset about the stolen money is cleared up!' said Charles, taking his grandmother's hand. 'It *wasn't* Elizabeth who took it, of course. The girl who stole it got frightened when the papers kept reporting that Elizabeth hadn't been found, and she suddenly owned up.'

'Who *was* the girl?' said Miss Wardle, indignantly.

'I'm afraid it was the one supposed to be Elizabeth's best friend,' said Charles. 'Lucy Howell – she came here to stay with Elizabeth last year, Granny. She saw the cash-box in the desk and took it on the spur of the moment, without even opening it. She hid it somewhere, waiting for a chance to break it open. She didn't realise that there was about a hundred pounds in it, and she was horrified when the police were called in about it.'

'I should think so!' said Mrs Sonning. 'I never did like Lucy – a sly little thing I thought she was. I was sorry that she was Elizabeth's friend.'

'Well, apparently Lucy was annoyed with Elizabeth and very jealous of her just then, because Elizabeth was ahead of her in marks and doing better at games – and what did she do but take the cash-box and put it into Elizabeth's chest of drawers! When the boarders' trunks and chests were searched – Elizabeth is a weekly boarder as you know – the cash-box was found – still unopened! Elizabeth had gone home for the weekend to Aunt Rose's, and the police went there to question her.'

'Poor Elizabeth!' said Mrs Sonning. 'But didn't she deny taking the money?'

'Yes, of course – but she wasn't believed. Most unfortunately she had actually been in the classroom where the money had stupidly been left, doing some homework all by herself, and had been seen there. Aunt Rose was very upset – and poor Elizabeth felt there was nothing to do but run away! I expect she thought she might have to go to prison or something!'

'Poor child! But now she can come back with her name cleared!' said Mrs Sonning. 'What a dreadful thing to happen to someone like Elizabeth. She's as honest as can be.'

'Yes. But how are we going to let her know that everything is all right?' asked Miss Wardle. 'We don't even know where the child is!'

'No. That's true,' said Charles, worried. 'But we *must* find her! She took only enough money with her to pay her railway fare down here apparently – that's all she had. She wouldn't have enough to buy food or anything else. She's hiding somewhere, all alone worried and miserable – thinking that we're all ashamed of her!'

'Don't,' said old Mrs Sonning, and began to weep into her handkerchief. 'Such a dear, good child – always so kind. Charles, we must find her – we must!'

'Well – the first thing to do is for me to go up and see this stable-boy who met Elizabeth in Gorton,' said Charles, getting up. 'Will you take me up to him, you two boys?'

'Yes,' said Peter and Jack, who had been listening to the conversation with much interest. 'We'll take you now. We are so glad everything's cleared up!'

CHAPTER SEVENTEEN

A funny business altogether

PETER, JACK, and Charles went to the gate at the bottom of
the little garden, and up the hill to Warner's Stables, the
two boys wheeling their bicycles. They liked Charles. He
reminded them of someone, but they couldn't think who it
was.

'Where's Tom?' Peter called to Harry, when they came
to the stables. He was saddling a horse.

'Somewhere about,' he shouted back. 'Over there, I
think.'

'You see if Tom is over there, and I'll go into the stables
and see if he's there,' said Peter. Charles went with Jack,
and Peter looked into the stables. At the far end he saw
Tom, cleaning out one of the stalls.

'Hey, Tom!' called Peter. 'There's someone wants to see
you.'

'Who?' shouted back Tom.

'You remember meeting that girl Elizabeth?' said Peter. 'Well, it's her brother, Charles. He's come over from France, he's so upset, and . . .'

He stopped, because Tom had suddenly flung down his rake, and had shot past him at top speed. He tore out of the door, and Peter stared in surprise. When Peter got to the stable door himself, there was no sign of Tom! He saw Jack and Charles coming towards him, and called to them.

'Did you see Tom? He tore out of here just now, goodness knows why!'

'We saw someone racing off,' said Jack. 'Bother! Just as we wanted him. Didn't you tell him someone wanted to see him?'

'Yes, of course. I don't know if he heard me or not, but he suddenly flung down his fork and dashed off without a word!' said Peter, puzzled.

Harry, the other stable-boy, came up with the big stable-girl. 'Don't take any notice of Tom,' he said. 'He's a bit odd! Isn't he, Kate?'

The stable-girl nodded. 'Hasn't got much to say for himself,' she said. 'Funny boy – a bit potty, I think!'

490

'But where did he go?' said Peter. 'Do you know where he lives? We could go to his home, and then our friend here could ask him a few things he wants to know.'

Neither Harry nor the girl knew where Tom lived, so Jack and Peter gave it up. 'Sorry,' they said to Charles and Peter added: 'We could come here again tomorrow if you like. Not that Tom can really tell you anything of importance. He may even have made it all up about meeting Elizabeth. He may have read about her in the papers, and just invented the whole meeting! He really *is* a bit odd, I think.'

'Well – thank you,' said Charles, who looked worried again. 'I'll go back. My poor old granny won't be herself again till we find Elizabeth. My parents haven't been told yet, but they'll have to be rung tomorrow, and asked to

491

come home. Dad's out in China on a most important job, and we didn't want to worry him at first. Apparently the police thought they would soon find my sister.'

'Yes – with no money – and wearing her school clothes it *ought* to have been easy to spot her,' said Jack. 'Well – good-bye – and good luck!'

The boys rode off down the hill. 'I'm really glad Elizabeth didn't steal that money after all,' said Peter. 'Though we've never met her, I thought it was rather strange that anyone said to be so honest and straightforward should have done such a thing. And now I've seen that old granny, and her nice brother Charles – he *is* nice, isn't he, Jack? – I see even more clearly that Elizabeth couldn't have been a thief.'

'It's a funny business altogether,' said Jack. 'And it's not cleared up yet, Peter – not till Elizabeth's found. Remember, *she* doesn't know that the real thief has owned up!'

'I know,' said Peter. 'Well – we'll have another Secret Seven meeting tomorrow night, the same time as today, Jack. We'll tell the others at school tomorrow. We'll have to report this evening's happenings, and see if there's anything further we can do.'

'Right!' said Jack. 'See you tomorrow!' and with a jingling of bicycle bells the two parted, each thinking the same thing. 'What a pity Elizabeth doesn't know that her name is cleared!'

Next evening the Secret Seven gathered in the meeting shed as usual, anxious to hear what Jack and Peter had to say. They were all very thrilled to hear about the brother Charles – and the exciting telephone call that had come while Jack and Peter were there.

'What a pity that boy Tom didn't stop and speak to Charles,' said Colin, puzzled. 'Do you suppose he made up that tale about meeting Elizabeth, and was afraid of being found out in his fairy-tale by Charles?'

'*I* tell you what!' said George, suddenly. 'I believe he knows where Elizabeth is! That's why he acts so strangely! That's why he ran off like that – to warn her that her brother was there!'

'You may be right, George,' said Peter, considering the matter. 'Yes – perhaps he *does* know where she is! Well – all the more reason why we should go up tomorrow and see him! We'll ask him straight out if he knows where the girl is – and watch his face. He's sure to give himself away if he *does* know where she is – even if he swears he doesn't!'

'We'll tell Charles to come too,' said Jack. 'If *he* thinks Tom knows his sister's hiding-place, I've no doubt he'll be able to make him tell it!'

'Right,' said Peter. 'Well – tomorrow may be exciting. We'll just see!'

CHAPTER EIGHTEEN

Peter goes mad

THE NEXT evening the Seven took their bicycles and went riding to Warner's Stables once more, leaving a message at Bramble Cottage for Charles to follow, if he wished. He was out when they called.

Harry and the stable-girl were carting straw about the yard, but Tom was nowhere to be seen.

'He asked if he could work down in the fields today,' said Harry. 'Not in the stables. You could bike down to them, if you want him. He's a bit touchy today, is old Tom!'

'If someone called Charles comes along, tell him where we are,' said Peter. 'That's the boy who was with us yesterday.'

They rode down to the fields, and saw Tom in the distance exercising ponies round the meadow. They shouted to him and waved.

He stopped and looked hard at them all. Then he waved back and came cantering over.

'Sorry I'm busy,' he said. 'Is there anything you want?'

'Yes!' said Peter, putting his bicycle by the gate and climbing over the top bar. 'Tom – I want to ask you a question. Do you know where Elizabeth Sonning is hiding? *Do* you?'

A frightened look came into Tom's face. 'Why should I know that?' he said. 'Don't be crazy!' And with that he kicked his heels against the pony's side and galloped off!

'He does know! He does!' said Jack. 'And he won't tell.' He turned to Peter and looked suddenly astonished. 'Why,

495

Peter – what on earth's the matter? Why are you looking like that?'

Peter did indeed look peculiar – astonished – bewildered – as if someone had knocked him on the head. Jack shook him, quite scared.

'Peter! What is it?'

'Gosh – of *course* he knows where Elizabeth is!' said Peter. 'Nobody in the world knows better where Elizabeth hides out! Nobody!'

'Peter!' cried everyone, wondering if he had suddenly gone mad. What in the world did he mean?

He didn't answer, but did something very surprising. He lifted his bicycle over the gate into the field, mounted it and rode over the grass after Tom, who was still cantering along, on the pony.

The Seven stared open-mouthed. No doubt about it – Peter had gone off his head! Now he was shouting at the top of his voice.

'Come here, you idiot! Everything's all right! Elizabeth! COME HERE! I've got good news for you! Elizabeth! ELIZABETH!'

'Mad,' said Jack, looking quite scared. They all stood and watched, really amazed.

Now Peter was cycling quite near to Tom and his rather frightened pony, and he was still shouting.

'Everything's all right, I tell you! Lucy Howell confessed *she* took the money! Everyone knows it wasn't you! WILL you stop, you idiot, and listen to me?'

And at last the pony stopped, and the rider allowed Peter to cycle up and jump off by its side. The six by the gate poured into the field to hear what was happening.

Peter was out of breath, but he still talked. 'You're Elizabeth! I know you are! I *knew* your brother reminded me of someone – and I suddenly saw the likeness just now at the gate! Elizabeth, it's all right. Your name's cleared. And look – there's your brother at the gate. Come now – you *are* Elizabeth, aren't you?'

Tears began to fall down the girl's face. 'Yes – I *am* Elizabeth Sonning! Oh, is it true that Lucy said she took the money? I thought she had – but I wasn't sure. Nobody will think me a thief any more?'

'Nobody,' said Peter. 'Well, you're a brave kid, aren't you – getting a job as a stable-boy, and working hard like this! Where did you hide at night? How . . .?'

'Oh – there's Charles!' cried Elizabeth, suddenly, though

the Seven still couldn't help thinking of her as Tom, of course! The girl galloped her pony over to Charles, shouting to him: 'Charles! Charles! Oh, I'm so glad to see you!'

She almost fell off her pony into his arms, and the two hugged one another tightly. The Seven went over to them, feeling excited and pleased. What a surprising ending to the problem they had been puzzling over so long!

'Well, you monkey!' said Charles, who suddenly looked much younger. 'What have you got to say for yourself? Bringing me over from France like this – having everyone hunting for you? Where have you been hiding? How did you get in and out of Granny's house? Why . . .?'

'Oh, Charles – I'll answer all your questions!' said Elizabeth, half-crying and half-laughing. 'But let's go to Granny's, do let's. I do want to hug her, I do want to tell her everything's all right!'

'Come on, then,' said Charles, putting his arm round his sister. He turned to the Seven. 'You kids can come too,' he said. 'We've a lot to thank you for – and I'm longing to know how you spotted that this dirty, untidy, smelly stable-boy was no other than my naughty little sister Elizabeth.'

CHAPTER NINETEEN

A jolly good finish

THEY ALL went out of the field, and took the path that led down to Bramble Cottage. The Seven were very thrilled to be in at the finish. To their great disgust they met Susie on her bicycle, riding along with a friend.

'Hallo!' she called cheekily. 'Solved your silly mystery yet?'

'Yes!' said Jack. 'And that boy Tom was Elizabeth – dressed up like a stable-boy. *You'd* never have thought of that in a hundred years!'

'Oh, but I knew it!' said the aggravating Susie. 'Shan't tell you how! But I knew it!' And away she went, waving her cheeky hand at them.

'She's a terrible fibber,' said Janet. 'I suppose she *couldn't* have guessed, could she, Jack?'

'I wouldn't put it past her,' said Jack, with a groan. 'Anyway, she'll keep on and on saying she knew. *Why* did I tell her just now?'

'Goodness knows,' said Peter. 'You'd better safety-pin your mouth, Jack! Well – here we are at the cottage. Won't the old granny be pleased?'

She was! She hugged the brown-faced, short-haired girl and kissed her, happy tears streaming down her face.

Miss Wardle rushed indoors and brought out biscuits and lemonade for everyone. Scamper, who was there as usual, of course, was delighted to have two fine biscuits presented to him.

'Elizabeth! Now where did you hide? And are those *my* riding-breeches?' asked Charles, pulling at them. 'Where did you get them?'

'From your chest of drawers here,' said Elizabeth. 'I knew nobody would miss them. They're rather big for me, though. And I've made them very dirty! I hid in the hayloft at the stables each night, with just a rug to cover me. I was quite warm and cosy.'

'So you *did* take that rug!' said Miss Wardle. 'I thought so! And all that food too, I suppose?'

'Yes. You see, I'd no money left after paying my fare down here,' said Elizabeth. 'At least, I had five pence, that's all. So I had to get a job – but you're only paid once a week, so I had to have food till my wages were due – I couldn't go without eating!'

'You poor child!' said Miss Wardle. 'Bless you, I knew you were innocent, I knew you weren't a thief! Yes, and I cooked special tarts and pies for you, my little dear, and left them out, hoping you'd come and take them.'

'Oh – thank you!' said Elizabeth. 'I did wonder why there was such a *lot* of food in the larder – and food I especially liked!'

'Why did you tell us that you had met – well, met *yourself* in Gorton, and all that?' asked Peter, puzzled.

'Only to put you off the scent,' said Elizabeth. 'I thought if people imagined I was off to France to find Charles, they wouldn't guess I was hiding near Granny's. I had to come near Granny's because of getting food, you see – and, anyway, I wanted to *feel* I was near somebody belonging to me, I was so miserable.'

'How did you get into the house, Elizabeth?' said Miss Wardle, and Charles chimed in with:

'Yes – how did you?'

And Peter added, 'Why, the other night we all watched here in the garden – but, how very funny, you were here too, Elizabeth, pretending to watch for yourself – you were Tom, up that tree! *Were* you up the tree?'

Elizabeth laughed. 'Yes, of course. That tree has a branch that goes to the bathroom window – and I know how to open the window from the outside and slip in – I'll show you, it's quite easy if you have a pocket-knife. But I'm getting too large to squeeze through it now, really! It really made me laugh to think of everyone watching and waiting – and there was I, up the tree, waiting to slip through the window. I got a lovely lot of food that night – did you see my torch shining in the downstairs rooms? And I was just sliding down the tree again when I heard the police knocking on the front door.'

'And you told us not to tell the police you were there – because you knew your pockets were full of food!' said Peter, with a chuckle. 'Yes, I think your brother's right. You really are a monkey.'

'But I was a very, very good stable-boy,' said Elizabeth, earnestly. 'Granny, Mr Warner said he was very pleased with me, and he even promised me a rise in wages if I went on working so hard! Can I go on being a stable-boy? It's nicer than being at school.'

'Certainly not!' said her grandmother, smiling. 'You'll go back to school and be welcomed there by everyone – and you'll work hard and be top of the exams, although you've missed a week and a half!'

'But what *I* want to know is – how did *you*, Peter, realise so suddenly that Tom the stable-boy was Elizabeth?' asked Charles.

'Well – I suddenly saw the likeness between you,' said Peter. 'And then somehow the bits of the jigsaw all fell into place, if you know what I mean! And I was so afraid that Elizabeth would run off again when she saw you, as she did when she heard you were at the stables yesterday, that I just felt I had to cycle at top speed after her pony and yell at her!'

'I was never so surprised in my life as when you came at me and my pony at sixty miles an hour on your bike, yelling at the top of your voice,' said Elizabeth. 'But I'm glad you did. Granny, I'm coming here for the holidays, aren't I? Can I have these children to play sometimes?'

'Of course!' said her grandmother. 'I shall always be glad to see them. There's only one thing I'm sad about

Elizabeth – your hair! *What* a pity you hacked it short like that. It was so soft and pretty!'

'I had to, Granny,' said Elizabeth. 'I did it with your nail scissors when I came one night to take Charles' riding-breeches to wear – and I took his jersey too, though it's so dirty now I don't expect he recognises it! Oh, Granny – I'm so very happy. You can't *think* how different I feel!'

'We'd better go,' said Peter to the others, in a low voice. 'Let's leave them all to be happy together. Come on, say good-bye.'

They said good-bye, and Scamper gravely shook paws as well. Then away they went on their bicycles, Scamper running beside them.

'What a wonderful finish!' said Jack. 'Who would have thought it would end like that? I feel rather happy myself! When's the next meeting, Peter?'

'Tomorrow – and we'll have a celebration to mark our success!' said Peter. 'Everyone must bring some food or drink. And we'll have to think of a new password, of course. What shall it be?'

'Stable-boy!' said Jack at once.

Well, it's quite a good one – but I mustn't tell you if it's the *right* one. Knock on the door of the shed, say 'Stable-boy!' and see if the Secret Seven let you in!